SO WILD A DREAM

BY LARISSA BROWN

THE COMPLETE STORY
BOOKS 1 & 2

SO WILD A DREAM:
THE COMPLETE STORY
Including 2nd edition of Book 1 and first printing of Book 2

ISBN: 978-0-9980835-2-0

Published by White Woods Press
LarissaBrown.net

Cover design by Brian John Park

For information about licensing, custom editions, special sales, or academic/corporate purchases, please contact Shannon Okey, Cooperative Press: info@cooperativepress.com or 10252 Berea Rd, Cleveland, Ohio 44102, USA. Larissa Brown may be reached at larissa.brown.writing.design@gmail.com.

Join the Larissa Brown e-news list at http://eepurl.com/bfjfdH

To fathers,

especially mine

who was the first Viking I ever knew

A NOTE ON WORDS & SOUNDS

I invented several of the old words and phrases in this book, by combining Old Icelandic and Old Norse words, along with speculating about how people thought of the world and put it into words. **Some of them are not real Viking or Icelandic words. Please don't expect an Icelander to know some of these. They're nonsense!**

Here and there, I've used letters that come from Old English, Old Norse and current day Icelandic alphabets, and are descended from early runes. English speakers, for that little voice in your head:

- **Ei** = long A sound, so Heirik's name sounds like "Hay'-rik" and nei is "nay"
- **J or j** = y sound, for example Jul is the winter Yule festival.
- **á** = "ow," so já sounds kind of like "yow" and Hár's name sounds like "Hower."
- **Þ or þ** = soft th as in "thing."
- **ð** = hard th, so broðr is "brother." Eðna's name sounds like "ay'-than" and Eiðr's name is "ay-thr."
- **í** = long ee; so the farm, Hvítmork, sounds like "Veet-mork."

A NOTE ON HISTORY

This is a work of speculative fiction, set in a fictional version of 10th century Iceland. Many of the places, customs, rites, Viking aphorisms and kennings are fictional. The characters whose grandparents were among the first settlers in the land are fictional and do not resemble any real Icelandic settlers.

BOOK ONE

ᛊ

C. 922 C.E.

Svana shoved a stick into a crack in the ground. A good stick, thick and bent, like an elbow crook without its flesh. She'd been saving it for a time when she could slip away from her husband to this far field. The grass would be tall soon, up to her waist. No one would see it here.

She knelt and traced its line with her fingers. It angled off to one side and toward the sky. It stretched blue and still over her head.

Ginn said that a thousand years from now, people travel by sky. Svana watched it always, these past two years since her marriage, yearning to go up free into its heights.

She dropped a leather bundle on the ground with a wet thud. She tucked her dress out of the way and untied her small knots. Why had she tied them so tight? A piece of her fingernail broke off, brittle as dead grass, and she cursed. Her fingers used to be soft and fine.

The cords pulled free and the leather fell open, baring the bloody head of a fox. A little one that had sniffed at her cooking fire that morning while Eiðr was away. She had thanked the gods over and over as she hacked its neck with her husband's old ax.

Its blood smelled just like that blade. The iron stink hit the back of her throat, and water came up in her mouth. She wiped her face on the shoulder of her dirty dress, and bits of hair like straw stuck in her mouth. Her hair used to be soft and yellow. Everyone said it was like heated butter.

She lifted the small head, and held it out in front of her. Would it be enough?

The gods preferred horses, but gods were practical beings. They would hear her.

She pushed the severed neck onto the stick.

Slowly, she twisted and pressed. She dared not break the stick—it was a good one—so she worked the head gently, a little at a time. She swallowed down sickness from the disgusting sounds, the sticky blood and empty eyes. No one else would do this for her. Her breath came soft and shallow as she worked.

Finally, the head hung on the bone-pole, eyes blank, seeing into the next life. The stick bowed under its weight, but it held. She turned it slowly, carefully, toward Hvítmork.

Svana wiped her hands on her skirt.

There.

The fox's dead gaze reached across the acres of grass and out toward Ginn's grand new house.

Svana bent low to speak into the stick where it met the ground.

"I raise this nithing pole and turn it on Ginn of no other name."

She felt foolish, but she pushed her words out stronger. Her voice was too small for the gods to hear.

"For my mother." She closed her eyes tight and pressed her palms to the ground. "For taking our places, forcing us from our home."

Hildur was a hard woman, but she used to hold Svana and rock her to sleep, when she was scared of spirits that walked in the night.

But nei, this was not for Hildur.

"For me." The words came faster. "For forcing me into a life of servitude, and the bed of a man I loathe. For leaving me alone. Crushing my life in your hateful hands like I am nothing but an egg."

Her words grew and blew a fire to life, as if flame climbed up the stick and lashed out of the fox's mouth.

"I turn this head also on Heirik Rakknason, chief and husband to Ginn. Already a boy is killing my own husband for me. Eiðr will be found with your family's ax in his back, and you will be blamed, Rakknason."

The fox's voice shook with rage and tears.

"I raise Hel against you."

Svana's heart stopped in her chest—the fox's head swung on its post. It looked away from Ginn's home and off into the highlands.

What did it mean? This sudden shift in a still sky?

She sat back on her heels and took shuddering breaths. Her clouds, her companions, did not travel. There was no wind.

She turned the fox head back toward Ginn and whispered an appeal for the curse to find its target.

BROWN

C. 922 C.E.

Brosa rested his shovel and looked out over the swells and valleys of his brother's land. Their grandfather had ringed this farm with fire, among the first men to claim the wilds of Iceland. His brother, chieftain now, owned it all.

On the brink of night, the land turned gray. The far-off hills changed first, the grass turning to ash. Then the valley was devoured by a creeping, shriveling deadness. It moved fast through the land, from the horizon right down to the dirt under his feet, so that he picked up one foot and checked the sole of his boot.

The dog beside him whined and sniffed.

Brosa bent again to dig. He leaned into the shovel, breaking up hunks of grass, over and over, stopping only to wipe his forehead with the back of his hand.

The sky dimmed, and the familiar sensation came, the one that had plagued him these four years since Esa's death. The sensation of his wife. The whisper of linen on his wrists. A dress whipping in the wind, hanging from a line. The feel of Esa's clothing, and through it, the shape and bones of her thigh. Slender and strong. Her laughter as he tried to slip his hands inside. All those moments, swallowed by crows.

"I welcome it, já?"

Words given to a stiff wind.

The shovel crunched, iron against colorless earth, faster and deeper until his muscles sang with the digging, and for one wild moment, he knew his thick body had been made only for this.

Sculpted by the gods so he could one day dig into her grave mound.

There she was.

Esa.

And next to her, the small bones of his son.

He climbed in beside them and laid down.

It would be his last act of usefulness, to complete his family. He would trade his family for a living one, for his brother, so that Ginn and Heirik could have a babe. Surely, some spirit would take his life in return for a new one to come. The spirit would find him here. He felt it nearing him, moving in the gray land, and its approach soothed him like a child's bedtime song.

"Finna mig." He asked to be found, to be taken. "Ta mig."

Brosa woke to a bird's call.

He caught the breeze on his face, smelled the damp earth. He flexed his cold fingers and felt a jaw bone under his thumb. Teeth. The long bones of Esa's dead leg pressed into his. He shifted, and they cracked.

He was alive, then, já. But the spirit was coming.

The call came again, and he jerked upright, eyes open. It wasn't the voice of a bird. It was a woman.

C. 922 C.E.

Eðna Jonsdottir crawled up out of the sea. Her dark wool skirt swirled in a wash of foam and sucked her down into the black sand. Salt water blasted up her nose, scraping out her sinuses, and she pressed her head between her palms, choking, coughing.

"Sodium chloride," she muttered, and the words burned.

The 22nd century lab she'd left behind was completely gone, its orderly vented air replaced by the madness of sea spray and fish stink.

Yes.

It wasn't a glorious arrival in the past, but it was right. The ocean, and black sand, were expected. "Confirmed, I'm on a beach," she recorded.

But what was the time?

She lifted her heavy head, hoping desperately for the wilds of the 10th century, dreading that if the machine hadn't worked, she might find the spindly, sky-high glass buildings of her city.

She saw nothing.

Only black.

Where were the waves? The foam, her dress? She felt for the ground, and her hands sank into sand. The ground was still under her knees. The waves still bumped at her back, but she couldn't see any of it. She'd gone blind.

She closed her fingers in the muck, steadied herself and shut her eyes. She let a stream of images pass. For just a second, she indulged in her birds. Vibrant, ancient ones, whose images she'd collected since she was ten. Peacocks, plovers, snowy owls.

Calm.

She tried again.

She blinked, and the landscape sprang to green-tinted life. Malfunctioning night vision.

Yes. She could see now. Her breath caught at the sight.

Eðna knelt in the center of an enormous curve of sand. Thrown through time, she had settled precisely where the foam met the land. Black cliffs rose before her, dominating a massive, white sky to what she presumed was the southeast, based on her memorized map and the assumption that she had come through on the same beach as Jen—the woman who would now call herself Ginn.

At Eðna's back, the ocean would stretch all the way to barren Greenland. It pulled, as if to suck her back, and she lurched forward on her knees.

"Alone," she said and wiped her mouth. "I've arrived, alone, in the water. As planned."

The sand was dark black, like winter night on her childhood farm, and her own fingers were ghostly green in the thermal glow. The silt transitioned to pebbles, and then bigger rocks, as her eyes moved up the sloping beach. Finally, the beach gave way to boulders, surrounded by thickets of pale silver plants. Their stems searched, reaching toward a blinding sun.

Eðna zoomed in on their round heads, like satellites dotted with tiny buds. Not yet flowered. Spring, then.

"Enhanced imaging and scans are functioning."

To her right, more of the same landscape continued into the distance, with no big spikes of white that would signify the churning heat of the city. Nothing lit the horizon or glowed from beyond the hills.

She blinked to seek/accept, and flowing script letters confirmed: *No coordinates found.*

In the corner of her field of vision, a timer counted the hours and minutes since she'd left the lab. She knocked water from her ear, and the numbers zinged through days and weeks, then settled back to zero.

"But the chronometer is haywire."

Would her lenses be stuck like this, in thermal imaging mode, counting time endlessly up and down?

Her contacts glitched, and the skeletal, gray and green image exploded into eye-searing color. A bright world of green and puce and a dozen shades of blue opened up before her – the naked colors of ancient Iceland's sand and ocean and sky.

Eðna raised a hand to shield her eyes from the glare. She scanned the beach to, presumably, the North and South.

"That would be a no. The contacts aren't stuck," she muttered.

In the distance, a bit of brilliant red flashed against the landscape. Her physical confirmation sat a mere half mile away.

A wooden hut, bleached by wind and salt spray, hunched at the water's edge. Two big A-frame tents stood back from it, natural canvas with wide red stripes, textbook Viking style. An animal-prowed, elegant boat sat on the water beyond the froth. These were the tents of Heirik Rakknason's family. She was within a generation of her target, if not spot on.

Exhilaration lifted her heart.

Here!

She rose to her feet, trembling, and stood tall. Icy water streamed from her hands and dress, and loose strands of her hair stuck to her cheeks and in her eyes. She lifted her chin to the clear, arctic sky. "Yes," she said, and a cloud of breath floated up and took off into the wind.

Here she stood, on the black sand beach of Jen's ravings. Eðna Jonsdottir had traveled through time. She would prove that it worked. And she would find Subject Zero: Jen.

Warmth came next on her list.

A short distance to the east, Eðna sighted a space between two big rocks—a cove or child-sized cave. That would be her spot.

Eðna's fingertips brushed the leather purse that hung from her belt, its vials of antibiotics and painkillers inside. She hugged the big bundle of supplies that laid next to her skin, under her skirt and shift. She'd make a full inventory when she reached the little cave.

As she trudged up the sloping beach, a map jumped to life and flickered in her eyes—the map that Jen had drawn of this coast, the fishing camp, the family's byway to the farm where Eðna would now go and find her.

"Contacts are erratic," she whispered.

When she reached the cave, she removed her two soaked, wool cloaks and unlaced her leather bodice down the sides. Her dress clung to her legs, frigid and heavy.

Jen had washed ashore when she time traveled, so this freezing water was expected, and Eðna had prepared. She carried a third cloak, folded in a heavy lump under her dress. She unfurled it, and out dropped a pair of light wool pants, a relatively dry underdress and a leather hat trimmed in fur.

Her skin prickled as she changed, and with a sudden pang she turned to be sure no one was there. The towering rocks hid her from behind, and the beach stood bleak and empty as far as she could see.

A surge of salty wind scooped into her little alcove, swirling as if it sought her. She shot a hand out for balance, but the rock was slick, and she slipped and pitched forward. She pushed silty hair from her face and allowed herself one moment of the misery she'd anticipated. Her head throbbed and nausea rose up, cold and unpleasant. She let herself vomit. Her throat burned, and her eyes watered.

She could do this.

She shook her head, and her braids fell out of their coils, thumping heavily on her chest. She stripped off her dress, dropped her wet undergarments and drew on the dry bloomers. She put the dry underdress next to her skin, the wet wool one back on over it. Finally, her leather top. She tightened the laces at her sides, pulled the fur hat down over her forehead, and began her hike to the fishing camp.

Her lungs woke with the glorious chill of arctic air, and relief and happiness surged along with the sound of the waves. She was alive. Here. Out of twelve million women in the City of Iceland, only Eðna walked across this sand, head high, wind in the bits of hair that stuck out of her hat, her dress trailing behind like the magnificent tail of a dark brown Sugarbird.

After years with her hands wrecked by leather, fingers pricked by countless sewing needles, she had stepped forward, courageous. Stood in front of important people and said, "I am the one."

The call came through on a Friday ten months ago. She'd been watching an arc about the earth's magnetic polarity on her wall screen, and she pushed it aside to answer a live call from one of the programmers she'd interviewed with. He was the lead on the project. Jeff. His messy blond ponytail fell over one shoulder, and he pushed a few loose strands out of his eyes.

"Hallo, Kona," he said in his clunky Old Norse.

Eðna's heart sped, and her mind zoomed. She had passed every test, large and small. She spoke the languages, Old Norse and Icelandic. Knew the history of the founders of this country and could recite the names and all known relationships of the people she would meet in the past. She was the right height for the time. And thanks to her father, she could swim and ride a horse. Make a fire. He'd even given her an old name. Eðna, with its long A and hard "th."

"*Ay*thna," she reminded Jeff.

Was he smiling, just a little? She'd heard about him from Vera. He always smiled at women.

"Will you do it?" He smiled wider. "If you will, we want you to test the primary tank for time travel."

Eðna's mouth opened and thoughts sped. The original tank. The one that transported Jen-who-was-Ginn to the past and back again. The only tank they had evidence for, after multiple non-events with copy tanks.

"Do you accept?" Jeff smiled a kind of half grin, and it made him seem even messier, like it matched his worn, ripped t-shirt. "You'd be doing me a huge favor."

"Yes," Eðna managed. Her heart beat hard, and her eyes stung. "Absolutely. Yes."

"See you tomorrow, then. 08:00."

Quiet settled on Eðna's impeccable room. Her belongings looked less defined, already irrelevant, and so she closed her eyes and dropped into a list.

She would learn and refine how to navigate and tell time by the sun. How to survive the cold beach. To walk a marathon and climb steep slopes in a ten-pound dress and belt. She would memorize the map for the hundredth time—the route from the ocean to the house where Jen-Ginn claimed to have lived. The White Woods. Hvítmork.

At the fishing camp, weak smoke rose from a ring of stones, but no men sat around the fire. That was clear to see from a half-K away. But as Eðna got closer to the camp, it wasn't the fire pit that drew her attention. The mystery of the untended embers, the hut, the tents, all drifted away. All nothing, compared to the boat.

Yes, Jen had called it a boat.

It was like calling a glacier big.

It was a ship that rocked gently on the water, just beyond the crashing froth, elegant and grave. Its enormous wooden swells and carved designs were burnished golden by the late-day light. A vessel built to ride like a steed over an endless ocean, its form that of a wave itself.

Her contacts tried to focus and estimate size, but they sputtered off, and she was left to calculate with her unaided eyes. A hull maybe ten men long. A prow reaching up out of the water four times her own height, curling inward first before rearing up to form an animal's head. Not the anticipated dragon, it had the ears of a dog, maybe a wolf. The artist had carved the beast's face with layer upon layer of finely carved swirls, eyes blank, jaws open wide.

Her heart reached. Eðna waded out beyond the foam, and a name surged up from rote memory and rocked with the tide at her ankles: Brosa Ulfsson. Yes. The chieftain's brother was a trader. He would own this kind of magnificent ship.

The carved wolf's gaze locked with hers. Its eyes—simple holes in the wood—glowed eerie blue. An optical trick, light off water. Eðna stood awash in half formed impressions. Pleasure.

Death. The elemental, harsh sounds of breath and beating heart.

A bird screamed, and Eðna blinked awake. A live bird!

Something cold climbed her calves, and she gasped and checked her legs. She was standing in water.

She turned in a quick circle, checking the beach. Empty. The bird was a crow, familiar, the one species that lived in her time.

Pulse settling, blush warming her neck and cheeks, she lifted her skirts up out of the waves. How could she have forgotten, even for a heartbeat, where she was? Who she was. The boat had seduced her and lulled her into pure sensation.

Ridiculous. A boat was not seductive. Planks and nails formed its swells, and nothing more. It couldn't lure her away from her mission.

To find Jen, she had to find allies, and that boat was empty. Useless. She turned her back on the shining ship.

The people she sought must be inside the tents. There would be someone here, someone designated to defend this beach and anything that drifted ashore. Someone to protect the boat.

"Hallo!" Eðna called.

Canvas flapped and beat the sides of the tents in a sudden gust, but no one responded.

"Hallo?" The quiet was complete and unnerving, without the hum of air conditioners and the small sounds of machines and screens. No natural sounds either. Not an animal in sight, and the wind had ceased, leaving not a breeze. Even the ocean seemed to suspend its lapping.

Eðna called again, closer, pushing away doubt, pushing open the tent.

Bodies sprawled on the floor.

Two men. One rested face down, a cheek pressed to the ground as if sleeping, an ax buried in his back. The other man, face up, stared without eyes. They'd already been taken by the handful of crows that pulled at his skin with sickening yanks. One of his arms was flung far away across the tent. Blood soaked both men's beards and clothes and the black sand floor lay dark and slick.

Eðna shrieked, and it stirred up a savage hurricane of black wings. Trapped inside the tent, crows flapped and beat the walls, cawing and screaming. She fell to her knees and backed away, dress tangling. Their wings shimmered with a deep blue tinge, just as they did in the city. But their talons were bigger up close, their foreheads intent with malice. Eyes like dark seeds watched her retreat.

Outside the tent, she gasped for fresh air and pushed sick fear down in her throat. Violence was expected in this time. She had trained to defend herself if necessary with her own small knife, but it came so soon. In the first hour of her journey, death.

Birds strutted across the sand. So big. Her eyes widened. They were not crows after all, but ravens. They turned to her with strange, jerky movements, and one of them spoke a single raw syllable.

The orderly, sophisticated words she wanted—*scapulae, severed*—came forward from the back of her mind. She stood and pressed her skirt to her thighs.

"Allies," she said. She drew away, turned from the tent and listed her objectives. "Physical and temporal location, warmth, allies, transportation."

The potential allies were dead. Being eaten by birds. Eðna pushed away her old terror, the fear she swore she would not allow to consume her. Fear of bodies and pain. Blood in beards, lost eyes.

—A horse shrieked, and Eðna jumped and put her hand to her heart.

Outside behind the tents, an animal stood tethered. It skittered and backed away at her approach, but its lead held. She spotted a wooden saddle leaning against the back of the tent. Blood pooled next to it, seeping out from under the canvas.

Bodies failed. She'd known that going in.

She hauled the simple saddle up onto the animal's back, secured the straps and climbed on, and she and the horse left the sand and boat and blood behind.

BROWN

Eðna welcomed facts.

They ran down the right side of her field of vision. Bits of information about the landscape and history of Iceland appeared the way she preferred, in fluid letters like old handwriting, bright white, overlaid against the evening light.

The earth's crust had shifted considerably over the past one thousand two hundred years, but the magnetic pole remained the same, and even without satellites, her contacts could orient her. She could see magnetic North, just like birds could—a pale gray arch on the horizon. So, she was heading generally toward Hvítmork, the farm she sought, approximately 40 kilometers inland from the fishing camp.

Just a few minutes into her journey, her lenses glitched, briefly in focus, and then out again. They threw up a mess of images: scattered scythe blades, cracks in frozen water, a bowerbird's decorated nest. The horse stamped and turned, and she was whipped around to face the way she came, to see the sun settling over the ocean. A garbled voice rose and fell in volume. And then nothing. The contacts died completely, leaving only ragged breath and heartbeat. Eðna was alone.

Vast sky and land rolled away toward sunset, not a single cursive letter flowering into life to describe and overlay the orange clouds. They streamed like jets of steam bursting from a fiery, sinking sun. Underneath, they were pink, with menacing plumes of steel and streaks of electric blue. She was facing west. That was wrong.

Above her head, the sky was a clear, yawning gray. It was so empty, devoid of clouds and symbols. She leaned forward over the horse and grasped its mane.

Not a word flickered. No Jeff, with his instructions and hypotheses scrolling by. No Vera, with her little notes about dinner and the beauty of the leather Eðna had worked that day. No map to lay over this immense world.

Her breath came short, with soft sounds of fear, uncontrollable. How would she know anything? How would she measure and record?

Toward the end of her training, she'd practiced disconnecting herself, for hours, and even days, at a time. Contact malfunction was more than possible. It was probable, based on Jen's experience, and Eðna had practiced sitting in blank silence in her room. But the world always hovered just on the other side of her isolation. She practiced turning off her contacts. Yes. But the world of knowledge and connection was there. She felt its hum, frantic and yet eternally patient, outside her room.

"Not the same," she said, and her voice made the emptiness bigger, worse.

She turned the horse to the east, and they moved on.

Night fell across their path, and everything turned gray and moon-like. Somewhere from the space era arcs, endless as an alien ocean-bed with no limit or form she could discern. A cold tendril curled in her gut. Maybe she had not become the first to travel in time, but had been flung instead to a far planet.

The ax handle, sticking out of the man's back, had been richly carved to look just like the ship's wolf. Blood spattered its wooden face, and its blank eye watched her retch. Now, her fingers tingled where she gripped the reins.

Stop. Stop it.

Eðna counted her fingers as she forced them each to relax. She imagined her favorite birds, one perched on each of the big rocks that spread to the horizon, and her mind's eye filled in the way their names would look, in white script beside their images. A violet-backed starling preened on a mat of mustard yellow lichens. The neon orange fan of a royal flycatcher waved in the breeze, and an incongruous swan spread its wings over dark pumice. She counted them as she slowly passed, always riding east, away from where the sun had been.

Yes. It was east, not a directionless moonscape. Some facts were timeless. She'd seen probably over 3,700 sunsets without the aid of lenses when she lived on her farm, and they always happened in the west. The sky always hung overhead, like it did tonight, dense and gently flickering with lights she had not seen since she was ten years old. They were pretty, and oddly comforting, giving depth and substance to what had been blank. An estimated 4,500 visible stars.

It was just like this—fine and starry—the night her Ma died.

Eðna, leave the sky for now, her father called. His typically expansive voice was subdued. She smoothed her dress and went inside their damp sod house.

Eðna lived on a fake farm, though she didn't know it. Her parents were fanatic realists—22nd century people who'd forsaken all the advances of humankind and lived like Viking settlers in the interior of Iceland. Her parents had given up all the knowledge of the real world, in an attempt at something "authentic." Little Eðna had no idea that out past the glacier there shone a universe of wonder and intellectual pursuit, more vast and varied than the stars.

A world where people did not die of elf-shot, an imaginary arrow to the gut, like her mother did.

Little Eðna had come inside at her father's call, and she watched Gida die in a terror of pain and fever. Eðna held Gida's hand hard and sobbed for her mommy. She rested her head on Gida's burning chest, and her mother touched her head with a slack hand. Eðna laid as though paralyzed, unable to bear watching as the unseen arrow twisted in Gida's belly. Yet, unable to let go.

While Eðna cried, Gida died of a simple, curable infection.

The next day, Eðna learned about the bigger world. She sat on the ground holding two sticks, drawing aimless shapes in a patch of dirt. Brenna, a young woman with wicked, witchy eyes came to sit beside Eðna. Vaguely dangerous and several years older, Brenna wore dresses that were too dark, too tight.

She took one of Eðna's sticks and drew a shape that she said was Iceland. She showed Eðna where they lived, a little way in from the edge, and then she dragged the stick all around the perimeter of the island. *And everything out here...* Brenna swirled her stick. *All this is full of people who could have saved your mother.*

The twig snapped.

Eðna's eyes flew open.

Darkness. A horse moving under her. Yes. She was riding in the night. Right.

She flicked her eyelids to scan for the source of the sound, but her contacts were still dead. She turned the horse in a circle. The animal snorted and reared, and Eðna yelped and clapped a hand to her mouth.

Three giants towered over her, massive against the dark gray sky. They had enormous rocks for heads, balanced on vaguely human bodies. All stone, like the sunlight-stricken trolls her Da talked about.

Only the horse had heard her shriek, but still she flushed with embarrassment.

Jen had described these massive cairns in her interviews. Eðna just had to put the stone women on the left, walk from shortest to tallest and follow their trajectory to Jen's farm. She was on the right path. And yet, in this negligible moonlight, even knowing what they were, the stone giants were not comforting. Gray night hung everywhere, dimming Eðna's world beyond just a few meters. Only mossy desolation stretched ahead and behind, and lichens that glowed like ghosts.

"I've reached the stone sisters," Eðna told her contacts, just in case they were picking anything up. Her voice wobbled. "Let's get this done."

She tightened her heels on the horse's sides, and they moved on, but the animal walked slower and slower, testing the way, afraid to touch something unseen.

Constant, shifting breezes sparkled on her skin. Before they died, her contacts had registered 10 degrees Celsius. Adjusted for the warmer averages in the 920s, it was likely April or May. Night would last approximately four or five hours.

She could make it in five hours. When the morning came, she would be there. She would watch the sun break over Hvítmork, and by the next night she'd be back in the lab with Jeff. Home safe to see Vera, her second mother, clapping her hands together. Eðna would establish that a person could be sent and brought back safely from the past. She would be the one who'd go down in history as proving it.

Yes. By tomorrow she could leave this world.

The horse drew up short. Something lay on the ground about five meters away. Not a lumpy stone like the thousand others.

Different. The horse hesitated, and she did too. She nudged him to investigate.

The shock was electric. A bird! Not a common crow like those she could see any time at home, or a raven, such a close cousin to the birds she knew in the city. This was the first real, different one that she could only see here in the past.

It lay dead on its side. Eðna dropped from the horse and knelt to observe it. She shouldn't touch it. Germs—tenth century ones—were dangerous. She pressed her hands to her thighs.

It was a small creature, about 25 centimeters from beak to tail. Its back and wings were speckled gray and white in the moonlight. She'd seen this kind of bird dozens of times in the arcs. Had breathlessly followed the curves of its wings with her fingertips, brushing the screens and leaving smudgy trails.

"Hallo, Singer." A kind of plover that bred in highlands and heathers, its song heralding spring. A group was called *a brace, a ponderance, a wing.*

The swirl on its breast became a line that traveled up its neck and curved back behind its eyes. It wound up around its forehead in a swoop, finally joining its small, dark beak. The shape of its coloring was like the curve of the ship rising out of the water—an image that seemed to hover, superimposed over the bird, but not generated by Eðna's contacts. It was her own recollection.

Eðna dug her fingers into her thighs, yearning to touch. She had to know what it felt like.

The sharply pointed beak was harder than rock, and slick like a fingernail. She let her fingers graze the wing. It was both slippery and rough at once, with pointy edges and tips on each feather. Little tines stuck to her callouses. She stroked in the direction the feathers grew, and her fingertips flew freely. When she stroked in the opposite direction, they prickled and fanned out, dividing and yet also clumping together. She drew her finger slowly along the edge and loosed the wing-threads into a fan.

"Vera," she whispered. If only she could record this sensation, so that Vera could feel a real bird's wing. Round, soft Vera who had taught her, cared for her, first shown her the birds in the visual arcs.

Eðna looked up, as if to show Vera, but of course she wasn't there. Eðna and the bird were alone on a vast plane.

The horse snorted, and Eðna snapped back to her mission. She stood and wiped her hands on her damp skirt. It was stupid to touch a dead animal. She drew out her flask and rubbed a tiny bit of whisky on her hands and fingers. In her pack, she had antibiotics and painkillers. She would be fine.

Her hands would remember real birds now, forever.

She rode farther. Small stands of bushes began to appear in the landscape. The sun was a pale suggestion coming up ahead of her now, confirming that she headed properly east.

Just like the day she first saw the city.

When she was ten, she'd run away. Gone with Brenna, and a man Brenna knew, to find civilization. She'd left her father behind without a word.

Now, he came rushing back, all of him, his charming smiles and silly winks, his worn ax handle with the shape of his hand in it, his giant shirts that she washed and hung on the line. She'd left him and gone unfathomably far.

"Da?" Her voice quavered. "Where are you?"

Eðna had prepared for many scenarios. In the simplest, on her way here to the past, she died. In others, she arrived in the wrong time or place. Someone saw her come through. Or no one saw her at all, and she wandered, just like now. Would she reach the X that marked Hvítmork on the vague maps and find that it didn't exist? Or that it did, but Jen had been cast out, murdered as a witch, like the men on the sand but worse?

Eðna was ready for all these things. She hadn't prepared for memories, for thoughts of her Da. For reliving her mother's death. Emotion hadn't even made the list.

She tried to review the last nine seconds of her recording to be sure the contacts hadn't captured her calling for her father, but they were dead.

Everything was dead here.

—A crack sounded, and she tensed. Nothing moved, but she heard the sound again. Something had definitely made a noise this time. Something that lived, after all the dead things she'd seen so far.

After a night of seeking something alive, an ally, a guide, now she hesitated, bathed in fear. Her heart rate increased. The ax in the man's back went deep. The blow was recent, blood still fluid.

Nei. She was prepared. She touched the knife at her belt. She had another in her boot, nothing to fear.

She called to it, whatever breathing thing it was, and she strained, as if she could hear its beating heart. In the lonely dimness, she craved life.

"Anyone?"

Brosa dragged a hand over his mouth and the tail of his beard. He blinked to wake his eyes.

It was a woman.

A spirit had come, and she would accept his trade.

He looked for his ax, and by the rising light of dawn he saw his situation. He sat in a dusty pit of bones. Hair still clung to his dead wife's skull. Sickness surged in his gut, and he struggled to stand, to climb out of the hole he'd dug. He covered Esa and his son with dirt as fast as a man could, and he staggered away, wiping his palm hard down his leg, grinding bone-dust into wool.

The woman called again. "Anyone?!!"

He'd expected his own name, when the spirit came for him.

He made his way up the rise, his leg still dragging with sleep, to meet her. Looking out over the land, he watched her approach.

His uncle told stories about the terrible goddess who roamed the highlands on a lame animal, herding the dead who were not destined for Valhalla. But he'd said she would be fierce. She would sit tall, her face smeared with blood and ash. She'd wear a belt adorned with forge-hot iron keys and the severed heads of children. Brosa expected hair writhing like eels, or braids clattering with knuckle bones, eyes lit from the inside as though her skull was filled with nothing but flame.

This woman did ride a tired horse, that was true. But that was the only feature she shared with Hár's vision of the reaper. Her long, tangled hair spilled like the ink Brosa had traded for in Norway – precious, dark liquid, staining her shoulders. Her chest folded in on herself, in exhaustion or weakness. A homespun dress clung to her legs, and the hems stuck to her ankles.

Nei matter. She was meant for him, and she had come.

"Here!" He waved his ax. "Over here!" The blade caught the early light, and she turned.

She turned her horse to Brosa, and he lurched toward her, the pull of the grave still in his legs.

He'd prepared for this moment, if a man possibly could. He imagined the reaper coming to him, but the details were formless as a moving cloud. She would burn his skin with her bony fingers and scrape his face with her savage nails. With the butt of her ax, she would shove him to the ground, raise her skirts and take him as a woman takes a lover, take his breath and heart into her.

This spirit was shivering and damp. Coming closer now, she was wrung out like a wet shirt. Her skin had a blue cast, as if he saw her through the thinnest sheet of ice on a milk barrel. Her fingers were frozen around the reins. Would she whisper with ice-breath in his ear? When her arms went around him, would they enclose him the way the sea might, searching with chilling fingers in his mouth and nostrils, under his wool and linen? He backed away, as if he could already feel her wintry fingers stroking his skin.

Stupid beast. He'd come here just for this, to lay down in the ground to signal her and call to her. And now she had come, and he was backing away.

He would have to touch her soon enough. He might as well help her from her horse. He took one step.

"Nei." She pulled herself up straight and jerked away, the horse stamping in warning. "Don't touch me. I'm fine."

"Já, alright then." Brosa held both his hands up. "Alright." This wasn't how it was done.

The spirit dropped from her horse and leaned against the animal. The sun was getting stronger, and it seemed that the milk-ice began to melt. Or were they tears on her cheeks?

"You are alive."

Was he meant to be dead already when she arrived?

"Have I done it wrong?"

"The bird was dead. Everything dead."

She swayed against her horse, and the animal stamped its feet and shifted. Brosa churned inside, wanting to help her stand, yet wanting to run from the damp horror that waited in her arms.

Was he that much of a coward, that he would come this far and then take back his offer to trade his soul?

The spirit's legs gave way, and Brosa caught her in his arms. She smelled like horse and seawater, and her braids had been taken apart by the wind and the night. She wore a kind of fine armor over her dress, a top of dark leather as thin as linen, and it was soaked to blackness.

She was damp and cold, já, but not foul. In truth, her shivering body sparked desire in him—a yearning to hold her small head against him and let her take his heartbeat. Take his living heart, and give it to a new child yet to be made.

She pushed him away. "Let go!"

Her hand went to a small blade, and she drew it quick as an eel. Brosa held his hands up to reason with her.

"Alright, Woman. I won't hurt you." Maybe she was a new reaper, sprung from the water to come to him. She didn't know how to do this either. "Can you tell me, do you have a name?"

"My name." She held her small knife still pointed at him. "Eðna."

"Eðna."

He'd expected something more glorious. A name that inspired gut-voiding fear.

"Everything was dead," she said. "The bird I saw on the ground."

These were not the words he'd imagined, in the moments before he was taken to the everlife. He'd thought, maybe they would talk about the life he'd led, what he was worthy of. The knowledge he had, of writing and boat design, the gift of his drawings that lay curled in the leather case at his waist. The years he'd spent obeying and upholding his brother, the courage he'd shown when he lost his mother, and when his newborn son died in his lap.

"It was about this big—" Eðna looked at her two palms, and for a moment Brosa thought she spoke of his baby. But she was speaking of the bird.

She lifted her eyes to him. And then her face went blank with wonder, as though she'd never seen a man before.

As though Brosa's face was the very air she needed to spark her fire, she began to turn from ash to delicate pink. An arrow of sun pierced through the clouds and bit her from one side, and it turned her hair all the colors of the woods after harvest. Brown leaves and deep shade, without a single child's bones in her braids. And while it was nei bonfire that lit her head, her dark brown eyes did flare with flecks of the flame he'd been expecting. Not a skull full of fire, then, but some. Like the promising glow before a flame leaps.

She followed his hairline with her ember eyes, followed his river of scars down to his beard. It was tangled and dusty and wrapped up in the leather cord he always wore and now regretted. She looked at his chest, his fine amber clothes, his arms where his bracers were tied, and she blushed, turning her pale skin pink.

Já, she was a new reaper he'd awakened, and she was finding her way. The sea-cold creature changed into a cream and woodland spirit. A spirit with thick, arched eyebrows, and full lips like berries that fell open, just a little, enough to kiss.

A memory caught him, as if by the tail. When he was a boy, Svana's lips had fallen open, just this way, before he pressed his mouth to hers. They kissed to see what it was like to be grown-ups.

If he kissed this reaper, would she be soft that way? Would she taste of mint and sea-dew?

"It's too bad I won't see my uncle again," Brosa said. He would tell Hár that he'd been wrong, so wrong about the reaper.

Surely he was worthy of this new one. Of being her first.

"You can put your knife down." He spoke gently. She seemed to like birds. "Let me tell you about the hawks I've seen in the old country."

"Hawks," she said, and she looked him over again. Her voice came so quiet, on a fresh and lovely breath. "Yes."

Eðna lowered her knife.

After all the death tonight—the men's corpses, the morbid bird, the grinding memories of her mother's last breath—this big man was alive. More than that, he was *lit* with life.

His skin was wind-kissed, his beard the color of the honey she'd once tasted, like sweet, liquid amber. His hair was electrified by brighter, almost white streaks, the same way the sun limned the morning clouds with white-gold.

He must be a shepherd. Yes. A blazing sun of a shepherd.

"My first living person." Here in the past, a living, breathing Viking, who was nothing like the rich men who played at being Vikings in her time, who went to bed at night in plush, heated beds, their clothes sanitized and warm from the dryer, dirt-free shoes tossed on the carpet. This man was visceral and messy, and he made everything wild. He spoke to her of hawks, and the old language—like sleek, tumbled stones—slipped from his tongue.

"Já, that's me," the man said. "Still alive." He stamped his foot, knocking dust from his massive boots.

Eðna blinked to capture his image, but functions were erratic. Even so, if her contacts worked, they could never register the wash of night-cold that rolled off his body as he came near. The scents of fresh dirt and grass, and the dust that stuck to the huge, scarred bracers at his wrists. There was no indoors for this man. He'd been sleeping here in the hills.

His lips were dry with dust, but they looked warm with the promise of charming smiles and murmured, private words. Eðna should confirm, with her fingers, just a touch. The way she had with the bird, so that her hands would know and remember this man. The same way they knew feathers now, forever.

What was she thinking?

Had time travel addled her brain?

She wiped her hands on her dirty dress, where the fabric clung to her thighs. She tucked loose strands of hair behind her ears. This shepherd looked kind and full of life, já. Not threatening. But she kept her hand on her knife hilt and stepped back. She scanned the environment. "Where are your sheep?"

"Sheep." The man spread his hands out, empty. "Was I supposed to bring an animal as well? I have none."

"But, you are a shepherd."

"Smalamadr?" He tilted his head, confused, and vividly colored waves of hair fell around his shoulders.

"I know I'm a mess, Lady," he said, and he stamped his foot again to loosen more dirt. "But I'm nei shepherd. I have a fine house, a warm fire. Silver and blades to bring you."

He hefted an ax, laid it across his two palms and held it out to her. His offering was so quick, a weapon suddenly in her face, she stepped back.

The ax gleamed. It was sharpened with the finest edge, and its gorgeous, carved handle glowed as golden as the man's beard. The wood was engraved with swirls and cables that ran down the length of the handle to the end, where it was shaped into the head of an animal. A dog or wolf. So familiar.

He was offering it willingly.

Eðna disarmed him. She snatched the ax and held it in both her hands. So heavy, it swayed in her grip. The man stepped back, hands up again, in peace.

"Woman," he said. "I'm doing my best, but I don't know how we do this."

"Do this?"

"I'm ignorant of death, já?" He ran a hand through his hair, and it stuck there, as though he was trying to hold something in. "After all the times you've come close enough to take so many of my family. Please, will you take my trade?"

"You want to trade your ax?" She looked to her waist and touched her pack, then looked to her horse. "I have nothing you would want."

"Gods," he growled. He kicked a rock and stalked away.

She called after him. "You're not a shepherd?"

He turned to face her, his frustration obviously rising. "I am Brosa Ulfsson. You've come for me, nei?"

Eðna sorted the seldom-used Old Icelandic words at the back of her mind. Brosa, an old word for mirth and light, for a smile.

"Brosa Ulfsson." It was easy and hot like whisky on her lips, and it felt good to say it. It felt as familiar as the ax.

Brosa.

Eðna's eyes snapped open. Her contacts jumped to life, and names, dates, sketches zoomed past, and her mission suddenly rushed back into focus. She'd studied the tree of their lineage, and the artists' drawings that tried to render the people Jen/Ginn described. Eðna superimposed the drawing of Heirik's darling, gorgeous brother over this real man, who loomed just a meter away with his arms crossed in frustration. The drawn image was all wrong. Too severe, unsmiling. But it was him. "Brosa."

"Já," he said. "Will you take me?"

Almost at the same moment, so that their words tumbled over one another, she said, "You can take me."

"I can take you?" What was the woman about? "I'm right here."

"Já, you are here. Brosa Ulfsson! Yes!"

The spirit brightened and burned with excitement, and his blood coursed with fear at what might come next. What would it feel like to die? To go with Eðna?

"But I'm not looking for you," she said, and those full berry lips closed into a sewn line. "I'm looking for Hvítmork. For Jen."

Jen.

Gods. That was the other name for Ginn.

"Gods, nei." She wanted Ginn, his brother's only happiness.

Brosa growled, turned from Eðna and trudged away. His boots drove hard into the dirt.

This spirit wouldn't even take the few things he had to give. Wouldn't take his life or even his comfort, which she surely needed. She only wanted him to act as guide, to take her close enough so she could grab Ginn and ride away into the afterlife. The two of them would fly away on her terrible, tired horse, suddenly made fierce and fast, with their ice blond and dark woodland hair streaming out behind. Too fast for him or Heirik to catch. His brother would be left alone.

Anguish twisted in Brosa's gut, and he held himself. "Take me instead, Eðna."

"You?" She called after him. "Nei, it's Jen I need to see."

"Ginn," he told her. "Don't take her. Take me, and give her a new life – a child of her own." He couldn't hide his bitterness. His voice was like knives. "Take my life, like you did my son's."

Her brows drew down tight. "What?"

"I'm trying to offer myself, Eðna. To go with you. I have waited, wondered," Brosa said. "If you would accept my offer. My life for a new one."

She lifted his ax, wary again. "I have no idea what you're talking about." She shook her head, her thick brows pulled tight. "I haven't killed anyone. I just got here, from one thousand-two years away."

Brosa's mind spun so that he had to put a hand out and steady himself.

Ginn had told him where she came from, já, though he could not fathom it any more than he could the depths of the sea. And now this woman Eðna was telling him she came from that place too, from years and years beyond reckoning.

Eðna was from Ginn's world. She was a real woman. "You're no spirit."

Eðna's brows drew down again, and she said, "A spirit?" She laughed. "No."

He turned from her and walked to the edge of the rise, and a tide turned in his gut. This Eðna was a flesh and blood woman. A threat to Ginn. And he had given her his ax, held her in his arms.

Esa's grave lay below him, disturbed and fresh. He narrowed his gaze, and his heart picked up. Was that a bone he had left sticking up out of the ground?

Gods, to defile and provoke the dead was the worst crime a man could commit. Worse than murder. A reaper would understand that he'd lain down with Esa. But Eðna was nei reaper, and he couldn't let her see what he'd done.

"Brosa?"

Gods damn her, she was right behind him. He turned on her and walked toward her, pushing her back down the rise, away from the view of the grave. "Why have you come? What do you want with Ginn?"

"She spoke about the beauty in this place, and I wanted to know if I could make it here too." Eðna blinked her eyes like a bird. "Is she here? Did she make it?"

Brosa's insides tossed again.

Eðna didn't know that Ginn had made it here.

What else would she not know, then? Nothing that had happened since Ginn returned two summers ago? Surely, Eðna would not know of Ginn's wedding to Heirik, nor the changes she had made as mistress of Hvítmork. Eðna would know nothing of the unbelievable solace his brother had come to know, in the midst of a bleak and solitary life. The different man, the satisfied man, Heirik had become. And the protective, fierce woman Ginn had become, at Heirik's side.

"Stop," Eðna said, and she raised his ax, shielding herself.

He was scaring her with his anger and his big strides, pushing her away from the top of the hill, from the view of Esa's grave. "Gods, I'm sorry, Woman." He dropped to his knee. "I don't mean any harm."

"Just tell me," she said, voice shaking, but strong. "Did Ginn make it to Hvítmork?"

Brosa's knee ground into the dirt, and his eyes rested on Eðna's dusty hems. He could tell this woman that Ginn had disappeared and never come back to Hvítmork. Maybe it would go better for Eðna. She could turn around, go home by the sea and never find out about Ginn's fierceness, the people she had ordered to be killed or exiled.

But something in him wanted to take Eðna home.

Last night, he dug into the ground and felt her coming through the land, through the night. And here she was. He lifted his eyes to her belt, slung low on her hips, and fine leather strands that laced up her leather top. The ends curled against her hips.

"Ginn is here," he said. "She is my brother's wife and lady of all this." He swept his gaze across the horizon.

Eðna brightened with a light he'd seen in the eyes of traders in the south. A hungry look, hiding the real price of things. She said, "Will you take me to her?"

The fact of Esa's bones behind him was a force. Brosa yearned to turn back and look. He could almost feel his wife rising as a wraith over the hill, wending her way like smoke to come whisper against the back of his neck. *Don't.*

"Nei." He shook his head. But he was speaking to Esa's ghost, not Eðna. Some force of will rose up in him that he hadn't felt in a long time.

He would not answer to bones.

To Eðna he said, "You can hold the ax, if it pleases you." He stood and brushed himself off, but the dust was thick. "But you'll need to stow it in your belt so we can ride."

Brosa whistled for Gull, and the animal came to him from over a rise in the land, eager and strong. Eðna looked amazed, as if she'd never seen a hale and healthy horse. Brosa mounted, and he gestured with his chin for Eðna to get up behind him.

"I'll take you, Eðna," Brosa said, "but you have to ride with me."

"I can ride myself." She looked around for her horse. It was on its side sleeping in the sparse grass.

"You may be strong, but your animal needs rest. He would take a day to carry you there."

She hesitated, and Brosa thought maybe she could not mount the horse behind him. Ginn said they had no animals. When Ginn came here, she could not even ride the slowest old girl.

But Eðna tucked the ax into her belt, with the blade snug against her side, as if she'd done so many times. She pushed her loose hair behind her ears, put her foot in the stirrup and pushed off the ground with ease. Her arms went around his waist, and she murmured against his back. "Þakka þér."

A low thrill crept through his bones. He looked in stark wonder at his hands, resting, dusty, on the reins.

He had no idea who Eðna truly was, or how she fit into the gods' plans. But her small whisper of thanks, and the touch of her head against his back, made him want to help her. She was small and brave, freezing, wet. She needed him. And she kindled something in him that he hadn't felt in a long time.

He reached down for her leg and touched her thigh to give some kind of comfort, and she slapped him away.

"Don't touch me," she said, and he smiled.

He kicked Gull's sides and they took off fast.

Eðna clung to Brosa's back on top of Gull, as they raced into the wind. Her arms impossibly, intimately wrapped around a man, her cheek pressed tight so that it jolted endlessly against his shirt, with the horse's footfalls beating in her brain. Everything in her recoiled. She had to let go of his rough, moving body.

She hung on. Senses overloaded, hair blowing into her eyes and nose, the lye soap scent of his dirty shirt, dust in her eyelashes. Grass and lichens went by fast as a data stream, their Latin and common names, in the script of ancient botanical prints, whizzing by. *P. Alpina, D. Octopetala, S. Herbacea.* Meadowgrass, avens, snowbed. A sky so enormous, ever brightening.

She could not see ahead.

Brosa's ax was tucked into Eðna's belt, and the long handle with its carved dog's head thumped against her leg. The knots and cables that adorned it shone warm and yellow in the sun. The dog's unseeing, wooden eye, was so familiar.

The ax.

Little wings of panic beat in her ribcage. This ax was familiar. It had the same patterns as the one she saw in the dead man's back.

Did she ride now with her arms around a murderer? A man capable of such a thing? She gripped Brosa's waist harder, fear pooling in the soles of her feet.

She breathed and let her eyes go soft and unfocused, her thoughts gliding like large birds. Spoonbills and cranes. Not flitting, hopping warblers.

No. Ginn described Brosa Ulfsson as a good man. The best, besides the chief himself.

This man had not killed the ones in the tent. Brosa, still had this ax, so there must be another just like it. And Brosa was working in the hills last night, still sleepy from a night in the grass when she arrived, not at the ocean. The scent and stains on the rough tunic under her cheek proved it.

"Hold on, Eðna." Brosa kicked the horse's side. Gull tilted forward to plunge down a hill, and all Eðna's weight fell into Brosa's back, hot and sweaty and unavoidable. Brosa reached back to touch her thigh—a simple, reassuring weight—and this time she let him.

He was the chieftain's brother. He would not hurt her.

"Thoughts like swans," Eðna murmured into his back. Breaths like long, slow descents into placid lakes.

A white wall shot up beside them, and Eðna blinked.

What?

A Latin name appeared, too fast for her to recognize before the letters elongated and disappeared. Eðna's eyes blurred with wind-tears, and the wall flickered like a massive screen, not quite opaque. Too tall and long to be any man-made structure they knew of from this time. She sorted possibilities, and a startling answer came.

Trees!

So many trees. A collective wash of white bark. Minute upon racing minute, a river of *Betula pendula,* birches never ending no matter how fast or far Gull flew. Their silver bark was unlikely to exist in the abundance that Jen described, and yet here these trees went by, shimmering just like Jen said. *Hvítmork.* The White Woods. The name of their farm.

Were they almost there?

The ends of Brosa's hair tickled Eðna's nose. His dirt scent mixed with the cool air that whistled in her ears. Her heart beat hard and Brosa's body echoed the rhythm, sending his own pulse back.

The grass underfoot was young green now, more tender, less tough than the weeds in the hills. They climbed again so fast that her stomach lurched. The horse topped a big rise and came to an abrupt stop, and Brosa turned Gull so Eðna could see.

"There, then," he said, breathless. "Hvítmork."

A stone dropped into Eðna's gut.

Below them, a green and savage expanse of grass and hills

spread out forever, untouched by the glittering towers of the city.

What had she done?

Hvítmork was a few buildings, more like humps in the land. Nothing more. Enormous land, without civilization. A few people and animals, all tiny, moved below.

"Gone," she murmured against Brosa's back.

Everything Eðna lived for was gone. Had never yet come to be. And she was gone. If she got lost, no one would ever find her.

Her contacts laid Jen's hand-drawn map over the actual landscape, Jen's circles and wobbly lines hovered over buildings, her words—*stable, forge, house*—floated next to each feature.

The points on Eðna's map moved subtly, adjusting themselves to reality. The lines matched themselves to the long, low grass house, more like a slope in the land, or a small hill, than a building. Dogs and children chased each other around its perimeter, a little girl's straw-colored braids bouncing behind her.

"Be careful with Ginn," Brosa said. And more words, about how it might go well for Eðna if she watched, waited.

Eðna half heard him. She stared in horror at the primitive house. Her contacts used Jen's description of its length—156 paces for a 1.75 m/5'9" man, her estimate of Heirik Rakknason's height—as a reference for measuring all the rest.

A stone-rimmed bath sent steam lazily into the air, right where Eðna expected. The forge crouched slightly uphill from where Jen had described it, a semicircle of stones, so big that a man now leaned against one, watching another man pound something into flat submission. Eðna could just hear their laughter and the clang of iron.

The stable stood in approximately the same place as Ginn had drawn it, about 30 meters from the house's back door. A round, low building, with wedge-shaped stalls. Chickens traversed the top of the waist-high earthen wall that circled the stable. A cow stood outside, chewing and swishing its tail.

And then, there was something that did not appear on Jen's map at all. Another house. This one majestically large compared to the first. It was about a half-K distant, and it stood more upright than the smaller dwelling, shaped more like the hall of a jarl or king in Norway, but covered in shaggy grass like an Icelandic settler's home. Nearly twice as big as the other house. Outrageously large.

Eðna zoomed in to see it up close.

Ornate double doors gleamed with a midnight finish. The contours of animal bodies spiraled and climbed above a tremendous arch. An imposing entrance. Something sizzled in Eðna's ears, a short zap and then her contacts broke down again. The carved animals rushed away, suddenly tiny, too far to make out clearly. They came back, with sickening jerks, suddenly huge.

"—Broðr!" Brosa's voice thundered in her bones.

Eðna looked up, and there was a man coming toward them through the grass. Silhouetted against the bright sun, far across a field, his face was in shadow. But even if Brosa had not called him brother, Eðna would have recognized Heirik Rakknason.

Eðna touched the knife-hilt at her waist.

Rakknason.

With streaming clouds and sun behind him, he was a dark vision of a chieftain, a settler in a rough land of ax-hewn justice. His tunic fell just above his knees, legs bound tight, ax swinging by his side. He moved with the loose, graceful gait that Jen had described so many times in her journal. The chief's long hair now caught in a breeze and streamed like the black feathers of a widowbird in flight.

Eðna zoomed in. Enhanced her vision.

Heirik Rakknason was smiling.

A small boy walked beside him, fumbling with a little ax, and the boy looked up, unconcerned by the chief's shocking appearance, which was clear to Eðna now. His tangle of black hair set off the crimson birthmark that covered one side of his face, and his eyes were the unearthly yellow Jen spoke of. But they were warm and amused as he spoke to the boy. The chief pointed out something on his own ax, and showed the boy how to heft it and turn his wrist.

Eðna had studied this man's solemn eyes on her wall screen. When Jen had accidentally traveled here to the 10th century, her contacts had recorded her experiences for a few hours before failing, and in that time, they'd captured an image of this man in the freezing foam at the edge of the sea. A man driven by logic, responsibility, wolfish curiosity. A man who did not smile. Whose eyes did not crinkle at the corners when he bent to speak with a child.

Jen had described the chief's calculating ruthlessness and physical prowess. The way he moved and spoke with spare gestures and words, his decisions all designed to protect his family and solidify his position. He'd cut the hand right off a man with one stroke of his ax, to prove a complex point about his power and that of the gods. Eðna struggled to reconcile that man with this one who laughed at something the boy said.

His tunic fell just above his knees, legs bound tight, ax swinging by his side.

The chief looked up with that smile still on his face, until he saw Eðna. In that moment, he drew himself closed like a gate, and she saw the distant and forbidding chief she'd been expecting. The change was so swift and complete, Eðna zoomed out fast and drew her head back.

"You don't have to fall to your knees," Brosa said, a tinge of bitterness in his voice. "You're my guest."

He wasn't kidding.

Eðna slid off the horse, and when she reached the ground, exhaustion hit. Her legs ached from riding all night, and she was suddenly aware of the cold in her bones and the damp dress clinging to her knees. She was acutely aware of the chief, just a few meters away and coming closer.

"Good," she said. She'd intended to drop to her knees in respect for the chief, but now she wobbled. She steadied herself on Brosa's arm, and her fingertips brushed the battered leather laces of his bracers.

"Herra," Brosa said, as he got down off of Gull's back. "I have news."

Herra. Brosa called his own brother by his title of honor.

The chief set the head of his ax firmly on the ground beside his foot and rested the long handle against his leg. His unnerving eyes flicked to the ax at Eðna's side, but he gave away no surprise, no concern. He crossed his arms loosely, and waited, resting those eyes on Eðna.

Rakknason's cheekbones were sharp, cheeks hollow, so that he looked hungry. The way his hair was pulled back tight off his forehead gave him an air of wild alertness, of instinct close to the surface.

Powerful. Intimidating. But not beautiful. Not like Brosa.

Gods, so many odd, stray thoughts kept coming forward from the mush of her exhausted mind. Eðna shook her head for the hundredth time. Her purpose here was an invitation to the house, to meet Ginn. That was her objective.

"Brother." The chief raised his brows, never taking his eyes from Eðna. "What is this?"

"She is Eðna." Brosa gave the slightest weight to the word she.

"Hallo," Eðna said. "Good to know you."

The old words stuck to her tongue, though she'd spoken Old Norse and Icelandic almost exclusively for months, practicing for this moment. Her dress was streaked with dirt, and stray bits of grass and strands of her hair clung to her skin around her neckline. A far more humble appearance than she'd wished for meeting the chief.

"She wandered alone," Brosa said. "Out past the walls."

"Alone." The chief still did not look at his brother, only at Eðna. Whatever shred of emotion the man had shown, whatever smile had touched his lips went she first saw him, was erased. "Where are your people?"

Eðna licked salt from her lips. "Far from here," she said.

Over the past several months, she'd had time to consider what she might say if she met Rakknason first. Words designed to appeal to the chief's sense of pride in his brave and remarkable wife, appeal to his sense of honor that would drive him to help another cold, damp woman from the future. Words that might make him trust her and bring her to Jen.

But Brosa broke in. "It seems the gods like to send them in spring."

The chief's eyes finally let Eðna go and shifted to Brosa. "Sjódottir also?"

Daughter of the ocean.

A beloved name, because his wife was from the sea too, but it carried no inherent honor. It was a backhanded compliment, or perhaps a fluidly delivered insult. As if Eðna did not have a father or mother to be named after.

"I am Eðna Jonsdottir. I—"

Brosa cut in again. "—Já, she is from the sea," he said. "But I met her in the hills."

Eðna yearned to tell Brosa to shut up, to let her speak.

The horse shifted behind them, tucking its nose against his shoulder, and Brosa reached up to pet the animal.

"You brought her to us," the chief said.

Brosa ducked his head, so slightly, as if to nuzzle with the horse, but she saw that it was in supplication before the chief, silently asking if he'd done the right thing. Big and beautiful Brosa, submitting to his own brother.

Eðna moved closer to his side.

"She knew the way," Brosa said. "Surely as an arrow."

Eðna had been wandering aimlessly, anything but sure and arrow-like when she ran into Brosa. Why was he stretching the truth?

Rakknason considered her.

Unlike Brosa's expansive force of life, the chief's strength was contained. With just a few words and the way he crossed his arms, the way he looked into her soul, and yet didn't look at her at all. He embodied everything that such a man—a powerful, cursed, physically striking man—might. Privilege and self-possession, protectiveness. Her father would have fallen down at this man's feet.

At the same time, he had a kind of endearing, worried look, questioning with a barely noticeable tilt of his head. As if he were rapidly working out possible scenarios and reasons for her presence.

"What have you come for?"

He cut straight to the marrow. Those unreal eyes that had smiled for the little boy were now emotionless. They saw everything, as if the chief had his own augmented vision to match hers. As if he could read all that was written in her contacts. Every bit of her plan was laid bare, insignificant and small. She had come here to learn, but suddenly it felt like a crime.

Crowded by two giant men, she backed away to see their faces.

"I've come." Eðna's throat went dry, and she started again. "I've come to see." That was all she could manage, and then her words gave out. The chief's black hair went in and out of focus, the land behind him gray, then green.

Sjódottir. The chief had asked as if Eðna were born of the water. As if her life had begun only when it came in contact with his sand. He gave no thought to who Eðna was before the beach, and no credit for her amazing journey, her bravery and intelligence. Nothing.

Brosa moved close to her side, and she shifted toward him. His palm was warm against the base of her spine. He steadied her.

She could do this.

Heirik Rakknason was intense, yes. But his gold eyes were no more unusual than any color that could be applied to contacts. She herself had once had pink. And if anyone was incredible here, it was her. She'd made it to Hvítmork, accurately traveling through time and space to stand here before him. She straightened her spine, leveled her own gaze back at the chief.

"I'm Eðna Jonsdottir," she said. "And I'm here to find your wife."

Did concern flicker briefly in those unreal eyes?

Jen had talked for hours about this man, and deep in her files, she'd left behind a personal journal that laid out her soul, and his, for anyone to read. Heirik had lived under the weight of profound loneliness until Jen came along. Untouchable, because of his appearance, his life was stark and hard. Jen had breathed new life into this man. She'd given him his soul back. She was important to him.

"What Ginn did was fearless and wondrous," Eðna said her practical words. Persuasive words. "A woman of her courage…I wanted to see if I could do what she did. I want to meet her, to learn from her."

A quiet moment passed. Two real birds flew in an enormous loop overhead. Eðna strained to ignore them, to focus.

The chief's words were so few when he finally released them. He told Brosa, "I'll find Ginn at the river." And then to Eðna, "My wife will want you to stay."

It wasn't exactly warm. For a second she thought the concern in Heirik's eyes was not for himself and his family, but for Eðna. He headed off toward the river to find his wife, his stride sure, but his shoulders tense underneath all that dark hair and wool.

Eðna turned to Brosa.

"Well, then, I guess I've been welcomed."

"Nei worry." Brosa began to walk up the hill, and Eðna matched him with giant steps. "My brother doesn't know how to talk to people."

Eðna picked her skirt up, so the filthy hems cleared the ground, and she stepped over spring grass and bunches of silvery lichens.

The land around the house was a sea of fresh green hills, with queasy dips and rises in all directions. Eðna was lost in the hollows and troughs, swimming against sickening waves.

The forge stood on one of the highest hills. Several big boulders were arranged to protect the fire pit. Iron hammers rested against the biggest rock, and a banked fire sent up ghostly wisps of smoke that remained from its last use. Just as Jen had drawn it. It was real, not an image on a screen. Eðna was so close. She was at the end of her strength, but she thrummed with excitement and dread.

Part of her wanted to sprint to the river, throw Jen over her shoulder, run the whole way back to the coast and plunge their hands into the water. Take Jen home with her to prove she'd made it. Another part of her just wanted to stop right here and shout with triumph and delight that she had made it this far at all. But something wrong and unsettling lurked underneath the excitement. The way the chief had spoken of his wife was disquieting. *She'll want you to stay.* And the dead men hung heavily in her mind.

Calm.

It wasn't possible that the chief could see into her heart, to her plans and secrets. Despite his extraordinary eyes, he was human.

"He's protective." Brosa slowed his huge steps, and Eðna caught up. "More than ever, now that he has Ginn."

"Yes," she said. "I got that."

Brosa waited at the top of the hill, leaning on one of the big forge rocks, with the steel sky framing him. Slanted sunlight touched his hair and hundreds of strands of gold seemed to wake up within the warm, dark blond. A sudden gust lifted it all, and it fanned out, a golden mane like extinct, big cats in the arcs. He smiled a little half smile.

"Are you going to stand and look at me, Woman? Or go see Ginn?"

"I'm not looking," Eðna snapped. "I'm fine."

"Eðna, be clear about it." He lost the mischievous smile. "You being here, it is unsettling for the chief. But Ginn is even more protective than he is. You could be in danger."

"Oh, come on," she said.

"You don't need to worry—"

"—I'm not afraid."

"Shh, Woman. Just, be careful with her. She's taken some hard revenge on women who have wronged her."

"What kind of revenge?"

"Nei matter right now," he said, glancing down toward the house. "Just know she is a wolf in her den."

Eðna looked to the ax that hung by his thigh, and its carved, unseeing dog. Was Brosa a violent enough man to kill for something he cared about?

"Like you?"

"Nei." He did it again, that small smile. "I'm no wolf. More of a house dog."

"I'll remember that." Eðna laughed, but it was hollow. Standing here at the very forge where Jen's husband honed his ax, it felt less triumphant, and a lot more dangerous and tense, than she'd imagined.

"You'll meet Ginn, and then we'll know how it will go for you."

They walked downhill to the house.

"Betta will have a dress for you, too." He looked to where she still held her hems up off the ground. "And dry socks."

Eðna looked down too. "Oh, you think I need a new dress?"

He cocked his head for a better look at her ankles, and a slow smile grew within the scruffiness of his beard. "Well, perhaps nei, if you want to stay in the stalls."

"The stalls?"

"With my sheep?"

She could see it already, how Brosa slipped into playfulness when everything was tense. He actually winked.

Sheep?

Oh gods, right. She'd called him a shepherd – one of the lowliest jobs in this time. A blush bloomed on her throat. "You need clean clothes yourself, you know."

He looked down at his own shirt and wiped it ineffectually. "Ah, já, I suppose I do." He brushed dirt off his thighs as they walked. "I was digging."

"Digging." She'd come across him so early. "In the night?"

His pace wavered.

"Twilight," he said. He smoothed the tail of his beard. "I worked until the day ended. Slept under the stars."

Eðna ran the back of her hand across her cheek, and it came away streaked with sweat and dust. No wonder, since she'd buried her face against Brosa's back.

"Digging for what?"

"Look," he brightened. He took a deep, preparatory breath. "The house. I'm sure Ginn will be here soon."

It stood strong and tall up close, with brilliant morning clouds rolling out behind it. *Stratocumulus.* Impossibly pale orange and mossy blue on their undersides. Eðna had prepared for Hvítmork to feel like her childhood home—the house her Da, Jon, had built. But this house was so much bigger, its walls alive with healthier grass than she'd ever known.

Lustrous, vivid grass grew everywhere, springing from dirt so saturated it was almost black. Fertile land. Children and men and animals wandered into the yard. Women with spindles and wary looks. Little boys with small spears and shields lowered at their sides. Two girls with rolled braids, one of them rocking a wooden doll.

Eðna used to play that way. Her doll was made of stuffed cloth.

The little girls looked up and stared. One by one, each of the people in the yard stopped and stared.

Brosa pressed his palm against the small of her back, and she moved away.

"I'll meet Jen on my own."

She wouldn't let Brosa scare her with undefined references to Jen's protectiveness. What did that even mean? Eðna had traveled through time to stand unafraid in this land, to watch Jen come up from the river and into her life. When Jen invited her in, Eðna would walk over this woman's threshold standing tall, with the crossed, open-mouthed creatures on the doorframe eating the sky above her head.

Brosa nodded. "You'll do well," he said, but he had a vaguely worried look, much like his brother's.

Eðna shook it off, along with the warmth where his hand had been.

Brosa turned to the kids in the yard and spread his arms wide. "Who can catch me?"

The children shrieked and went after him, leaving Eðna to meet Ginn alone. She breathed deep and looked toward the river.

ᛋ

Svana drew her sharpest needle through fine fabric, the color of a rain-soon sky.

She did not dare think of Eiðr dead. Nei.

Her mother always told Svana that the color of this dress made her eyes light up like a shimmering pool. She mended it by the outside fire, looking up every few minutes. No one came, and so she kept at her needle.

Stitch, stitch, stitch.

She did not think of Rakknason. She did not think of the chief's dead yellow eyes, his bloody face gone pale with loss when he was cast out as a murderer for killing Eiðr. Heirik's face that she had once touched with tenderness and revulsion. Though it sickened her just to untie the chief's bracers and stroke his cursed arm beneath, she had done it. She had once listened to her mother and tried to get him to marry her.

Her hands shook, not thinking about him.

A bird shrieked.

"Frigg!" She jumped, and the needle bit her again. She sucked her finger. Her lovely blue dress had blood on it.

So much anger sewn into this dress. Her one remaining fine piece of clothing. When she wore it, it pulled close against her hips and breasts and drew men's' eyes. She smiled and ran her fingers along the elegantly shaped sleeve. One man was all she cared about, and he was a man who liked a woman in a well-cut dress. He came to her, in her thoughts sometimes, golden and hale, driven by a gods-given fire. His sea-strong eyes. His ready laughter, warm breath on her cheek as she leaned in to trim his beard to a fine point. Brosa.

"I'm the chief," he'd said to her, when they were small children. "You be the wife of the house." And she hung sticks at her belt to be the keys. She told him how many sheep to slaughter, and to wipe his boots.

Now, she had a real husband and a real house—a cramped room with a small, smoky hearth, with a single roof vent that let in little sun. It smelled of old food and dirty clothes, with no thralls to wash their small collection of shirts and Eiðr's filthy pants.

He kept an old fur coat of his dead sister's, Esa's, hanging from a hook in the corner, as if the woman weren't several years gone. Esa had once been Brosa's wife, and sometimes when Eiðr was not home, Svana would nuzzle into the fur on the collar of that coat, where Brosa had rested his cheek so many times during his marriage. She could just smell the scent of sea-dew and dust that always clung to him.

This was not the life Svana deserved, smelling a dead woman's coat to seek the scent of her man. In her true life, in her heart, Heirik Rakknason was dead and Brosa was risen to chieftain, with Svana close by his side.

The gods and fate had taken that life away from her. But it must be possible. The gods took, but they also gave back, time and again.

She counted out the times with her stitches.

First, when they were young, the family decided the chief would never marry, because of his bloody curse. That was when the idea took life in her mother's mind, that Svana would marry Brosa and become head of the great Hvítmork household. But then Brosa was wed to lovely Esa.

Stitch, stitch.

The gods gave Svana hope again when Esa died in childbirth, but then Brosa was sent away to trade. He came home and was betrothed to Ginn, that conniving beastess. The gods gave Svana hope again when Ginn rejected him. Rejected him! The woman's head was loose.

Stitch, stitch, stitch.

Soon Svana would wear this blue dress to the widow Ginn's house, when Heirik was cast out for his crime – the crime that had been done at Svana's own bidding. The murder of Eiðr.

Rakknason would be an outlaw, as good as dead to the world of men.

It was a dress like the sky, to travel in, to go get something better.

Hoof beats pounded on the other side of the rise, and she stood from her sewing. The job was done. The shepherd boy would crest the rise now, with news that Eiðr was dead, as planned.

The horse thundered nearer.

She didn't expect the man who came over the hill. Oh, nei. It was not the hired boy.

Nei, nei, nei.

His greasy hair and sneer were too familiar, his rough clothes, crooked nose, one good hand on the reins. Eiðr. The gods sucked all breath from her body, pushed her forward, stumbling toward her husband. He was not dead. Everything fell apart, fell to the dirt with her mending.

He pulled up short before her, breathless. "Wife! I have news.'

"You are not at the sea."

"Of course I'm not, Woman. I'm here. The chief changed the work today." He turned dark with rage. "But I have been to the hills."

"The hills." What matter were the hills? Had he found her nithing pole?

"My sister's grave," he said. "It is defiled. Dug up and her bones revealed." His voice trembled with anger, almost tears, with raging love for his dead goddess-sister Esa.

Her grave dug up.

This was not part of Svana's plan. Gods. After all she had plotted, all she had paid and had yet to pay, here Eiðr stood before her, alive.

"Nei!" She wailed like a widow and hit the ground on her knees. She sobbed, "Nei, nei."

Eiðr dropped to his knees beside her, his arm rushed around her and his touch made water come up in her mouth.

"Wife," he said. He touched her cheek. "Svana."

She choked down sickness, the way he said her name.

"Nei worry," he said. "I will take care of her honor."

He thought she howled for Esa. Good. He had no idea that she'd hoped to never see him alive again. Never feel his foul breath, hot in her ear. Eiðr whispered, "He will pay."

Her breath stopped.

He will pay.

Eiðr swore, "He's gone too far. This feud between us…it will end with his downfall."

Svana's blood quickened with hope. Even though Eiðr still lived, a sickening act had been committed against his sister's corpse, and he blamed Rakknason.

It made sense. The chief had been insulting Eiðr's family for many years. Rakknason was a twisted, disgusting man, who caught Eiðr up in a living trap. Instead of feuding outright, he gave Eiðr land and work. But he took Eiðr's hand.

Now, Eiðr blamed the chief for defiling Esa's grave. It was an offense worthy of outlawry. Svana's nithing post had worked after all, in ways she did not expect. The gods would still give her her due. The chief would be blamed for this, and he and Ginn would pay

Eðna opened her hands and bunches of skirt fell out.

At her back, sweet laughter bubbled up, and she yearned to turn and go with Brosa. He would be playing in the sun, wrestling with a bunch of children, distracting them. But she kept her eyes straight ahead, where a shimmering girl approached from down at the river.

Ludicrous. A woman could not iridesce. It was her white dress creating an optical illusion against the dark earth. It billowed around her knees and ankles, moving with the erratic wind and her big, purposeful strides. Pale blond hair whipped around her waist and elbows.

"Jen is here," Eðna attempted to record.

Up close, the luminescence held. Jen wore a light, gauzy apron and dress, made of the finest white fabric. But it was not the dress that shone. Jen herself seemed to glow with a soft, silver light.

A woven crown of twigs and lichens circled her forehead. Long wisps of ice-blond hair were plaited into loose braids, decorated with bits of grass and more lichens of minty-green and gold. A deep blue tattoo of a whale's tail curved up the left side of her face to wrap around her orbital bone. The ghostly green of the lichens accentuated Jen's silver eyes. A penetrating gaze, with hints of wild, unexpected fierceness.

In one hand, she held a knife. It dripped red liquid, staining her apron gruesome pink. A flash, a trick of the light, turned her into one of Helgi's Valkyries, an apron in place of blood-drenched chain mail, rays shooting from her spear. The dead man's bloody face came and went in a heartbeat.

But Ginn's knife did not stream with blood. The smears on her dress were too purple. Trails on the backs of her hands were bluish, so that it looked like her veins were on the outside of her skin.

"I am Ginn," she said, and she blinked slowly as though she were catching Eðna in her eyes. "Welcome to Hvítmork." Ginn dropped her knife, and it hung from a leather strap at her wrist, but she did not offer her purple-streaked hand to Eðna. A relief.

"Hallo, Ginn. I'm Eðna."

Ginn tilted her head, as if tasting Eðna's voice. She waited, patient as a hunter, for Eðna to say more.

"I'm so happy to see you here, safe. To finally meet you." It was the truth. After so much preparation, so many hopes for this journey, Eðna was thrilled to see Jen here, secure and whole, the subject of her mission.

"You're from the future," Ginn said. "You made it."

Eðna smiled. "Yes, I'm from your time."

Ginn's brows drew down into a vee, but she didn't comment. With those disconcerting purple-blood hands, she lifted her skirt to step through the grass. "Come," she said. "We'll get you some blankets and a seat by the fire."

They walked side by side, Ginn's pink skirt edges and Eðna's murky hems snagging on the grass.

"What was it like for you," Ginn asked. "Coming through?"

"Much like you described. Brutal, sickening."

Ginn stopped walking and looked to the sky, then off down the hill toward the river. Eðna could just make out women working around fires, smoke and steam rising from giant, black pots.

"It was worth it all."

"Yes," Eðna said. "It was." Another truth. Ginn meant this place, this family, but Eðna felt the same about her mission, that it was worth all the pain and risk.

Then she told the lie she'd practiced, with a deep breath. "Your home, your house, your farm, it's all gorgeous."

Ginn stepped onto the threshold of her house, and she smiled. Her eyes warmed, and the gap that Eðna had seen onscreen now showed between her teeth, but her voice was unsettlingly deep for such a girlish creature. "Come," she said, and she turned to enter. Stronger, more confident than she'd been in any of the vids. Ginn must have become accustomed to giving commands here.

Eðna tugged on the strings of her top and stepped into the house. Smoke burned her eyes, and she struggled to open them wide and accept the darkness.

Unlike the lush, green exterior, the inside of the house felt like the home that her Ma and Da had made, with murky, dark corners and shafts of blinding light. But it was huge compared to the house where she grew up. Its big posts supported two stories of sleeping berths, and as her eyes adjusted, she confirmed what she'd expected. The posts and beams and beds were all made of wood. Extravagant wood. So much of it, all cut up and used for sleeping and sitting on. Benches everywhere, all made of trees. The scent wrapped around Eðna, familiar from all the times she'd buried her nose into the bark of her few birches.

In an overlay of memory, she sat in her childhood house. A square room, not grand and long like this one. It had a few beds made of stacked dirt and turf, covered with tufted grass pads and blankets and dolls. The single hearth sat at the center of the room, and they had a sturdy wooden table. How had they gotten it, when trees were so scarce? She hadn't wondered then, when the world was just the world, the way it had always been, and there had always been that table. Worn soft with millions of brushes of fingers.

One side of the table was nearest to the fire and always hot. Gida would seat little Eðna there, with her back to the flame, so she could be the warmest. Eðna would always twist around to see the fire burn. So many hours spent slowly chewing her flatbread and butter and watching the pictures of swans and goddesses that sparked and flew there.

Just as her contacts had thrown up random images earlier, now her mind did the same. All the things from her past that she had practiced facing, when she was alone in her room at night—things the company could never know about her. Jeff knew only that she grew up on a farm, not how much she loathed it. He might never have chosen her.

"Sit, Lady! Come sit." A little girl drew Eðna close to the hearth. "I'm Ranka."

Eðna shrugged off the girl's grubby hands, but she welcomed the fire. It warmed her ankles and knees, and finally she admitted the misery and cold of the last twelve hours and let it roll through her. Ironically, now that she was wrapped in a blanket and seated on a warm, fur-lined bench, she trembled.

"Come close," Ginn said. "Come get your strength back."

A chill crept deeper into Eðna's bones. Just as the chief seemed to see her plans laid bare, Ginn could see her weakness. Could see plainly that even though she'd found Hvítmork, Eðna was lost.

Ethereal Ginn, looking shrewdly into Eðna's heart.

The woman slipped a silver ring onto one of her stained fingers. Those tiny fingers that Eðna had seen in vids, sketching and pointing at maps, were, in person, stronger. Capable. Nails rimmed with plum and violet, as if she'd been hacking up strange-blooded creatures.

"I've been dyeing cloth."

"Ah," Eðna said. Dye. Common, benign. Ginn was human. And for the first time in hours, Eðna felt her shoulders relax.

Ginn drew another gleaming ring from the little purse that hung at her waist, and she slipped it on another finger. A rich woman, adorned with grass and silver and such fine leather.

It was almost impossible to see underneath the woman's knives, shears, firestriker, and ring of toothy iron keys. Her belt was almost hidden. And yet. Eðna sucked in a sharp breath.

She knew its strands and contours. A masterpiece of a belt, formed of dozens of intertwining strips tanned and dyed to subtly varying hues of brown and amber. The style was atypical for the 10th century. Unique in any century, actually, with its wide braids threaded and woven with whole tiny words of intricate sub-plaits, made with strands as fine as snowbit stems.

Eðna made that belt.

Back at the company, when she made costumes for Vera, using her childhood skills all day so that she could earn her keep, and then read and learn all the facts of the wide world at night. She had worked those fine strips of leather herself, braiding them as the design came to her.

Everything was here, physical and solid, after so many weeks of screens and plans. Brosa's words came back to Eðna from just an hour ago. *You are real.*

Eðna made it.

She'd made it through every obstacle, through time and distance and memory. She swayed, dizzy with exhaustion and fear and accomplishment. Drowsy with the blessed warmth of fire and wool. Ginn took a seat across from her and leaned in as though they were friends, and fear slipped from Eðna's shoulders like a blanket.

Ginn leaned closer. "When did you arrive?" She gave off the scent of the fields and an unfamiliar, earthy smell, perhaps from the dye. "You came through the tank."

"Last night," Eðna said. "It's somewhat blurry. I went into the tank some time yesterday."

Ginn took Eðna's hand, and Eðna tensed and pulled back, but Ginn did not let go. She looked straight into Eðna's eyes. Could she see the thin film there? She turned Eðna's hand palm up, as though she were going to tell her fortune. "You made it."

Eðna drew her hand away and fixed the blanket around her knees. "I'm right where I thought I would be, yes."

The girl Ranka had returned with a wooden cup of something steaming and scented with herbs. Tucked in between Eðna's palms, the cup warmed her. All this wood, burning, wasted. It scratched her palms with splinters too tiny to see.

"I should be experiencing hypothermia after my ride through the night." Eðna set her drink aside and bent to untie her boots, and her head swam with sparkles. Her wobbling mind and optical abnormalities could be her contacts struggling to function, or the first signs of overexposure to cold. Unsafe. Frostbite in her toes would be serious, if she didn't move this process along, gather her facts and return home.

Her fingers were suddenly thick and useless.

"Let me do that," Ginn said, and she helped peel off Eðna's soggy boots.

"Takk." Eðna took the cup up again and sipped at the drink—a delicate ale, laced with a floral taste. "I'll be fine."

"Já," Ginn said. "Your feet will. But your dress isn't going to make it. You'll need a new one."

Eðna laughed. "Just what Brosa said."

Ginn gave Eðna a wry smile. "He's been known to watch women's hems."

A tall, thin woman came to sit beside Ginn. "That's the truth. Since he was just a boy."

Beside Ginn, the woman could not have been plainer. All her brown hair was bound up in girlish braids that accentuated her angular features, without a single blade of grass or bit of whimsical lichen woven in. But something about her knowing eyes, her smooth skin, was captivating. A baby laid curled against her shoulder, and she held it by one hand, her long dye-stained fingers supporting its tiny back. Eðna had no names in her eyes now, but this could only be Betta, Ginn's best friend.

"This is Eðna," Ginn said. Then quickly, "You don't need to look up Betta. My friend. And this is her son, Haldi."

"Look her up?"

"I can see you want to check your contacts," Ginn said and she blinked, too. An old habit still ingrained in her eyes? "Are they working?"

"Some," Eðna said. "On and off."

"Mine worked for a couple hours, nei more," Ginn said. Ginn's had worked for a while! Eðna yearned to take notes, but she couldn't record anything.

Betta kissed her baby's head and cradled him close. "You were not prepared," she said to Ginn, but she narrowed her piercing gaze on Eðna. "Not like this woman is."

"I am prepared, yes. Thanks to Ginn's bravery, I knew what to expect." Eðna turned to Ginn. "Since you left, Jeff made some improvements."

"Jeff," Ginn said, broke into a smile. The gap between her two front teeth made her even more human, a normal girl, and her icy eyes warmed. When she smiled, the whale's tail gave her a look of arch mischief. A changeable creature, her demeanor different in a heartbeat. "How is he?"

"Tall, Nordic," Eðna said. "A flirt." Jeff spent his days in second tech revolution coffee houses and built old-fashioned computers that were functioning works of art. He was brilliant enough—or lucky enough—to send Eðna here to the past. He admitted he didn't really understand what made it happen.

Right before he sent Eðna, he reviewed the risks with her. "They all but dissected Jen when she came back," Jeff told her. "If this machine works, you'll be examined and interrogated."

"If that happens, then we've both succeeded," Eðna said.

He tried to take her hand, but he settled for a gesture, to encompass the lab and everything in it. "Then for this, I owe you one." He'd given her his charming, immoral grin right before he sent her hurtling back in time. "A big one." It was a sweet smile that touched even Eðna, who didn't have a shred of interest in men beyond their role in her achievement.

"He's happy," Eðna said, taking another small sip from the wooden cup to hide another lie. In fact, Jeff had been on a lonely and driven quest to duplicate the time slip effect, but still only the original tank would do it, and he had tested it only on objects, recorders, cameras. Eðna was the first person to go.

It worked, and she was the only one in the universe who knew that.

She needed to get back to Jeff, to report on their success. Back to the person who had waved to Eðna, a quick goodbye for her short trip, here, or to oblivion. He'd mouthed the words, *I owe you,* when in fact, no one owed her anything. This was her dream, to take the risks required so she could contribute to one of the greatest breakthroughs in human knowledge.

"He would love to see me here, safe and sound."

"Good." Ginn's smile lingered.

"I remember my first day here," Ginn said. "My time on the sand. I was near death when they found me."

Eðna sipped the warm, grass-scented ale, and it soothed her throat. A drink that smelled, like Brosa, of rosemary. The scent of the spiny little herb was everywhere here, on his skin, on Ginn's clothes, in the ale. Rare here, and a show of wealth, just like the rings that now covered all of Ginn's fingers.

"Betta and Ranka bathed me and dressed me to meet the chief." Ginn's voice softened on the last two words, and she let out a tiny puff of laughter. "It seems impossible, I didn't know my husband then." She spoke of him reverently, as if he were a god. As if the moment she realized she was stuck here in this hard and dangerous year was the best day of her existence.

"Já," Eðna said. "I just met him. Without a bath. He was not pleased."

"He's wary." Betta said. "No one comes here."

"He shields us," Ginn said, and she took the baby from Betta. She laid tiny Haldi in her lap and touched his cheek with a ring-laden finger, her eyes going soft and distant. "Many have hurt him, hurt us."

The fire and the drink were so pleasant, but thoughts of death and sand intruded.

More people were hurt than Ginn even knew. But keeping quiet about the dead men seemed prudent. Eðna had to observe, first. But those designs on Brosa's and Heirik's axes were exactly the same as the twists and knots on the weapon in the dead man's back. How many axes were there like that?

"For you it was different," Ginn went on. "You intended to travel here."

"Yes, I did." Eðna sipped her ale and looked up over the rim of the cup. "I was looking for you, of course."

"I don't blame you. It's beautiful here. A world completely untouched by the city."

"The city." Eðna turned the cup in her hand. "I miss it already."

What was she saying? Her plan didn't include revealing irrelevant feelings.

"You miss it?" Ginn drew back slightly. She pressed the baby close to her chest. "You miss the city where buildings cover the sky and people have burrowed into the ice to hide?"

Not everyone saw it that way.

Eðna counted silently. She had to befriend Ginn, not antagonize her. She had to say the right things. "Well, I have been gone only a day." She drew her blanket close and smiled. "And I've been wet the whole time I've been here. I do miss towels."

Ginn did not smile in return. "There was only cold and fear there," Ginn said, and she sounded like Eðna's Da. "No one looked in each other's eyes."

"There is knowledge there," Eðna said.

She counted again, silently. She had to be careful, but her thoughts twisted and climbed like vines. Ginn thought it was cold in the city? This place was all ignorance and threat. A few benches drawn close to a miserable hearth.

Eðna suddenly felt trapped by the shadowy house. She spasmed with the desire to stomp out the small fire that hissed at her feet. Without a hood to draw the smoke out, the air in the room lacked oxygen. The shadowy house contracted around her. "We have air purifiers, too." She placed a bare foot on the hearth stone and nodded toward the fire. "You know this is dangerous."

Betta stood. "We have plenty here."

This was all wrong. Eðna's emotions were flying out everywhere like sparks. She smoothed her skirt. Regrouped.

"Yes," Eðna said. "It's just as I dreamed it would be. I'm just in shock. I rode all night."

Ginn said, "We've kept you long enough. You need a bath and some rest. Ranka, get some dry clothes for our guest."

"Já, Lukla," the girl said.

An almost-Norse word, maybe early Icelandic?

"She calls you *key*?" Eðna asked in the future tongue.

"My honored title, as the head of this house," Ginn said, and she rose to stand along with Betta. Both women loomed above Eðna, Betta gently bouncing Haldi. "It's a word-song, luklaheima, meaning *key* and *home* and also *to confer a title* all in one phrase."

A hint of wild pride came through as she looked down on Eðna. And that excitement that Jen always betrayed in the vids, whenever she spoke about language and voices. For a brief moment, Eðna was intrigued by the language, too. For a brief moment, they shared a common curiosity, a craving to know and understand this place. This name for a chief's honored wife was previously unknown. Eðna could take it back with her.

"*Key-home*," she said in the future language. "Yes."

"Eðna," Ginn said, still hovering over her. "If you love the city, then why did you come?"

Eðna couldn't say. She couldn't look at this woman with her word-poem title and her god of a husband and tell her, I've come to study you. To take observations back to a future you despise, just as much as I reject this place.

In her most elaborate and intense dreams, Eðna was able to do more than gather information. She was able to bring Jen home with her, the proof in person.

Eðna laughed to herself. This woman no longer Jen. She was Ginn, and she was already home.

Eðna had thought—everyone had thought—that Jen would be just as fascinated with time travel as they'd all become. That if Eðna could locate Jen, she would find a curious woman, wanting to know more about how the process worked. Ginn was the complete opposite. She'd taken this place into her soul and body, and she had become the home of the keys. Exactly where and when she should be. Now that Eðna had met Ginn, the mission to find her and ask about her experiences with the tank made little sense.

Eðna saw the moment that Ginn got it.

"Nei," she breathed. Then stronger, "Nei." Betta stood closer to Ginn, silently at her friend's side, so that Eðna looked up at them both like a guilty child.

"You're not here to find refuge." Ginn was cold. "You want to go back. You want to find out how it works."

Eðna stood to meet Ginn's eyes. "I'll leave you in peace and return to the city as soon as I rest a little."

"I'm sorry," Ginn said. "I can't let you do that."

Eðna woke in darkness so complete that her eyes invented pinpricks of light. She blinked, but her contacts were still dead. Nothing revealed or explained.

Pain sat deep in her hips, in the bones of her pelvis and legs, all her weight against a hard bench. Fear pooled in her stomach like sour milk, and she reached for words to clear her mind. *Upper femur, patella.*

She actually smelled whey. Was she dreaming?

A tiny, cold baby foot kicked her in the spine, and Eðna jerked away. A bigger, warmer body shifted behind her, and warm breath brushed her back. Breathing so close to her back. Soft whimpers came and then dissipated.

She wasn't dreaming, nei. She was in the pantry. Right.

Eðna had been put in the pantry with Betta and her baby. They slept on a bench covered with sheepskins and wool blankets. Barrels of milk and cheese stood a meter tall at the foot of what passed for a bed.

Eðna drew as far away from the woman as possible. She was here at Hvítmork, her dream within her grasp. But Jen was Ginn, the home of the keys, and Eðna was her captive.

The whimpers stopped. The baby must have found his mother's breast.

Eðna reviewed. Her failure of will. Mortifying, weak tears. Fear of a simple shepherd in the hills. Desperately accepting help from Brosa. The little foot pushing into her back, the food stink in this tiny room.

Her fingers and lips tingled with an unexpected dread of the small, pitch-dark space. Betta's body, the baby's body, were too hot and too near. She had to get out. Her feet touched the dirt floor, cold and gritty, and her panic mounted.

She made it across the pitch black room without stumbling and without waking Betta. The woman was a hawk in the daytime, but she slept soundly. Important to know. Yes.

The door handle rattled, but held.

Locked.

They'd actually locked her up.

Eðna's chest seized and breath came too shallow. She was locked in this space that was too small, walls and ceiling much too close, a living grave. The air would run out in some number of hours, and she couldn't even look up how long it would take. Nothing worked. She sought blindly with her palms for any cracks in the wall. Her fingernails scraped at the lock.

"What are you about?" Betta's deep, sleepy voice came out of the dark.

"What am I about?" Eðna laughed, a crazed laugh, and slumped against the cool wood, her cheek against the door. "What am I about? I'm a prisoner in this hot pantry, sleeping on a hard board with you and a newborn, about forty kilometers and one thousand two hundred and two years from where I need to go. And I am trying to get out." Her voice rose, hysterical. "I have to get out."

"Já then," Betta said with resignation, and the bench creaked as she got down out of bed. "We'll go to the trees."

Betta's arm brushed Eðna's shoulder, and Eðna jumped. A key turned with a solid thunk, and Betta pushed the door open to reveal the soft light of the weaving room.

Eðna gulped relatively fresh air and squinted against the flickering lamps. The room opened up over her head and all around her, big enough for her to stretch out and breathe.

A couple of oil lamps were guttering, giving off chaotic, jumping strobes of light. All that remained of the fire in the hearth was a collection of embers that glowed red and orange. The softly smoked air spoke of comfort and safety, the discussions of grown-ups, tugs on her pigtails.

Stop.

Her personal past was not part of this mission.

Time travel worked. Her remaining task was to return to Jeff with information, observations. The jackpot would be instructions, if Jen had somehow discovered the mechanism.

Eðna followed Betta, counting steps toward the back door. She would get away. Not tonight. She still needed to gather Jen's – Ginn's – knowledge and impressions. But soon. And when it was time, she would know the distance to the door. She would get past Betta somehow, past the people who slept all around this room, the man who slumbered, propped against the wall by the far door. A failed sentry, asleep at his post?

She would memorize everything about this family, until she found a way beyond them.

Eðna stopped short. The sleeping man was Brosa.

The stream of white scars along the side of his face flared in the lamplight. Betta's torch brought out silvery blond streaks in his hair, and his cheekbones stood stark without the fullness of his smile.

Eðna felt the pull of the boat rocking on the water. Proud. By itself. She wanted to sit down on the floor beside him and nudge herself into his arms, hang onto him the way she did when they rode Gull. He would wake just a little and smile for her again.

What?

She shook her head.

The dark, tiny room had affected her mind.

She shook her hands out, shaking off the pantry, the blackness, the strange, unsettling thoughts and desires.

"This way," Betta said, almost as if she could hear Eðna thinking about routes and maps and plans. She guided her toward the blond wooden door that led to the back mudroom—the anteroom to the outside world.

With a torch in her hand, Betta led Eðna down into a tunnel in the earth, out to the bath. Eðna reviewed the map of the house in her mind, reconciling the root-rich smell with the diagram she'd memorized. The schematic that Jen, Ginn, had drawn in the future.

The night air prickled her skin. Temperature and humidity unknown. The bath steamed, and under the gray night and rising mist, she could just make out the ring of stones that rimmed the water.

So familiar, and yet so entirely foreign. The dirt and odors of her childhood combined with her father's fantasy of a raw, authentic life. And a nameless energy, rising like the wisps of water vapor.

There was no way to fight him. Her Da. He kept breaking the surface of her consciousness.

"My father had a bath like this."

Betta's angular nose and cheekbones were sharper than the chief's. Sharp eyes, too. Even in the near dark, Eðna could see how they searched. "Your father had a bath like this in the *city*?"

She spoke with disgust, and the word city—spoken in Eðna's modern language, obviously taught to Betta by Ginn—oozed out of her mouth, turning her voice as sour as the dairy barrels.

So, Ginn had taught them hateful things about the future.

Eðna added it to the litany of things gone wrong. Ginn's decree that Eðna could not leave. The locked pantry. Her own Da and his stupid farm. All those wasted years floating in just such a bath, absorbing nothing, no ideas, no intelligent thoughts expressed by anyone, just discussion of animals and weather. Betta's words were more sticks on the fire. The woman's derisive attitude toward Eðna's crystal-clear home in the future—the home she cherished, and this woman had never even seen.

"I grew up on a *farm,*" Eðna said in the old language. It came out just as disgusted as Betta's *city*.

Past the bath, they reached a stand of a few trees, not many more birches than Eðna had as a child. The bathroom would, of course, be a primitive hole in the ground. Right.

And Betta would let her go to it.

Hope rose. The woman was strong, no doubt, and at least 15 centimeters taller than Eðna. She could probably run fast, but Eðna could surprise her.

Betta's insulting tone turned curious. "Ginn says there is no more land to farm."

"Ginn probably says a lot of things about our home."

Eðna waded into the brush to pretend to pee in the makeshift toilet. She rustled around, as if lifting her skirts, and spoke loud enough to reach Betta.

"Has she told you how cold the buildings are and how much better farms are? She never saw a farm like mine. Forty-seven trees total, and such sparse grass, the few animals were thin."

Eðna's eyes watered with the smell of this place. "My father thought it was wonderful."

Betta's answer came from beyond the bushes. "He thought it was the best place for you."

"It wasn't."

Eðna drew all the fabric of her skirt up tight against her waist and moved as quietly as she could, hardly breathing, toward the opposite edge of the trees.

Could it be this easy? When the time came, could she just say she had to visit the trees?

"Well," Betta said, her voice smaller, farther away. "It is good here. The farm is green and the animals and babes are fat."

Eðna reached the open edge of the bunch of trees, on the far side from Betta. The sky was enormous and dense with stars that she hadn't seen in a decade. The land was vast, the horizon horribly far. She'd forgotten the sky could feel so heavy over her head. It pushed against her, held her down, as though she could actually feel the motion of the earth.

She let her skirts go, let her eyes soften and her gaze flow into the distance, until her eyes filled with stinging water. She blinked, and in a snap, night vision sprang to life.

Contacts! Yes. The grass and trees turned eerie green, and pale words rose up beside them. *Betula pendula.* The bath was a white hot circle teaming with writhing tendrils of light. Owl mode, she and Vera called it.

An advantage. An advantage that she might not have again.

Eðna stood at the edge of the brush, while Betta hung behind with unaided eyes. And right now, the night sky was as dark as it would ever be, affording the most cover Eðna could hope for in the spring dimness. Maybe enough to obscure a dash downhill.

The forest at the bottom of the long slope formed an endless stand of green stalks, laced with the Latin words for juniper, angelica, birches. Eðna's heart reached for those labels, desperate to run down into the orderly letters. The trees looked small from up here, but they were big enough to hide under, and the cover would be deep. Once inside the forest, she would be virtually invisible.

She'd trained physically and could walk, climb and run from this farm to the coast, about an ancient marathon's distance, on rocky, hilly terrain. In ten hours she could be there, if she ran over open land. But not inside the woods. She'd never trained inside a tangle of a million trees—an enormity that no one in the future could really simulate.

Possibilities branched, including some she never would have considered before she actually met Ginn. Punishment at Ginn's hands, servitude, lifelong imprisonment in a space too small for breath. Injury in the woods. Deep brush without shoes made no sense. Instead of hours, it would take days. And real animals. She reviewed the short list of mammals in settlement era Iceland: just one. The arctic fox was significantly smaller than Eðna and complacent, nonaggressive.

She moved one toe, testing the damp grass, testing the idea of running to the sea.

Yes, she could run.

Without any clothes. Only a shift, and slippers on her feet. Without her medicine and her leather top. No food or water. No knife. No time to grab a horse. No time to gather the fullness of knowledge she came for. No time to say goodbye to Brosa.

"—Come, Woman," Betta's cold hand closed on her wrist.

Eðna gasped. "Get off!"

She turned on Betta and yanked away. In the light of the raised torch and Eðna's night vision, Betta's face was all prominent bones, and big, sinister green teeth. Her eyes glowed bright with heat, two greenish orbs. "Ginn and I both fought hard for this life. You will not take it from us."

"I am not here to take your home."

"You didn't come here like Ginn did," Betta said, and it was low and calm, like a growl. "I saw all your things laid in the pantry. You came with supplies, a purpose."

Eðna backed away. "I'm here to learn about something greater than all of us. To unlock a secret that no person has ever been able to figure out."

Betta shook her head, ready to pounce. "Nei. You may think that." The woman's eyes flared white-green, and her increased heartbeat and body temperature blinked in Eðna's field of vision.

"Moving through *time,*" Eðna said. "It's the most—"

"—Nei matter." Betta shot her words out. "Time belongs to Saga and Idun. They sent you through it. But we can't know their reasons."

Owl mode vision abruptly turned off, and Eðna stood in mud-thick gray.

Her chance to dash was gone.

"Get inside," Betta said, and her hand closed on Eðna's arm again, nails the way that talons might feel. She turned to enter the tunnel, dragging Eðna behind.

Eðna stumbled along, twisting her arm in Betta's grasp. The tunnel walls were wickedly lit by torchlight, and the scent of dirt chilled her bones. Underground, buried. She saw the blind, dead man in her mind, his eyes eaten. She'd come to the shore right on top of a murder. If anyone found out, would she be in danger of worse imprisonment than a pantry?

She had not thought about who might be blamed for the murders. The dead men must have families, people who would miss them and would want reparation, maybe even revenge. And she had been at the scene.

She might never get away.

And she had just given up a chance.

Betta dragged her into the weaving room. Brosa still slept, propped against the wall, and he turned toward Eðna as she passed, unconsciously, deep in his sleep. He folded one arm around himself, the way he might hold a woman while she dreamed.

"Get in bed, Eðna."

The pantry door opened, black and depthless. Betta stepped inside, and her torchlight flickered on the ceiling, too low, too cramped. If they locked her in there again, she would never get out. Never see the brilliant city again.

"Nei." She shook her head and backed away. "Let me go!"

"Come, Woman," Betta said. "I'm sleepy."

Eðna, and she backed away and shouted "Nei!"

"Stop now," Betta said. "You'll wake the house."

"—Leave her." Brosa's voice was rough with sleep. He'd come to his feet and stood behind Eðna. "What's going on here?"

Eðna backed up, just a little, and felt him solid and big behind her. Standing tall, she would fit completely, perfectly under his chin. He wouldn't let Betta take her.

"The woman will run," Betta said. "Ginn wants her kept."

"The door was locked," Eðna said, turning to him. "I couldn't get out."

"Locked?" Brosa's voice was dangerous in the dark, no longer sleepy. The manic lamplight threw shadows all over his face, and his sleep-mussed hair. "You locked her behind a key?"

"It's Ginn's wish," Betta said. "I only borrow the keys."

Back in the pantry, the baby wailed, and Betta turned first to the cries, then back to Brosa.

"Well," he said, "Ginn can find me in the morning and get her revenge." He spoke gently, and reached out to Betta to take her torch. "You go to Haldi. I'll watch this one."

This one? Meaning Eðna. "Excuse me?"

Brosa stilled her with a half smile and a wink that made her fume, ready to fight him as well as Betta.

"Give me my pack." Eðna fought inside, struggled against both of them.

Calm.

Brosa was helping her.

Betta gave her a sharp look. "You want to run."

"I just want my things," Eðna said. "I want to hold my pack."

Betta got the pack and handed it to Eðna with a warning in her eyes. Before she closed the pantry door, she turned to Brosa and said, "Ginn will have my head, *Nephew*."

Brosa laughed, a single hard syllable. "Nei, *Old Woman*." He said it with a wry smile. "You take care of yourself and the babe. I'll take care of Eðna."

Brosa smiled. The woman was so small, sitting by the fire and holding her pack to her chest. Her dark hair faded into the night-room. Only the embers lit her face, making her chin into a point, everything like a fox.

He was maybe four years old the last time he trembled before a dark door. This Eðna was strange, coming to him in the fields, yet drawing her knife. Brave, and yet frightened of the pantry. She huddled inside her own arms and refused to take his blanket.

Brosa nudged new logs into place. They would catch soon and warm her up.

"I need to go home."

"Sit still, Eðna," he said. "You're shaking. Just rest a minute."

Her eyes darted again, like earlier, like a bird. "It's not safe."

"It is safe here," he murmured. "No harm will come to you."

"Hah!"

"Well." The woman was right, in truth. His good sister, Ginn, had done terrible things to woman who crossed her. "I will nei let Ginn or Betta harm you. And it is worse outside. It's darkest night."

"It's summer. There's light."

Brosa sighed. "Já, but can you stay the night by my fire before you get started on your escape? I'm tired." He settled against the wall and stretched his cramped legs. "I'm not looking for a trip to the coast tonight."

She pressed her pack to her chest.

"Fine," she said. "But I won't sleep."

She pulled her thin leather top from her pack, and pulled it on over her head. When she reached up, he could see her curves inside her shift.

"Stay awake as a hawk," he said and closed his eyes. "Just don't go anywhere if I nod off."

Brosa opened one eye. Eðna was watching him. He sighed and sat up.

"Tell me a story, Woman. To pass the time."

She drew something out from her pack, something with the dull metal look of a honed blade. A silver drinking flask. She opened it and held it up to him, as if to toast.

"Skál," she said, without joy. She put it to her lips, wheezed and spilled drink down her chin. "Oh, holy hell."

Brosa fought to hold in laughter, but he couldn't keep from smiling.

"You try it." She pushed the flask toward him.

It was rare, a vessel hammered in Norway or farther south. He tilted it back, swallowed, and was seized with coughing. "Gods, Woman, what is this fire water?"

Her eyebrows rose on her forehead. "Whisky." She considered the flask in his hands. "For unknown *factors*."

One of her future words, mixed in with his language.

He took a small sip this time. "Northumbrian drink?"

"Indian." she said. "From the East."

He ducked his head and wiped his beard. He hadn't tasted anything like it in years, not since his travels to the old country. Its taste brought memories of villages set against the water, boats pulled up on sand, places to drink and mourn. He let it burn his throat raw, washing away those thoughts.

"I don't know all of Ginn's logic," Brosa said, and he handed the flask back to Eðna. "But I wouldn't have thought they'd turn the key on you."

"You didn't know?"

"That you were locked up? Nei."

"But, you were stationed here to watch in case I got loose."

"What? Here by the door?" He dropped his voice, looked her straight on. "I had no such reason to sleep here."

"Don't you have a nice bed somewhere?"

"Not as fine a bed as you just gave up." He nodded toward the pantry. "My uncle was thrown out so you could sleep there."

"Oh."

Brosa smiled, and it felt fresh and strange. He had smiled a few times this past year, já, but not like this, with joy in it. "You didn't find it to your liking?"

"The pantry is…small."

"Já, I was afraid of it when I was a boy."

"When you were a child," she said. "I'm a grown woman."

"That you are," he said, and he looked in her eyes and reached for the flask again. It would be good to see her in the light, to know if she blushed. "This is a drink from your time?"

"From a distillery built on old plans." She stopped, started again. "An older time, but somewhere between mine and yours."

"You can travel freely on Saga's river?"

"Well, no." Her words were already soft and slurred from the drink. "But where I live, people with money play at being from different times. That's why Jen and I know your language. Why I had the right clothes."

"Why?" Brosa asked. "Do you not like your own time?"

"I love my time," she said, and she smiled, brilliant as stars. "It's full of wonders. Clean homes without dirt for our floors." She stirred the ground with her boot. "Fires that burn without wood or smoke to singe our lungs. Enough food, always. There are no more mortal wounds. No killing fevers."

Her shoulders let down, and her fingers unclenched from her pack.

"The walls in my home light up from inside. The insides of my eyes fill up with written words, like runes, and I can dip into a thousand years of knowledge."

Either she was sick in her mind, or she truly was a handmaiden of Saga.

"I keep moments from childhood in my mind," Brosa said. "It is like that?"

Eðna went cold again. "A little like it."

She tugged on the ends of the ties that bound that strange shirt, and the leather hugged her tight.

What had he said wrong?

Brosa ducked his head to find her eyes. "You must have been a headstrong girl. Your brown braids flying." He got a smile from her, but not a laugh. "You don't keep those moments, from when you were young?"

She took a drink, this time without sputtering. "I try not to."

Ah.

"Alright then," he said. He leaned back against the wall and settled in to rest. "I'll tell you some of my old moments, and you can fall asleep."

"I'm not going to sleep."

"Good, then, you'll know all about me by morning."

"Good, I will." She smiled, so tired.

"Will you please take my cloak?"

"Nei," she said. "I'm fine."

"Good, then, Fine One." He smiled, and touched his boot to her leg, which she also drew away. A tough woman. His usual charms didn't soften her much, and she wouldn't let him wrap her up in his arms for comfort.

He'd rock her to sleep with his words then, if not his body. "I was just about four when we turned over my father's ship."

It was the first time he remembered going to the coast, though he must have gone there tied to his Ma's back, or tucked in the sleds, many times. "When we were small, we stayed with the women and gathered things. Berries and leaves and eggs. Shells for cups and scoops, and to build elves' houses in the sand."

Eðna nodded, like a little girl trying to stay awake through a bedtime story.

"I drew away from my Ma, to see what Heirik was doing. He must have been a big man of six or seven." His brother, so serious, even at that age.

"My Da's men had dragged the boat out of the water and turned it, to lay new wood on the hull. I'd sat in it before, já? We played at rowing and sailing in the wind, but I'd never seen it pulled up on the land. It stuck up from the sand like bleached bones, and I could see the logic of an animal in the turning."

"An animal?" Eðna's voice was drifting.

"A whale, I thought. The biggest animal, the one that rides the sea."

"*Megaptera*," she said.

Brosa raised one brow. He would have to get used to her strange words.

"I got underneath to look at the ribs. To be inside the whale's belly. The boat so massive, and me so small, I could stand up under there. Men pounded iron nails into the curved boards all around me, over my head, and the sound rang in my bones."

He felt the echo even now. Smelled the wood—not on fire, but simply wood, set to a purpose. Gods, he hadn't felt the lure of that simple purpose in so long.

"I was little, já," he told Eðna. "But I knew that someday it would be my boat."

"I saw it," Eðna murmured, half in slumber.

"You saw my boat?" Pride came, like an unexpected wave. He cared that she saw his ship, tall and strong in the water. "I wish you could see it under sail."

She still fought sleep. Fine then, he would do what his uncle had done, when he and Heirik were just babes.

"Do you know the parts of a boat, Eðna?"

"Of course I do," she said. She crossed her arms in place of the blanket she refused. "The hull…" She left off, too sleepy to speak.

"Já, the hull," Brosa said, smiling in the dark. "The hull and the mast and the sail. The raven's roost. Oars and benches and boards underfoot."

He put the rhythm of the waves into his words. "The stern and the bow and the wolf to clear the way. The keel to slice the water, and the steerboard to make the fate."

Eðna breathed steadily. Brosa lay his blanket over her and pulled the wool up under her chin. "I will not let them hurt you," he whispered. "Not like Hildur and Svana."

He sat on his heels beside her, and the light moved on her face. Without her waking spirit in her eyes, she looked peaceful, almost free. Her hair fell loose over her shoulders, deep as forest shadows, and now that she'd bathed, she smelled of mint and not the sea. Her dark brows arched over her closed eyes, not quite as pointed, not drawn so tight as when she was awake. She'd been scared all the time since he'd met her. It was good to see her calm. He'd done that for her. Helped her let it go.

She would not want him to touch her cheek. He drew away, pushed himself up to stand and stretch his legs. Even in sleep, Eðna pushed the blanket away, just a little. Stubborn kit.

"—I see."

Ginn's voice came from the door to the mudroom. She stood on the threshold in her pale shift, so fine he could see the shape of her body under its fall. Her hair hung long and messy, and Brosa felt a familiar stab of surprise, that this woman and his brother slept in the same bed. He was struck with longing sometimes, when he thought of it. He never knew why.

"You see what?" he asked. "That this woman is free from your locked pantry?"

"I have to protect what we have here, brother."

"Don't." Brosa turned to the fire, nudged the embers with his boot. "I will watch her."

"You'll stay awake and be sure she doesn't leave?"

"I said I will." Brosa would not look at Ginn.

"It's life and death, broðr. She yearns to leave here, and she'll destroy Hvítmork with her journey. A horde from the future will come down on us."

"I will watch," Brosa growled, turning on Ginn. She stood tall, but her breath came as fast as Brosa's. He'd never used that tone with her, not once nei matter what they went through. "But you need to talk with Eðna tomorrow. Settle this."

"Já, okay," Ginn said. "I will talk to her in the morning. Show her the beauty here."

"Já," he said. "The beauty."

Eðna followed Ginn up the hill toward the forge. With her hair clean and twisted up on her head, the sun warmed the nape of her neck and her leather vest. Tough grass bunched up under her feet in the soft shoes they'd loaned her. The little leather shoe-tips peeked out from under a dress that was made in all the natural colors of linen and wool.

An impractical dress. The big skirt would get caught up in a cooking fire. The creamy colors would get stained when a woman worked in the fields or by the hearth.

Or when she ran away.

"This is the place I first saw the farm," Ginn said. "First met Heirik."

"But, you saw him at the coast." Eðna came to stand beside Ginn. "I saw the image from your contacts."

"This is where I learned his name, and he showed me the woods." Ginn turned, and Eðna followed her gaze out over the valley, and then her eyes traveled farther and farther, kilometers upon kilometers into the hazy world beyond. All trees. Infinite as last night's stars. The most studied estimates had never come close. The enormity nearly drove Eðna to her knees.

And while each single tree was alive, she saw them now as a single silver-and-green organism that rippled and tossed like muscles under fur, moving with the wind.

"Listen," Ginn said. "Do you hear the men talking?"

There were several of them, just far enough away that Eðna couldn't make out individual words.

"Já, sure," Eðna said.

"Their voices move like the rumble of hoof beats, of a dozen horses about to come over a hill."

"They sound just like men to me."

"Nei," Ginn said. "Nowhere in the future could their voices expand and echo inside a valley."

The men laughed. More like the ravens on the beach than a herd of horses.

"Eðna," Ginn said, looking into the distance. "If you succeed, all this will be lost."

Eðna tore her eyes away from the forest. "I didn't come here to destroy anything." Ginn was from Eðna's world. She must understand what was at stake. "I'm here to add something. Something astounding and…fundamental, to the vast knowledge of human kind."

"We are humankind," Ginn said. "Heirik's grandfather Magnus was one of the first people to ever step foot on this island. Your city comes straight from him, from us."

"We don't know how this family fits into the settlement records," Eðna said. "Some of the earlier names, you know they disappeared."

"Brosa told me the history," Ginn said.

"Brosa is a storyteller," Eðna said. Last night he'd tricked her, lulled her to give up and go to sleep, with a list of words about a boat. His last whispers, barely caught up in her consciousness. About Svana?

"He helped you last night." Ginn smiled, warm and sly, as if they shared a secret.

Eðna didn't need to look up Ginn's history to know where that smile came from. Ginn had almost married Brosa. She'd held him, yes, kissed him. More than that?

So what? What should Eðna care? She had nothing to do with men. Brosa was an ally. "He's kind."

"His grandfather and grandmother traveled weeks on a boat from Norway, with all their belongings, even animals on board." Ginn was wistful for a time even farther in the past. "Magnus built fires in a ring, enclosing this land, claiming it. He explored the hills and valleys and found such beauty. I'll take you to the ravine. You'll see what he saw. What I see."

"I am seeing what you see. That's what I'm here for. Nothing more."

The lie stuck to her tongue. She had seen more, at the coast, than Ginn knew about. Should she tell Ginn about the dead men?

She yearned to know who they were, who had killed them, but Brosa's vague warnings whispered in the back of her mind.

Ginn looked away, far off into the endless trees. She rested her hand, heavy with rings, on one of the boulders. "They'll put an espresso stand right here."

"No," Eðna said, and she turned again to 22nd century words. "No, it's for enlightenment, not for tourists and espresso stands. You learned something amazing when you came here, Ginn. If I don't return, everything you accidentally discovered will be lost."

"Good." Swift and sure, Ginn turned hard, and Eðna saw the threat that Brosa alluded to. In a breath, Ginn was no longer the gossamer Viking princess with twigs in her hair, or even the protective keeper of the keys. She was the wolf Brosa described, with a gleam of berserker madness behind her silver eyes.

Eðna backed away. "I'll promise."

"You'll promise what?"

Ginn's voice was chillingly even and calm.

"I won't reveal anything about how it really worked," she said. "I'll tell them I landed in the wrong time. The contacts didn't respond."

"Why would you do that?"

"Because I want to go home."

Eðna stopped. Everything she'd practiced and needed to say—the compliments and smiles that would allow her to earn Ginn's trust—all dissolved. Anger and fear filled her mouth with bile, and the truth tumbled out. "I'll never find this place beautiful. I know too much about what it's like."

Ginn flared with anger, like a predatory crowned eagle, head and feathers rising. "How do you know what it's like here?"

"I grew up in this," Eðna said, rising too. "In this ignorance."

"What do you mean you grew up in this?"

"I grew up on a farm, out past the glacier," Eðna said. "And until I was ten years old, I had no idea." She shook with old, familiar rage. "I didn't know that the city existed. That history or math or reading or science or medicine existed. Nothing."

Ginn went still and quiet. "A realist." She breathed the word, and her fascination, her reverence, chilled Eðna. Ginn looked like she wanted to reach out and explore Eðna. Or dissect her.

"I got away," Eðna said. "And I learned enough, became knowledgeable enough to get chosen to test the tank. I had the experience, the language. I left the costume shop behind."

"The costume shop? You worked for Vera? We called her the blowfish."

"What do you mean by that?"

Ginn pursed her lips. "She got all puffed up and angry whenever anything happened to the costumes."

Was she ridiculing Vera?

"She cared for me." Tears fought to come out, and her heart reached for her second mother. "When I was a little girl, alone. She gave me work I was good at, working *pleather* for people with money. Leather for the really rich ones. All those belts and scabbards and bracers people wore on the city streets to play."

At night, Vera taught Eðna to read. Eðna would sit snug beside Vera's round body, and they would look at incredible things on the screen. Eðna liked birds, and so Vera showed her how to find records and vids of them. She practiced reading about them and listened to their calls and songs.

In the daytime, while Eðna's fingers made saddle stitches with synthetic sinew, she discovered and sorted images of raptors, shorebirds, pigeons and doves in their orderly divisions. Vera checked on her handiwork sometimes, but Eðna was meticulous with the needle, and so Vera left her alone with her wings and facts.

"I didn't mind making belts like my mother taught me," Eðna said. "As long as I didn't have to make dresses and aprons, didn't have to touch anyone. Just the leather."

"I'm sorry," Ginn said. "That's why you're wearing that gorgeous bodice. You made it."

Eðna ran her hands down her top and nodded. She gestured toward Ginn with her chin. "I made your belt."

"This very one?"

Eðna nodded. She'd spent over a week, always keeping track of the dozens of fine strands.

"It's gorgeous," Ginn said. "All the first year I was here, women wanted to look at it and touch it."

Vera had said the same, that it was a work of art with its intricate braids of the finest strips of leather.

"You wore it into the tank that day, because you spilled coffee on a priceless dress."

"I did." Ginn ducked her head. "I'm sorry, Eðna. It was careless. To ruin the dress, and to talk that way about Vera."

It was a genuine apology, but meaningless. Eðna needed home, with a desperate burning. Would Ginn ever let her go?

"What happened to Svana?"

Ginn looked up, startled. "I married her off to Eiðr." She said this as though it were the obvious course. "The two of them belong together." Ginn thrust her chin at Eðna. "Go ahead and adjust your records."

Eðna almost blinked, but she steadied herself. She would not try to access her contacts now. Ginn would see it as weak.

Eðna sorted her own real memories of the world she'd studied, and found him. Eiðr had been part of a feud, a fight in which Ginn was threatened. The chief maimed him, took his hand off with an ax.

Now, young Svana was married to him.

"And what about Svana's mother?"

An eerie smile crept onto Ginn's face. "She's in Greenland."

"I see," Eðna said.

Icy dread stirred in her stomach. Brosa's vague sense of unease, his hand at her back, supporting her, his vague warnings. He was right. Ginn had been ruthless with the women who crossed her. What might she do with Eðna?

"A seeress is coming, to bless the new hall, before we travel to the assembly. We've had news that she'll be here in two weeks. She'll tell all our fates, including yours, and then I'll know what to do." Ginn rested her hand on the braided belt, as if protecting it. "I'll decide about you then, Eðna."

The land seemed to slide out from under Eðna like mud, and she reached out for the boulder.

Ginn was mercurial and vengeful. She might briefly regret her callousness about Vera, but she was, after all, dangerous. She was something Eðna had hoped to never see again. A fanatic. She believed in Saga, in her Viking logic, retribution. Protectiveness at all costs. She believed in a seeress, just as completely as Eðna's father believed in a land full of elves and a sky full of gods.

If Eðna wasn't gone by the time the seeress came, some addled crone would tell Ginn to lock her in the black pantry for the rest of her life, until Eðna went insane. Ginn would drag Eðna to the assembly of all the men and women of Iceland, where she'd find her some disgusting man to marry, who'd want to touch her, keep her, take her to an even worse place than this land. Eðna would be condemned to a life of ignorance and pain. And no one, not even Brosa, would stop Ginn.

Eðna couldn't let that happen. She would learn this family's habits and schedules, find her way out from under their constant supervision. She'd get to the woods, and then beyond to the great valley and the sea. She had two weeks.

Brosa crushed his dirty shirt and dropped it next to his uncle's in the hot stream of the bath runoff. Cool morning air cleansed his chest and thighs. How many baths would it take to shake off the grave?

"Carry the dust," he spoke to the air, rubbing his arms. Take every grain of Esa's bones from his skin, já. And gods take this unease in his gut, too.

It had been a long and strange two days. He left this house two nights ago, meaning to never see another sunrise, and yet last night, he'd carried a spirit to bed, a woman from another time.

Eðna looked so cold on the floor by the mealstone. He couldn't stand to see her slumped there on the dirt. Once she was deep asleep, he'd lifted her, blanket and pack and all, and carried her to a better bed. Not the pantry that she feared, but a berth in the main room, close to the heartstone.

Now, Ginn decreed that Brosa would watch Eðna. And in truth, he was glad to, but the woman did nothing but sit and brood and watch hens with her wide brown eyes. And he needed a bath more than a man needed air.

He laid a clean shirt and wool pants to warm on the stones and joined his uncle Hár.

His second-father lounged in the water, up to his chest in steam, head thrown back on the rocks and a giant cup of ale in his hand. Small rivers of drink ran down his beard and into the pool.

Hár lifted his head and opened one eye. "Careful you don't float too long, nephew. You'll grow fat."

This from a giant who had become even bigger than he was ten years ago, when Brosa was a boy.

Talking with the man was like batting at insects, but Brosa couldn't help himself. "Even so, I'll find a small space to cram in next to you."

The bath was big enough to hold ten men, and Brosa slipped into it, the water slopping over the edges and into his uncle's cup. Hár smacked Brosa on the back of the head, playfully pushing his face into the water.

"Beast."

His uncle's affection came at him sideways most of the time.

The old man smiled. "Only my wife calls me that."

"Já, well. She is right." Brosa wiped his beard with the back of his hand.

They both settled in to the heat. Brosa's confusion, a rock forming inside him, started to relax. Hard thoughts, unnamed worries, blended into the steam.

"I see you float enough, Uncle."

"Everything is planted and sheared." Hár's great sigh rocked all the water in the pool. "And I have a son of two months."

"So you can lounge."

"So I have to lounge," his uncle returned, "Else I'll end up spending endless hours by the fire holding a crying babe."

Brosa still felt sick at the thought of his uncle bedding Betta. He forced the images away, but one or two crept in. "She's a little sister to me, you know. Much too young for you."

Plain, good Betta, eighteen years old and in love with this mountain of a forty-year-old man.

Hár smiled. "Well, a man doesn't always get to pick."

Brosa raised his brows, a familiar frustration stirring his guts. "What does that mean? You've chosen every bride you ever had."

Brosa's own wife had been handed to him like a calf, to forge an alliance with a family long since declined. Three years later, she was gone, and her older brother killed by Heirik, her younger brother maimed by Heirik's blade. An unsettled feud hung between them, ready to erupt. So much good his marriage had done any of them.

Hár took a deep drink. "Your life was not so hard, já? She was as her name said, fair as a breeze." Esa Svakavind, her byname, after the beauty of sweet air lifting her pale hair.

Brosa closed his eyes against the old pain. Against what could have been, in the year before Esa and their newborn son died. He started to climb out. "Perhaps I'll go bathe in the hills."

"Nei." Hár turned soft, his gruffness gone. His hand was rough on Brosa's shoulder, his ale-breath so close. "Nei. I only meant to say that this time I fell in love, and there was not a damn thing I could do about it."

Brosa took in his uncle's touch like a long drink of ale. A Da's touch.

"The great passion does not grow like a lamb," his uncle grumbled. "It throws you like a horse."

"You're a poet, Uncle."

"I should be, after so many women." Hár returned to drinking, his eyes closed, cup raised high.

"Did you love any of the others?"

Hár swallowed and wiped at his wet beard. Contemplated the sky. "There were times I thought I did."

Brosa sank down until the back of his neck rested on the rim of stones. In the quiet, the leather knot that held his Thor's hammer rolled against his spine.

When Hár spoke again, it was with caution. "About this woman, Eðna."

Brosa's eyes snapped open. "She is no threat."

Hár eyed him with one raised brow. "Nei?"

The bath felt suddenly deep, opening underneath Brosa like a dark sea, shifting with water spirits, warning him about something not yet said. It would bring trouble, whatever it was, and he felt in his bones that Eðna had a part in it.

"Nei." Brosa was final.

"Well, I didn't say so, Nephew. Calm yourself."

Water kissed the rocks, over and over, until everything settled.

"The woman came from nowhere," Brosa said. "Calling for help. I was out in the hills, and I heard her." Even as he laid out his frustration, the talking eased him, and he laughed at the image of Eðna as a reaper, hair braided with bones and a fire inside her head. Limping on that poor horse.

"May not want to laugh yet," Hár said. "It's for Ginn and Heirik to decide what happens to her."

Brosa turned his face to the sun, wishing for his uncle to let him be. But he could feel the old man's eyes.

"Will you go trade again?" Hár asked. "There's still time to leave this year."

"I don't know."

"You'll need to know soon," His uncle kept on. "The assembly is coming."

What was he doing here, talking with this man? It was like running a gauntlet.

"What else, Uncle?" Brosa sat up, and the hot pool sloshed. "Should I trade or not? Should I marry someone? Hide Eðna from this family, maybe, and live out our days in the elf hollow. Or do you think I should have married Svana, kept her here in the house, under our gaze?"

His uncle did not rise to it. "The seeress is coming," he said with a wry grin. "I'm sure she'll tell us all what to do."

Brosa laughed. "Já, the seeress. She'd have to get in line behind his brother, his uncle, Ginn, everyone else who had a vision of Brosa's life. He settled into the water, willing it to deepen again, to let go of his ankles.

"She is a beauty, nei?" His uncle threw back more ale.

"Which?" Brosa drew his brows. Hár couldn't possibly mean the seeress, or mean Svana, after the girl had done so much damage.

"The woman. Eðna."

"Eðna, já." Her name hit Brosa without warning, and he answered without thought. "Her eyes are fire."

"Ah." His uncle might as well have permanently raised his brow, so high it disappeared in his mess of hair. "Well, then," the old man said. He leaned in to Brosa and spoke low. "Your brother's wife has eyes that burn, too. If you value Eðna, shield her from Ginn."

A stone dropped in Brosa's gut. He'd left Eðna alone.

Nei matter. Stupid beast, listening to his uncle. The old man was talking in superstitious riddles. Ginn would not hurt Eðna.

Not outright. But still, he saw Eðna that first night, her eyes sparking with anger and tears as Betta hauled her to the pantry.

When he carried Eðna off to bed, she made soft sounds, and her eyelashes stirred like insects' wings. Like she might wake and find herself in his arms. She would have punched him in the face, nei doubt.

Brosa floated in a warmth greater than the water, his heart churning over and over, wanting more. What would it feel like to slide his hands over that thin leather top, with its tight laces down her sides?

"And nei," He coughed and shifted, answered his uncle. "I won't go trade."

"You should." Hár gave him a long look. "And take her with you, to the old country. Get her away from here."

"She doesn't want to go to the old country."

"You know what she wants, then?"

"Já, I do."

"Well, a goat's balls in hell, I can't fathom what a woman wants. Especially one sent by Saga. But I think you should get in that boat of yours and take her."

"—The woman stays."

Brosa and Hár turned at Heirik's voice. The chief stood behind them, at the entrance to the tunnel. How long had he been listening?

He came to sit on his heels beside the pool. "Ginn wants her kept for now."

Brosa broke in, "Why don't we find out what the woman herself wants?"

"She is sent from Saga," Heirik said. He dipped his hand into the bath and moved the water. "She may not know what she wants."

Brosa closed his eyes for a long moment. He would not erupt like Hekla. Nei.

Sometimes Brosa saw the curse on his brother, even though most times Heirik's mark was just part of him. Now, it stood stark against his two homespun shirts. His bloody fingers stirred the small waves. To Heirik, anything strange was a threat.

"A horde will come if Eðna is allowed to return."

"Eðna?" Brosa drew his brows together, dumbfounded. "Leading a horde? The woman is a brave little thing, but she's no shieldmaiden."

"She does wear that armor," Hár said. "It makes a man want to pull the strings."

"Gods!" Brosa hauled himself out of the water. He struggled with his dry shirt and pulled it down over his sopping wet head. From under the twisted linen, he heard his uncle still talking.

"Perhaps what you need is not a light breeze, Nephew. Perhaps what you need is a strong wind to knock you on your ass."

Stuck inside his shirt, he had no answer. Just as it settled on him and the hem hit his thighs, his cousin Magnus came running. He skidded to a halt at the bath's very edge, breathless.

"On the sand at the fishing camp," Magnus panted, hands on his knees. "Two dead men. Ivar and Torg. Cousins of Eiðr. No one's been down to the fishing camp. They're two days gone."

"What? How?" Brosa and Hár answered at once.

Magnus stood tall, eyes and voice grave. "Murdered. Right where they stood. Done by ax."

Hár was out of the bath in an instant, faster and more graceful than Brosa thought possible. Heirik was on his feet, too, any emotion hidden behind cold eyes.

Brosa himself stood like a troll frozen in the light. Two days gone on the sand. The time when Eðna arrived. Could it be true that Eðna was a harbinger of death after all? That she brought destruction?

With those hands that smoothed her skirt and clutched at her leather strings? Those fiery, but frightened eyes?

Nei chance. His mind was getting away from him.

"There's more, Da," Magnus said, while Hár dragged pants up over his wet legs.

Hár stopped. He growled, "What more?"

"I went to bring in the far horses. I was out by the grave mounds." Magnus looked straight at Brosa, and his gaze said he was sorry for the news he had to bring.

"Say what you know," Heirik stood with his arms crossed, dead calm.

"There were hoofmarks of many horses." Magnus swallowed. "Esa's grave was dug up."

Brosa stood stunned.

He had to react as a good husband would do, in the face of such a vile crime. React with outrage, so they wouldn't know of his own terrible act against her bones. He ground out words, any words he should say now.

"The bastard who did this—"

But his brother and Hár were gone, Hár's voice bellowing inside the tunnel. For a moment, Brosa stood dripping, watching the men of his family all heading to the house. Then like a shot, he raced. To get to Eðna.

Eðna sorted her belongings on the bed. She separated things into piles, moving beads, a needle case, extra socks to the left. On the right, antibiotics and painkillers, wool bloomers, protein bars, a big cloak that could double as a blanket. She brushed her fingers along the impossibly sleek, brown pelt that she had found under her cheek on the first morning she woke here.

Brosa had tucked her into bed, and tucked her pack in under the blankets, close to her side. Did he stay with her for a while, after he put her to bed? Had he pushed wisps of hair behind her ears?

Ridiculous. It was of no consequence if he sat beside her and watched her chest rise and fall in sleep. Guarding against her escape. Or guarding her from the dangers of this house?

Now, the little bed, with its half-sheer apricot-pink curtains, had become her refuge from all the bodies, faces, voices. A good place to huddle and plan. This morning, diffuse light entered the curtains and fell across her arms, almost exactly the pale orange of the clouds that spread across the enormous sky.

A rough and yet song-like whisper filled the space. A couple days ago, she'd finally placed it. It was a mixture of women's low speech, shuffling boots on dirt, and rhythmic stone against metal. The sound of more than one man sharpening knives or ax blades. Gods, what kind of barbaric people needed so many blades to be sharp and ready?

Take only what's necessary.

Brenna's voice rang clear and conspiratorial in Eðna's memory, from a dozen years ago, when they'd escaped their childhood farm. They'd taken two real sheepskins, wrapped and tied around their handful of belongings and bits of food. Angry little Eðna had left almost everything behind. She took none of her toys or the big-girl pack that Gida had helped her make. Just the woolly skin to hold her food together.

It was 12 years ago her time, but the sheep that was killed to get that skin would not be born for a very long time. Its pelt laid in Eðna's room, 1200 years away, among her heat-conductive blankets, her pristine bed and crisp sheets.

She would get there. Soon she would sleep between those sweet-smelling sheets and breathe that crystal-clear, healthy air again.

She would take only a little water. It was heavy, and it was everywhere in this place and time, seeping up out of the ground and running free on the surface. Often sulfurous, but potable. She would take dried fish and berries. Just a little. If she had to take a circuitous route, had to hide, it still couldn't take more than two days to reach the ocean, but calories were important.

She would steal a hatchet on the way out. A small one, just enough for emergencies. That was all. She wouldn't take this fur that smelled of Brosa, scented with his rosemary and leather.

—Sudden shouts came, and Eðna sat up, alert. Men yelled, and their horses snorted and cried out.

Eðna opened the curtains a bit, to see just a slice of what was happening in the house. Women dropped their sewing and grabbed their little ones to go outside. Men picked up axes and let go of their wood carvings and sharpening stones. The commotion drew them all away. Everyone gone.

Eðna opened the curtains all the way. She stood with her toe just touching down onto the ground, and she froze. The flames inside the ring of the central heartstone fluctuated, casting light onto golden hued benches and deep piles of furs and skins. Oil lamps, thick with liquid fat, stuck out from the walls along the rows of berths. Firewood cracked and settled, the only movement in a still house.

She was alone.

Alone!

She grabbed a handful of things from the "take" pile and covered the ground quickly to slip out through the wide, wooden door to the weaving room. She pushed gently, opening the door just a crack. The iron hinges creaked, and she held her breath.

There was the small hearth, the mealstone, where she'd fallen asleep with Brosa, and another door beyond. She moved quickly through the mudroom, knocking over a stack of baskets. A handful of wooden handles clunked and a handful of scythe blades clattered to the floor. She grabbed one and plunged into the tunnel. She had no time to fear its low, dark ceiling.

When she emerged, she spared a second to look back, but the house and yard were empty. She heard men shouting and women talking wildly at the stables, but she had no view of them.

That meant they couldn't see her, either.

She ran past the steamy bath and almost stumbled over a pile of shirts that lay soaking in a stream. Gods, they threw their clothes on the ground like savages.

She looked around, in a short panicked search for direction, then she leaped over the bundles of abandoned clothes and ran east—the opposite of the direction they would expect—not toward the ocean, but into the green valley and toward the white woods.

Wind whistled in her ears. Her lungs, startled by the sudden sprint, burned. She'd still be visible from up at the house, when the commotion—whatever it was—died down and Brosa noticed she was gone. She had to move faster than she'd ever run before.

Fresh air washed her inside, awakening her muscles, and as if they were fueled with her excitement, her contacts flared to life. Yes.

A street-eye schematic, based on saved data of Jen's drawings, floated a meter out from her eyes, jumping and changing wildly as she surged toward the forest. She sought the boundaries of the farm, scanned the curved edge of the woods, to ascertain the best spot to enter the trees.

She could almost feel Brosa's hand about to close on her shoulder, any second now. She ached with the desire to look behind her, to be sure no one was following, but there were no hoof beats. Only the sound of her own ragged breathing and her skirts billowing in the wind around her ankles. Sounds that felt like silence, like water after thirst. No more metal being honed. No more sheep complaining or babies crying. No more Betta denigrating a future she'd never seen.

Brosa had called Betta a hawk, and it was apt. *Accipiter nisus.* In just a few days, Eðna had spent enough time with Betta, listening to her talk of wool and men. Eðna searched in her contacts for her stacked information, dipping into the birds of Iceland. Maybe Betta was more like *Falco rusticulous.* They killed with their teeth, not their feet.

Eðna called up a snapshot of her gear spread out on her cramped little bed. The opportunity to run had come suddenly, and she'd left many things behind. Her definition of *necessary* narrowed and re-formed.

She had her medicine, a little food. She wore soft leather slippers, with thin lining, and they squished in the moist grass. Her purse and belt whapped at her hips—too loose. She buckled her belt tighter as she ran, never stopping. Not for anything. Not until she rounded the enormous edge of the woods and was out of sight.

Yes. She reached the curve!

She steadied her pace and scanned the trees. When and where should she plunge in? She balanced options: The woods would slow her down significantly, but they would also shield her from pursuers.

The chief and his family knew this land intimately, completely. Going directly to the coast would be useless. If she went straight toward the water, Brosa would find her quickly.

A pang hit her chest hard, and she stopped for a breathless moment, hands on her knees.

Brosa.

What matter was he?

She shook her head, but the image of her belongings stuck in her contacts, no matter how she tried to dismiss it. Her meager things hovered over the mud and grass at her feet. The valley was wet and green, and water seeped up farther into her slippers.

Yes, Brosa would come for her.

He'd ride on Gull, along the edge of the white woods, calling her name. Sitting tall on his horse, he would push into the wind, looking for her. His golden hair would tangle and whip, and his brilliant, ocean-blue eyes would search. Just for her.

Had Da even looked for her, when she ran away?

With a violent dash of her head, she made the "take" and "leave" piles disappear. She picked up running again, parallel to the forest's edge, looking for the most tangled place to hide.

A dozen years ago, Brenna told Eðna about the City of Iceland that surrounded them everywhere. People beyond counting filled all the habitable spaces of the island's perimeter, with buildings that sat on top of each other, climbing up to the clouds. And such knowledge! Other ways of living. Brenna told Eðna about writing and showed her some of the shapes that made up words. Not just runes like pictures. People wrote them on smooth, frosted surfaces like frozen water, but their breath did not make them disappear. They didn't write in the dirt with a stick.

Brenna got so excited when she talked about it all. She introduced the concept of history, and how their families were just mimicking it, living as if it really were Viking times.

When Eðna challenged her Da he said *my sweet girl* and tried to hold her. She asked him about what Brenna said. Did the city exist? Was it true, that people could have saved her mother?

He took her, shaking, inside his big arms. Surrounded by wool and the smell of his sweat and metal, Eðna longed for him to say the words that would dismiss Brenna's madness. She waited in brittle suspense for her big, safe Da to refute the older girl's lies.

Little One, he said, holding Eðna tight. *That world out there is not right.* He drew back to look in her eyes. *It's all plastic and glass.*

Dread flooded in.

Her father said words she'd never heard before. *Plastic?* He didn't deny what Brenna said. So it was true.

There is no blood out there. He traced a curl by her ear and spoke with love. *No animals or big sky. No honor in living that way.*

Eðna ripped herself out of his arms.

"This is the world that's not right." Her throat was raw, like she'd swallowed shards of a frost cup. She spit the words out at him. "You're a kind of person who doesn't exist!"

Her Da smiled, one of his sly, sweet smiles. He raised his arms out wide as if to say, *Look, here I am. I do exist.* It was just like him to wink and tease while her world crumbled.

He told her that honor meant keeping promises and protecting each other.

"Like you protected Mommy?"

Now, a small sob came out, a harsh gasp. Look at where she had come. Ironically, to a land, a house, a lush valley that her father would have loved. She laughed and sniffled. How many times would she have to run away from farms?

Eðna touched the vial of antibiotics in the purse that sat snug now against her waist. Smooth and cool. With the back of her hand, she wiped her cheek. Wet.

She would arrive home soon, triumphantly appearing in the lab. She saw herself taking shape there, against every possible rational explanation. She'd made it and returned, from this Viking Age valley, where arctic breezes gathered from oceans away, with no buildings to stop their advance, and the ground was so wet it squished with every footfall.

She listed the things she would have again, easing her breath, matching it to her strides. Clean dishes, healthy air, wall screens that glistened like ice. Impeccable floors, watertight shoes, thousands of facts inside contacts that didn't glitch and sizzle.

Her eyes darted to the woods. Every inhalation sucked in an unfamiliar, musty scent. Dirt. But also fungus? Or maybe rotting leaves. What did an enormous carpet of wet leaves smell like?

Ginn would have noticed by now that she was missing. There were so many trees, with their secrets and turnings. It was time to enter the woods now, into an unknown and alien place, with no solid plan, or Brosa would find her.

Would he fly on Gull, and lift her in a single, heroic swoop? Throw her across the horse's back and drag her to the house? When she struggled, would he bind her with rope? No. He probably wouldn't have any rope on such short notice. Maybe he'd tear off his shirt and shred it, so he could bind her in linen. Her sweet captor and guard.

He would come, yes.

Brosa tapped Gull with his heel, and the horse picked up its walk into a gentle lope along the edge of the woods. The woman, Eðna, would not be far ahead, but he couldn't be sure which way she'd run. Losing her would be easy enough. And he couldn't lose her.

She'd run away at the very moment they got news of two of the worst crimes in the land – defilement of the dead and cold-blooded murder. As for the first, well, he knew who had committed that act. As for the second, with Eðna running now, her guilt would be clear to any but the dumbest man. One like him, a beast so stupid that even with her fleeing before him, he still didn't believe she had anything to do with the deaths of two of his brother's tenants.

Brosa had to reach her. She would not know her way through these woods. He had to help her get to the coast and home, before she was accused of murder.

The surge of sadness in his gut, at the thought of losing her, was only because she could be lost or hurt at this moment. She could be deep in the woods by now, a place she didn't understand.

He smiled. Eðna swore she knew the parts of a boat, but she could only name the hull. He hadn't even gotten past the simplest terms before she fell asleep. She couldn't steer through these trees any more than she could navigate the ocean between here and Norway.

The idea of the old country had come to him now and then, since Hár brought it up. A whisper only, not a plan, but the possibility drew him. And it was wrapped up with Eðna. Could he take her there, instead of sending her to her time? They could jump onto his ship today. They would only need a few men.

She would kick and yowl the whole way, and knock Brosa off the boat. He smiled, but his gut ached with the truth, that he would be a Viking then. Stealing a woman, nei matter that he meant her no harm. Nei matter that more than the whale road separated her from her home.

He let his eyes run over the tree line. Her dark hair would disappear in the forest, but the dress she'd been given was bright and light, the loose fabric like a bless around her small wrists, her ankles. He looked for it now, among the trees.

"Ho," he spoke to Gull, and the horse slowed to search along with him, snuffling and watching the birches. Brosa had been to this part of the woods many times, hunting foxes alone or following Heirik. But Eðna would not know the place, and that worried him.

He rounded a curve of forest, and there she was, running along the edge.

She wore no dress, only her shift, and it flew behind her, brown with mud. She covered the ground with strong strides, like a mare racing to the sea.

She heard him. Her head snapped up. She turned to face Brosa, and the look in her eyes pulled Brosa up short. It was horror. It speared Brosa in the gut, that he could make Eðna look this way.

Eðna turned in desperation, like a drowning woman, and then she dove and crashed into the woods.

Brosa slid off Gull and followed her.

"Eðna, stop," he called, pushing branches full with new leaves out of his eyes. "Come, Woman!"

"Never," she called back.

He laughed to himself. He would not reach this woman with commands, the way his brother controlled men and women. Despite Eðna's anger, and her blindness to the pattern of these woods, her spirit was strong.

She moved slower now, fumbling with the branches. He was close enough to see her clearly now. Her dark curls hung in a loose tie down her back. Just like Heirik's long, dark hair that he had followed on hundreds of boyhood days, chasing his brother into these woods.

Heirik was just as desperate to get away from Brosa. Everyone, always trying to escape him.

His laughter died in his chest.

"You'll be lost soon," he called.

"I have a map," she snapped, still pushing forward.

Nei doubt she did have a map of the island, but nei map had ever been drawn of these trees. No ink had placed these woods on a cured hide. She had no way to know that they were approaching a small clearing—a room inside the woods no bigger than a house. He would catch up with her soon, and he slowed his pace and let her tangle herself up in confusion.

Eðna broke through into the clearing and stopped short. She turned, as lost as he'd warned that she would be. He hung back, at the trees' edge, and coaxed her.

"Come to me, Eðna."

"Nei. You're keeping me prisoner here." She held herself close, shielding herself against him, but something about her reached for him. Something in her eyes. "No better than a woman you grabbed by the hair on the way from some island."

"Eðna, don't ever—"

"—Don't talk to me." She raged, but she didn't run. "I'm prepared. I'll do what it takes to get home, and I'll keep trying, no matter how many times you drag me back."

He smiled, by half. "I would not leave you alone in the woods, even if you did have such a map, and were in your proper clothes. Certainly not in your shift, without a stick of knowledge about where you are."

"Like you know where we are, either."

"Já, of course I do," he said. "I know where we are, and I know the route back to Gull and to home."

She stopped for a second and her brows drew down tight. Did she not believe him?

"Eðna, I know you had nothing to do with those men."

"Men?" Her brows came to an even sharper point above her nose.

"The dead ones, on the sand."

She froze, a sudden sheet of ice between them. "I don't know what you're talking about."

Brosa's mind tossed with lies and truth. Did she really have no knowledge of the crime? Was it an accident that she had arrived here the same day they died? And that she had fled today of all days?

"I won't come with you," she said.

"Já, you will." He finally broke, exasperated, and raised both his arms to show her the world. "Look around you, Woman. There is no map of these trees, except the one in my head."

She pressed her lips together.

And then she nodded. She was angry as a prodded horse, but she agreed. She wouldn't run anymore today.

In truth, he'd expected more of a fight.

He slid off of Gull's back and went to Eðna. He stood close enough to smell her clean hair and herbs.

"You have the scent of the woods, now," he said. Stupid beast. Words spilled without thought.

Eðna had a reply on her lips, but then those brown eyes widened. She turned slowly, looking at the trees, and her mouth, so like the color of fall berries, dropped open in wonder.

"There are so many trees," she said.

Brosa tilted his head back. There were nei more or less trees than usual. "You did know you were entering the woods, nei?"

"I've never been inside." Her voice was nothing but breath.

She swayed for a moment, as if she might sink to the ground, and it was all he could do to stay back and not catch her. The grass caught on the linen around her ankles, showing the shape of her calves, strong and lean, bringing Esa to mind.

In years past, Esa's calves would peek out while she sewed, when she sat across the hearth from him and he honed his blades. Months of marriage passed before he realized his wife was flirting. He pictured Eðna, the image like a flicker of flame, sitting across a fire from him while he worked.

"Have you never seen birches?"

"Never this many," she said.

The ends of her dark hair lifted in a breeze and stuck to her cheeks. She was intent, listening. Did she feel what he did? The shifting of the woods, with its breath of leaves and insects and animals. Her fingers and eyes drew knowledge from the trees. She absorbed them. And her strength began to show from underneath her hesitance and anger. He saw a force in her, trying to lift a sheet from across her eyes. He saw her under there, under her bluster and fear and leather ties. He thought her name, and it bit his heart. Eðna.

The linen was lifted from his own gaze, too. The thing that had been dividing him from the living for these two years.

He saw his old horse Fjoðr in his mind. His beloved animal, racing on the horizon, coming to him. The sensation was strong, and after years of feeling nothing, he looked at his own hands and arms to be sure they had not changed.

A savage feeling came to life in one beat of his pulse. He wanted Eðna.

With a dry throat, he stood in this realization. He had to lean against a tree.

The woman's fingers brushed the bark, and her skin and eyes glowed. Brosa ached to touch her, and he recognized it now for what it was. Not a desire to touch her for strength when she met Ginn, scared and alone, or to warm her by the hearth. Nei. It was a desire to caress and know her.

Her fingers explored the peeling bark, and Brosa moved silently. So close to her now. He had to speak.

Dumb beast. This was nei time to tell her such a thing. Not when she ran from him, not when there were dead men on the sand and Brosa had come to drag her home.

Even so. He had to give her his broad smile, had to say something to make her laugh, make her want him, too. But in the face of such raw desire, all his past ways with women seemed puny and wrong.

He laid his hand over the back of hers.

He covered it completely, and trapped her skin against the skin of the tree. A breeze blew her hair so that a dark strand caught in his beard and tangled in the bark and with their locked fingers. It felt good and simple.

He breathed like a hidden fox.

A widower already at 21 years, a father once, if just for an instant. A grown man. Touching Eðna, he was a boy again, full of unshaped dreams.

She lifted her eyes to him, and she blushed across her cheeks, her throat. He wanted to put his lips there, where her skin lit, and say her name against her bones. He shifted closer, easy in case she might bolt. And as he did, Eðna slipped away and turned her back on him, looking deep into the woods.

"I want to go home," she said. "I have fourteen more days until the seeress comes. Ginn says the blind woman will decide my fate."

"Eðna, I can't let you—"

She swung toward him, and now her eyes burned. "—I have to be gone by then. Or whatever that freak woman says, I'll have to live with forever."

Her voice shook, and he saw her for a moment as that eternal force he had awaited in the grave. Not the force of death, nei. Her hair was not braided with skulls, but with leaves and bark in her tossed curls. She had a fire behind her eyes, já, but not burning for the dead. Burning to live. Gods, she was glorious.

And she wanted nothing to do with his life. She was a prisoner of his house, her heart already riding the waves to home.

"Fourteen days, já?"

He had fourteen days to make her stay.

Eðna slipped the reins around her wrists and twisted the ends over and over, letting them slide through her fingers. She let Gull carry her at a slow walk, his gait like a tide, washing her back and forth, and she watched the trees pass slowly. So many.

Brosa walked a few paces away, his huge boots crushing the slender spring grass, his shoulders tense. He let her ride the horse alone, and he held onto a long lead, gently, almost incidentally, as if he hardly cared if Eðna ran. He hadn't tied her up and lashed her to the horse's back. He hadn't even touched her at all.

Except for what he did in the woods, with his hand on hers.

She felt it again, his hand, her hand. It was a simple touch. But it wasn't, either. Not just a lift up onto a horse or a palm against her back to guide her to the house. It was not accidental, the way he laid his huge hand to cover the back of hers, with a deliberate pressure, an angling of his body to get close. So close that she felt the movement of his breath in the hair on top of her head.

Brosa's body was not the same as others. Not vulnerable, like her mother's or her own. His bones, and his pulse under his skin, were not fragile. They were powerful, animated by a will beyond anything she'd felt before. Had she actually spread her fingers, to let his slip between hers? She had no reference for such a thing, a man holding her hand. Maybe she had opened her hand, just a fraction of a centimeter, before her brain engaged and she pulled away.

She returned to absorbing the trees.

They were different underneath the skin. Among the millions of specimens, an infinite variety of colors would shine under their bark, underneath the silver-white. Amidst their secrets and facts to be ascertained, she wondered how one tree became bronze and one copper when they stood in the exact same soil, touching and intertwined.

This forest contained knowledge that could not be learned in the future, where there were no stands of trees bigger than two dozen. Density, size, colors, light transmittance, the scent and scratch of the bark under her fingernails. What it felt like to be down inside, in the middle of so many. She felt a surge of something familiar and light returning. She didn't even need the answers yet. The wondering itself was like food. Like water slaking thirst.

But it could never work. She could never measure those things here in the past. Never create a model of the woods, turn it on its side and upside down, manipulate, label and save. Without her technology, she couldn't do anything.

Gull swayed with each footstep, carrying Eðna in waves.

Soon, a seer would tell Ginn that Eðna was a threat. At the assembly—the althing—Ginn would find someone to take Eðna in a ship, far from here. Too far from her only route home.

She would run again. Brosa would catch her again, and it would only make her look culpable, the harder she tried to flee. Or she would go back to the house willingly, just like this. But she might be imprisoned forever for her desire, her wish to gain knowledge about time travel.

One thing was certain. If she'd ever thought of telling Brosa about what she saw at the fishing camp, that impulse was gone. More than ever, she wanted nothing to do with the dead men.

It didn't matter. Eðna's mission was her mission, and the lost lives of men who'd turned to dust a thousand years before she was born had nothing to do with it.

She leaned far off the saddle and brushed leaves with her fingertips. She wouldn't struggle right now and try to tear away. She would allow Brosa to hold impassively onto the lead and take her back to the house. She had time enough to visit the woods and gather as much information as she could. And when the time came to escape, Brosa would assist her. He had taken her hand. He seemed to like her. He would want to help. Yes.

Brosa rested his palm on Gull's cheek. His hand was massive, his fingers clean and rough. His old bracers were tied loosely around his wrists, as if he'd thrown them on in the rush to chase her.

"Your bracers are a mess," she said.

Startled, Brosa looked to her, and gods, Eðna could drown in his eyes, such a complex sea-blue.

"My bracers?"

"They're all scratched," Eðna said. "I can repair them, make them nice again."

It would give her something to do. To occupy her hands, while she observed, befriended, looked for another chance to run.

Brosa got that half-smile on his face. "I would like that, Fine One."

Brosa closed his eyes and drank in the feel of Ginn raking his head with a comb. His uncle was right. He had let himself go. His hair was so tangled, Ginn could barely get the teeth through it.

Since his brother married almost two years ago, Ginn had lit the house like a hundred lamps. She had lit Heirik's life on fire, and Brosa had slowly moved into the shadows. He did the work that was required of him, smiled while he put on his own wrist bracers, mended his own shirts, the way Heirik once did. And like Heirik, Brosa left the hearth for long and useless walks. Visits to his secret place in the woods—the one that no one knew about. He came home and drank ale until he fell down into sleep.

He'd wallowed like the pigs he saw in Norway. But less satisfied than the pigs.

Now, sunlight warmed his eyelids and Ginn fixed his hair.

It had been just a day since news of the crimes. Just a day since Eðna fled. One day since her hunger for knowledge, and her body, had knocked Brosa on his ass, just as Hár said. He was supposed to feel rage about Esa's grave right now. Supposed to be a devastated widower, driven to revenge. But the weak spring sun on his face felt like life had returned to him after a long, dead winter.

Ginn yanked on the comb.

"Gods, Woman, you'll rip my scalp off."

"Sit still," she said, and she scraped at him with the bone tines.

While she combed, Brosa unwound the cord from his long beard. Many months ago he'd tied it up in a tail. And then the next day, he tied it the same. And so on, until a year had passed, and no one cared any more what he looked like.

"Do you think my beard will hold this shape forever?"

"Nei," Ginn said. "Don't worry. I'll make you handsome."

He laughed. "I'll settle for smelling fine."

"You smell good," she said, and she leaned over to sniff his hair. "Like sea-dew and soap."

"Good," he said. "A man should be clean."

"Right," she said, drawing out the word. She must be curious about his sudden request for a shearing.

"But you can make my hair like it used to be, já? Prettier than Heirik's?" He was kidding, of course, but also unsettled. Could she? Or had he let himself go too long to ever come back?

"Hah!" Ginn laughed, and she came around in front of Brosa and crouched down to work on his beard. "If you want, I can compare you to my husband, but it won't go well for you."

His words shot out before thinking. "At least I can talk to women."

Stupid. Why would he goad Ginn? The woman could go cold as quick as his brother. One minute a smiling friend, a past lover, now a sister. The next minute a wolf.

Like frost, she said, "I thank the gods he never did."

Brosa swallowed, Ginn's shears close to his throat. "Now is as good a time as any to ask you, Sister. About Ivar and Torg. What will Heirik do?"

Now that Ginn had come, and Brosa had drifted off into the wilds of his heart, away from home, Heirik rarely confided in him.

"He'll watch," Ginn said. "Let fools tie themselves up in their own ropes."

Brosa could almost feel those ropes tightening around his own ankles.

Then Ginn warmed again, smacked Brosa on the head with the comb, and all was well. She returned to shearing him.

He closed his eyes and tipped his head back. For a quick moment he thought of Eðna doing this, caring for him, making him look just the way she wanted, and he gave a lazy smile.

"Eðna shies away from touch," Ginn said.

"Gods. The women in this house can truly read men's thoughts."

"A blind woman could read yours right now."

Já, then, he would have to smile less. Try not to stare at Eðna's hips.

"Believe me," Ginn said. "She's afraid to be close. I've seen it before."

"Já, you know I have too."

They both knew Heirik's way. His brother had always longed for touch, but withheld it out of fear for others.

Eðna was different. The moment they met in the hills, she pulled away. Not silent like Heirik, nei, but in her own way, with flashing eyes and pushing hands. So many times she'd refused his comfort. When he placed his hand on hers in the woods, she'd slipped out from under, quick as an eel.

"I don't know why," Brosa said. "No curse follows her."

"Well, something does follow her. She's as brittle as straw."

"She is driven," Brosa said. "That's all."

"As a hawk," Ginn said. "And we are the plovers. She hides something."

Brosa grabbed the comb and stilled Ginn's hand. "Listen, sister!"

Ginn went still in his grasp.

He hadn't meant to sound so hard. But Eðna was no bird of prey gliding over their house. He leaned in, elbows on his knees. "I want to offer her my worth. Make her choose to stay."

The words were new, never spoken out loud, and they tasted good and right. And yet, they scared him as much as the idea of a sea-cold reaper. He wanted Eðna, já. He had wanted women before. But he hadn't said, even in his own heart, how much he desired this one. That to hold her, he would offer Eðna everything he had, and it still might not be enough.

Ginn sank back on her heels and set the comb in her lap. Her lips curved into a slow smile, and her eyes took on that sheen like Heirik's, that he always had when he was thinking about which sheep to kill.

"Good," Ginn said, no doubt considering her own needs. "That's good. But you will have a challenge on your hands. Almost as impossible as I did."

"Impossible." Brosa sat up straight. "And yet here you are, keeper of the keys."

She smiled wider, showing that small space in her teeth. He hated to think that he'd kissed her long ago. Followed those teeth with his tongue.

She must have seen him scowl.

"It's alright, brother," she said. "We'll make a plan."

"Nei, Woman. Stay out of this." He smiled, but he was serious.

Ginn considered him. "You'll need more than a haircut."

"I said, put your claws away."

Ginn was undaunted. "You must see, Eðna craves knowledge."

"Já, she does. So?"

"So show her, there is so much to learn here. Show her you're an intelligent man, not a savage."

He laughed again. Nei matter that Ginn was driven by her own desire to keep Eðna close, but she was right. There were thousands of things that Eðna could learn here, some as big as the sky, and many small enough to fit into a moment between man and woman. And Eðna seemed to have no knowledge of most of them.

"So, Beast," Ginn said, "Besides this very good haircut, you'll need some snowbloom-water in case of a kiss. And this beard. Almost all will have to go. I'll cut it to a point, the way you once wore it."

Years ago, he did wear his beard in a short point. Svana was the one who always cut it that way, but he let that memory pass. He would never mention the girl in front of Ginn.

Ginn kept talking, while everything turned in his mind. "This could solve everything," she said. "Eðna is drawn to you. She just has to realize that she wants you."

"If she does, I'll be a happy man."

"Every woman wants you."

Brosa shifted uneasily.

It would be nice to be known for something other than his charming grin and fair looks. Yet, even his sweet sister Ginn would use them to her own ends.

"Well, this one doesn't, not by a boat length," he said. Eðna had slipped her hand from his grasp. As quick as water she'd run through his fingers and turned from him. She didn't want to stay with him, didn't want to stay in his world at all.

"She does," Ginn said, and her shears sliced. "We just have to get her to see it."

Eðna pressed her bare toes into the mud, at the very edge of Ginn's river. It rushed through this lush, little ravine—a miniature canyon, with rock walls that towered an estimated 15 meters overhead.

It was absurdly gorgeous, all espresso-black earth and moss and ice-blue water. The place gave the impression of a stillness and silence almost sacred, despite the water's twinkling sounds and Betta's relentless presence just a little farther down the bank.

The river was only a few meters across here, where it wound around slick rocks and islands small enough for her father's elves. It turned crazy corners before expanding, free of the little canyon, and charged off across Ginn's land, to eventually join the sea. If Eðna were small and weightless as a leaf, she would be there by now. Going home.

Ginn sent Betta with Eðna to work here by the riverbank. She thought this place was so beautiful, it would persuade Eðna to stay. Ridiculous. As if soot-brown cliffs and small, dark caves enclosing her, would endear Eðna to this time.

She stirred up the muck with her foot. With her toe, she drew four lines in the moist ground. It had been four days since Ginn made her pronouncement about the seer. Ten days left before the crone would arrive.

Brosa's bracers laid beside her on the bank. Also, a hunk of lye soap, lanolin for her hands, a knife, small iron shears. She'd cut the cracked and stained leather out of the center of each bracer and craft two braided panels to insert along each wrist.

She picked one up and smiled. It was so huge, it could spin around on her upper arm.

Betta had put her to work when she learned about Eðna's skill. Fine. She needed this work for her hands, so she could think and plan. Brosa made her the blade she needed to cut the finest strips of leather—a wooden cylinder, with two small blades on it, a few millimeters space between them. That space became the width of the cord as she drew leather through. Even pressure and reasonable speed made a consistent strip for braiding.

The smell of real hide flew up into her nose, with a flurry of fibers as small as pollen.

She hadn't known the difference when she was little. Real leather was beyond rare in her time, and so the material her mother taught her to work with was fake. *Pleather* that her Da got in return for chickens and small rabbits when he went on his mysterious trading missions.

It was one of the few instances when her Ma cheated and used an impure substitute for anything. Gida's hands yearned to cut and stitch and plait, and she couldn't stand to live without working the soft hide. Little Eðna sat close by her side and watched her mother's bony, strong hands. She had skinny fingers and wrinkly knuckles that looked too big. Eðna tried to match her mother's motions, but her own hands were chubby and she fumbled at first. Later, she got very good.

Eðna's mother's scent was animal, but with a slight chemical burn that Eðna later learned was the mark of *pleather*. A concept—that something would be a fake version of something else—that was entirely new to her in the city.

"It doesn't soak up water, see?"

Vera's fingers, soft and skilled, had cast a few drops onto a piece of faux hide, and then a few on a precious real sample, to show Eðna the difference. The water stood on top of the *pleather* in round, reflective beads.

Here in the past, Eðna dipped her fingers into the river and flicked sprinkles onto the leather in her lap, and for a moment she sat in the safety and kindness of Vera. She swallowed a sob. Wanting her Ma and Vera all in one mixed-up ache.

The water was absorbed, darkening the leather in abstract shapes.

Eðna braided.

It wasn't just work, drawing strands together. Her own mind and hands had always needed this, just like her Ma. She organized the cords between her fingers, closing her eyes during the most complex maneuvers, because her hands knew better. Her hands knew pattern and repetition.

Here by the little river, a familiar consuming attention and satisfaction came over her.

Her contacts tried to display and sort things, the way she always did while working, bird after bird. And then, the images sped up. Instead of birds, the contacts threw up flotsam, picture after picture, faster and faster. A cairn as tall as a man, a bone comb, half-carved wood, complex ink drawings of indistinct shapes. They went by too fast. Soon, the images went by so rapidly, they turned Eðna's stomach. She tried to stand and fell back down, and her eyes showed her the word, *vertigo*. She looked up, and the roar of pictures obscured the sky.

Eðna felt around the rocks for the soap. She washed her fingers in the river as best she could while pictures of water and wings and frost on a window sped by. She held open one eye, touched her fingertip to her contact and drew it out.

Everything stopped. Only the stream passed by, reflecting soft, painless light.

Relief.

Her insides slowly settled.

She turned the contact to the sky, like a glistening bowl on the very tip of her finger. Could she really see the lightning flicker of images still flashing inside its curve? The savagery and stupidity of the pictures, messages, news from groups that strangers had added her to, about things she didn't understand. People had shown her things, over and over, and now they all spewed forth and flashed and changed in this tiny cup.

How long would her contacts be like this? Working, not working. Uncontrollable. Irrational. How long would they last? Long enough for her to escape? Or would they die here?

"—You need to eat, Fine One."

Eðna sat up straight, startled by Brosa. She closed her hand around her contact.

He leaned against a nearby rock wall, arms folded, smile full of mischief. She thought he would be angry over her running away. But ever since that time in the woods, he'd seemed even more playful, ready to smile. Today, there was something especially different.

"Your beard!"

"It was time I showed you what I look like."

The cords that bound his long beard into a tail were gone, and what remained was clean and brilliant golden-blond, trimmed to a devilish point. It made him look immoral. He smiled and stroked it. "How do you like my face?"

"Beautiful," Eðna sighed.

What?

Where did that come from? She blushed and rested her forehead in her palm. She'd never thought of a man as beautiful before.

"I'm working on your bracers," she said.

Brosa came to see, and as he lowered himself to sit close, Eðna slipped her contact into the folds of her dress.

Brosa sat close, so close, and Eðna's toes flexed with a quick impulse to run, but something held her near to him. Some instinct even more powerful than fleeing.

She smoothed the leather in her lap. "I cut them up the middle, and I'll put these braided pieces in the place of what I removed."

"Beautiful," he said, and Eðna blushed even harder. Was he serious or just mimicking what she'd said about his beard?

He spoke low and private, earnest. "I'll be proud to wear them when they're done."

She brushed her fingers over her contact, where it was hidden. She yearned to put it somewhere safe, until later when she could clean it. But then it would be between them, and she and Brosa would talk about her contacts. She liked this instead, sitting the sun and gently talking about his wrists, his face, her braid-work.

"Eat," he said.

He'd taken out squares of flat bread, and spread goat cheese on one of them.

"I can't," she said. "My hands are dirty."

"Come then," Brosa said. "You can't starve, Woman. Open your mouth."

Brosa held out a cracker with fluffy, white cheese. The idea that she would take it from his hand was absurd. But the contact was rolled up, moist in her fist.

She opened her mouth.

He placed the cracker between her lips, and she accidentally closed her mouth on his finger. Gods, it was mortifying. Impossibly intimate. Had he moved closer to her? Too close now.

"The way a small bird eats," he said.

Eðna went rigid.

"No more." She scooted away and clutched at her skirt to protect her filthy contact. Brosa had spoken out loud about her love of birds, and she felt herself descending into the dirt and earth with embarrassment. Her skin shone with it. And even if she wasn't mortified, she was no helpless chick.

Brosa wiped his hands on his thighs and sighed. "Come then, Woman. You can eat at the house."

Brosa turned a piece of wood over in his fingers, and he measured it against his hand, from fingertips to wrist. He'd sharpened a small awl for the purpose, and he used it to dig a long center line up the wood. It gave a satisfying sense of clearing the way for something.

In only a few days, he and Eðna had fallen into a pattern that warmed him.

She worked in the mornings on leather, repairing packs and belts, and he stayed a safe distance away, both of them ignoring the truth, that he guarded her. Now, he sat with his back against a forge stone, carving in soft birch. He could just see Eðna, sitting against the wall that ringed the stable, her braided head bent over the work in her lap.

He smiled, warmed to know that she especially worked to make his bracers glorious. She worked and re-worked the plaits and cords that would hold his sleeves tight against his wrists. He wanted her fingers there, too, underneath his shirt. That would be good, já.

He pressed with his awl, deepening the gouge, moving forward and yet down toward the wood's heart. Up and out again.

Starting at the center line, he carved out fine, angled shoots. Soon, a feather would come to be. He saw it now, in his mind, the way that Eðna saw the design of cables and twists she worked, before they took visible shape. Some true things could not be seen with the eye.

With short strokes, he worked on the feather.

It was like that with Eðna's traveling. Some unseen force had brought her to him exhausted and hurt, pulled apart by wind and time. Why did Saga need to batter Eðna's body to send her here? The water of time must be violent as a storm-wracked sea. The thought turned over in his mind, of unseen hulls and sails that Saga filled with wind and life. If he could see that water, could he build the right boat? To follow her?

She looked like a girl, so young, hunched over his bracers. He smiled, thinking she would smack him if he said so.

Later, he would bring her food. They both worked in the mornings, but she did not stop until he brought her bread and cheese and ale. A few days ago, he fed her like a small bird and felt a brush of her lips against his fingers. His hands were so rough from work, he barely felt her soft berry lips. He could have leaned in and followed that bread with a kiss.

But she hissed at him and pulled away.

What did he expect? He smiled and smoothed the half-carved feather. She was Eðna, and she was fine without his help.

A shadow fell across his legs.

"Get out of my sun, Áki."

"I'm not a little boy." Eðna bumped his shin with her small boot, and Brosa sat up straight and tall. This time, Eðna had come to him. He shoved the half-formed feather into his pack, and he shielded his eyes with his hand so he could see her beautiful face.

"Já then, *Woman*. Are you through working?"

"For a while," she said. "Betta has me repairing a pack, and more bracers. Your uncle's are a mess."

"I would imagine so," he said.

She sat beside him and crossed her legs, her skirt dusty and apron green from grass. She picked the small yellow flowers that were strewn everywhere in spring, and the house dog came and sniffed at her hand. It was good, being here with Eðna in the sun.

"Does this mean you've brought the food today?"

She smiled. "No," she said. "Just me. I thought we could go down to the house together."

Já, he would go with her, anywhere she wanted. And soon, he would take her to the woods early in the morning, when the ground birds were nesting. She had never seen them, in all her life. She wanted a world with words in her eyes and writing without ink. But in truth, as Ginn said, there were many things to learn here, and many things she did not know.

Eðna woke to a whisper. "Vakna, Finen."

She climbed up out of sleep and turned to the voice—an amber honey voice, with the cadence of old, old language—telling her to wake up. Calling her an unknown compound word that meant something like "fine one." The scent of wood and rosemary came next, and she opened her eyes. Brosa leaned over her, like the sun coming in to the sleepy dim of her bed. His hair fell forward and hid his scar, but could not obscure his sea-blue eyes, wide awake and twinkling.

With a quick stab of annoyance she pressed her lips together. She'd been here eleven long days, and he had called her Fine One more than once. He was amused when she pushed away his assistance, but she didn't need his help, at least with the simplest things, like smoothing out a blanket or eating a cracker.

"That word, fine," she said, sitting and drawing her blanket up to cover her shift. "I'm not sure you use it the way we do in the future."

"Já?" He sat back on the edge of her bed, a ridiculous number of knives clanking on his belt. "How do you use it?"

"Well, it does mean okay, as in not needing help." She sounded pricklier than she'd intended. "But also, someone who is fine is..." She searched for old words. "Beautiful. Strong, and...attractive to a man."

He smiled and closed those ocean eyes for a moment, savoring some thought or remembering someone. His wife?

It stabbed Eðna's heart, but why? Why should she care? If he thought of women past, then he would stop using the word on Eðna.

"Get up," he said, and he patted the bed beside her. "It's early. I thought we would find some birds."

"Find birds?"

Brosa sat on her sheepskins and furs, half inside her curtains, tying his newly-braided bracers. They looked good on him, the thin, fine braids climbing up his thick wrists.

"Well, some are talking now, before the sun comes up," he said. "Soon they'll go to their ground nests and we can get close. But you need to learn stealth."

Eðna drew her blanket up higher. "You think you'll teach me to be stealthy."

"Já, I think that."

"It doesn't come naturally to me," she said.

A couple of days ago, he'd trimmed his beard into a point, and when he smiled, he looked impossibly even more mischievous and alive. "You'll learn."

They waded through the wet grass and slowly descended the hill to the woods. The sky was gentle and pale lilac, like a martin's breast. Feathery clouds moved across the expanse. At the tops of the highest hills, long trails of mist rose from the ground to meet the clouds and disappear, incorporated. A hint of gold gathered just below the horizon. The sun would change the million tree trunks of matte white bark to silver in a quarter hour.

Her contacts worked sporadically, jolting her to attention once or twice a day, then slipping back into oblivion. Perhaps quietly continuing their work of recording and remembering? Eðna couldn't be sure if they were recording anything, so she memorized facts and images on her own—the delicate and complex patterns of light and shade, the variations under the white bark, lined with infinite metallic colors. She would remember them, já, but could she ever describe them?

At the edge of the woods, mist curled out of the trees and around their feet, then rose and dissipated, revealing her little boots. They were covered in bits of sticky wet grass. Brosa's boots were covered in green too, and the damp brought out the scent of true leather, so different from her mother's sharp tang of *pleather*. This scent was Brosa's. Part of his persistent presence beside her.

She studied him. Not because she enjoyed him, of course, but to learn his habits—to identify the lax times when he tended to be busy or not paying attention. But he was attentive, always watching her, sitting by her, trying to feed her. She'd look up from the fire, and he would lift his eyes to her over the rim of his mug of ale. His leg sometimes accidentally brushed hers when they sat on the fur-deep benches to eat. She'd actually let him place a piece of flatbread in her mouth.

Ridiculous. And mortifying. She'd dropped her eyes, hoping that no one had seen.

Now she scanned the woods with her naked eyes, reviewing the scenarios she dreamed up while she braided.

In the simplest scenario, she found another chance to run—a moment when Brosa's attention finally wavered and his eyes settled on some other subject. Maybe he had a woman somewhere, from another farm, who would come when the seer was here.

Eðna dashed the image out of her mind. She would be gone before ever seeing such a thing.

The option with the greatest chance for success was to become friends with Brosa, to continue to get close to him. He would help her get to the coast, and so she talked with him, went with him to meals, went on this walk under this pastel sky, away from the hearth. She looked up to his face, far above hers.

Should she tell him she'd seen the dead bodies? She yearned for him to be an ally in all ways, a confidant. And the family all knew about them now—two murdered men who worked for the chief, but men of no consequence to anyone, with no reason to be killed. They were cousins of Svana's husband. Brosa said his brother was waiting to untie the logic of their deaths before he retaliated.

Every time she thought of speaking about it, an inner voice told her to hide. To not get involved, not get Brosa involved. She didn't like the lie of omission between them, but she would be gone long before it became an issue.

As if he could sense her churning thoughts, Brosa's shoulders tensed. He was not as easy in his body, here at the forest's edge. "You won't see many birds if you crash through the woods."

"Right," she said. "You're going to teach me to walk softly."

Brosa smiled that gods-damned half-private smile. It always started at one corner of his mouth, as if he tried, but failed, to stop it from growing.

She crossed her arms. "What does that mean? When you laugh that half-hidden laugh?"

"Not a thing, Woman."

"Right." She brushed her fingertips over the ties of her bodice. "I know it's about me."

His smile widened. "Já, alright," he admitted. "It's only that sometimes you look like a lamb getting its first legs."

Her skin blazed, and she turned away. "Never mind the woods today."

"Eðna, don't," Brosa said gently to her back. "You must see that it's friendly."

She should walk away. He made her feel stupid. But Brosa was easy and good at everything. He didn't know how it burned Eðna to not know something, to be ignorant about a subject. And, too, the trees held her, and her curiosity was stronger than indignation.

She wiped her boot, but only picked up more sticky grass.

"Okay," she said. She smeared grass with her other foot, too. "I'm not used to *friendly.*"

Brosa muttered something. An oath? Louder, he said, "We'll practice here." He stirred the brush and twigs with the toe of his big boot, and it didn't make a sound. "In the morning, the ground and sticks are full with dew. The wet brush makes less noise."

She moved a few sticks with her toe, and though it made a shushing sound, it wasn't overly loud. She took a step, and a twig snapped.

"When you step, press your foot into the ground first, before putting your full body into it," Brosa said. "Don't walk on top."

They stepped into the edge of the woods, and Eðna pressed first the ball of her foot and then her heel into the moist ground.

"Listen to the sounds of the woods," he said. "The birds, the scratching animals. Don't try to hide from them, just become another sound."

Esoteric nonsense. She turned to him with a raised brow. "Become one with the woods?"

"Okay, Woman, I know I sound like a fool. It's just what my Da told me."

"Fathers are full of advice." Another twig broke under her foot. "You know I grew up on a farm."

"Já, you said that much."

"It was nothing like this." She stopped still, and she placed her hand on silver bark. "We had forty-seven trees where I grew up."

"Forty and seven. Surrounding your house?"

"Forty-seven in all. Anywhere. There were no more big trees in any direction, even after hours of walking. It was blank, brown land with just sparse grass and our few crops."

Brosa looked at the woods and blew out a deep breath.

"A thousand years from now, the city surrounds all of Iceland," she said. "In the center, the land is tired and lifeless, most of it covered in volcanic ash. There are a few farms like my parents', where people are near to starving all the time. There are very few animals left."

"A farm without animals?"

"They're all dead."

Brosa backed away just a little, as if the dreadful truth of the future could infect him. "A farm of the dead."

He'd never shied away from her before, and Eðna reached for his wrist. She couldn't get her fingers around half of it. "The bracers are working?"

"Já," he said, and he brushed her hand with his thumb. "Tell me about your farm."

Eðna slipped her hand away and took another quiet step.

"I left it. When I was a little girl, I came to the city alone. There was a woman..." She smiled. "Vera. She took me in and helped me. She worked making clothes that are from your time, and I worked with her, making belts and purses and bracers."

"And this," he said, and he reached for one of the laces at her side, playful again. She slipped away from his hands.

"I did," she said. "This top is the only thing I made for myself. Vera let me have the real leather."

He must have heard the warmth in Eðna's voice.

"This Vera taught you things," he said.

"I was little," she said. "She taught me to read, and to search for words. I saw pictures for the first time." She spread her hands, trying to find the words, the essence, of a photograph. "The way that things looked in other lands, other times, that I could never—"

She stopped, flushed with excitement. Brosa was resting his back against a tree, just watching her. He was truly something, the streaks in his blond hair sparkling almost white in the lacy sunlight, his big shoulders rounded and arms crossed. Almost wastefully comfortable, taking for granted that ease in his own skin.

"There are many things worth saving here," he said. "You could stay for a while, Eðna."

She didn't move, didn't even shift her weight on the brush underfoot. Her pulse sounded like a terrible, raging surf in her ears.

He wanted her to stay?

What did he mean by a while?

Brosa's assistance was her greatest hope. Had she waited too long to ask him? She'd formed a friendship to endear and recruit him, and it had worked too well. She'd observed and hesitated and lost her chance. Lost her desire to go, too?

What was she thinking?

Brosa was asking that she remain here, for some reason, when no reason could ever make her want that. She knew that for sure. So why couldn't she raise her eyes to Brosa, and raise her voice to tell him that she would never stay here out of choice, not for a week, not even a day? Her throat had closed up, dry as dust.

Silently, with easy grace, he pushed himself off the tree. "Come quietly, Woman. There should be awl-beaks," he said. "Just past the small clearing."

Brosa leaned into the wooden door—the back entrance to Ginn's new hall. Well-made, the hinges still shone with seal oil, and it opened without a sound. Brosa shushed Eðna with a push of his palm and motioned for her to enter the dark.

She'd been here two weeks now, and he hadn't shown her enough of his mind and heart. He had to make his feelings known now. He had little time left.

He pressed the leather cylinder to his thigh. He would show her his plans, and she would see him clearly.

Her voice was small in the cramped space. "Brosa?"

She reached for his hand, and Brosa's heart stumbled at her touch.

He'd taken her to the woods several times over the past days, always watching her look and learn, answering her questions about the trees, moss, birds, worms. He showed her plants they used to make touchwood to spark fire, and the lichens Betta used to dye wool for trade. He showed Eðna fox tracks and the ground nests of birds with beaks like the needles she used to sew leather. He'd stood by, or stooped to sit on a nearby log, while she *saved images.* But he hadn't tried to take her with a kiss, or take her body against his. Pull her down to sit on his lap.

He wanted to, like a man wants air. Many times he had to walk away and press his forehead to a tree, or shift his weight where he sat, to get rid of his desire. He kept his eyes on a piece of fungus or moss, and not her hand that held it, her wrist under the stitching on her dress. At night, he walked away from the house, where he could be alone with his thoughts of her. She was lovely, courageous, tense as a trap, and then she would soften.

Now, she held his hand tight in the dark.

Her bones were small, her fingers strong and cool. He could push her gently against the wall here in the mudroom, find her with his hands and body in the dark. Would she want him in return?

"I can't see," she said.

"Just a back room, já?" His fingers tightened around hers. "The next room has light."

He pushed open another door, and they entered the dim cooking room. A place made for preparing meals and feasts, it sat empty now, without comforts. No pelts on the benches or logs ready to set fire in the mealstone. A single roof vent let in watery light. It made Eðna look as though she stood in morning mist, her features softened, skin like cream. He would drink her in, taste her throat, her wrists. Gods, he wanted her.

She let his hand go.

"I thought it would be decorated all over. Carved."

"This is a room for cooking," he said. "Come with me, one more door." He drew her with his words, to show her the true inside. The heart of the hall.

From the first days building began, he'd felt the hall take shape like a massive boat, its ribs going up first, open to the sky. Standing inside the beams was like riding in the hold of a great ship. A house bigger than any he had ever seen, even during his travels.

He took a deep breath. "The biggest house in Iceland." He smiled. "Come see."

Eðna stepped into the grand hall and gasped. "The eyes!"

"They do leap out of the darkness."

The animals of his family.

For months, skilled men had worked carving their snouts and teeth and paws, into doorways, beams, table legs, chairs, even the walls themselves. Carved beasts lurked in forests of wood-knots and rode on waves made by men's knives and hands. The wolves and foxes of his father and mother. The ravens and whales of Heirik and Ginn. Their eyes looked out from every post and beam.

Eðna's animal would be a great bird, its wings spread and amber-stone eyes glinting. What would his animal be? Maybe a house dog, following his brother around.

He dashed the ugly thought away.

Eðna had gone ahead into the room and explored the carvings with her hands. Her small fingers stroked the animals that were cut into the wood. She pressed her fingers into the jaws of a carved wolf.

"Ginn believes in big gestures," he said. "She is building this hall to give him a place where his loneliness doesn't linger."

"I wondered why." Eðna pushed a dark strand of hair behind her ear.

She stepped into the empty hearth, just a large ring of stones and dirt that lay still until the day the house would be blessed by the seer. The crone, and the dozen or more companions she brought, were near now. Two days away. Maybe three.

Eðna looked up into the fall of light that came through the roof, as though under a waterfall, and turned in a circle, her little boots kicking up dust. A sudden surge of sun hit her, and she turned to him, a small smile on her lips.

"I have a tiny bit of whisky left." She raised one brow and said this like a secret, though they were alone. She slipped the flask out of her belt and took a small sip, then handed it to him.

"Do you always stand in the hearth?"

She laughed. "Nei, never. I don't have a hearth like this."

"Ginn says the houses are massive in your time, bigger than this by far."

"I suppose." She looked up toward the sun. "But they really can't be compared. Have you seen the frozen plains?"

"Glaciers," he said. "Of course."

"Where I live, we have *stabilized* the glaciers." She wove together his language and hers when she was frustrated or excited. "Steadied one of the last ones. People carved it open in the center and made a great hall of ice."

Brosa swigged the harsh drink. "It sounds cold."

Eðna stopped circling, and her dress settled around her ankles.

He'd hurt her.

"Nei, nei," he hurried to make things right. "It sounds pleasing and cool." He spread his hands as if warming them over the empty hearth. "When they light all the fires in this hall, it will be too warm. We'll roast alive."

Eðna laughed.

Good.

She ranged farther into the hall. A long braid swung against her back. He wanted her to take the strands apart for him, let her hair fall into his open palms. He sipped more whisky and shook the flask. Almost empty.

"This is a fireplace!" She called from far across the hall.

"Já," he called, and he went to her. "Ginn told us about a place for fire built into the wall of the house."

He ran a hand along the stones that formed the hole in the wall. "She drew it, so it could be built. It has a shaft that carries the smoke outside. Like a þakinnlogi, but big."

"Þakinnlogi?"

"A hidden flame. You haven't heard of this?"

Eðna shook her head, her brows drawn in the center of her forehead. "Nei."

"You've never built a fire in a bowl in the ground, to hide the smoke?"

"We don't need to do that." She turned to look at the fireplace, and he cursed himself again. He'd embarrassed her. Eðna didn't like to not know something.

"It doesn't belong here." Her words echoed up inside the fire shaft.

"It's in the wrong place?"

"In this time, in this place at all." She closed and opened her eyes, narrowed them the way she often did. "The first chimneys were invented in the 11th century, not for another hundred years or so."

"You know so much about them?"

"I just looked it up." She met his gaze.

"You looked up." Brosa cast his eyes to the ceiling. "And then knew this?"

"I have…" She began again. "I told you about how I have words I can read in my eyes."

"Runes that only you can see, já. When you told me, I thought you were half asleep and dreaming."

"It's true. The symbols are inside tiny bits of material, like the finest cloth, that fit over the surface of my eyes."

Brosa sank onto a bench and let out a deep breath of whisky.

"And this cloth, it tells you about fireplaces?" He placed his hands on his knees. "Come here, into the light. Let me see this linen."

"We can try," she said. She knelt before him and tilted her head back, and his blood raced. "You might be able to see."

Eðna smelled of the herbs Ginn used to scent her skin, and when she knelt at his feet, some sly goddess threw boat dreams at him. The usual workshop he imagined, with tools to work the wood. An image came, of kissing Eðna among his half-built, upturned hulls. Something rose fast in him, in the space of a pulse, some lost emotion, without sense.

She lifted her eyes, and it didn't matter that they were covered in the thinnest piece of linen. His own were, too, já? He knew what it was like to look out from under a shade. Her eyes ignited him, from behind their veil of words. Desire reared up suddenly, and the truth rolled in under him and pitched him like a boat.

He didn't just want her hips and waist in his hands, and her body under his in the furs. Much worse, he wanted her beside him, always. Wanted to look into these linen-veiled, woods-brown eyes all his life. The dream of days together formed in an instant. The vision of shared, urgent need and understanding. The wish to never be apart.

"They're called *contacts*," she said. "Everyone wears them in my time. Well, everyone in the city. They help show me direction, and I can ask them for things like when and where a certain kind of animal lived. I can get and keep other peoples' knowledge."

With his elbows on his knees, he leaned close. He peered into her eyes while she continued to speak about words and facts. He came near enough to feel her breath on his cheek, her hair touching his face, mixing with the strands of his beard. Even so, he could not see her *contacts*. Only a twinkling of her eye that could have been caused by her spirit just as soon as a bit of cloth.

He struggled to speak. "Why do you need this, Eðna?"

"Why?" She asked as though he were the dumbest beast. "It's everything. Everything in the world."

A flash of life lifted her voice, and her lashes brushed the soft skin under her eyes. "Everything anyone ever learned, in all of time, is saved here."

He held still, wanting to protect her happiness, to blow softly and feed it like the tiniest ember in a nest of twigs. He was very close. He could slip his hand into her hair and hold her head, touch her lips.

She would hit him, surely.

"Not everything," he said, hardly breathing.

"I was ten," she said. "I liked the pretty birds, so that was what I learned about, to get better at reading the letters...like runes. I could save each bird's image in my eyes, in the walls of my house. Each one's name."

"There are many things worth saving here," he said. "Many things you can learn in this time. As many as there are kinds of birds."

She blinked. "There are 10,081 known types."

"That many, já?" How could he best that? He let out breath, forced his lungs to work. "What else can you see, besides words? Just me and these benches?"

"Well," she sat up on her knees and looked around. "The contacts can light the hall up for me, if I want, if it's too dark. Either by sharpening my own gaze or by using other forms of light. Light waves..." Her words left off. "I don't know how to tell you."

He drew his elbows up off his knees and sat tall.

"Don't worry, Woman. I live here in a wood and earth house, without knowledge in my eyes, but I'm not a dumb sheep."

"Brosa, nei—"

"—I know a great deal about the ways of waves."

"Já, I'm sorry. I know you do."

She placed her hand on his knee, and he thought, for a heartbeat, that he should be showing her his drawings. But all thoughts and plans dissolved. Did she realize she was touching the inside of his leg? He would stay still as a stone, stop breathing entirely, if she would just leave her palm there with only a thin layer of wool between them.

"I'm sorry," she said again, and she ducked her head, spoke softly. "You must know more than I do about waves."

Did she know her fingers were moving against his thigh?

"Já, then?" He coughed and swallowed. He listened to her words, tried to forget her hand. "If you weren't weighing my ignorance, then what were you thinking about under those brows?"

She drew her hand away and stood. "About the pantry."

"Gods, a chaotic wind drives you, Woman."

"In the pantry, I could have lit the room up. But I didn't want to see how small it was."

Brosa didn't know how to feel anger and disdain at his brother, at Ginn, and yet it rolled hard through him. They'd locked Eðna up, like a criminal, and it made him burn every time he thought of it. Of her in the dark, her hands against the door, trying to get out.

"And with you posted outside my door." She wiped her small nose. "To guard in case I somehow escaped."

"I told you, I was not there to watch you."

Já, he had been sleeping at the back door when she went past. She had said as much at the fireside that night. And he could see the situation—himself curled up against the wall, with his knives still on his belt. It could easily have looked like he lingered there to catch her if she tried to go outside. He'd told her nei.

"You fell asleep at your post."

"You are wrong." He spoke sharply. He hadn't meant to let it out, the force of his anger at Ginn. "I would never be part of such a thing."

"Why, then? Why would the chief's honored brother sleep on the floor?"

"I didn't sleep there to watch for you," he said. "I sleep there often, because I have no real bed I belong in."

Eðna didn't speak.

That was something.

In truth, he had no real bed anymore. The bed he'd shared with his wife was right there in the pantry. Where Esa had lain in his arms and laughed into his shoulder, the sleeves of her long shift brushing his face. The same bed where Eðna now slept. His mind turned inside out at the thought of Eðna lying there, against the furs and boards where he'd known Esa over and over.

The silence was like the rushing of water on sand. He tossed back the last bit of drink from the flask, and he wiped his mouth with the back of his hand.

"Every corner of that house holds dangers for me. Places where I did stupid things, where I grew up. Where babes were born and people died." Words came like a tide. "Beside that back door, asleep, I am halfway gone."

Eðna was silent.

"I sleep outside sometimes," he said. "I'd rather spend time with the stars." Under the sky, where his thoughts could roam, he felt too insignificant to worry about things past.

Eðna took the flask from him and held it to her chest. "My da did, too."

"Your da?"

"Já, he lived to be outside. To see the horizon the way the Gods made it, he said."

Her eyes shut tight. Against pain?

"He believed in living in the old ways." She turned to take in the hall. "What he imagined were your ways. He could never have dreamed up a place like this, or men like you and Heirik."

He didn't know what she meant by men like him and his brother, but she threw him in together with Heirik and the grand hall and all the things her Da dreamed of. That might be good.

"Men like me?"

"Big, powerful," she said. "Honorable."

These were good things, ferocity and honor, já? She saw him that way.

"Your Da was not these things?"

"He let my mother die."

Gods, he wanted to comfort her. "Eðna, I know the same. My Ma is gone, too."

He'd said goodbye to Signe as she lay on the bier. He'd drawn himself up and held his breath so he would not cry.

Eðna spoke. "He lied. I didn't know until I was ten that there was a city, that there was another way. He chose to ignore all the help we could have gotten. He chose my life for me and didn't tell me there was another way." Her voice shook with anger, but her eyes were not full of rage. She was wounded.

Brosa yearned to hold her, to tell her that he would give her everything her Da had not. He'd give her honor and loyalty and truth. But he sat in silence, his own lies, his omissions about Esa's grave, swaying in his mind like meat on heavy hooks. And the dust from his wife's grave still clung to his skin, nei matter the number of baths he'd taken.

"Eðna," he said. "I've lost many people, too. My parents and...others."

He wouldn't talk about a dead wife and child, not while he sat here hoping, and failing, to seduce this difficult, passionate woman.

"I'm sorry," she said.

"Nei," he said. "Nei, don't be sorry to talk of such things. Just know that I understand."

She nodded.

This was the moment he'd kiss a normal woman. But Eðna was so far beyond the women he knew. Confusing and brave and fragile. The moment was like a frost cup. He would hold it lightly.

"Does my face resemble a rune stone?" He grinned.

"What?"

"With your *contacts.*"

"Nei," she laughed.

"Don't twist the truth," he said. "I have symbols across my face, don't I?"

He backed up around the high seat to draw her with him into the dark. He would kiss her here, behind the high seat. And he would show her he was not ignorant like her Da. That he had a heart that beat beside his lungs.

"The contacts are not working all the time," she ducked her head. "Some things I see with my own eyes."

"Can you see me now? In the shadows?"

She followed him. "I can see your teeth. You smile a lot."

He blinked, surprised. In days past, he did smile a lot. He hadn't for some time.

"Come see this," he said.

On the back of the high seat, where his parents once sat together over the heads of all the people of Hvítmork, there were letters carved deep in the wood. His name.

Eðna brushed her fingers over the runes. "Brosa."

"Já, that is me." He smiled again. "I do write."

She followed each symbol with her fingers, with such care, as if she might disturb his fate if she pressed too hard.

His voice cracked. "My mother was a rare woman. She made sure we knew the symbols. That we could wield their power."

He traced his brother's name, where it stood next to his own. Heirik had carved his first. Then it was Brosa's turn.

"I have been to the old country and can speak the dansk tunga. Some."

"Norway, yes," she said. "For two years, you went to trade."

"Já," he said slowly. "I did." So Ginn had told the people in the future more about him than he imagined. What did Eðna know about his family? Did she know about Esa and Arulf?

Even if she had every detail of his past there in her eyes, she could not know what it felt like to hold his child and watch him pass into the everlife. She couldn't know that he'd destroyed their resting place. Eðna knew he once had a wife, já, but she couldn't know that he'd never felt for Esa the way he felt now. The way he'd just begun to feel.

"Brosa." She whispered in the shadows. "Will you help me go home?"

The moment broke like a delicate glass in his fingers. He saw himself at the bow of a dark ship, nothing ahead or behind. It was useless, feeling anger at fate, but it came, and he struggled against it.

"There are many things you don't know, Eðna. More than your ten thousands of birds."

"Help me learn," she said. "What do I need to know to get out of here?"

"You don't need to go home," he said, passion building. "You say your knowledge is everything, it is life. Well, what about hidden fires, and how a boat is turned? How it feels to be surrounded by the deep woods? There's knowledge to be had about real waves, teeming with eels and greater beasts."

He was good at giving up what he wanted. Smiling and saying já, sure. He would marry Esa. He would go trade. He would marry Ginn. But now his voice deepened like his uncle's, his own desire, his own dreams building like flames and wind.

"The things Ginn told you about me, they are not all there is to know."

"What things?"

"That I'm loyal as a house dog?" His words were bitter, like shark on his tongue. Growing in fierceness. "I wink at the ladies and drink and laugh with the men. A charming beast, who doesn't know what he himself wants."

Eðna backed away from him, and his heart broke. He was scaring her, but he couldn't stop. "The life your Da gave you is not the same as what I can give you here."

"Brosa, what—" She shook her head, her eyes wet. "Give me? Here? I can't stay here."

This was it, then. He was losing her. So fast, he'd hardly had a chance to know he loved her. "Shh," he said, and he pressed his fingers to her mouth. "Give me a breath, before—"

—The door crashed open, and both of them went silent as stones.

Eðna scooted farther behind the high seat and hid beside Brosa.

Ginn smiled, playful, and spoke in her unexpected, deep voice. "The hall is not blessed, Husband."

"Nei matter, Wife." Heirik spoke playfully, too, loose and free in a way that Eðna hadn't seen. "Come."

Heirik let an ax slide from his grip, to rest alongside the bench, then he picked Ginn up by the waist. With a swing of her skirts, he placed her on the table. Ginn's sweet laugh lifted into the cool hall air.

And then they went quiet and still as snow. Filled with awe, as if they'd never dreamed of such a glorious and impossible thing as one another. Their wonder settled around them and drew them together, and Eðna felt the muffled silence of a winter night, a blanket wrapped around her. She remembered her father's arms, carrying her through the cold.

The chief brushed Ginn's cheekbone with the backs of his fingers, and she lifted her chin to let him continue, so slowly, down her throat. He traced just above the neckline of her dress, and Ginn breathed deep and slow. Her eyes went sleepy and unfocused, but open, never leaving Heirik. He smoothed the bone over her eye, where the whale's tail curved, and she pressed her forehead into his hand.

Ginn's voice was hoarse. "The hall is not ready."

Heirik traced her lips with his thumb.

"I was not ready for you, Litla." He placed his palm on her cheek.

Eðna breathed, her lungs tight and painful.

Ginn touched Heirik, then, just the same way that her husband had touched her. She curled her fingers and drew her knuckles along his cheekbone and down his throat. Eðna noted the order of touches, the way that Ginn reflected the exact series that Heirik had done to her. Ginn's fingers circled the pendant at his neck, slipped inside his untied shirt, and he watched her face.

"It will come to be, Love," he said. "In this house."

"Shh," Ginn said. "Don't speak about it."

The chief closed his eyes and leaned in to Ginn's fingers. He rested his forehead on hers, and she reached behind him and untied the leather that held his hair. Black waves fell around them, hiding them from the world, from Eðna and Brosa.

Ginn dropped a hand to Heirik's hip and slid it up under his shirt, and he ducked his head to breathe deep against her throat. She drew him in, murmuring secrets of desire, devotion. Such loving touch. No fear. No weakness.

The chief kissed his wife, a growling kiss, hard. The words Eðna needed—*luscious, consuming*—fled, her brain drifting. Heirik wore no bracers on his wrists, and Ginn pushed her hands up inside his sleeves. He ground words out, called her *wife* and *love* in one word, "Ástkkván." His respiration came hard. "We will bless the hall ourselves."

Eðna gripped the high seat, riveted, unable to look away or even close her eyes. She saw what Ginn saw, Heirik's intensity and control, his mind lost, and yet giving orders. To come to him. To bless the hall themselves.

Wait.

What?

Oh, no. Were they going to have sex here, now?

Like fuel on fire, Ginn responded, wrapping her legs around her husband.

Eðna looked to Brosa, desperate for direction. Shouldn't they say something? Shouldn't they tell them they were here?

Brosa stood with his forehead pressed into the back of the high seat, eyes tightly closed. A fleeting image came, of him with the letters of his brother's name pressed into his forehead, slowly vanishing as blood returned. *Does my face resemble a rune stone?*

He glanced sideways at Eðna, helpless.

She looked at him from under her fingers, hiding.

This was wrong. Eðna would speak up. Now. She opened her mouth—

—A sound burst out from behind the cooking room door, and the girl Ranka dashed in, her braids swinging. The chief and his wife separated instantly, and Ginn slipped gracefully from the table, smoothing her skirts.

"Lukla," the girl panted. "The seer is early. Just a half day away."

Ginn was impossibly serene. She spoke with control beyond belief, as though the furious fire with Heirik had not just burned. "Thank you, Ranka," she said. "Let's find your mother."

"She's already sent word to bring up the ale and the frost cups and swans, and—"

While the girl charged forward on her list, Ginn listened and nodded. And she discreetly traced her husband's palm with one finger, drawing a line up his wrist. The chief pressed his other hand against the small of Ginn's back. A secret touch, unseen by Ranka.

Eðna couldn't swallow, couldn't breathe.

Ginn stepped away, drawing the girl out the door with her. She glanced back at Heirik and smiled, a darling, promising smile that she thought no one could see. She winked at her husband, then closed the door.

Heirik pressed his palm to the table where Ginn had sat, then lifted it to his lips and softly kissed his own hand. He picked up his ax and left.

The door closed, and Eðna let out a long breath. "Gods," she said, and that was all she could muster. Her mind and body whirled with images and thoughts of Heirik's seduction, Ginn's tender and raw love, her hands under his clothes. Bodies, unafraid of one another. Eyes so clear and unafraid of death.

"Já." Brosa still rested his forehead on the high seat. "I'm happy for my brother. But I did not want to see that."

Was he upset by their touching, their devotion?

No. He smiled, simply relieved. He took Eðna's hand, to draw her into the night, and an afterimage swiftly came, of Ginn's finger stroking Heirik's wrist, a touch both teasing and sacred. An image now burned into Eðna's mind.

Brosa's hand lingered in hers for a moment.

He opened the back door to the hall just a crack, and after searching the yard, he pulled Eðna out after him. He drew her into the growing dim of night, and they leaned against the house beside each other. A swift wind, smelling of sweet grass, came and ruffled her skirts. Brosa's hair whipped her face, and it smelled of soap.

They watched Ginn, who was halfway up the hill to the old house. She was all blond and blue, her hair and dress whipping around her shoulders and ankles, as natural a part of this landscape as a flower, or an elegant, twisting tree. She stood tall, owning all that surrounded her—the land, the sky, the house. The man who now walked up the hill toward the forge, his black hair untied by her hand.

The air tasted clear as water, and Brosa's voice came low, as though speaking to himself. "There is no place for me here."

Eðna had been forming similar words. "Lesser," she murmured. That's what she would be if she didn't find a way out. Less than the woman she'd worked so hard to grow into. Nothing but a farm girl, after all.

"Já, I am," Brosa said. "But you don't have to rub in the ashes."

What?

"Nei." Eðna corrected him. "Nei. Not you." She adjusted her belt, straightened the sheath that held her small knife. "I'm thinking of myself. If I were made to stay."

Brosa's eyes hardened, the blue now seeming less like the sea and more like a winter sky casting freezing rain. His scar showed bright white.

"Never, Eðna. You would not be lesser than any woman here." He began to trudge up the hill, grinding small stones into dirt. "But I know your meaning."

She trailed after, but then stopped and let him go.

He didn't know her meaning at all. It wasn't about being lesser than Ginn or Heirik. Nei, it was about being less than she could be in the city. Eðna's life would be smaller here, meaner, her opportunities diminished to almost nothing. She'd learn nothing ever again, and hardly have a chance at living long enough to care.

What was it Brosa had said before Heirik and Ginn burst in? Something about her Da's life not being the same? He was wrong. It was just the same here.

She tugged on the ties at her side and watched Brosa get smaller as he attacked the hill.

ᛊ

Svana snatched the broom out of the corner when she heard her husband's horse approach.

Eiðr's cousins, Ivar and Torg, were dead. When they'd heard the news, Svana knew it was that idiot shepherd who killed the wrong men. Since the news of the murders and Esa's grave, Eiðr had been in a foul way. He pushed his rage down every day, as though he would drown it under the surface of a bath, waiting for his time to move against Rakknason. As if such a man could challenge a god.

Most days, she cooked and sewed and cleaned only enough to get by. But in her less dark moments, she felt sorry for Eiðr and did more to feed warmth into their home. When he came home, she made small gestures.

She swept.

She knew how to do every task well, of course. Her mother, Hildur, had been a legendary keeper of the keys, her house tidy, men clean, blankets stacked tight. Svana and the other girls spun thread until their fingers were slippery with sheep's oil. They made soap and dyed cloth, though Svana spent less time at the pot and more time lying in the grass and looking at the sky. Even then, when her life was good and easy, her spirit had wanted to go up into the clouds, just to see Frigg's handiwork.

The first days of their marriage, Eiðr patiently told her how to sweep properly in the corners and spark a better fire—things any child knew. Já, Svana was able. She just refused.

She dragged her broom in half circles, watching her skirts sway.

Some men would rage at a wife like her. But Eiðr had not harmed Svana. Nei, at first he treasured her. When she was given to him as wife, she was dishonored, but so was he, for all that their families had done to the chief. Eiðr struggled to do the simplest work with one hand, because Rakknason had cut the other hand off. That he would be given any wife, let alone one as stunning and sweet as Svana, strained belief.

She swirled, and the broom-straw crackled.

Their wedding had been a mockery of a feast. The wedding Ginn should have had, with snowblooms and banners and cool ale in the midsummer sun. A hundred guests in their finest clothes, night fires across the farm, frost cups of drink, everything lovely. It was an honor Ginn never got to have. Instead, Ginn had been married to Heirik in the field, on the way to meet his fate, with no feast or blessing. And so Ginn placed that honor on Svana's head instead. Did she see Svana cry, crouched behind the forge when no one was looking?

That night, her wedding night, Svana choked on Eiðr's ale-breath. She shrank from his ghost-hand when it touched her. A man partway in the afterlife, his arm a smoke-vent for death to sneak through.

That was almost two years ago.

Svana made a poor wife, and Eiðr's sense of good fortune was gone by now.

Outside the door, he kicked the stone foundation of the house and loosened dirt from his boots. Svana stiffened and gripped the broom handle.

"I feel like I've waited a year to eat," he grumbled, then called again. "Woman, are you in there?"

She breathed deep and smiled.

"Já, Eiðr," she said. "I'm here."

With a gust of air, he entered. He filled the room with his bulk of wool, his clunking boots, his sharp knife and simple ax. He looked to her with his grim face, long crooked nose and the ever-sneer of his family. But Eiðr was not as ugly as the chief. His eyes were always alive, green as grass.

He sat on a bench and pushed his foot toward her, for her to remove his boot. She knelt to undo the bindings, and she smelled the sweat in his clothes and leg wraps. He ran his hand through his hair, and the strands left filthy oil on his fingers. Her own fault. She should comb his hair and trim his beard, wash his clothes, be proud.

His other arm - the one without a hand - rested on his thigh, right before her eyes.

It felt like a slap, the way the truth hit her. Eiðr was Svana's own severed hand. He was her punishment. Every time she looked at him, some lost part of her, a severed dream, throbbed with pain.

"There is food in the pot." She stood and picked up the broom again.

"Good," he said, and he went in his sock-feet to find it. His footsteps made cloud-puffs of dust.

"We worked all day on the walls." He stirred the stew and served himself. "The far ones are crumbling, and the chief sent me with just two boys to help."

Svana choked. Her husband trying to lift stones. The image made her cringe.

"Another five days' work, at least." Eiðr sat and swished a pitcher of ale, sniffed it and drank.

She swept dirt into small piles and snaking lines, little hills like the walls he went on about.

Brosa would not sniff and gulp when he drank ale, and dribble it in his beard. He would beam like the sun, his beard neat with the tracks of Svana's own comb.

Eiðr spit a piece of fish bone on the floor, and she swept it up into one of her little hills.

To have Brosa one day, she would have to get rid of Eiðr. Not just divorce him, even if Ginn and Heirik would allow it, but get rid of him completely.

She had no poison around, except an abundance of snowbloom. She took it every month, to keep a child away, and she gave it to Eiðr for good breath. But it was not strong enough to knock the life out of a big man.

She shaped another small hill of dirt.

She could put lye in his ale. It would stink and bubble, and he would know right away, but if he took a swig without smelling first, just one gulp should seize his chest. The burning would take his lungs. Or she could hit him in the head with the pot, with a heavy swing.

With the side of the broom, Svana wrecked one of her dust-hills and began to gather it up again.

She could cut his throat with her fish knife.

Nei. Beheading the fox was horrible enough, and the memory made her throat close. Could she handle cutting the throat of a strong man? Could she bring herself to do it, if he turned those green eyes to her?

Eiðr talked, and Svana did not listen. He waved his ghost hand, and spirits flew like sparks. She ducked her head, drew herself in small so they wouldn't land on her.

"...and Brosa," Eiðr said.

Svana stopped.

What about Brosa?

She wouldn't ask Eiðr to repeat himself. She wouldn't ever say Brosa's name. It would come out cracked and sad and soaked with passion, and Eiðr would know she still dreamed of him.

"...the woman he found."

Svana stood still as snow. "A woman?"

"Wandering in the hills, another stranger like the chief's wife."

Svana forced the broom to move. She cleaned around Eiðr's feet, and he lifted them to let her in.

"The long-haired chief. Everyone falls at his feet." Eiðr laughed, a ragged sound, and he threw his arm around Svana's waist and pulled her tight to him. "Afraid to bed a woman. Ginn herself had to force him to take her."

Svana swallowed hard and did not struggle against Eiðr's embrace. "I'm sure she did." She couldn't say much or her voice would betray her.

"The whole family has lost its wits," Eiðr went on. "Ever since Ulf died, they've gone down knees first like a long-dying beast. This last thrust—to kill my innocent cousins—is too much. Soon they will lose everything." Eiðr kissed Svana where her keys hung. He lifted his green eyes. "And you and I will be repaid."

He let her go.

"Soon," she vowed, though it was more of a plea.

"It would be better to let the revenge simmer longer," he said. "But the seer is a good time for an accusation." He chewed. "She's come early."

He tossed off the news like a piece of stale bread. "I hope you're ready with my shirt. We go tomorrow."

Eðna tightened her belt, fitting it snugly so she'd be able to run without her purse and knife slapping at her thighs. This time, she'd be ready.

The sky was winding down to dusk. Calm and slow, she walked uphill to the forge. Nonchalantly, as though wandering, lost in thought. "Bee Hummingbird," she whispered. Just the size of a bumblebee. She named her birds, one bird per step, starting with the smallest. "Lesser Goldfinch." Not to be confused with the Goldcrest with its miniscule frown, a bird just a centimeter longer than her old sewing awl that fit inside her palm.

The seeress was here.

Eðna hadn't seen her yet, but the woman's arrival had consumed the household. Ginn and Betta especially burned to find out the truth that the woman would supposedly tell. They were in their element, serving the woman and making an honored place for her and her entourage of a dozen other women in the new hall before revealing her at tonight's feast. Everyone had lost their minds and their vigilance, and now Eðna was completely alone.

Eðna reached the top of the hill—the place where Ginn first took her, when she tried to show Eðna the beauty of Hvítmork. Electric peach cumulous clouds were quickly lowering and turning to ash and steel. Three birds glided through the darkening sky, unbelievably graceful and high.

Eðna ducked behind the biggest forge-stone. It stood at least 20 centimeters over her head. She leaned against it, finally hidden, and let out an anxious breath. She would be fine. Yes.

She'd wait just a minute or two and then go, once the sky darkened to indigo.

She would succeed this time. The alternatives were not good. Tonight, some wizened crone would tell Ginn what to do with Eðna, anything from imprisoning her forever to sending her to toil and starve in Greenland or Canada.

She tucked her hair behind her ear, and her fingers snagged in intricate braids. Ranka had drawn Eðna's hair back from her forehead and plaited it in a complex pattern, woven with sprigs of fragrant evergreens. Juniper and extravagant lavender. Betta said that with her full brown lips, Eðna did not need berries for color.

Now, she stood high above Ginn's two houses, the old and the new. Dozens of milling, shouting, laughing people, had come here to get a glimpse of the seeress. They'd arrived all night and day in their best dress clothes, with knives and cups and horns hanging at their belts, ready to drink from the barrels of ale Ginn provided. Men with big beards and raucous laughs, and women with braids coiled up or hanging down their backs. All drunk already.

Not one of them was Brosa.

He hadn't come to find her today, the way he usually did. Instead of working leather, Eðna had cleaned glasses and sanded the rims of dozens of wooden cups. She curled birch bark into cones for the children, brushing her fingers over the papery tree-skins. An extravagant waste of wood. And Brosa never appeared with his usual bits of food for her, and his wicked smiles.

She'd seen him walking around scowling, rolling barrels of drink, digging a fire pit. He threw his weight into the shovel like an angry ram, and Eðna got a glimpse at what that big body could do. His muscles moved with pure purpose under his long shirt. He stopped to wipe sweat from his brow, where pieces of his hair had come free and stuck in his eyes, and he saw Eðna. He only nodded. No smile.

He must know—they both knew—that this would be Eðna's last day here. That she would have to run. It was her only remaining chance.

Stupid. She'd thought Brosa cared about her enough to help her. Several times, she'd imagined them making their way to the coast together, Brosa hiding her from Ginn's wrath, them laughing together among the trees. Instead, when she asked for his help, he spit fire at her. In the shadows of the great hall, he'd sharpened his eyes and his words, telling her she didn't know things like how to hide smoke or build a boat.

He'd never taken her hand again, never mentioned it. These past several days, Eðna thought maybe it was the way a man touched a woman. But after seeing Ginn and Heirik together, she wasn't sure anymore.

What would she know? Growing up, she absorbed all the advances of science and technology, like a series of shocks, each one more awe-inspiring and embittering. She did not spare any time to think about boys, or later men, except to sometimes feel a ridiculous longing for her Da.

She tied a big knot in her dress and underskirts, and she yanked it tight. What did it matter, anyhow? If Brosa touched her with desire, all the worse. He would never help her. He wanted her to stay.

She knew her way to the ocean. She could get away without him.

The sky was as dark as it was going to get. Time to go.

"You're a pretty one."

Eðna tensed, and her hand went to her knife hilt. A drunken man reeled up to her. He smelled of ale and sweat, and something metallic, maybe blood. He narrowed his eyes, and he swayed, almost unable to stand. "Come to me, Maid." He grabbed Eðna's arm, tearing her hand away before she could draw her knife.

She struggled. "Get off!" She pushed him, but he weighed as much as the forge-stone. The man leaned into her, forced her back until her spine was pressed into the rock. The stink of ale and bad teeth hit her nose and throat.

"Let me go." She tore at his foul shirt, his giant body so hot and horrible underneath. Too close. Smothering her. "No!"

She brought her arms up underneath his, trying to pry her way out. She got an arm free and went for his eyes with her fingernails.

"Fiery bitch." The drunk grabbed her behind her head and bent to kiss her with his disgusting mouth.

"Back away, Ansig."

Brosa's voice was cold and level, and Ansig hesitated, but only for a single breath. He slurred, "Go away, Ulfsson. I'm busy." He ground against Eðna, and she choked, panicked. She called to Brosa for help.

Brosa dragged Ansig off of Eðna with a growl of rage, and he spun the man around and punched him hard in the gut. The drunk man wheezed and went to his knees, spewing saliva.

"Look at me," Brosa said, and he kicked Ansig to get him to look up. Brosa held a knife pointed toward the man's face. "Look at this blade. It will be the one that cuts your balls off if you touch this woman again."

"Já, já," the man sputtered, wiping spit from his beard.

"Get downwind of us," Brosa said. "And don't come back to this house as long as you live."

Ansig's eyes went wide. "But, rikbróðir..." It was a word like high-born-brother. Brosa was casting him out forever from the great house, and Ansig begged. He bowed and touched his forehead to the dirt, then looked up to Brosa. "Please, I won't—"

Brosa lowered the knife so that it pointed toward the man's crotch. "Go."

Ansig crawled until he was far enough away, then got to his feet and stumbled down the hill.

"Eðna," Brosa came to her, pulled her into his arms and pressed her head tight against his chest. "Are you alright?"

His arms were too tight. He smelled of soap and clean wool, so different from Ansig, but he smothered her the same way, and Eðna panicked. So much bigger than her, his arms binding, too tight. She pushed her way out. "Don't."

"Já, okay," Brosa said, and he backed away and put his hands up. "Eðna, I should have been with you."

"Nei," she said. She was suddenly so cold, she wrapped her arms around herself. "It's not your job to protect me."

"Oh já, I forgot." Brosa kicked a large stone down the hill and folded his own arms, too. "You're fine."

"I can take care of myself. I just..." Eðna smoothed her dress, and she ran into the big knot. She folded her shaking hands. "It's just, I've never kissed a man before."

Brosa's eyes flew to hers. "He didn't, did he? I was in time?"

"Já, you were," she said. "You were."

Brosa turned toward the dark expanse of land where Ansig had run away, and he picked up a rock. He yelled after Ansig, an incoherent roar, and threw the stone into the night. He turned back to Eðna, radiant with anger, everything about him alive and raging so that he seemed to light up the forge.

His hair was braided tight around his face, and his scars and eyes were clear and sharp. Amber wool spanned his chest, over a shirt so fine and pale it shone like the moon. It laid untied at his throat, where a silver Thor's hammer rose and fell with his rapid breath. He wore no bracers, and under his loose shirt cuffs, his thick wrists were solid with silver bands. His knife hung from his fingers.

She thought of larger birds. Regal ones that blazed with yellow and bronze. "Golden eagle," she murmured. That was Brosa, now.

"What are you about, Woman?"

"You're stunning." Her Brosa. And she did not need to fear his embrace.

"So they say," he spit out. He jammed his knife into its leather sheath so hard, Eðna winced.

Yesterday, in the grand hall, he'd wanted her to understand that he wasn't just darling and pretty. He was more than a fancy bird.

"Nei. Not like that. It's just that you got dressed up," she said.

Brosa stopped railing at Ansig and at the sky and the night, and he looked at Eðna. He looked at her hands, where she gripped her pale skirt, and at the big knot that laid against her thigh. He looked at her feet, where her little boots showed from beneath three layers of skirts. His eyes rested on her neckline, her throat, and she drew a braid over her shoulder and covered her skin, that right now felt like it was glowing.

He looked at her in a way she would not have recognized until yesterday. But she had seen the same expression, on a similar face, just before the chief's black hair fell forward and hid his desire for his wife. Brosa looked at Eðna the same way the chief looked at Ginn.

She dropped her eyes to his golden leather boots. They were wrapped tight around his calves, and the laces climbed all the way up and under the hem of his wool.

"I—" She cleared her throat, and she tried again to smooth her hair, running aground on her braids. She looked down the hill toward the house, where people still laughed, and drinking songs blurred together, punctuated with shouts.

And then it all stopped and a profound silence came over the farm. People backed up to make a path through the crowd, and they all dropped to their knees, foreheads touching the dirt the way that Ansig had bowed to Brosa.

Heirik and Ginn rode in on their black and white horses, side by side, slowly moving among their people. Ginn held her husband's hand loosely, and even from this distance, Eðna felt their grace, their serene and powerful presence. She could just make out the marks on their faces that seemed supernatural to these people. Here, where everyone believed in gods that dumped blood on Heirik and drew runes in ink on Ginn's face.

Once the chief and lady had passed, men and women swarmed into the great hall like insects, dressed in all colors of wool. Children followed their parents, happily, blindly, into the heat and smoke. Soon, she would be part of that if she didn't flee.

"I have to go," Eðna said. "Or I'll find out my destiny now."

"I hope you do," Brosa said. His voice was neutral. "I hope the seer says you'll go by sea, a thousand years and worlds away."

He might as well have punched her in the gut like he did Ansig.

It was what she wanted. To go home. So why did it hurt?

"It's what I came here to do," she said, matching his calm.

"Já," he said, and he glanced toward the knot in her skirt. "You were expecting to run off without me."

"I asked you to take me."

"I asked you to stay."

They were silent, at a fiery impasse. A fierce tension held them locked together, both breathing hard. Down by the hall, the last few men and women were wedging themselves in through the double doors.

"It's time," Brosa said. He looked toward the woods, and he nodded once, then twice, as if convincing himself.

He kissed his own palm, the way Heirik had done in the hall, and he pressed it to Eðna's cheek. Electric heat flowed everywhere.

And he released her. He took his hand away. He left her alone and set off down the hill.

He'd plainly asked her to stay. But he wouldn't stop her when she fled. If she moved swiftly, he would let her slip away, slip back into the water and off to home.

Fine. She would say goodbye to him silently, too. Without telling him that he meant something beyond his undeniable gorgeousness. That his beauty was just part of him, the way his thoughts and will and kindness were. Without telling him that he had saved her from her own fear over these past weeks. She would remember him. She wouldn't say any of that out loud. An unvoiced goodbye.

Just the kind of goodbye she'd given her Da.

Seeing Brosa now with his back to her, coiled tight with frustration, Eðna felt a wild, unknown tenderness for him. The honored brother, below Heirik, who day after day comforted and protected and taught her. He headed toward the chieftain's hall alone, among so many. She'd left him that way, so alone among so many people. How could she have thought she'd leave him without a word?

"Wait," she whispered, too quiet for him to hear. He was almost to the hall now. "Wait!"

She ran down toward the double doors, with their gleaming black wolf's eyes and waves. The smoking, deliciously carved mouth of hell.

Eðna took a deep breath and dove into the crush of people who filled the hall. Too many bodies, too close. She was too short to see, and she twisted away from hands on her back, her waist. Spit out braids that hit her in the mouth. She turned around, but it was too late to go back, to find her way out.

And then she was up against a familiar back. The back she had clung to as they rode on Gull. The strong back she watched ramming a shovel into the earth. Watched walking down to this hall, defeated. "Brosa!"

She slipped her fingers into his belt, desperate not to lose him. He turned, irritated, and then his eyes awoke to her. His heavy brows lifted, and he said her name, amazed.

She was shoved from behind and trapped against his chest.

He bent to tell her, quiet and private. "It's only men and women, Fine One. Nothing to fear."

"They're all over me." She struggled against the bodies that pressed into her back.

"Shh," Brosa said. He took her hand, and his palm was warm and dry, the pressure of fingers reassuring. He guided her through the crowd.

Eðna had been in this hall just the day before, sneaking around the back of the high seats with Brosa, but it might as well have been another world, another time. The intimate place where they'd talked, where she'd explored carved animals' teeth and watched Ginn touch her husband, was now lost under the weight of a hundred churning, sweating people. They crowded around long tables and in the alcoves that lined the walls.

The air was heavy with laughter, shouts, and the smoke of burning seeds and herbs. The hearth where she had stood yesterday was full of flames.

Handwoven tunics and embossed leather belts jangling with the cups they'd brought. Their legs were bound from ankle to knee in fabric, or for Brosa and Heirik and Hár, leather. The women were adorned with pounds of beads and big brooches, their dresses all the colors of sheep and dye. The finer the colors, the closer to the high seats. Colorful, better-off women.

"Come, we have an honored place." Brosa pulled Eðna in toward the head of the hall, where a few tables were placed apart from the others. He drew Eðna down beside him on a bench that was soft with furs and skins. One of the same benches where she'd knelt at his feet so he could try to see her contacts.

Betta and Hár sat across the table—the old man's arm slung around his wife's back. The changes in both of them were astounding. Hár wore a torc around his neck with two cats' heads meeting at his throat, their eyes gleaming, amber gems. His hair was clean and combed, with silver strands glinting with light. And gods, Betta was a joyful, young girl. Dressed in grass green silk, with her hair cascading down over one shoulder and flowers tucked behind her ears.

She and her husband both looked at Eðna with questioning eyes, over a table set with sparkling glass cups and polished, shining drinking horns propped up in stands made of metal and bone. Bowls of ale were already set, their rims hung with delicate bone ladles. Ale-swans, they called them, after the lovely birds—spoons named for the elegant curves of their necks.

Their table sat perpendicular to the biggest hearth—the one that cut across the room and divided the high seats from everyone else. It formed a moat of fire one would have to cross to reach the chief and Ginn. They sat far above the crowd, silently watching.

Each of them was a strange creature, but together they were stunning. Heirik wore a midnight-dark wool tunic, with trim woven from silver threads. He'd drawn his hair back severely, aggressively showing the mark people feared, and his cheekbones stood out sharp as blades. A long braid fell over his shoulder and down his chest, with pale ivory beads—gods, were they some animal's vertebrae?—caught up in the ends. His birthmark did, in this firelight, look like blood. His gaze was neutral, taking in everything as though recording, but there was a violent edge to his stillness.

At his side, Ginn was dazzling as a glacier. Her hair looked almost white and was braided just like the chief's, falling down over a silver-blue gown, trimmed with white fur that moved with the whisper of her breath. The color of her hair, her skin, her clothes made her seem as solid as arctic ice, yet as insubstantial as a ghost. Her silver eyes looked over the hall and all its people with ownership and pride. And with a keen, barely hidden excitement.

Under Ginn's and Heirik's feet, a plush landscape of furs and rugs spread out all around—each one the skin and fur of a real animal. So many lives given, so many priceless treasures. Ginn casually rested her boots on a fox's hide.

Ginn set her arm on the carved arm of the high seat, precisely alongside the chief's, so that they almost, but did not, touch. Both their wrists flashed with jewelry, and a giant ring wrapped around one of Heirik's fingers.

A third, empty seat sat next to Ginn. "For the seer." Brosa nodded to the vacant chair.

Eðna struggled to focus on Brosa's voice, on the people, their shapes, but the air was thick with grassy smoke that turned her thoughts soft. Heirik's hands elongated and blurred. Ginn, beside him, turned gray, and then brilliant blue, sparkling with error messages in dramatic script. Eðna blinked her contacts off, and focused with her own eyes. She scanned the room for anything she could rest on, anything that wouldn't jump in the firelight and blur in the herbal smoke.

It would be a mixture of dry weeds, probably angelica, moss, and the seer's hallucinogenic seeds. The smoke would put everyone into a pleasantly drugged, accepting state, so they would be awed by the seer. Awed in a way that Eðna would not. She knew intellectually that she was being drugged, deprived of oxygen. That the woman had no spiritual powers.

People were crammed into alcoves all along the walls, and swags of juniper branches and wildflowers—the green, satellite-like angelica plants, not yet bloomed, that Eðna had seen at the beach her first day here—brushed their heads. The swags drooped and melted like candle wax. Eðna's mind was listing. Flowers melting. Lamps so small that they each held a single handful of oil flickered on every table, so that the room spun like a sugary galaxy all around.

"A little help, Eðna?"

Brosa held out a drinking horn for her to take. The big tusk was smooth, and so heavy it tipped in both her hands. An enormous curl, encrusted with decadent swirls of metal that, in the smoke-light, writhed like snakes.

She shook her head. She would remain lucid. Yes.

Brosa poured ale into the horn, and then he poured ale into a rare and lovely glass for Eðna. She drank it down in a few quick swallows, and he raised an eyebrow and filled it again.

A woman sat down heavily beside them, and her swinging hair smacked Eðna in the face. Brosa drew Eðna close. He rested his chin on her head, and his hand came up around her back.

"You stayed," he said. He whispered, words like a soothing lullaby, and he held her. It would be alright in this crowd, just for a minute, to rest her cheek against his chest. To close her eyes and fall into soap and rosemary and wool. The metal of the Thor's hammer at his throat.

Her father's scents. Jon would have loved this night.

"I'm still leaving," Eðna said.

"Rest your head, Woman." Brosa's words hummed in his chest, against her cheek.

The crowd hushed. Ginn and Heirik stood, and so did everyone else, to welcome the seer.

A woman came haltingly into the room, one leg dragging. Brown hair floated in a messy cloud around her face, spilling out of a large, black hood that was lined with even blacker fur. In her bony hand, she plied a gorgeous wooden cane. Her fingers curled over the handle—an extravagantly carved head of a cat, eyes shining with black inlays, neck adorned with a copper collar.

The seer's attendants helped her up onto the dais next to Ginn. She paused and looked out with cold, sure authority. One eye wandered over the tops of dozens of heads, the other milk-white and unseeing—the pupil filled in with a white film, perhaps caused by an infection, but not by advanced age. No, the woman looked young. Shrewd. Her lips pursed for a moment, then she turned to sit in the third, empty high seat.

The chief made toasts to the seer, to his wife, the abundance of his farm, the loyalty of all the people in the extravagant new hall. Ginn served ale first to her husband, then the seeress. Young Magnus's wife took over serving the honored guests. She winked at Eðna when she poured more ale into her glass.

Then Ginn brought the seeress an elaborate bowl brimming with sticky, red liquid. It sloshed like stew, and large lumps broke the surface. One thin stream of blood ran down the outside of the gleaming bowl.

Eðna swallowed hard. "What is that?"

"The hearts of every living creature on the farm."

Eðna's throat spasmed. "Why?"

"It honors the seeress." His breath ruffled her hair. "With all the spirits of our farm, from the smallest bird to the greatest soul."

Ginn's eyes gleamed with the thrill of this night. It was the incandescent gaze of a fanatic. On this night, her big night, to bless this hall and her union with Heirik, would she have asked even a man or woman to make an extreme sacrifice?

"A person, too?"

"Nei, Elskan. Shh," Brosa whispered. "Beasts only. A hen." He stroked her back, lulling her. "A dog, a fox, a sheep."

Eðna let out an unsteady breath and anchored herself on his list.

"A goat, a sheep," he listed, quietly soothing her. "The greatest soul is a horse. An old and honored one."

She nodded with each name, sleepy from the thick air and his slow, seductive words. He spoke of the seer. "With her damaged eye, she can see inside doors that are closed to us."

"Cataracts," Eðna mumbled, and Brosa ducked to hear her.

"Eðna?"

Oh, her name sounded rich and delicious when he said it.

He was stroking her back. The idea of him holding her, and the weight of his hand, sent fresh blood through her veins.

What was she thinking?

"Her eye," she said, extracting herself from Brosa's touch. "In my time, it would be fixed."

The seer's entourage of at least a dozen women stood tightly packed around the dais and began to chant, wordless tones that joined and began to vibrate in Eðna's mind, merged with the herbs and flames. She could get lost in here forever.

"Two are here," the seer's voice cut through the droning, louder and more commanding than Eðna expected. She had seemed feeble. Her half-gaze swept the room but did not land on anyone. The woman's proclamation was overly dramatic, something about two here "who have seen Ragnarok, clearer than I do."

Eðna drifted softly in the clouds of smoke, slack and sleepy from oxygen deprivation.

The droning deepened, expanded, and the woman spoke cryptic nonsense. Words about fields and babes, birds and clouds, swans, waves. So that anyone might find themselves and their own worries and dreams in her chants.

Eðna's mind moved slowly, everything, everyone tipping and sliding, absorbing the seer's list of various, irrelevant things.

Wings and waves. Wings and waves.

Wait.

Wings. Eðna's birds. And the waves were her way home. Yes. It wasn't irrelevant. This part was about her.

What would this crackpot woman tell Ginn to do with her? She leaned forward, hands flat on the table, ready to spring up and fight whatever fate came next.

Were she and Jen the ones who'd seen Ragnarok? And what did that mean, anyway? Fine. If her clean and literate future world was the end times, then Eðna longed for Ragnarok. If knowledge and science were two wolves devouring the sky, then she would take the gnashing of their teeth over ignorance.

"You burn for your home," Brosa said.

Eðna jumped.

Brosa. Yes, he was here, so near, and she was snug against his chest again. He ducked to speak close to her ear, underneath the rustling all around them. "I long for you to catch fire like that for me, já?"

She closed her eyes. "Me?"

"Nei matter what the seer says, do you think your eager glimpse of your future could be me?" Brosa pulled away so she could see him. "This face?"

He smiled, not a half smile but a full, beautiful grin. He lifted her knuckles to his lips and pressed Eðna's hand to his mouth.

She swayed, drawn under by waves. She was missing what the seer was saying. She twisted in her seat, half here with this gentle, gorgeous man, half listening for the promise of a way home. Brosa's voice rocked her as if she was in a sturdy boat, safe and dry, under a clear night sky. What were the words she wanted?

"Seductive," she murmured. "Sensual."

"I'll give you my worth, Eðna, whatever it might be." His ocean-colored eyes were intense, despite the smoke. "For all my life."

"All your life," she echoed.

What was he saying?

All his life?

Brosa stilled her fingers, wrapped them in his own. He slipped his other hand behind her head, fingers in her hair. He held her head in his palm, and she was lost in the forest with him, branches caressing her as she turned and turned. Lost in a boat that rocked and rocked, curled up in a blanket in his arms, lungs swirling with smoke, sliding headlong into pleasure and danger. The silver on his wrist was cool against her face.

Never any man like him, ever.

"Don't go, Fine One. Stay beside me all our years."

No one, not even an uncanny seer, could have foretold such a thing. Such a man, wanting her.

Her eyes stung, and there was a pop, a sizzling, and pain in her temples. Her contacts bloomed into life, a red warning symbol flashing the oxygen content of the room. Temperature, humidity, scrolling at the top. An image match: Brosa Ulfsson, son of Ulf Magnuson, son of Magnus Heirikson. The family tree grew like a vine of glowing letters, overlaid on Brosa's face. The chief on his cheek. Names of people who were not blood related, but were vital, sprang up across the bottom. Svana Hildursdottir on his lips. Like a stamp that said NOT FOR YOU.

Eðna sat up straight.

When she was so little, and in so much pain, she'd wrenched herself away from a farm like this one. She'd fought hard and broken her own heart, and no doubt her father's heart too, to make it to her shining city.

The cool song of the future soothed her smoky insides. She was meant to alight here in the past, record everything she could, then go. She would make it home. Brosa was impossible.

Irrelevant.

Her heart clenched at the thought, and she leaned into him, her body proving her mind wrong. And in that moment, everything changed.

Cold air rushed in, as the giant double doors opened. The seer's litany, and her entourage's droning, stopped. Intense silence descended on the room, and everyone strained to see. Who would disturb this night?

A man stood silhouetted in the big double doors, his face and clothes as dark as the chief's.

"Eiðr?" Brosa asked under his breath.

The chief and Ginn both watched the man, coldly evaluating. The chief nodded almost imperceptibly toward someone in the dark of the room, and two men moved to flank the newcomer.

Eiðr came to stand before the main hearth, and his face was deranged by the jumping flames. His boots and pants were coarse, his hair stringy, but he wore an elegant, long cloak that swept the ground. He fell to his knees and dropped his head in deference to Heirik and Ginn.

"Herra, Lukla." He looked up, and in the flames, his eyes glistened.

"Eiðr, my honor-feeder. Welcome." The chief spoke without emotion, though it sounded more like, *I will cut your heart out for this, right after the seer leaves.*

Eiðr stood, trembling all over, with madness or fervor.

"Herra, I am grateful. But I cannot sit and take your drink and hear my fate while in my chest I grieve." His voice broke, then steadied. "I am here to state a case, before all in this hall. A case to be carried to the althing for judgment."

The fire spit and crackled, joining its hissing with a hundred surreptitious whispers. A faint and ghostly whistle of wind moved over the roof vents. Branches snapped, and a log shifted.

Eiðr turned to address the room. He scanned the crowd and found Eðna and Brosa, and he raised his cloaked arm to point.

"Two of my kinsmen lay dead on the sand with ravens picking at their bones. I accuse Brosa Ulfsson of their murder."

A great gasp moved through the hall, and Eiðr rose his voice above the shocked crowd. "And of defiling the grave of my fair sister, Esa."

Someone wailed. A woman's keen rose above all the tide of whispers. Eðna scanned the crowd, and her contacts sputtered out, yet she easily found the source. People had parted to make room for the woman, who was on her knees by the hearth.

Blond hair fell around her shoulders and hid her face. When she looked up and her hood fell back, Eðna knew her at once. Just a moment ago, she'd seen the woman's name scrolled across Brosa's face. Svana.

Gods, she was just a girl. She clutched at her gown, ripping at herself, crying, her gaze zooming everywhere at once, until she landed on Eðna. Or nei, not Eðna, but Brosa beside her. Svana looked to Brosa with such yearning and terror, such sadness.

Eðna opened her palm, but Brosa did not take her hand. She turned to him, and he was no longer there. His chin no longer rested on her head, and his warm thigh was not pressed against hers. He was gone.

A great murmur rolled along the ground, around benches and feet, climbing fast. People were in motion, shouting, crowding, and Eðna was knocked sideways. She stood, and she was lifted and swept into a rush for the door. Where was Brosa? She wrapped her arms tight around her chest and pushed her way through the stifling bodies, until she was expelled.

She staggered into the cold, moist world, and her lungs awoke with clear air. The night had sunk into an odd midnight violet, deeper than a spring night should be, and Brosa was nowhere—not up at the forge or the stables. Eðna turned to the sky, the woods. She looked to the old house and up every hill.

This was it.

She should run.

This was an absolutely foolproof diversion that would cover her tracks without a trace. No one would miss her until much, much later.

No one but Brosa. He wasn't here, but she saw him clearly in her mind. A dozen images of small moments came, of Brosa's rough fingers peeling back white bark to show her the copper and bronze underneath, winking and feeding her a bite of cheese, sitting with his back against a tree, carving, telling her she was fine, even after he knew what it meant. His arms crossed, a shield against pain. *You were expecting to leave without me.*

The first time they met, he reached to help her off her horse, and she'd held a knife to him and snapped at him. *I'm fine.*

She breathed the fresh air, her hands on her thighs, lungs burning, and her heart wept.

She couldn't go.

She could not leave Brosa accused, facing an unknown fate. She knew something that Eiðr did not. Something that no one else could stand witness to but her. She knew that Brosa was not at the coast when those men were killed. He was in the highlands, and he'd been there all night.

She had to tell someone. Everyone. She had to stay long enough so everyone in this world would understand he was innocent.

Eðna stood on the threshold of Ginn's house and turned her palm up to the early morning sky. It was dry.

Too bad it wasn't raining. Hard. A snarling, howling storm could wash her mind clear of last night's smoke that still lurked in her lungs. Even a thin, needle-like rain might break up this sky—a suffocating sky of ash- and stone-colored clouds that closed absolutely over her head. *Stratocumulus* or *nimbostratus*?

She pressed her fist to her forehead. She couldn't remember which to call it when there was no sun visible, only a gray ceiling, with a line of burning white across the horizon. A small space where Eðna could breathe, if she could only reach it.

Last night, she'd stood in the center of a churning mass of people, stood alone in a field, watching her perfect opportunity go by. She waited in the dark, watching as dozens of men and women finally settled in around a big fire, glugging ale and laughing, and the incredible accusation began to become legend.

They moved off in pairs or families to find places to sleep inside the old house. Dusty, brawny young men slept against the grass walls outside. None of them truly cared about Brosa. The challenge to his honor—the startling, impossible accusation—was a diversion in an otherwise monotonous life.

This morning, they'd awakened to an early start, heading off to the althing. A few men gathered over by the stables, tying packs onto horses and securing axes, blankets, knives. They murmured to each other, presumably about the trip that stretched out before them over the next four days. The chief and a few of his closest men would leave early and ride ahead of the crowd.

They swung themselves up onto their animals. Heirik Rakknason spoke, dark and low, and his uncle answered with undecipherable, gruff words. But where was Brosa?

She hadn't seen him since last night, just before Eiðr's accusation. Her brain threw out fuzzy memories, of Brosa whispering about a life together, of him holding her hand. He was wearing the bracers she'd fixed for him. Her own handiwork on his wrists. He'd buried his fingers in her hair, hadn't he? He held the back of her head and talked about her burning eyes. Talked about his worth and years.

Where was he now?

Gods, what was wrong with her?

Of all the unexpected and terrifying things that had happened here in the past—the dead men, the pantry, the seer—it was this constant, low-level searching for Brosa that was the strangest. Like a hum she couldn't hear, or a pair of contacts on seek/accept, just for him.

She looked again, and this time he was here, and her pulse rose. On Gull's back, Brosa was striking. His hair was pulled tight into a single braid that lay over his shoulder, and it highlighted his facial bones, his white scar and bleak eyes. His skin looked red and raw, as though scoured by wind or tears. He looked to her, and his eyes were as gray and unmoving as the clouds.

Eðna stood, her boots untied and hands empty. Moving toward him. If she could just hear him say something, say her name, call her Fine One, so that the corners of his eyes crinkled with laughter, she would know he was okay. If she could hear him say anything, any word at all, she would feel secure.

He shook his head. It was a movement so small, only she could have seen it. He lifted his fingers off the reins, as if to put up a hand, push her away, but even that gesture was abandoned. He turned the horse and rode away after Heirik and Hár.

Eðna stood alone.

What was she doing here?

She let her head drop back, and she stared into the stifling sky. She'd had her chance last night, and instead here she was, waiting to get up on a horse and ride deeper into the past, away from her goal, away from safety. And the man she stayed for had just turned away.

Brosa didn't deserve that broken, desolate look in his eyes. But, damn him. He'd just ridden away on his golden Viking horse, after giving her a look, a shake of his head that said clearly, *Don't come to me.*

Something moist and cold bumped her cheek, and Eðna gasped and almost smacked a horse that had come to bury its nose underneath her hair.

"This is Vinda," Ranka said. "Daughter of Vakr." The child introduced her, as if the horse were royalty. She held the reins out for Eðna to take.

Vinda was a dark beauty, with an espresso coat and silver mane. Eðna combed her fingers through the animal's thick, stiff hair, and a warm scent of dust and mane rose up. Vinda snuffled Eðna's neck again. Eðna gazed after the dust cloud, the evidence of men, diminishing in the distance.

"—You'll ride with me," Ginn said.

Eðna woke from her thoughts and shook her gauzy head.

"With you?"

"Next to me and Betta. We'll catch up with the men tonight."

On all sides of Eðna, women had started to pack. They worked efficiently and with solid grace, not wasting a moment of time or a speck of energy or space. They hauled blankets onto horses' backs, tightened packs full of bread and cheese and berries, and loaded sleds with bolt after bolt of the finest wool to trade, woven of threads so slender it could float. Vera would love the complex and multi-layered colors. Amber-pinks and mustard-greens from Betta's hands and dyepots.

Betta wore her baby on her chest in a sling – so small – and directed Ranka to cover the precious fabric with canvas. In between bundles, they tucked the littlest children, with boiled eggs to keep their hands warm and to eat along the way.

The clouds began to lower and churn, but still there was no rain. Eðna kept her eyes raised and tried to see the sky as Brosa would. Maybe as a great, overturned ocean, the waves just beginning to move after a long time becalmed.

Her father told her once that the clouds were thoughts moving in Ymir's skull—storm clouds were angry thoughts, bitter memories. Ridiculous. An ignorant way to look at atmospheric phenomena.

She was still going home, as soon as Brosa's trial ended. Yes. But right now, despite the shake of his head that said *go away*, she would follow him. Far behind, under a demonic sky, she was with him.

She swung a leg up onto Vinda. "Fine."

Brosa brought his ax down on a fallen tree at his feet. Two days gone on their journey to the assembly. Two more to go. A dozen more strokes and this fallen birch would become firewood.

Riding far ahead of the family, he stopped alone to make his own small fires when he and Gull needed to rest. He chopped wood at the edge of a massive forest that wound toward the meeting plain. Many trees were tossed on the ground from the winter's storms. Beyond them, birches and snowblooms massed and continued into darkness.

This trip to the assembly felt like a journey of the damned. The land had passed by, brown and without meaning. Walls that needed work, a flat, gray sky. Brosa rode Gull without passion, or walked beside the horse sometimes, one boot plodding after the other. The grass was halfway up Gull's legs already.

The althing was a time for his family to gather in warmth, forge alliances, renew friendships, laugh and drink in their rich, comfortable booth with its beds and furs and hearth. It was a time for his brother, and Brosa along with him, to drink and plan with other rich and powerful men. To arrange marriages and further feuds. To trade for honey and nuts, and buy jewelry for a fine woman.

And here he was traveling alone like a raven-starver, too humiliated to look anyone in the eye. The only woman he would ever want to adorn with silver and amber must surely be ashamed to know him.

Once or twice, he had slowed his pace and lurked in the trees to see the women go by, and Eðna was still with them. Why? If she'd once thought he was ignorant, now she had her proof. And yet, she continued to travel with his family.

Every time he wanted to join them, his rage rose up. A strong desire to snarl, to destroy something with his hands. If anyone, even his brother or uncle, so much as looked at him the wrong way, he would respond like a beast.

He hacked at the fallen tree, raising his ax far above his shoulder with every blow. It tore at his heart the way Eðna looked for him before he left, but he couldn't risk such a mood around her. She would see his savagery. She might even fear him. Maybe she should.

He lowered his ax and breathed deep. He rearranged the wood with his foot, and Gull came to snort and bump Brosa with his nose.

"Go!" He snapped, and the horse backed away.

Gull was a good animal, but his thundering footfalls did not match Brosa's pulse the way that his old horse Fjoðr's had. Fjoðr, the horse he had chosen and named as a boy. Named for the wind. Even if it hadn't been Eiðr's own hand, someone from his family had slit Fjoðr's throat while Brosa was gone trading.

Brosa swung at the birch again, swamped with memory. Drifting at sea for days, the men freezing and hungry, Brosa had warmed and sustained himself with thoughts of Fjoðr. His greatest yearning, when he rowed into the shore, home from his long travels, was to see his golden boy. The horse would toss his mane and bump Brosa hard with his head, his bright eyes asking, *Where have you been?*

But Fjoðr was not there, and Heirik gave Brosa the news. Brosa crouched in the sand in the dark, holding himself. He would kill the people who murdered his horse. He paced the shore, growling with anger, and finally settled on a desire to wade back into the ocean he'd come from and numb himself.

Now, Brosa stopped hacking up wood. He rested, with his hands on his knees, panting like a dog.

He hadn't thought about Fjoðr's death. Gods, it wouldn't go well, at his trial, when they brought it up. Brosa had every reason to hate Eiðr's family. What could he do?

Could he lie?

If he told the truth, would anyone believe he had committed one crime, but not the other? That he'd dug into Esa's grave, but hadn't killed any man in all his life.

It was unlikely he would face death for his crime, but humiliation was sure. If he was found guilty and forced to pay, his heart and mind might curl up in sickening dishonor. There would be a pall over his memory. Murderer. Defiler.

He looked deep into the woods, full of spirits and animals, a living part of this place where he was born, where his grandmother gave birth to Ulf, and Signe gave life to him and his brother. The woods moved gently, patiently. Leaves sighed like a maid, and streams moved toward river and sea.

When he traded, he'd seen the island from a distance for the first time. It was a great animal, maybe a whale, thrusting up from the water so that men like Brosa could be born and live their lives on its back.

What would Eðna see?

She called the edge of the island a city, a place where people lived in stacks of homes like giant cairns, each stone a dwelling. Or maybe not cairns, nei. Trees that reached the sky, rivaling Yggdrasil—the tree that encompassed Brosa's whole world—with people living inside. Glittering with frost as if kissed by bright sun, even in the night. Homes as big as the whole world he had understood just weeks ago.

He wiped his forehead with the back of his hand, and Eðna's leatherwork grazed his skin.

Brosa had meant to give his life in return for a new one, but in truth, also because he was afraid. He laid down in the ground, because his usefulness to his brother and family had come to an end.

That was a dismal night. But in the morning, Eðna came.

He smiled. Já, she limped into his life on a tired horse, hair tangled and smelling of the sea, and she wrecked everything. His knowledge, his heart, his plans. She woke him from the dead, and upset his resolve as easily as flipping a rowboat. His desire to die meant nothing in the face of her bravery and devotion to her dream. She came, proud and alone, with a wind from Saga at her back. What did the boat look like that brought her here? What unseen waves carried it?

Eðna's traveling would be a beautiful journey.

He stooped and weighed a small hunk of wood in his hands. This piece would work for carving. He would make her a bird, one of the small flickers that flew from tree to tree.

Brosa sat in the brush, and with his knife, he shaved away the white bark. A deep fiery color glowed inside, as if the wood contained its own burning fate.

Gull came to sniff at it, and he was skittish, nei doubt thinking he'd be shouted at again. Brosa ran his palm down the horse's nose with affection. It wasn't Gull's fault that he was not Fjoðr.

Brosa shaped the wood with his knife, shaving off layers to get to the essence in the center.

Eðna could have run a dozen times by now. Why was she still here?

He didn't want her to be part of this mess, and yet he did. He wanted her to be at his side nei matter what happened. He couldn't fathom her reasons for still riding along with Ginn and Betta and his cousins. And in truth, part of him didn't care *why* she stayed, only that she did.

Not long ago, he was ready to lay down his life for a noble purpose. Now, he wanted to keep it. He had a reason to fight for his life. Not because it would help Heirik or his family in some way, but because he himself wanted it.

He smoothed his thumb along the long lines in the wood.

Things came naturally to him. Everyone said so. Brosa could spark fires, carve toys, sail, make men and women happy. But to fight for himself—he had no idea how to do this.

Only Gull stood by his side now, chewing grass. And nei matter how smart and loyal the horse might be, he could not help Brosa with his thoughts and questions. Could not help him consider logic. About the trial. About his own heart.

His brother knew about such questions. More than anyone, Heirik had changed his whole way of being, all his beliefs, in order to take hold of happiness. It was time to talk to Heirik.

Brosa stood and dropped the unformed bit of wood into his pack. It was hardly shaped at all, but it held the promise of becoming a bird. He called Gull, and he secured several dry logs on the horse's back.

Gull would not stray from Brosa, but Brosa picked up the lead anyway. It felt like holding the horse's hand. Brosa had ridden ahead of his family, and now he and the horse turned and headed back, away from the althing, back toward Eðna. Back to Heirik.

Eðna slid off of Vinda's back. She smoothed her skirts and walked in a circle, forcing blood to circulate through her cramped, numb legs.

They'd ridden farther today—the third day—so they could reach this place that was special to Ginn. Just ten meters away, a massive cairn stood to mark the lady's favored sleeping spot.

They'd had caught up to the men, and together there were dozens of people, maybe fifty or more, setting up camp. Eðna and Ginn walked through the crowd, people making way for Ginn. Eðna's heart was alive and eyes alert for Brosa, but the smoke from small fires obscured her vision. She searched the wind-chapped faces and blond heads, many of them bowed as she and Ginn passed, but he was not there.

Gods, she was lost. Day after day without him, her reasons for staying grew abstract. Riding on Vinda, hour after hour she questioned herself. But morning after morning when he did not appear, Eðna was more sure than ever that Brosa needed her. So she rode through the long hours, thinking until her mind swam, yearning, finally, to tell someone what she knew.

Here at her favored camping stop, Ginn drew Eðna toward the edge of the trees. She had a special place, a sacred place here, that she wanted Eðna to see.

Eðna looked behind one more time before she ducked into the trees, scanning with her naked eyes for Brosa's broad shoulders and golden hair. He was big. He'd be visible above anyone else. But there were only men and women in dusty homespun clothes in every shade of gray and brown, children chasing each other with sticks or sitting by their parents, drinking from wooden cups. A dismal scene. Half of them would die from lung disease. Eðna touched the purse that hung safely at her waist, with its medicine inside.

She turned to follow Ginn into the woods.

Eðna pushed aside branches that sprang back and whipped her cheeks. Delicate spring leaves brushed her face. She stooped to make it through the small passageway in the brush, following Ginn's dress, as it disappeared and reappeared ahead of her. The passage narrowed and tightened, until she dropped to her knees and crawled. A fox trail, not quite big enough for them to fit through.

Eðna yanked at her bunched-up skirt and spit out bits of leaves. How had Ginn ever found this ridiculous place?

"Not much farther," Ginn called. A minute later, Eðna burst through the bushes, on her knees, into a tiny clearing. It was just big enough for the two of them. A streamlet, no more than a meter across, took up half the clearing. Tender young grass lay velvety at their knees, and sunlight and breeze made shadows flicker. Leafy impressions. The scent of fresh dirt and grass made the place familiar, though Eðna had never been here. It was only the smell of Brosa's dusty shirt and the grass he'd been digging up when they met.

Did the leaves actually shimmer?

It must be an effect of her dying contacts. They hadn't worked much at all since the seer. Combined with this late-day, angled sunlight. Yes.

Ginn threw her hood back, and bits of platinum hair flew with static electricity, escaped from her coils of braids. She breathed deep, ran her hands through the baby grass and beamed with love for her little hideaway.

Eðna could easily imagine Heirik falling in love with her. Her fierce sweetness, punctuated by moments of steel and shrewd observation. A silver gaze that could flick on and off like a switch. She regarded Eðna with a hint of that shrewdness.

Too late, it occurred to Eðna to be scared. "Why have you taken me here?"

"You see it, don't you?"

"See what?"

"The light," Ginn said. "On the water and leaves. This is her place."

More cryptic weirdness. "Whose place?"

"Saga's," Ginn said.

The goddess who drank from the river of time, who saw the future and the past. Eðna's mother had whispered stories about Saga, warm in her ear when she was a little girl, drifting off to sleep in Gida's arms. Her mother's belief was strong and sure.

Eðna picked a piece of dead leaf from her tongue. "A folk tale."

Ginn bristled for a second, just a flash, but she controlled her features. "Nei," she said. "Saga sent you here. She sent both of us."

"Jeff sent me here," said Eðna, shifting from the old language to 22nd century words.

"Jeff is a sweetheart." Ginn smiled. "But what does he know about sending a person through time? He's fumbling at controlling a beautiful mystery. Staying up all night, drinking whole pots of coffee, straining to understand something that can't be explained."

Ginn's vision of Jeff was accurate. He spent hours asleep with his forehead resting on the old-fashioned computer. He had little-to-no idea about why the tank—and only that one tank—did what it did.

"It must depend on your contacts," he'd said, his hand in his hair, frustrated, and worried for Eðna. "That's all we can guess. Jen wore hers into the tank by accident the first time. On purpose, the second. So it was the same."

Whisperings of more inexplicable reasons floated around the team like the small, cold breezes that Da had called spirit breath. That the machine only worked because of the runes inside Jen's eyes—her Viking diary that she saved in her contacts. It was some combination of runes and contacts and a quirk in this one machine. They tested copies of the tank first, and no one ever traveled anywhere. No one had fallen through the floor of the simulated hearth and landed in another time. Not until Eðna.

Here in the past, the most outlandish explanations seemed to make sense to everyone. It was not difficult to believe—or even very surprising—that the goddess who sat by the water of time might send the chief a wife. Might pick Eðna up in the future and bring her here. The gods could do these things, and they didn't have to have a reason beyond their own entertainment.

"Well," Eðna said. "Jeff successfully sent me."

"Já, okay," Ginn said. "Jeff waved goodbye and flipped some old-fashioned switches. He sent you to test the tank and return.

But here you are, on your way to the althing, entangled in a man's life."

"I'm not tangled up with Brosa."

"Right," Ginn said. "That is the man I mean."

Eðna pressed her palms to her thighs. "I did not come to the past to hang around with Brosa."

"Then why are you still here? You could have gotten away when Brosa was accused. You haven't tried to run since the seer."

Eðna tucked her skirt under her knees. How could she parse all the mixed up factors and explain to Ginn? The unexpected sense of duty toward him, her explosive anger and frustration, confusing tenderness and devotion. The flood of memories and images, the men who had died, Brosa's hand on her back. In the smoky hall, she might have seen a tear on his face, sliding down toward his golden beard.

"You are hiding something." Ginn was sure.

She was hiding something, já, and it was churning in her head and in her heart, and finally, now, the dam broke. "I'm a witness," she said. "I need to exonerate him, before I return."

Ginn was instantly taut, alert. "What do you mean at witness?"

"When I landed here, I saw two dead men at the fishing camp. Their blood was fresh, but Brosa was up in the hills that night." The relief of telling someone was a sudden rush. "It couldn't have been him."

Ginn was quiet too long. She looked like she was turning Eðna's words over in every direction.

"But, you rode from the fishing camp to the hills. Couldn't Brosa have done the same?"

"No!" Did Ginn actually believe Brosa could be a murderer? "He was just waking up when I met him. He'd been sleeping all night, nowhere near the coast."

"Good." Ginn let out a big breath. "This is good." She smoothed the grass with her palm, as if sealing Brosa's innocence. "Does he know this?"

"No."

"That's good, too."

"I had that same thought. That it was good to keep it from him, at least for now."

"He'll do anything to get you away from here, if he thinks you're in danger." Ginn gave a wry smile. "That's what the men of this family try to do."

Eðna shook her head and looked off into the trees. If Brosa was so concerned with her safety, where was he now? She needed him so much. She swallowed hard.

Ginn must have seen her struggle. "Eðna, I didn't want to come here the first time. I didn't know my fate. But I came to love my home and to love Heirik."

"The way you say his name, it's like you worship him."

Ginn laughed. "Nei, not at all by now."

"What does that mean?"

"I did for a while. I would stand outside his room and just touch the door. I actually fainted when I saw him fresh from the bath, he was so gorgeous."

Eðna sniffed.

"There's nothing wrong with loving someone that much," Ginn said. "But he pushed me away over and over. Every time we got close, he slammed the door, because of his curse. For the love of the gods, he wanted me to marry Brosa."

"I heard that in your interviews," Eðna snapped.

Ginn smiled. "That bothers you."

"Of course it does. Brosa was good to you, and you threw him away."

Ginn raised an eyebrow.

Eðna breathed. She needed to find out more about time travel. She had to reset. She would be calm and befriend Ginn, ask her important questions. "Why did you come back to the lab?"

Ginn smoothed the grass with her palm. "Heirik pushed me to the breaking point, and I left him."

"But you came back here again."

"I had to try. This is where I belong. But by then—" Ginn cut her own thought short.

"By then things were different, after months had passed."

"Nei," Ginn looked up. "That was the strange part. There I was in the future, worried that a hundred days had passed. That Heirik had moved on with his life, maybe married Svana and already had a child on the way. But when I got here…" She shook her head and looked at Eðna, a real question in her eyes. For the first time, Ginn wasn't completely in control of her world. "I came back in the same moment I had gone. I woke up in the water just a few meters away from the men I'd been escaping."

The same moment. Eðna's mind zoomed with this new information. "Down to the second?"

"Já, the very same moment, wading in the ocean right where and when I had left."

Eðna's mind tilted and her thoughts swirled. This was new, critical. "You must have been thrilled. You hadn't missed anything."

"I was furious," Ginn said, and her voice dropped, low and dark. "Mostly at Heirik. For all the lost time and pain. Once we married, it was as I had hoped, já? All the small moments I'd dreamed of. Helping him prepare for the day, making decisions about our farm, our lives. But sometimes I'd look at him and what he'd put me through was there, hard between us."

"You stayed anyway."

Eðna hadn't waited around to find out what things would have felt like between her and her Da.

"Let's just say the first year of our marriage was not what I expected."

"Not much here is the way I expected, either."

"Listen, Woman," Ginn said. "Brosa will not want you involved with his trial. When you see him, don't say a word. Do not tell him you plan to speak at the law rock."

Eðna nodded. "He's just a good man."

"He is," Ginn said. "But that's not all. He's your good man. I can see that you feel the way he does."

"What way is that?"

"With fire."

Fire? "Say what you mean. I don't understand your Norse magic words."

"Alright, then," Ginn said. "He lusts after you, and he loves you."

Eðna blinked back sudden tears. She knew intellectually that Brosa wanted her. He'd said so, hadn't he? He'd held her hand, pressed her close when she was scared. He'd told her confusing, old-language things about giving her his worth, while they sat in a smoky, drug-induced haze.

Love was not something she'd considered, ever, let alone on this mission, which had already gone off on a treacherous, time-sucking tangent. This trip to the althing had eaten up the last of her contacts' abilities, it had delayed her so long, she had no idea how it might affect her return. The notion of love was distant as a moon rock, something from another world.

"Ridiculous." Eðna smoothed her skirt. "I met him two weeks ago."

"Love rage is quick," Ginn said, steady and sure.

"Well, it has nothing to do with why I'm here, and nothing to do with me."

"Okay, then," Ginn said, gentle, serene. "If you say so. Brosa has nothing to do with you. You're just here because he's a good man."

"That's right—"

—A splash drew her up short. A small bird perched on a stone by the stream, cleaning its wing.

"A meadow pipit." Eðna's words were just a breath. The bird sat right here, breathing, preening. It blinked at Eðna, and she could almost feel its rapid heartbeat.

This was the closest she had come to a living forest bird. Not a shrieking crow, like she could see in the city, or a chicken from Ginn's yard. A delicate, wild creature of the woods. It's tiny, glossy black eyes, round and lonely, were unafraid.

It puffed itself up and then plunged its beak underneath its fan of brown feathers, grooming itself. It hopped and made small adjustments so it could drink.

Alone. So tiny, it could sit in her palm. Brosa's hand would enclose it entirely. The bird hopped to another stone. Eðna shifted on her knees, dying to touch this little creature. Maybe if she waited, completely still, it would come.

Ginn drew something from her purse, and she carefully, slowly held it out to the bird. A piece of bread. The pipit hopped closer.

"My husband is a powerful man," she said, holding the bread out to the bird in her silver ring-heavy fingers. Out of nowhere. And yet, of course! Her husband.

It all locked together now, the moving parts. Rakknason was the richest, most feared and revered man in this world. He could command anyone, make the world work any way he wanted. Brosa's life hung in the balance. His brother could tip the scales, with the currencies of silver and fear.

"Heirik will save Brosa."

"Nei," Ginn said.

Nei? "Just no? Why on earth not?"

"Honor is complex." Ginn let the bird take a tiny bit of bread from her fingers. "Heirik's ever-life, after death, is shaped by his honor in this world."

Eðna's fists closed around her dress. She stared, unable to speak, astonished. Would the chief really turn his back on his brother? She spoke softly, so she wouldn't scare the bird away. "A man's honor is more important than his brother?"

"A man's honor is more important than anything."

With a swift motion, Ginn picked up the bird and tucked its tiny body against her chest. It struggled for just a second, and Ginn twisted and broke its neck.

"Gods!" Eðna stood and stumbled backwards, a hand to her mouth. "What is wrong with you?!"

"The bird is for Saga," Ginn said, her eyes shining. "For bringing us here." She laid it on the rock, and a lattice of weak sun and shadows spread over its body.

Eðna struggled to get away from Ginn, get out of the clearing. Her dress got bundled up in branches and leaves, and she yanked and ripped it, tears in her eyes. Suddenly it was dim, and she panicked, looking for her way, then plunged forward, pushing aside branches that smacked her face, leaves that stuck to her tears.

Ginn didn't follow, but still Eðna felt her like a savage thing at her back. Ginn's relentless, cold faith drove Eðna forward in the failing light. Drove her, breathless, out of the woods and into the dusty, twilight camp.

Brosa dropped his pack and unrolled his furs on the ground, far from his family, though he could see their small fires.

It was the third night, the night they stopped at Ginn's sacred place. The family would rest here, and in the morning they would make the final leg of the journey to the althing.

He could just make out faces, children drawn up in parents' arms, men and women entwined. He heard the crackling flames, women laughing, a drinking song winding its way up to the night sky. He'd returned to be with his family, to find Heirik. But now that he could hear them and see them, he lurked at the edges. He didn't know how to talk to Eðna—a foreign sensation that he could not shake.

He walked quietly, the way he'd taught Eðna, until he could see the nearest fire. His brother's, where only the closest family sat. Heirik sat sheltering Ginn with his body. She leaned back against him, love-blind, eyes half closed like a sleepy babe. Eðna wasn't there.

That night two years ago, when he'd returned from trading, Heirik had more to tell Brosa besides the terrible news about Fjoðr. Most of it was about Ginn, an ice blue and silver spirit-woman who had come from the sea, and who wanted Heirik.

It was impossible to believe, and Brosa thought maybe Heirik had finally given in to his loneliness and lost his wits. But Brosa wanted so hard for it to be true, that there was a good, beautiful woman for his brother. He'd turned his mouth up into a smile and listened to Heirik talk about her for hours as they rode home.

When they got to the house, Brosa sat by a fire much like this one. He'd looked into all their long-missed faces. He gave them generous tales of all he'd seen and listed the many things he'd brought back from places they would not lay eyes on in all their lives. And Brosa saw her, Ginn, across a fire just like the one where she now sat. She'd looked at Brosa the way that women do, with lowered eyelids and a shy smile. His brother's gods-sent woman flushed when she saw Brosa. She'd come into his arms more than once, já? It hurt his heart.

And yet, here they were.

What did it mean that Eðna turned from him, and yet followed him? Looked for him? Maybe the time for those questions, and for seeking answers in her arms, had passed. But he had to speak to his brother.

When Brosa approached the fire, all talk died. No one spoke. Heirik simply got to his feet and followed Brosa off into the night.

They didn't walk far before they came to a dark field with low grass and a scattering of fist-sized rocks. Just enough moonlight to see their jagged edges and odd shapes. Without a word or a glance, they both stooped to collect them.

Brosa went down on his knee beside Heirik and placed a flat stone on the ground. Heirik always let him go first, since they were small boys, taking turns to see whose hand would make the rocks fall. His brother's familiar presence comforted him.

Heirik added a stone. "What will you do about Esa and Arulf?"

Brosa managed not to choke.

Heirik knew. Of course he did. Somehow, with an unnatural sense, Heirik knew all that happened in his house and on his land, down to a lamb's sneeze. Brosa had spent hours walking beside Gull these past days, pondering what to say to Heirik. How to say the truth, that he had taken a shovel to Esa's grave. Never realizing that of course the chief would already know.

Heirik nodded and turned his gaze to the night over Brosa's shoulder, not quite looking Brosa in the eyes. An unnerving habit of the chief's, calculated to make a man feel like he was below looking at. Brosa knew it well.

"The woman Eðna," Heirik said. "Why didn't she run? When we were taken up with Eiðr's accusation."

Brosa placed another stone, and an unfamiliar feeling crept into his bones. There was something Heirik didn't understand.

Too bad Brosa didn't either.

"I can't fathom what a woman wants."

Heirik's eyebrow raised.

"Já, then," Brosa said. "I can't fathom *this* woman. All I know is that she wants to get away from me with a bright passion. She doesn't want me. A quick-witted woman, considering my situation."

Heirik actually laughed. "The woman wants you more than any I've seen. It makes her hiss like a cornered fox."

"Oh, já, that's good, then. I'm like a ring of iron teeth around her leg."

Brosa's words hung in a sudden silence.

"I won't be able to help you," Heirik said, without looking up from his rocks.

Brosa knelt still as a log, soaking in his brother's regret. It was plain that Heirik was not speaking about Eðna. He was speaking of the trial.

"You are my other life," Heirik said. "My other mind and heart. But on my honor, I cannot steer the law speaker and the men to your favor."

Brosa placed his stone too hard, and the pile tumbled and crashed. "Are you suggesting that I would ask you to do that?"

"Nei," Heirik said, unmoved by Brosa's surge of anger. He weighed a stone in his hand. "Nei. Only that I thought of it myself, and the desire to do it burns hot. To help you, always, is what I want. But it's not possible."

Brosa was stunned. "That you even thought about it is not possible."

Things were very bad—likely hopeless—if Heirik's mind had turned this way. Brosa gripped a stone hard. He brushed the ground with his palm and flattened a space to start building again.

"You don't know why I did what I did to Esa." Brosa closed off his heart so he could say the words. "To my son."

"I know pain, Brother."

"Nei," Brosa said, quick and hard. He hurried before Heirik could say more, his words building. "It wasn't grief. I don't know a name for what it was. But I do know that what I did, digging that grave, somehow called Eðna to me that morning. Some strong spirit has been at the steerboard ever since, and I'm at the oars rowing like a fool." He looked up from the stones. "What do I do?"

"The trial itself will determine how to go about the truth."

"Nei," Brosa said, balancing a stone that might be the one to tip it all. "Nei, I mean about Eðna."

Spoken out loud, the question was raw, this moment tender, in a way he'd never dreamed or expected. Heirik, sharing his thoughts on women was more unfathomable than any maid's heart.

Heirik smiled. "You'd ask me for such advice?"

Brosa smiled, too.

"You have Ginn now," Brosa said, and he was unsure if his words were for Heirik's comfort, or an accusation. He quickly laughed and said, "A rare woman. You must be an expert."

Heirik raised his eyebrow again, more like their uncle every day. "I am an expert on women?"

"Já, well, at least the desperate causes."

Heirik was silent so long, Brosa feared he had hurt him. The chief placed a stone, lifting his hand from it slowly, with great care. "What I can tell you is not about women. I can tell you that I finally allowed myself a life. Allowed Ginn a life. Thank the gods she was still willing."

"You did wait too long," Brosa said.

"Part of her still rages at me."

"You were fighting against your honor. It's not an easy thing for a man to do."

The cairn swayed. One or two more stones and it would go down.

"Shh," Heirik said, and he thrust his chin toward someone moving in the dark. A figure wrapped in blankets lurked behind some larger stones in the distance, a wave-froth of white underdress giving her away. Brosa hadn't seen her in days, and his pulse surged with confused hope and lust. Eðna was looking for him. He stood, his whole body and mind drawn to her. He stood to go to her.

She darted away. A wraith come to hover by him and then slip into the night.

"Já," Brosa said, with no particular meaning.

He turned to Heirik, who had also gotten to his feet. "That is the most unknowable part. The woman wants nothing more than to go home, and yet she's here, traveling to the althing."

"More than here." Heirik turned away and tossed a stone far into the shadows. "She's hiding to get a look at you."

Brosa yelled into the night, “Then why won’t you have me, Woman?!” But the skirt hem was gone.

Heirik said, “There are greater bonds holding her than Ginn’s wishes.”

Brosa swallowed, his throat sore from sudden shouting. His body ached from wanting Eðna, his hands begged for her skin. Her flashing skirt ducking behind that rock like a fox’s tail bounding away into a warren of brush, asking him to follow.

A rush of understanding hit him, so that the ground pitched under his knees.

Heirik thought he couldn’t help Brosa. He was wrong. He had been helping him all along.

All these years, his whole life, Heirik had led Brosa to this quiet talk together, when it seemed like nothing had been learned, nothing decided or gained. But Heirik had been his guide, since he was born. Had taught him how to live. And in the dark, Brosa looked into the past and saw the hundreds of times Heirik had denied himself everything. The nights he sat apart from his uncle’s stories by the fire, the days he spent brooding in the woods, the agony it cost him to give Ginn away. Tonight, Heirik had told Brosa the one truth that could only come from all those years of hiding and denial.

Brosa had to live a life. Not a life dedicated to his family, to Heirik, to anything that anyone asked. A life of his own.

He had let his shame drive him ahead of the family on this journey, always making sure Eðna could not see him, could not reach him. A dumb beast, hiding from the one person he wanted. He had avoided her too long.

He wouldn’t make the same mistake his brother made.

For the first time in his life, he gave the chief an order. “Go to your wife,” Brosa said, and he laid a hand on Heirik’s shoulder. “I’ll go to Eðna.”

Brosa found Eðna in the dark, her back against a boulder, eyes to the sky. She wore a shawl the color of a new lamb, and her dark hair fell in tangles over her shoulders, as if she'd been tossing in her furs. The night was warm, but Eðna held the shawl tight, and she shook as if she'd been pulled from the freezing sea.

"Finen?"

"I looked for you, so long." Small Eðna, so scared. Seeing her this way tore at his heart, and he couldn't answer for where he'd been, hiding when she needed him.

"Let me hold you, Woman."

Like a shot, she ran into his arms and knocked the wind out of him. He wrapped his arms around her, stunned.

"Tell me, Elskan, what's wrong?"

"She just....killed it." She shook her head and her breath hitched. "Just...dead."

He was a giant next to Eðna. All the times he dreamed of holding her, he worried she would disappear in his arms and leave him with dust. It was not that way. She was small, but with solid bones, strong hands on his back. She laid her head against his heart, breath rising and crashing against his own breath, until she settled and joined him, breathing together. Her hair smelled of herbs and sun from the long ride, and he whispered against the top of her head. "Shh, good."

He closed his eyes. He would be happy in her arms all his days, but not like this, with her in tears.

"Do you want to tell me?"

She nodded, and she spoke so close to his chest, he strained to hear. "There was a bird that came close to us in the woods. I thought, if I could draw it to me somehow, I could maybe hold it. I wanted to feel its heartbeat." Her breath hitched and chopped up her words. "Ginn broke its neck in her hands. To leave it for Saga."

Já, so it had to do with Ginn.

"She made an offering?"

Eðna stiffened in his arms. "The bird wasn't hers to offer."

"Nei, nei," he said, and he smoothed Eðna's hair. He wouldn't argue with her. Not now, while she rested against him, her curves round and soft, her arms tightening around his waist. He sent his own silent thanks to the goddess who brought Eðna here, into his life, into his arms. Saga deserved more than one small bird laid out on a rock in the woods. But he knew Eðna's meaning. He had not thought about it from the bird's point of view. Now that he did, the thought felt natural, familiar to his own experience. It was an honor for the animal's spirit, but not an honor that the creature chose.

"It was only little," Eðna said.

Brosa smoothed his hand over her back—he could cover half of it, if he spread his fingers. He brushed his thumb against her wing-bone. "Will you come sit with me, by the fire?"

She pulled away and checked the surroundings, skittish. "Ginn is there."

"Já, she is, with my brother's arms around her. And there is my uncle, holding his wife, and my cousin and his wife. I don't have much time until the trial, Eðna. I won't get the wrong idea, if you would just sit with me by the fire, in my arms."

He waited for the quick stab of refusal. Eðna pulling away from him again, always away.

She looked like a cloud of dress and pale skin in the moonlight. Gods, he wanted to lay her down, watch her chin lift to him, her lips open for a kiss.

"Okay," she said. "I will."

Brosa's mind had to catch up, and he almost stumbled.

She said yes.

"Come, then," he said, and he led her to the fire.

He sat and leaned his back against a big log, and he lifted his arm to let Eðna climb inside his embrace. She angled in like an untamed creature, not familiar with closeness and warmth. He settled her in his arms, and she leaned stiffly back against his chest. She looked around at the family, rigid. Nervous maybe, full of rage about the offering. Ginn had reminded Eðna of her fears.

She needed gentling, like Gull when he was young. Brosa brushed the soft part of her wrist with his fingers, just inside the edge of her dress.

"Brosa." He thought she would tell him to stop, but she said, "Lean closer."

He bent to listen, and his hair fell forward against her face.

"I don't know…" She stopped and started like a guilty child. "I was…"

"You can tell me," he said, and he smiled. "My father said the fall of a man's hair is a place for women's secrets."

He held Eðna so close, he felt her take a deep breath. "I've never had a man's arms around me like this before."

His chest ached for her. She was unsure, not of him, but of tenderness itself. She let him, among all men, be the one to hold her. "I hope I do well, then. So you see how it should be done."

Brosa pressed his lips to the top of her head, and she let him. Did she even fall into him a little closer? She smelled good, and the bones of her shoulders and back were sturdy against his chest.

Across the fire, his uncle sat beside Betta. Hár held his wife's hand lightly in his lap, turning her ring over and over while they watched the flames. Hár winked at Brosa.

Já well, his uncle had been right after all.

They didn't speak any more. It was just as he'd yearned for, Eðna in his arms, just sharing the fire and the night. As the sky darkened into midnight, and the firewood settled, something shifted between him and Eðna, too. A movement toward one another, in spirit and in body.

Two by two, his family left the fireside, until he and his woman remained, her breath coming deep and steady.

"Are you awake?"

"Mmmm," she said, heavy with sleep. She sat up, blinking and looking around. "Everyone is gone."

"Já, they went to their beds."

It was done, then. The settling together, the easy moments, taken by the night. She would leave now, with that familiar tuck of her hair behind her ear, or a press of palms to her skirt.

But, nei. She twisted around to face him, but she did not pull away. Didn't run.

He smiled and brushed her cheekbone with his thumb. "Did I do well, Finen?"

"Do well?"

The woman barely breathed.

"Holding you," he said. "I told you I'd show you how it's done."

Eðna laughed and ducked her head, and he almost couldn't hear her answer. "Já, very well."

She liked his arms, his body around her. And Gods, she was still here. So near, he could taste her. His body strained, and he forced himself to breathe, to charm her, draw her, not take her right now.

"If you liked that," he said, and he bent to brush his lips against her throat. "You should try a kiss."

Eðna held very still.

She didn't speak, and so he kissed the strong bone of her jaw, underneath her hair. She exhaled against his cheek, a small sound. "I'll try," she said, and she turned so that his mouth was just a breath away from hers. Brosa kissed her, and he dropped into glimmering ocean, far, far over his head.

Brosa set Eðna down in his furs, and he sat beside her. He brought her close, pulled her into his arms, and his hands caught in her hair and shawl. It slipped from her shoulders, down her back and around his arms. She was shaking again.

"I'll warm you," he said. "With my hands." He kissed her throat. "My words, my body."

She drew back, then tucked her head against his chest, as if hide. He wanted to push her dress down over her shoulders, up over her knees. Get in to reach her skin any way he could. But she'd just told him by the fire that she'd never felt a man's arms around her before. She feared touch, and he wouldn't scare her. Never.

"Bodies fail," she said, her voice lost in his shirt.

"Nei worry," he said. "I'm sturdy." And then, he promised her in truth. "This body will not fail you."

He kissed her shoulder, just at the edge of her dress, and she made the smallest sounds of lust and desire. Gods, she was testing him, though she didn't mean to. He pressed his forehead hard to hers, and she pressed back.

"I want you, Elskan," he said. "But I want you slowly, without fear."

She nodded, even as her forehead still touched his. Maybe she couldn't speak.

"Will you sleep here with me? And I'll hold you. Nothing more."

She nodded again. He gently laid her down, and he laid down beside her and touched her anxious brows and thick, berry lips.

"Or, maybe one thing more." He kissed her again.

"Brosa." She stopped him. "I don't know...I do want you."

"Ah, you admit it."

She laughed a little. "I don't even know how to want someone."

Eðna had never even felt a man's arms around her.

This was too much for her. She had no idea how to seek comfort and pleasure. Maybe she could, if he didn't scare her away. "Shh, Woman, just give us some time. Rest, and I'll hold you."

He laid behind Eðna so that he could wrap his arm around her and shelter her, feel the length of her body, her curves. Maybe his hand brushed her breast, just some.

She didn't truly speak, though he could just hear her murmuring the names he had taught her, instead of her long future words. "Awl-beak, flicker, sand-eels' bane."

"Sleep, Love," he said. "We will both be here tomorrow, and the next day." He could not promise anything beyond that.

Eðna nodded, and she did begin to fall asleep. When she spoke, she was so close to dreaming that her question surprised him. "Why are you still here?"

"Me?" Why was he here? She was the one who could have run.

"You could have gone to Norway, nei?" She was so tired, she slurred like she'd had too much ale. "Or anywhere else already?"

He had asked himself this question many times over the past few days. Eðna did not understand all the logic of honor, of feuds that simmered like water over flame, of men's ways. He would not flee from an accusation, even one that was half true. Maybe it was even more important to stay since it *was* true. A man would own up to such a thing. Not run.

But there was more. "It's my home," he said. "The place where I was a boy, and then a man." That was enough. That was why.

"Why are *you* still here, Fine One?"

But she'd fallen into sleep, with her secret reasons for staying.

He felt sleep coming too. The pleasurable moment, when a man closes his heavy eyes and lets go. Holding her felt good like that.

He imagined for a moment that this was a true bed, in a home of their own, his and Eðna's. Imagined she could be happy living out her days by his side. Vonfjara surged in him—the wash of hope and hopelessness in one tide. And then the tide settled, and a moment came that was like a calm sea, the ocean so still that a man floated above everything that teemed and struggled. He and Eðna held still like that.

For now. Soon, she would go home to her world and he would go on to whatever the trial held for him.

In the meantime, he would give her everything.

He tightened his arm around her and curled his body against her back. He'd already given over his wits and his heart, and he would give all his body if she let him.

Tomorrow, he would give her the leather case with his words and drawings, his thoughts and plans. She would hold and care for them, nei matter what his fate may be. Maybe later in the day, he would get them back, a free man. Or maybe she would hold them for a very long time. Maybe a thousand years. At least, she would see his work—truly see him—for a moment.

"I will give you the truth," he said, quietly enough not to wake her. "Soon I will, Elskan." He would not lie at the trial. He would not withhold truth like her Da did. He'd be the man he promised he would be.

Eðna crossed her arms against the morning chill and tucked her hands into her sleeves. She stood and shivered, a safe distance from Brosa. He still slept, warm and big, under the same wool blankets where she'd spent the night by his side.

He'd kissed her.

A kiss like a sweet sigh against her mouth, and she closed her eyes, and her mind and heart flew and dove like elegant seabirds. His mouth so warm, his lips curled in a smile even as he pressed them to hers.

And then he carried her—carried her!—to his bed of sheepskins and wool, and he laid down beside her. He touched her face, her chin, the line of her nose, as if she was the most delicate thing he'd ever seen. She burrowed in under his huge arm like she was some kind of animal in its den, lulled to sleep with the most unreal sensation of *wanting* to be enclosed. Wanting to know Brosa—not just the way his hands felt, the way his beard felt against her skin, but also his thoughts, his heart.

An impossible series of events.

Arousal was caused by a rush of blood, which led to a physical state receptive to intercourse. Pulse and respiration became rapid, the female body was flooded with moisture that made everything softer, lush. That was all.

So, how could she reconcile those facts with what it felt like last night? The exhilaration when he kissed her for the first time? And then every following time, more and more? Something fundamental, terrifying and good, had moved in her and over her. It couldn't be encompassed or explained by physical reactions. Never. When Brosa wrapped his arm around her from behind, she felt how he wanted her. For the first time, she felt a man's body aroused against hers, and in an electric instant, the words she sought—*conditions? conducive?*—flew away, useless.

This morning, she stood in the mist alone and touched her chin. It was so slightly raw from his beard. Could she really still feel the whisper of his hair on her cheeks? Taste, now, the angelica from his lips and tongue?

Several meters away, still asleep in his furs, he turned and closed his arm protectively around the space where Eðna had been. The surge it caused was shocking. Eðna wanted more. She could go to him right now, and he would let her in under that strong arm. She could snuggle against his broad chest and close her eyes. Not trapped. Safe. Brosa's body could be hers, right now.

She shook her hands out. Eðna Jonsdottir, snuggling?

She stretched her fingers, yearning for work. Her hands needed leather. Needed strands moving over and under one another, forming organized plaits and knots. She had no contact function, but in her own natural memory, she called up complex braid patterns. Gods, she'd slid these fingers into his hair, at the back of his neck, and pulled him to her.

Brosa stirred as if to wake, and she ran.

She plowed straight into Ranka, who was passing by carrying a pail of freezing cold water. It splashed on both their feet.

"Oh Lady, I'm sorry!"

"Nei," Eðna said, breathless and shocked. "It was my fault. I just..." Weak and light-headed, her pulse pounded fast and hard enough that she felt it jump in her wrist. Yes, she was shocked. She displayed the symptoms of actual, physical shock. Dizziness, nausea, chest pain, moist skin.

"Lady?"

Ranka's fine little brows were drawn down, and her head was tilted, worried. She took Eðna by the arm and guided her. "Maybe we can sit by the fire."

"Já," Eðna said. She flexed and opened her fingers in order, easing her grip on her shawl. "The fire."

Ranka made Eðna sit, and she dipped a cup into a pot of warm drink. The little girl's hair—golden brown and long—fell forward over the steaming pot. The familiar herbal scent rose up and tickled Eðna's nose, relaxing her.

"You are a bad mess," the girl said.

Eðna laughed a little. "Why? What do I look like?"

"Like the nest of an awl-beak. Did you roll around on the ground?"

Eðna choked on her drink. "Umm."

Ranka didn't wait for further explanation. She assessed Eðna with a narrow-eyed gaze. "I can help you. Make your hair pretty."

Eðna had seen Ranka braid her own hair many times, her little arms reaching up behind her head. Eðna could almost feel the burning ache in her own arms, from working complex braids in her own hair. She wanted that ache. She needed thick strands of hair to hold between her fingers, four strands on each hand, to weave and control.

"Later you can," Eðna said. "First I'll braid yours."

Ranka lit up, delighted. "Yes, please!" She handed Eðna thin leather strands for tying, and she sat at Eðna's feet, legs crossed, her whole body vibrating with excitement.

Eðna balanced her cup at her feet, and she drew her fingers through Ranka's long, wavy hair. She combed it with her fingertips and divided it into thick sections. Hair was so different from leather. Slippery, and that made it satisfying in a different way. The fine strands kept coming apart and flying up with static electricity, and Eðna drew them back in.

For a moment, Eðna was with Gida again, very young, learning to work with her hands. "I'm especially good at braiding," she said.

"I am, too," Ranka said, turning her head and messing everything up. "I've made up my own patterns."

"Me too!"

Gida had told Eðna she was an artist.

Eðna moved her hands like her mother always had, while Ranka spoke of a dozen things. "When we get to the assembly, we'll see the green rock ocean, a land of boulders covered with moss that are as big as a sea. And the hole in the earth where the assembly is. There are cracks all around the land, small enough to hide and seek. And I'll get some fine thread for weaving."

"Weaving? What kind of weaving do you do?"

"Trim for aprons and dresses and shirts," Ranka said. "I make up crossings and patterns."

The girl did tablet weaving, something Eðna had done many times. Impressive. Some of the Viking era trims and patterns required deft movements, the handling of so many strands, mathematical and spatial abilities that Ranka must possess.

"...Even silver thread," Ranka said.

"Silver-colored thread?"

"Nei, lady, it's really silver. The metal worker from the old country brings it, and it's very rare. My Da buys it for me. It's made from the finest slivers of silver, wound so tight you can't even tell that it's not string."

String made of real silver, so fine it could be threaded through the holes in a tablet. Amazing. Eðna longed to see it, touch it.

It hit her then, that she was here for the althing. She could see things like silver thread. She *could* touch it.

"And my day will happen while we're there," Ranka said. "The day I was born. I get to wear a flower crown and have honey to eat, and I'll be ten."

Eðna froze for a second, all her fingers threaded with hair.

Ten. The same age Eðna was when she left home.

Eðna had similar braids in her own hair, then. They crowned her little head, as she trudged through brush and mud and over rocks to escape her lying father. To a bird, she would have looked like a speck—a tiny speck full of anger and dreams. Fear foremost, but also fierce determination to push the scared parts back, push them deep inside.

The night that she and Brenna and Gren first saw the shining city, Eðna had huddled, silent, in her wool blanket. The city twinkled, like a thousand stars had fallen to earth, Ymir's thoughts fallen from his head. She held herself that night, tight, inside her blanket, and she shivered with dread.

She hadn't allowed many people near her since. Too mad at her Da, too afraid, too hard on herself, too driven.

Now, she smoothed Ranka's hair back from her forehead. Had she really been this little?

She could have let someone hold her, for the gods' sake.

Ranka asked Eðna, "Will you teach me some of your braids?"

"Sure," Eðna said. "I'll teach you."

It was too bad she couldn't take the child back to the city with her and give Ranka the chance that Eðna had, to learn more than new braid patterns. To see such wonders and live in safety and warmth. If Ginn still had her old contacts, could it work? Could the contacts make time travel possible for Ranka, even if they were defunct and dried out?

Nei matter.

Ranka was excited about *this* journey to the assembly. She was happy here.

Could Eðna be happy here, just for a day or two? Would it hurt to open up a little, just for now? She could let herself have Brosa's affection and comfort until after the trial. Maybe give those things too, if she even knew how. She had a job to do at the assembly—a new, smaller mission within her larger one—to exonerate Brosa. After that, she would return to the lab. But right now, this two-day period floated, suspended like a bubble. Inside it, she could allow herself to want him. She could revel in his half smiles, and his silly, sweet humor. The way he winked and called her *Finen*, quiet and secret against her lips, in the second before he kissed her.

They both hurtled into an unknown future. She could let herself be held close for now. For the gods' sake, she traveled through time. She could be brave enough to kiss this man. Could hold him in return.

She tied Ranka's hair with a leather strand. "I can show you something else, too," Eðna said. "We'll get a few sharp sticks and I'll show you how to make letters."

"Such a pretty maid," Brosa said.

Eðna blushed, just from his voice. He blocked out the rising sun with his big body, and he ran his hands through his hair, making it even messier.

"Thank you," Ranka said, and she twisted around to show him her braids.

Over her head, Brosa winked at Eðna, his eyes twinkling like the light within woods. Eðna's hair might have looked like an awl-beak's nest, but he'd meant the compliment for her.

He wound his own hair up and tied it in a knot. That hair that had slipped through Eðna's fingers. Those cheekbones that were so strong under her palms. That sinful mouth, smiling now. Gods, she was staring at him, her own mouth open, just enough to kiss him. He looked awake and alive. Her brilliant shepherd.

"Já, then," he said, and he rubbed his hands together. "Where is some food?"

Brosa walked several strides behind Eðna, watching her explore the market. She dove into everything with a kind of wonder he had not felt since he was a boy, holding Signe's hand and walking these aisles of men and women who loomed over his head. Then they had been nothing but a blur of skirts and boots and cups and knives. Now a grown man, taller than most, he looked out over the heads of hundreds of men and women.

Eðna slipped among and through them like water, down aisles and around merchants' booths with joy. None of her usual fear. Perhaps he had given her some ease and joy, at least for a time.

He kept his eye carefully on her. Her pale linen dress was lighter and cleaner than most, and her top with its laces up her sides was unlike any other. Here and there, the crowds thinned, and he could see her underskirt showing at her ankles. Her belt was slung low on her hips, and her dark scabbard and purse moved with her gait. The colors of Eðna. Cream and deep woods.

Her long braids swung behind her, each one trailing its curls of leather, whispering to be undone. They brushed her waist, where he wanted to put his hands again, the way he had last night.

Gods, last night would burn in his memory until he was an old man. He had not bedded the woman, far from it, but it was as if they'd joined themselves for all time. She let him kiss her. She fell asleep in his arms. He yearned for her now, even as they walked through this crowd.

He had this day, this one morning, to act as a man should. To hold up her spirit, help her understand she did not need to shield her heart all the time. To please her. It gave him a warm purpose.

He caught up with her when she stopped to sniff at herbs. An old man, bent and wrinkled, was selling dried juniper berries and bláber to toss into skyr, and baskets full of rare lavender, field mint and rosemary.

Eðna bent to take a deep breath, and the sweet skin at the back of her neck, where her braids divided, made Brosa swallow with a dry throat. He could place his lips there, now, but she might not like that show of affection, among all these people. She had kissed him last night, but that was not the same. She had not given herself to him in spirit, as a woman and wife. She was not his to kiss in front of this old man, and the white-haired woman at his side.

Brosa tugged on the end of her braid.

Eðna turned and gave him an evil look, as if she might smack him, but then she smiled and placed her hand on his bracer. He imagined he could feel her through the leather, her skin against his wrist, the way he had felt her arms in the furs last night, just before they both fell into sleep.

"This one smells like you." She spoke softly to him, as though they were alone in all the world. She twirled a twig of rosemary under his nose, and he was suddenly glad he had a habit, since he was a young man, of washing his face with sea-dew and his teeth with snowbloom water.

He picked a small handful out of the basket, handed it to her and tossed the man a coin. Eðna slipped a single sprig into her hair, and when it slipped out, he fixed it, with the lightest touch.

They moved on to the next merchant. Dozens of ale horns hung from cords, and Eðna's fingers moved through them gently, tracing the metal work on each one. She knelt to look through overflowing baskets of horns of all sizes that weren't yet adorned with pewter or silver. Baskets of sheepskins and furs overflowed onto the ground.

A woman stirred a pot as big around as a dairy barrel, full with a thick stew of lamb and barley and rare greens. At the next stall, a woman sold boiled eggs in their shells, and salmon smoked over a fire of dry wood. Rounds of flat bread, with holes in the center, were strung on a wooden rod above the fire. He bought several rounds, and for a high price the woman added honey and ground nuts from Norway.

These were sights and smells he had known dozens of times, but today they felt as new to him as they were to Eðna.

Brosa took her hand and licked the honey that had dripped there, and her skin turned fiery red along her neckline. She turned to look around them, but they stood in the midst of bustle and hurry and laughter, where no one would notice a single kiss—a man's lips on his woman's wrist.

"No one sees us, Fine One."

Shy Eðna, as well as brave. Her strength and yearning, intelligence and worry, all written in those arched brows. He could watch them all his life.

His thoughts would not rest on how short their life together might be.

After speaking with his brother, he was more confused than ever about his trial. But now, watching Eðna move, curious and sweet, through this crowd, he was sure of what he had to do.

She valued honor, já, and so he would tell the truth. That he was no murderer, but he did dig up Esa's grave.

"Elskan," he said, when she was too absorbed in looking at a tray of silver rings. After weeks of wanting her, it was cruel how short a time he might get to love her. Once she learned the truth about what he'd done, she would fear and revile him. Nei matter what price he paid at the trial, he would lose Eðna to the ocean, to time.

She deserved to know that truth now, before she watched his trial. She deserved as much—this bold and fragile woman who smiled and held up a silver and leather scabbard for him to see. Who set him on fire with every glance and smile. He grumbled to himself, "I should tell her."

He felt an answering whisper, a breeze against the back of his neck. Esa's spirit voice. *Don't.*

It was unlikely he would face death for his crime, though possible by the law of the land. It was more likely he would lose many things. Some money, some status, a good deal of honor. It was likely that after tomorrow, he would have nothing of worth to offer Eðna.

He would give her things before the trial, then. Too much of a coward to tell her what he'd done, he still could give her his heart, the shelter of his arms, his drawings and plans. Things that were better than a handful of rosemary and a dribble of honey on bread.

ᛊ

Svana peeked out from behind a tent that was pitched close to the assembly lake. People gathered here to eat and drink at sunset. To touch and sing. Families laughing. Strong young men searching for girls. Women's eyes downcast, flirting. Wives and husbands who wanted each other's company.

Svana looked at each face, one by one, and they seemed strange and shifting as figures drawn in Frigg's clouds. Out of her reach.

And then there was Brosa.

She almost darted out from her hiding place to go to him, the current of desire was so strong. She twisted her boot into the dirt to keep still. She would not talk to him, nei. Not now that her own husband had accused him of vile crimes. Not on the night before his trial.

It was knife-pain to hide, when he sat on a waterside rock, smiling, right there. She'd seen him for only a moment at Ginn's great hall. A sickeningly short glimpse, after all the weeks she waited. All the time that passed with no reason to go to Ginn's house, no reason to see Brosa. With only her memories, and the ghost of his scent on an old coat. The assembly had finally come, and here he sat only a house-length away.

He truly did shine like an evening sun. He always sent off sparks and heat, like a hearth. His big body was so strong, but soft, too. Not full of blade-lines and hunger like the chief's. Brosa's face was alight with sweet thoughts and laughter. His blond hair was tangled, the way it would look if she took him to bed and rolled with him in the furs.

Her bones ached for him.

A stiff breeze came, and she caught Brosa's rosemary scent, even above the smell of lakeside moss and water. And then, he opened his palm, and he did hold a handful of sea-dew. She squinted to be sure. Já, he held several sprigs, tied in a small bundle.

Svana could almost feel those little spines between her palms. She would rub them together and then stroke Brosa's hair, back when she took care of him. Tonight, his waves were so messy. Didn't anyone care for him now?

She had to get him free from Eiðr's charges.

Fear crept into her blood, thinking about what she had to do. Knowing Ginn, it would cost Svana her life, or worse. But she could not let beautiful Brosa pay for a murder that Svana herself had caused. Tomorrow, she would stand and speak.

She wouldn't think about what would happen after that. Nei. She wouldn't think of the ropes around her wrists, dragging her away, a murderess. Would not think of Eiðr, furious with a green-eyed rage.

She would think about her and Brosa, finally together. Once he was free, he would save Svana. Take her away, to his boat, and off this island, into the world. He would stand tall on the deck of the ship, and the ocean and all its fish and beasts would welcome them.

Brosa held the bundle of sea-dew out like a handful of wildflowers. Playful, like a small dog, he tapped someone on the nose with the spiny ends.

Svana's heart closed up, hard as a stone.

It was the woman. Eðna.

Svana tried to swallow. Brosa sat there, so near. Her own love, and he was touching that daughter-of-the-sea.

Svana had seen her for only a second, when Eiðr went to make his accusation. An accusation that Svana thought would be directed at the chief himself. She had meant to watch Ginn's icy face change to pain when she heard Eiðr's charges, but all she could see was Brosa, in his honored place below the high seats. That night, he wore his best amber wool and his braids the way she loved them. And beside him, there was a short, brown-haired woman, with thick eyebrows and strange leather clothes. The one her husband spoke about.

Who did she think she was, coming here and taking Brosa?

Now, here she sat across from him, with the lovely sunset-water at their feet, and Eðna closed her eyes and let Brosa draw a line down the slope of her nose.

Brosa leaned in close to Eðna, and he kissed her.

Svana sobbed, an uncontrollable sound. She clutched the tent with shaking claw-hands.

Again, Brosa was leaving her. Again, the gods were taking him, and he would go with Eðna, without a look behind him to find out if Svana even lived and breathed.

Eðna must be sent by a dark goddess, to have the power to draw him like this. She wore her shining hair braided in pretty plaits, her leather top laced at her sides to show off her curves, a smile on her full lips, but Svana could see plainly. Eðna was Hel, and Brosa was her willing prey.

Brosa took Eðna's face in his hand, his rings grazing the woman's face, his other hand on Eðna's thigh, moving up to her waist.

Gods take them both.

He could find his own fate tomorrow at his trial. Svana would not speak, after all.

Eðna climbed toward Brosa, where he stood at the top of a steep hill, awaiting his trial.

He stood with one foot up on a big, flat boulder, and his arms crossed, tall and beautiful against a steel sky. The clouds were streaked with gold where the sun came through. It brought out the lights in Brosa's hair, like he was part of the land and weather, and Eðna was amazed, again, at his force of will, his startling life. Now that she knew him, she saw his deep sadness, and his sweetness. His seductive pull, like waves bringing her closer to the top of the rise. To him.

"Fine One," he said, and he gave her one of his smiles. "I was afraid I wouldn't see your ember-eyes again."

She ducked her head, still shy about how he talked to her.

Gods, she had to focus. She'd had allowed herself two nights, and one luxurious day here at the assembly, to forget everything else and just be with Brosa. Now, she drew her mission back into focus. Stand up for Brosa, get free from Ginn, and return to the future.

She faltered and almost twisted her ankle.

The future. She hadn't thought of it that way before. The 22nd century was home, not somewhere far away in comparison to here.

She came up beside Brosa and looked out into a vast distance. They stood on a rocky point above a gigantic rift in the earth, the long rent that ran down the middle of Þingvellir, the assembly site. The rift was not as deep as it would become by the 22nd century. Rugged and rocky, it was so different from the canyon she knew in her time, lined with glass and laced with elevators for tourists.

"They say Odin made this rent with a great knife," Brosa said. "To cleave this side of the land from the other. I suppose you know better."

Eðna wished for her maps. For more to give Brosa than the crude numbers and facts she could remember: 64 degrees North, 21 degrees West.

"They call these *tectonic plates.*" Eðna spread her hands. "Giant slabs of earth..." She stopped and looked across the valley. A boundary where big portions of the earth met. A coming together of vast and unimaginable things.

She and Brosa both knew their idyll was over.

"Nei," she said. "What I know is no better than Odin's knife."

"My case will be heard over there." Brosa pointed to another outcropping, farther to what she thought was the South. "When I was a boy, we loved to hear justice dealt, to see the crimes paid for with silver and with fists. Once, we saw screaming horses, and two men fought to the death."

Eðna could only imagine the horses rearing back, their terrible shrieks. Brosa and this other man, Eiðr—his face compiled from half-seen impressions in the great hall—fighting with axes.

"To the death?"

"Nei worry, Woman," he said. "It won't be like that today. Most likely, I'll pay Eiðr an outrageous price in silver."

She wouldn't say what she saw, as plain as the sky—that he didn't believe it himself. He was afraid.

"Come, Eðna," he said. He took a leather case from his belt. "I've waited too long to show you this."

It was a leather cylinder that might have been a quiver for a child's small arrows, but it was tied tight at the top with long leather strips. Brosa lowered himself to kneel beside the big, flat rock.

"What is it?" Eðna knelt beside him, and she tucked her thick skirts under her knees.

Brosa's hands were big, but he worked the tiny knots with elegant quickness. In the city, she only knew women who worked with leather. She'd forgotten about men and their knots.

Brosa drew a roll of some stiff material out of the tube.

Paper?

"It's hide," he said. "So fine, the merchant showed me he could hold up seven sheets and still see right through."

Vellum. Real vellum, from an animal.

Brosa unrolled it, and Eðna's eyes widened, her breath caught, stunned. The page was covered with a thousand lines and swirls of ink—unknown shapes, with curving arrows and embellishments that swirled in front of her eyes like a moving image of a galaxy. Small runes lined the margins, drawn with intense concentration. The intricate ink lines wobbled thick and thin, where Brosa had used the finest tipped stick or quill.

A column of shapes rose up the page, each one a sort of curved V with its wings raised, like a faceless raven coming straight out of the page and flying toward Eðna.

At the top of the page, the bird-forms were simple, thin stick figures. But as they neared the bottom, they became more detailed, drawn with ridges on the wings like scales, their wingtips turned up. Brosa's thumbprints showed here and there. He must have spent countless hours drawing, forming the tiny runes that surrounded each bird, with the smallest arrows marking key parts.

A schematic. But of what?

She only saw birds.

Of course she did. She knew them better than anything in the world. The one thing she drew when she was a little girl, over and over, her hands forming the wings, until she felt the whole meaning of a bird in the motions of her hands over screens.

What did Brosa feel in his hands like that?

What did he see?

She let her mind open to him, let her eyes go soft, and then, yes. Everything shifted, and she saw what Brosa drew. Saw the figures not as upturned wings, but as cross sections. Fine parallel lines and swirls curved together into comprehensible shapes, and her breath came out in soft wonder.

"These are boats."

"Já," he said, and he turned to her in surprise and delight. He shifted closer to her and spread the page out flat.

"You spoke about waves of light," he said. "I spent time on the ocean when I went trading. I have thought since then about the forms of waves. I have an idea for a different shape here." He ran his finger along the line of the lowermost hull. "To fit with the ocean and slide over her curves."

If Brosa was alive before, he was brilliant as the big glacier now. In profile, absorbed in his schematic, he'd lost that hint of sadness that lurked behind his smile. Energy rose from him, so strong she thought she could see its light. Everything in his face was open and free.

"—Do you think? Eðna?"

He was waiting for an answer. He'd been talking to her.

"I'm sorry, I…"

"I see," he said, and he smiled, beginning with just a curl of one corner of his mouth. With his thumb, he gently traced her jawline. "I see."

Eðna held her breath, still and dizzy. His eyes were on hers, his thumb warm and rough, and it hit her like a wave of whisky. A shot of searing heat and drowsy bliss.

She used to think of bodies only when they needed to be adorned with leather bracers and purses and sheaths. She'd never thought about caresses. Never once considered thumbs across lips.

What was she doing?

She shrugged his hand away. "I was not staring at you. You're just vain. Nei matter what you think you see."

Brosa laughed and held both his hands up. "Okay, then," he said. "I was only asking you about your boat, Eðna, and you didn't answer. Did it look like this? The vessel that brought you here."

Her boat? The one that brought her here?

Yes. He was asking asked about the machine, the tank that sent her through time, as if it were a physical boat that carried her here on Saga's river. As though something as complex and unknowable as the tank could be compared to a ship. Impossible.

And yet so was Brosa. Here he was, a tenth century settler using ink and vellum to draw plans for more hydrodynamic hulls. Hulls like wings, more mysterious and elegant than any of Jeff's computers.

She let her eyes go soft again, and it took shape—the lab as a boat.

"Longer than your ship," she said. "And it sits inside a building at the heart of the glacier, not on open water. Its hull… well… its walls are made of steel and rock. But inside, it has sections of glass."

"Whole walls of glass," Brosa said. "I've seen only cups, small things."

"Yes, so imagine a whole building of it, all around me," she said. Clean walls, so perfect they were transparent. She could see Jeff there, waving goodbye. Mouthing the words, *I owe you one.*

"And a hearth in the center, where I would kneel by the fire."

A simulated hearth, without any real warmth. And Jeff and his team had no idea why. They just kept the fire, because that's exactly how the simulation was set when Jen traveled through time.

"A burning fire in the center of a steel boat," he said. "It sounds like it's designed to sink."

She laughed. "Já, I suppose so."

"So you knelt by the fire in this sinking ship and then you were here?"

"Well, I guess that's how it's done." She laughed. "Behind one of the glass walls is a box, not much bigger than this rock. And that box is what sends me."

Gods, it sounded so much stupider than a sleek, wooden vessel that went over a supernatural ocean. But Brosa listened with intent, absolute belief and wonder.

"There is no man at the steerboard?"

"The steerboard?"

"You have not been listening to my lists, Woman. The piece here," he said, and he touched his drawing, where one of the cross sections showed a long pole extending down off one side. "It's the limb that steers the boat."

"I see," she traced it with her eyes, careful not to touch the paper. His thumbprints here and there illustrated what could happen in a world without the ability to delete, to clean up mistakes or copy masterpieces. She couldn't bear to touch, to make a mess.

"When I was really small," Brosa said, "I sat in our boat many times, já? To play at being a big man."

"A big man." Eðna smiled. "Like you are now."

She tucked a strand of Brosa's hair behind his ear, and he smiled too.

"I knew the rocking of the water as a gentle thing, like a babe in a mother's arms. The smell of wood felt good in my lungs." Brosa dropped his eyes, deep in memories. "My Da told me, the steerboard helps you go the right way. End up where you want to be. I asked him how a piece of wood could do this, and he told me you also need the man who holds it."

"So you wanted to be that man."

"Oh, já, I wanted to say where we would go." He looked out over the rent in the land. "I had no idea how little a man gets to choose."

"I understand the feeling," she grumbled, and a shock jolted her. She and Brosa were the same. Today, he would be steered into some future that was not of his choosing, maybe against his will, just as she had when she was a girl. As if he felt the recognition, too, Brosa's eyes snapped back to her.

Eðna started to speak, but he did first.

"Shh, Woman," he said, and he took her hand. "We don't have much time. Just sit with me."

"Já," she said. "I want to look at your drawings."

He settled again, like a little boy wanting to show her what he'd drawn. Just like Eðna when she showed Vera her drawings of quails and auks. She called Vera urgently, the time she finished drawing a great scarlet ibis, and Vera clapped for her.

Eðna held her fingertip just above one of his illustrations. "They look like they could fly," she said. "Your boats."

Brosa took her hand and laid it flat on the drawing, pressing her gently to the paper, just as he had done that first time, in the woods. His hand was so big, it encompassed hers entirely, and his silver bracelet lay cool against her wrist. She glowed with the sweetness of him wanting her to touch his work, not caring if she smudged it, just wanting her to know it. She wished his hand would stay there forever. But he took it away and left her to trace the inky blue hull.

"Everyone says I have the sea in my eyes, and my fate is to sail and trade. And so I sailed and traded," he said. "But I don't love the sea. I love the boat."

"You need to build these," she said. "You have to test your plans."

"Ah, já," he said. "I'll get started on that, right after my trial for murder."

It was like a strike in the face, and Eðna turned away. Salt stung behind her nose, and in the corners of her eyes.

"Oh, nei, Elskan, I'm sorry." He took her hands both in his. He called her sweetheart. "Eðna, I know you must leave today. Please, remember me well."

This couldn't be happening. Her mission hadn't gone this absolutely, fundamentally and utterly wrong. She wasn't really at the althing, holding the strong hands of a Viking man who was on trial for grave crimes, who had held her up, brave, when she faltered. He'd captured her heart, and now her mind with his wave theories and boat plans. A gorgeous, rugged 10th century man, sad and courageous, and oh gods, he slid his fingers into her hair, and a million little stars flared into life on her skin.

How could she give him up? And yet, how could she ever give up her dreams and her city?

Men's voices floated up the rise.

Brosa pressed his forehead to hers and closed his eyes, turned to brush his lips against her temple. He spoke soft and low, only to her. "Take these drawings, Eðna. While I still have anything of worth to give."

"Brosa Ulfsson," a man said.

Three men stood close by, then five were there, and unexpected dread came. Eðna grasped Brosa's hand hard and pressed her forehead to his. They couldn't take him. Nei. Not him.

"No!" She panicked. "I'm not ready."

"Take the plans to remember me." Brosa's breath was warm on her temple. He just had time to say, "While I'm speaking at the trial, run."

Eðna opened her palm, and a twisted ball of wildflowers rolled out onto the ground. She'd been braiding the grass on the hill, above the assembly of dozens of men and women who'd come to hear cases.

Brosa's trial would follow several others—a sort of "main event," because of Heirik's status and fame. To see the brother of the powerful chief brought low was the most exciting thing that would happen all year, and as the time drew near, more and more people joined the crowd.

Where was Brosa? Why couldn't she have these last moments with him, instead of him waiting alone somewhere for his turn?

The trials were particularly Viking—dramatic, self-important, grave as a funeral, and yet punctuated with catcalls and jokes from the dozens of men and women assembled.

Eðna's brain swam and began to overflow with details of inane cases. Issues of stolen cattle, damaged fleeces, an untrustworthy dairy maid and two cheating husbands. So many small indignities, so much energy and jealousy and desperation, so many crimes paid for with coins saved up over a year, that would have bought less than a cup of coffee in her time.

So many wads of grass lying beside her.

"The case of Eiðr Olaffson against Brosa Ulfsson, who is accused of the murder of Ivar Njalson and Torg Njalson, and of the defiling of Esa Olaffsdottir's grave."

Eðna's throat closed, her hands still as claws around another lump of grass. She opened her fingers one at a time. Made herself stand when Brosa walked into view.

She stepped forward, drawn by his light. He was glorious in his amber wool and silver bands, golden braids tight against his head and waves of hair falling loose behind, his face open with kindness and fear. So generous and good. How could anyone fault this man for a thing in all the world? Believe for even a minute that he could commit such crimes? She willed him to look up, but he looked only into the eyes of his accuser, Eiðr, and calmly, courageously listened to his claims.

The woman, Svana, stood behind Eiðr with her head bowed and a miserable look on her little, heart-shaped face. Eðna's fist closed, and she seethed with the desire to punch the girl in her tiny, perfect mouth.

What was wrong with her?

She had three simple steps to complete—help free Brosa, slip away from Ginn, and run to the sea to tap out. Svana was of no concern. The girl played no part in Eðna's plan.

The speaker's voice carried like a song up over the crowd. "Does anyone else wish to say words?"

Eðna wiped sweat and chlorophyll on her dress and smoothed it over her thighs.

"I do," she said. She meant for her words to ring out strong and sure over the heads of the men and women below, but her voice was more like the croak of a sick crow. She cleared her throat and took a long step, and then another slow stride down the hill. "I want to speak on behalf of Brosa Ulfsson."

Brosa whipped his head up.

Eðna was here. For the gods' sake, she hadn't run. Worse, she was walking with grave purpose toward him and the law speaker. Her dress billowed, fair underskirts peeking out at her ankles. Her dark hair spilled out of her braids and flew in the wind. Men gasped, and women looked at Eðna with stark anger, but his courageous woman looked only ahead.

It was his nightmare come to be, the woman he wanted more than life, putting herself in danger in front of men and women who held deadly grudges against him and his family. Eiðr, whose brother was killed at Heirik's blade. Who believed that Brosa had killed his sister by making a child with her. Svana, whose mother was banished from this island by Ginn. Eðna didn't understand how the wolf grew slow and silent in their hearts.

Brosa was struck with desire for something simple and good, a sharp need to ask Eðna once more. *Sit with me, in my arms.*

"I was with Brosa that night," Eðna said.

Men and women laughed and talked behind their hands.

She kept on, with her brave face. "He was in the highlands, working."

Eiðr locked bright green eyes on Eðna, as if to slap her with his gaze, and Brosa fought hard to hold himself back from stepping between them and shielding her.

"Brosa Ulfsson?" Eiðr sneered, and he cast his eyes over Brosa, as if to point out his soft body and fine clothes. "Working?"

There were hoots and more laughter.

"He was digging," Eðna said.

"Digging," Eiðr repeated, and then a light grew in his green eyes. He looked at Heirik and the law speaker. "Digging in the hills."

Eðna looked from Eiðr to Heirik and back. Brosa saw her confusion, and then dawning horror. She was a small animal in a trap, and only Brosa could get her out. It broke his heart, but he had to release her.

"Nei," Brosa said, stern and sure. "I was not with her that night."

"The truth, Brosa." Svana stepped out from behind her husband. He hadn't heard Svana speak in so long. Her voice was ragged in her throat, but her face and hands brought memories of sun-soaked days in his boyhood, back when no one ached with anger.

Small Svana spoke. "You were not in the hills with this woman." She threw a disgusted look toward Eðna. "Who is she, anyway?" Svana asked.

Another woman shouted from the crowd, "Já, who is she?" The crowd picked up her words. Voices rang loud in the crack in the earth. And then a single chilling voice. "How does she know this? Was she part of it?"

"Stop!" Brosa said, and he turned on the crowd. "Svana Hildursdottir is right. This woman—" He looked to his beautiful Eðna, and he put steel into his heart. "I don't know her."

A gasp blanketed the crowd, and Eðna's sweet, dark eyebrows drew together. She begged him, silently. Why?

He turned his back on her. "I don't know her. And she doesn't know me."

"Brosa!" Eðna's voice cut him, straight through to his bones. He heard other women murmuring, men's voices climbing with interest, and Eðna pleading. "Brosa, I met you—"

"—I did not kill those men at the sea." His words echoed in the valley, so commanding that he stopped and let them ring like a final nail in a hull doomed to sink. He turned back to Eðna, and he gave her the truth he'd been intending to give her all along. Too late. Far too late. "I did not kill those men. But on my honor, I did dig up my wife's grave and sleep beside her bones."

Eðna gasped and her arms flew to her gut, as though he'd kicked her. Tears sprang up in her sweet brown eyes. It was the last thing he saw before he was dragged away from the closing crowd. Dragged away to wait, while his brother and Eiðr negotiated his fate.

Time passed slowly, long minutes seeming like days becalmed at sea. Brosa looked down into the rift in the land that made the law speaker's words ring. A rift so big that he could not fully hold it in his mind. Deeper than fifty men, and farther across than the whole world he knew as a child. Longer than the span of all of Hvítmork. Shaped like a colossal eel, it slithered into the distance, until the heavy walls joined at the horizon. There was no end.

It was his grandfather's country, his family's place. His own.

Gods, he hoped Eðna was riding away from it right now.

He smiled to himself. The woman was fierce, and she'd been willing to stand up for him. This was why she stayed. His chest ached to think that all this time she was here for him. She'd traveled all this way to speak for him.

He hoped she'd stolen Gull and was riding back to the sea. Refusing to know her was like ripping his own heart from his body—the worst lie he had ever told. But maybe it had released her. After what he admitted, after denying he knew her. He would never forget her eyes. "Freya, let her run."

"It's time," a man said, and Brosa turned from Odin's rift. "Come with me."

The man's voice was gentle, apologetic, and he held a spear in his hand with the butt end planted in the ground. Brosa followed it with his eyes, up to the sky, and black birds moved through the clouds there. A terrible omen.

The gods would not let the innocent be punished. But what about him? The partially guilty?

The question was how big an ax Eiðr had hanging over Heirik's head. Two years past, Heirik killed the man's brother Ageirr in bloody combat. And now Brosa had dug up Esa, an even worse crime against a good woman's ever-after pride and honor.

Brosa did not want his brother to use his power and silver to bend justice. And Heirik never would do such a thing anyway. He would glower, sit silently and ply the fear of his stained face, but his honor would prevent him from saving Brosa straight out, now that Brosa had confessed to the worse of the two crimes.

Brosa came to the circle of men. He did not look at Heirik or Eiðr. Nor at his uncle, at Svana, at Ginn. He couldn't bear to ask any one of them with his eyes about what had transpired when they met and decided his punishment. He wanted to hear only from the speaker's mouth, what decision had been made, what mortifying fee would be paid by his great and honorable brother.

He looked out to the horizon, imagining Eðna's brown hair flying free behind her as she rushed toward her home.

"Brosa Ulfsson," the speaker said. His voice carried at ten times the strength of a normal man, deep into the jagged wound in the ground. "You have been found guilty of murder and of the desecration of a good woman's grave. For these crimes, you are cast outside the hearths of men and women, and outside the protection of the law of this land."

Brosa had imagined high fines, public shaming, even a sentence of death. But nothing in him had prepared for this. Outlawed.

A dirty path opened up before Brosa, with men lined up on either side. They passed small rocks from hand to hand, weighing his punishment. Brosa would leave the world of family and law by passing through this gauntlet of stones.

It would be a dishonor, but not a mauling. In truth, many men would run a gauntlet laughing, diving for the end, tossing stones back at their brothers and friends. But most men were guilty of hogging ale or harassing sheep—crimes worthy of an easy kind of humiliation. At the end of the line, a horn of drink waited for them.

For Brosa, only the open land waited.

For weeks, since Eðna called him from the grave, he'd hoped to find something worthy in himself, an honor as sturdy as his body. He'd hoped to put his family's bones behind him, and find something good to offer to Eðna. All he found was shame. At the end of this path, he would become an outlaw. The truth opened up in his chest, the horror of it.

He did defile Esa's grave. He would atone for that. But he did not kill those men. His brother's tenants – men who were guarding his own ship when they died – chopped down like saplings with no weapons in their hands. It was not fathomable that he would do such a thing. But the crimes were weighed together, and he was guilty.

Now men shuffled and clutched their stones.

Eðna was not among the dozens, maybe fifty, men and women who'd come to watch him slink away.

Good.

To see her now would crush him. He would stay clear-eyed and strong. And yet, he searched for her, to look in her fire-eyes one more time before he left the world of home fires and friendly talk and women. But he'd denied knowing her. She wouldn't be in this crowd, she would have finally run away, and it was time.

Dread spread its wings in his chest.

Brosa looked up and met the eyes of the first man, and it was his brother. Heirik balanced a small stone in his blood-stained hand. Those gold eyes, clear and regretful, settled on Brosa.

Nei, not Heirik first. Not yet.

Brosa yearned for his big brother's touch, a hand on his shoulder, his voice low in his ear, so that no one else could hear, and Heirik did touch Brosa's forehead with his thumb, as if to wipe away dirt. "I did try, after all," he said.

"If I could borrow your will," Brosa said. "I could use some now." He could use some of Heirik's skill at hiding his heart, so he could walk this gauntlet with his head high.

Heirik leaned close and whispered, "I will find you."

A reassurance, but somehow it felt like the final blow. The crow-like dread opened up fully and beat its wings.

Brosa would not look at any of the other men.

Not Egil, the powerful chief in the west. Not Rafnson, the rich trader with six boats. His breath caught on his simple dream to build swifter hulls, a dream shredded like a torn sail.

He would not look at his uncle Hár, who had raised him. That would destroy his will. He would keep his eyes on the land ahead, wherever he might be going. Would he become a fugitive on the sea? Or a forest dweller? He almost laughed.

Heirik raised his rock high, a dark blot, an offering against the sky.

Brosa bowed his head. Body tense, bones alert, he prepared for pain. Every nerve strained. Palms wet, breath short. He raised his eyes to Heirik. He would keep his eyes open, nei matter what happened. He would not shame himself by closing them.

Heirik let the stone drop, and it hit the dust with a thud and rolled to Brosa's feet.

Brosa stared at the rock. Heirik let it drop?

The next man did the same.

Brosa took one step, then another, and as he walked, each man dropped his stone to the ground instead of throwing it. A soft thunder of stones rolled before and behind him. Brosa walked slowly. His pride had died, but still some shred of dignity did not allow him to run. He stepped over each stone, following them as he might follow the cairns that marked a byway.

He forgot to be ready for pain. When it came, it was sudden and swift, like a knife through rotten fish. Someone had thrown a rock at his back. It hurt.

Eyes ahead.

Yet, he couldn't. He had to know who had done it. Was it Eiðr?

Nei, it wasn't his accuser. He turned, and found a stranger had thrown the stone. A man with wet brown eyes, gleeful and sick. Brosa's shoulder exploded when another rock hit, and the soft murmur of tumbling stones erupted into shouting. Rocks flew freely at him, and fresh pain broke over him again and again. His will strained, trying to handle so many blows, pain spearing his knee, his foot, coming from everywhere.

Walk with dignity.

He could hear his mother's voice, sharp as the winter sun. *No running!* He was a boy, barreling through the house, chasing a chicken. Like a swift crack in ice she said, "Nei, Little Horse!"—one of her names for him. And then she laughed, bright and sweet. Her voice was so clear, he looked for her in the crowd. Instead he saw Eiðr with a big stone held high in his only hand.

Eiðr was a man like Brosa himself, a little brother who'd blindly followed his own big brother into disaster. Look where it had gotten them both. Eiðr without a hand, Brosa without a future.

Eiðr's face creased with rage, mouth open and ugly. He wasn't here to dishonor Brosa. Nei, dishonor was not enough. He wanted blood. He threw his stone.

Brosa had time to balance all his stupidity and his strength, and he found no answer. Would he go into death this way, then, a rock to the head, sailing on an empty ship?

His old vision came again, of the island as a creature that bore and sustained him and everyone he knew and loved. He looked up, beyond Eiðr, and hills of every shade of sun and shadow rose and dropped in wild, shifting patterns.

Somewhere, Eðna was flying on horseback, to the sea. Never giving up on her home.

He would not give up, either. He lifted his head once more. He would fight for his place on this creature's great back. Hold on to it, like a boy holds fast to a wild horse.

In a heartbeat, this came to him, and he raised his hand and knocked Eiðr's stone out of the air to fall at his feet and tumble in the dust. A brief stillness followed.

"You take nothing from me," Brosa said, and he wiped his hands of Eiðr's rock-dust. "Nothing at all."

Eiðr sputtered, enraged. He raised another stone, even higher than the first, and this one sang true, straight for Brosa's head.

But the blow came to Brosa's gut instead. A force rammed into his side—something much bigger than a rock, more like a sheep out of control. It landed hard against his ribs and knocked the air from his chest. He stumbled, reached out for balance, and his arms found Eðna.

Eðna?

She'd rammed into him and knocked him out of the stone's path. Her small body had driven him to his knees.

She grabbed him by the head and pulled him down, and she screamed like a fury. "Bastard!" She clung to his back, hands ripping at his hair, covering his face.

Eðna believed them. She believed he was a common murderer, and she had stayed here again, this time to vent her rage. The pain was worse than a thousand stones, a thousand ax blades, raw as an open wound. Didn't she know him?

And yet, he had denied knowing her.

She let go of Brosa, and turned to face Eiðr. Furious, her skirts ablaze in the wind. "Murderer!" She spat at Eiðr's feet. "Keyta! Foul water."

Angry, strong Eðna, a ferocious thing.

Brosa's head throbbed, and his senses caught up slowly. Eðna was not cursing him. She was shouting at Eiðr.

Gods, the woman did not believe the worst of Brosa. She was protecting him! Tiny Eðna was covering him to shelter him from the shower of rocks.

Laughter strained against his ribs. Of course, Eðna would do this. Her hand slipped into his, and her bones were strong, her voice low and urgent.

"Run now." She gripped his hand. "Get out of here."

Then, her fingers opened and slipped from his, and she dropped to the ground. Felled by a stone.

Brosa growled. The dumb beasts were still throwing stones and laughing like a sky full of crows. He lifted Eðna over his shoulder, and he ran. He ran until they passed the last man, and then a bit farther, so they were safe.

Brosa slowed to a walk, and he shifted Eðna so that he held her not like a bale of hay, but like a bride. Her head rested on his shoulder. Her eyes were closed, and her blood smeared his shirt, where the stone had cut her face.

"Elskan, wake up." Brosa grazed her hairline with his lips, a brush of a kiss along her forehead. He pressed his nose to her hair. "Please wake."

Back at Hvítmork, he'd asked her to stay with him all their days. Gods, what had he done?

He stepped over the threshold of his family's booth, into their assembly-home, and he saw the order of things. The carefully made beds, well-swept floor, banked fire, the evidence of good people. Everyone had gone to watch his trial. A deep sense of family settled among the stools and fire stones.

He laid Eðna on a bed of furs. He would have to wait until she woke. Make sure she was alright. He found an ale skin and cup, and he brought drink to her lips. Ale dripped onto her chin, and he lifted her. She didn't wake.

He sat with Eðna limp in his arms and shook his head.

Gods take the men who continued to throw stones even after she was in the way. Gods take the men who condemned and convicted him – all of them. And gods take her! Eðna was as dumb as he was.

He snarled like a dog and dropped her head to the pillow without care. Her eyes shot open, bright and fire-like.

"What is wrong with you?!"

Brosa laughed, bitter and sharp. "You would ask *me* this?"

He turned away before he might spit and shout. Turned from her fiery, bright force and shoved food and a shirt, any shirt, into a saddle bag.

"I saved you," she snarled. "Twice! And you're mad at me?"

He threw more things blindly into the bag. "You should be running already to the sea."

He forced one more bundle of food into his pack and called for Gull who whinnied and stamped outside the open door of the booth. Brosa got up on the horse in a heartbeat.

Eðna came to stand below him, and he bent low for one last goodbye. He pressed his palm to her face, and he covered her whole cheek in his one hand. "Go home, Fine One."

She didn't push him away, but her gaze was cold and mean, and there was only frost and tears in her voice. "You said you didn't know me."

"You don't understand the ways of the law here." Brosa's own voice sounded like cracked ice. "It was the hardest thing I've done in my life."

Eðna's breath hitched, and her eyes were fierce.

"It's my last glimpse of you, Eðna." Brosa brushed her brow. "Could you be soft for me?"

"Soft?" She laughed and yanked away from his touch.

"Já, I want to remember you sweetly, Woman."

"Oh, you will remember me just fine, Beast. I'll be right next to you."

She moved like a fast bird, all wings and speed, and mounted the horse behind him.

"Oh, nei, Woman." He shook his head, "You are not coming with me."

She wrapped her arms around his waist, and he hunched forward away from her touch. But gods, even now her embrace sent fire coursing through him. Her head against his back was a bittersweet weight—a feather, and yet strong.

Nei. She could not come. The men who would hunt him in four days' time would have no honor and no mercy for a woman.

How could he tell her what life stretched ahead of him? Convince her to complete her work here in his time, and just go? For the gods' sake, she needed to go. But he didn't find the words.

Nei matter. It was Eðna. She would not give in to any talk, any reasoning.

"It's not your decision," she said. To leave the assembly together with him was her choice. Weighing everything, all his wishes and lies and promises and mistakes, all the dangers they would face on the plains that stretched ahead of them, he could not do it. He would not take Eðna's power over her own fate.

An outlaw had four days' grace to return home for the things he needed to live, the things that were rightly his, before his punishment began. It was enough time to explain things to Eðna, talk to her, get her to change her own mind. If they rode hard for the sea, they could make it in time.

Gods damn her.

He dug his heels in to Gull, and he and Eðna flew from the althing, into the vast land, together.

ᛋ

Svana put down her knife and watched Eiðr struggle to open the knot on their bedroll. His one hand fumbled, and he growled and tossed the big roll of skins in Svana's lap. He stomped off toward the fire to sit and drink.

The knot was wrenched sideways. Svana yanked on it and made it worse.

Who cared if she got it free? She would only unroll a dusty bed where Eiðr would sleep next to her, and she would stare into her beloved sky, and feel and hear him breathe.

They traveled with only a handful of men, moving quickly through the land. Halfway home in just a day.

Svana drew her jagged fish knife from her belt and slipped it under the cord. She would just cut it. She pulled, and the leather strained against her blade.

The men talked over their ale, a bunch of spitting animals.

"Ulfsson is soft. He'll make a pitiful outlaw."

They laughed.

"He's got four days," another said.

Svana yanked against the cord.

Outlawed.

Her Brosa.

Every time she thought the words, her head wheeled like crows.

Brosa had four days to go home and gather the tools he needed to live and the things he treasured. After that time, any man could kill him on sight.

She would not think of Brosa cowering in the trees, hiding like a filthy, wounded animal. Would not think of his golden hair matted from sleeping on the ground, his blue eyes gone murky and dead.

She sawed at the cord around the bedroll. Why would the knife-teeth not get through?

"So you think the chief's brother will live in the woods," another man said. "Who will shine his jewelry and comb his hair?"

They laughed like savages.

"He did take a woman with him."

Svana would not scream. She sawed harder against the leather ties. Nei. She would not think of that woman Eðna. It was satisfying, seeing Brosa reject her at the trial, já? But still, she would not think of that Eðna ducking her head, and Brosa handing her rosemary, so tender.

Svana would think, instead, of the things Brosa cherished and might save from his home to take into the unknown. The things that would sustain him. Would he take a bowl that they had shared for the hundreds of meals they ate together, and a shirt that Svana had spun and sewn for him, when he headed into the wilderness?

Eiðr spoke. "I'm sure Ulfsson will make a fine place for himself in the woods, if he lives long enough to get there."

Svana's knife stopped.

Her throat closed with sudden knowledge.

That was it.

That was the reason they were racing so fast to get home. There were four days' grace for Brosa, but that was a rule not all men would honor. Eiðr planned to get to Hvítmork first, to kill Brosa now, before the time was up, when Brosa hadn't yet had a chance to hide.

"If he has any sense, he'll head for the sea," one of the fools said.

"If he has any sense, he will not," Eiðr said. "His ship seems an obvious place for us to wait to attack. He's sentimental. He'll go home."

Svana shoved the sheepskins off her lap and stood. Her anger surged so that she felt she could kill Eiðr with her bare hands right now, but his men would never let her.

She headed uphill. It was the only way out of their camp, without passing by the fire. The whisper of her boots on the dust sounded like thunder. But the men's voices got smaller, and no one followed.

Every decision in her life, no matter how small, was determined by her mother, by Ginn, by Eiðr. Taking a step, and then another, was her own. Right now, she would just walk.

Step after step. She climbed, now inside a stand of short trees and brush. Steeper still, her breath coming hard, she pulled herself up by grasping juniper branches.

The woman Eðna was with Brosa right now. The sting was sharp and brought water up into her mouth and eyes. Again, Svana watched him go away with another woman. Why did Eðna get to be with Brosa, while Svana was stuck with a pack of foul hogs who mocked a good man? Svana wanted to crush Eiðr. She wanted to crush Eðna, too.

Svana stood still in the brush.

Could she? If she went along with Eiðr and aided in an ambush at Hvítmork, there she might find Eðna. If Brosa had not carried the woman to the ocean first, then she would be at the house, and Svana would use her hands and feet and knife to destroy that beiskaldi.

The little woods around Svana stood quiet and still, and the light moved like quick wings, changing here and there. Different from any place she'd ever been. In just these few minutes, she'd gone far enough so that she couldn't hear Eiðr. The smoke from his fire was the merest breath.

She came over a final rise, and her stomach dropped.

The land ended, and there was only open air. She threw her arms out, and her toes fought for balance, spraying dust down into nothing. Svana stood on a rock's edge, far above a frozen valley.

The vision below her sucked the air, the very essence, out of her chest.

"Freya?" Her soft word formed smoke that floated away into a vast place.

No farm house waited right over the rise. No coast. No wolf-jawed boat. Black earth and white ice was all that existed, except for a thin blue strip where earth met sky. The ocean was just a thread across a horizon unfathomably far.

Wind tried to force her back, but she held her ground. The late sun made the sky catch fire. She raised her hand to shield her gaze. From high on one side, a white expanse swept down into a black valley so big, it could only have been gouged by a god's knife. The ice led down onto flat, dark earth, that was threaded everywhere with frozen streams like fine stitching.

Still as death, and yet somehow the ice was seeking, like fingers in the land. It melted into pools that glowed white-hot. Svana covered one pool with her hand. From up here, the lake was the size of her palm. Surely, up close it was bigger than the whole yard at Hvítmork. Each pool, bigger than her girlhood world. Brosa would be a single grain of dust kneeling at the edge of even the smallest one.

The wind whipped her dress behind her like a sail and streaked her face with tears.

The world was bigger than she'd ever known. Big enough for Brosa to get safely lost. If Svana could keep her husband away, mislead him somehow, Brosa might make it to his boat.

What about Svana herself? Could she get lost, too?

"Woman, get back here!"

Eiðr's command startled her, and Svana threw her arms out for balance. She turned to him and put her back to the endless drop. Eiðr pushed his way through the brush, his brows heavy with rage.

Svana stretched her arms wide, and the wind sucked at her dress and limbs. More little stones fell from the edge, from under her heels.

She had dreamed these two years of going away by sky, soaring into Freya's clouds, never to be seen again.

Could she? Just fly?

Nei. She laughed. Of course not.

It would destroy her to go by air. She had tried to destroy so many people—Ginn, Heirik, Eiðr—but she had failed every time. Destruction was not the way to get free.

Eiðr's eyes were green fire. "Wife, are you dumb?"

Then again, maybe it was.

"Nei, husband," she said, and she put on a sweet smile. "I was just looking at the land. Come up and see."

BOOK TWO

ᛊ

912 C.E.

Like a little goat, Svana Hildursdottir followed the other girls up the slanted roof. Everything was night-dark except for her hands, silver as rings in the moonlight. She grabbed fist after fist of grass, climbing on her knees. She would ruin her dress, but she didn't care. Svana was almost nine years old, and she would make it to the top of the house.

Whispers and laughter tumbled down to her, but she could not see. Thora's dirty boots and hems were in her face.

Svana was last, because she was the new girl to the farm. The one who was not family. Did not belong. Whose mother was a match for the disgusting, terrible chief. Hildur did not marry Rakknason, thank the gods. But taking care of his house, holding the keys, was enough to make Hildur's daughter last among girls.

Svana let go of the grass just long enough to touch a worn stone that hung at her belt, just like Ma did when they spoke of Rakknason. Svana didn't know what it did, to touch the stone, but she copied Hildur, and so far, she had not died.

The night was cool and crackled like the forest leaves this time of year.

Svana might be last, but she was quick and pretty, and she had evenly spaced teeth. Thora was twelve years old, and already you could tell she would become a cowfoot.

"Shh! Shh!"

The first girls made it to the top. Up above Svana, just a few more handholds away, they gathered around the roof vent. Laying on their bellies and peering down in, their faces were made into skeletons—bones and angles called forth by the flame-colored light. Dalla pushed her hand out to shush them all. Dalla, Thora, two more cousins, all four of them crowded around the vent to listen to the grown men talking down inside. There was no room for Svana.

She whispered, small as a bug, "Can I look, too?"

One of the cousins hunched closer to the vent. "There's no place for you, Svana Sviðauga."

Svana's throat filled up, like a river pouring in.

Svana Sting-Eyes.

She could never stop her burning tears, when the girls were mean and said things and held their dolls and combs from her. She stirred soap and wet wool, carried butter to the table, spun by the stable—all with blood-rims around her eyes that her mother griped at her about.

Thora moved to block Svana's way. The girl's foot slipped, and she kicked Svana's cheek.

Nei!

She could not let Thora do this. Could not let Sting-Eyes become her byname. A lifetime of sorrow and ugliness would follow such a name. If she was strong, she would be glorious and beautiful. If she allowed herself to be a weakling, she would never command a great home, never join with a worthy man.

She shoved her way past Thora and crawled to the top. She came to her knees at the very point of the roof and swayed with the height, feeling almost as though she could rise even higher, right off the peak.

Up here, the spirits flew on a free course, with no hills or houses to slow them. The wind came and dried the wet place on Svana's cheek where Thora had stepped with her soft, moist slipper. Svana's hair blew and whipped along with the horse's long grass mane, and she trembled in the sharp air.

The heavy stink of old smoke clogged her nose and mouth, but the wind was sweet as cream on the edge of butter. It had a taste of turning from one thing to another.

Just a few steps away, all the girls looked down into the hole in the roof, with their harpy faces, listening for men's secrets and plans.

Svana looked up instead.

The darkness was vast, Ymir's skull—the dome they lived inside—bigger than her imagination. She lifted a hand to smooth the sky. Sviðauga meant eyes that smart from burning, já. And she would not let it become her name. Starting tonight, she would stand tall with her eyes clear and free of pain. She was no coward underneath this dome.

If she was strong, maybe the girls would want her. The boys would want to be near her. And she would tell them nei. "I am going where I want." She said it to the sky, to practice. "Without you." One day, she would go far away, já. And not see anyone ever again.

ᛒ

912 C.E.

Brosa stepped into the little cave and breathed in the gods.

He was not tall yet, not like his brother. The rock sloped up and away far over his head, so high that Odin's ravens might glide there, or Frigg's distaff shine with slick new wool, just like his Ma's. He tipped his head back to see, and his wet hair fell down his back. Fingers of frigid water reached under his shirt and tickled his spine.

It was quiet here, after the powerful rush of the stream he had crossed. And dry as a warm bed full of feathers and furs. Clean air filled his chest, and the smell of wings and foxes. It was nei grand hall, but it was good. The floor was thick with juniper bones and dust. And right in the rock floor, built just for him by the gods, was a stone firepit with a passage for air. The spirits that came and went with flame were alive in this place.

He would build his fort here.

Heirik never came this way. His brother had his own hideout, far to the south, that he thought was secret. Brosa had followed him. He'd learned from Heirik—a man of ten years old should have a place of his own.

He would build his right against this rock wall, tucked under this cave-roof, and no one would ever know.

Brosa twisted his hair to get the water out, and he looked out over the way he had come. His route was marked with his special cairns, and with his passing he had claimed all he could see. The silver-white, grasping trees. The underbrush that left burst-berry stains on his legs. His bindings and boots were washed clean now by the water that coursed just below. The gods had put a river right in the woods. It even had a shining waterfall, small enough to fit inside a forest ravine. The river split the woods in two, and on this side, everything was his.

He should show his Ma. She would like it here.

He slid the thin roll of birch bark from his pack and unrolled it, slow and easy, but it still crumbled at the edges. He took out his sharp little sticks and stoppered horn full of dye, stolen from the pantry. His chest seized with guilt, for just a moment.

He licked his lips and started to draw his plans. The lines were uneven and looked like scratch marks, but they were powerful. Writing put life into the bark. His Ma had made sure he could do it, to read the runes and learn what most other men could not.

The light moved and changed across the bark, as he drew the rafters and walls and door he would make. The bed he would build. He scratched marks for the wood he would need to gather. He longed to draw a picture of Heirik—the main person who was not to come here ever. But writing invoked vague things, powerful things to come, and so he did not.

Brosa rolled up his plans and hid them in a pile of leaves and brush.

He sat and rested his boots and arrows, and he was quiet for a long time, claiming this space with his silence. The forest spirits sent two dozen flickers to land and chitter on the stones right beside his feet. One or two walked across his arrows where they were strewn. Then together the birds rose, turning as if drawn like smoke to a roof vent in the sky. Circling and protecting Brosa's new place with their blanket of wings.

He set his palm against the rock.

Sturdy. Good.

He gave it a smack, the way a man smacks a strong house. He would live here one day. Já, he felt it. He was already chief of this small place.

2121 C. E.

Eðna pushed through knee-high grass, her skirt in a knot, her little bow and quiver bumping on her back.

She was ten. Far past time to learn to shoot. So said Da. But when she went out to practice, she always ended up wandering and filling her pockets with stones and blooms.

Da was different. When his arrows flew, they sang a note like windsong, and they went so much straighter and faster than Eðna's. She dreamed sometimes, in her bed, of becoming small as a wight. One of the tiniest land spirits. She could ride on one of her da's longest and most graceful shots. Jon's strong arm would pull the string back so that his fingers brushed his beard, and with a wink to Eðna, he would let her go. She would feel the wind in her face and become a creature of the sky.

How would the house look from up there? Or the sheep mowing trails in the ground, searching for green shoots in the far fields? There would be a pattern to all their movements, like a great and intricate braid. She could see it just by looking around. The turnings of streams and animals' paths would look, to Frigg in the sky, as if they crossed over and under like weaving.

She pushed sweaty hair from her face and drew her eyes back to where she was going. The black rocks could turn an ankle in a second, and they lurked everywhere in the land. But those rocks were where the snowbits took hold, in the cracks and along the edges. Flowers so small, they must be tended by land spirits, to pick and make tiny bundles for their tables underground. The roots were the thinnest tendrils, almost too fine to see.

The grass swished against her bare calves, and her skin tingled and itched.

Eðna stooped among the stalks of grass. Her bow and arrow got caught up in the plants all around her, and her breath came slow and shallow as she worked to carefully pry the flowers up without crushing the petals. The only sounds were her breath and her skirt rustling. The fanning grass in the breeze. So quiet, she heard the dirt smearing under her fingers.

So many petals could fit into one of Eðna's palms. She tried to count them one time. She lined up flowers in the dirt and started over counting again and again, but there were too many and they kept crumbling, so that the separate petals increased the number of things to keep track of. She made images instead. She nudged the petals with her fingertips, turning their neat lines into shapes with tails and arrows and the mane of her mother's horse.

One day when she was a mommy, maybe she would have her own horse and name it Snowbit, after these flowers.

It was nei matter that she collected stuff from between rocks instead of practicing shooting. There wasn't any reason to get good at it. Nothing to shoot but the hillocks and marks on the walls of the ravine. It was just one of the ancient skills Da wanted her to have.

Around the fire, Jon told stories about warriors with arrows, about women who stood alone and defended their homes with just a bow and a handful of fletches. He told of Baldr, whose Ma Frigg had convinced each and every thing in the entire world not to hurt him. But she missed a small bush called mistletoe, and so Baldr was killed with an arrow made of that wood.

Baldr's father pushed him away in the sea in a flaming boat, and Baldr's wife gave up her life and laid down dead next to him.

Eðna yanked at a stalk of grass. She wished she'd never heard of Baldr.

She stood and put her handful of blossoms into her pack. These would be for Ma. It might make her feel better, to have a crown, and so Eðna picked some long strands of grass, too. Maybe sitting together to braid the grass would ease the pain of the unseen elf-shot that was in her mother's belly.

Eðna's chest twisted inside as if an elf-arrow speared her, too.

Her mother was going to die.

She kept forgetting Ma was sick, and then she'd think of something like a crown.

Would Da lay down beside Gida and die too, like Baldr's wife? If Eðna lost both her parents, she would be alone and have to make fires and carry water and cook for herself. She'd have to send them both to the gods. She would need help. She was too small to push away a fiery boat.

She brushed her palms on her skirt, leaving green streaks.

Nei matter. She'd never even seen a boat, and they had no big water.

Eðna walked up from the field and crept to the back of the house, so she could surprise Gida with the grass and flowers and they could weave them together. Eðna was so sneaky. The dog came to sniff at her bow and her hands, but he didn't bark. She was almost to the door when she heard her parents' voices.

Her mother's words were strained, like they were pushed through pain. "Jack, no," Gida pleaded.

"Love," her father said to her mother. "Please, let me." His voice was strangled with pain, too.

Eðna had never heard their voices this way, and she'd never heard this name, Jack.

"Nei." Her mother gasped, and she stopped talking and whimpered like the dog, as though the pain surged hard. Then she said, "I want to be here. Under the sky, with the gods."

Eðna dropped her flowers and crouched low to hide. She held herself in a small ball, close against the house. Her mother was really going. Going soon. But Eðna's dread wasn't just because Ma was dying. There was something else about it, about them talking—something big she didn't understand. She could feel how big it was, but didn't know why.

She set her eyes on the ground and the green stains on her skirt. She refused to look up at the sky full of gods. One of them might be swooping down, coming for her mother right now. Something even more terrible lurked underneath and around her, and she was squashed in the middle with nowhere to go.

Nei, she would not look up or down, or inside either. Not look anywhere. She pressed her eyes shut tight. So tight.

She was ten then, before death came, and the city.

Eðna was more than twice that age now. Those moments, those flowers—her parents—were over a thousand years away, and Eðna was here in the tenth century, on a wild and unruly mission that had gone so wrong. Eyes closed, she rode on a horse that flew into the wind, her cheek and temple resting against the giant back of a glorious, bruised and angry man.

That time with her parents was unimaginably long ago. Eðna opened her eyes to now.

922 C.E.

Eðna dug her fingers in under Brosa's belt and held on tight, as they flew on Gull's back, away from the assembly. The ground rushed by at terrifying speed, and she clutched the horse with her thighs. Good, kind Brosa had been shamed and beaten. Tears stung her cheeks, and Brosa's hair whipped her eyes.

The air between them, in the tiny spaces between his body and hers, vibrated with tension that rose and grew like the questions she wanted to ask. She swallowed her thoughts. Brosa would never hear her anyway, over Gull's hoof beats and snorts and the wind and speed.

He was so angry. Sweet Brosa had snarled at her, back at the assembly and shoved her onto the bed. Eðna had protected him, stood up and spoke for him. She took a rock for him. And he was angry at her!

"What the hell is your problem?!" She shouted into the wind.

No response.

They rode.

The evidence of volcanic eruptions went by, rocks of all sizes spreading for untold distances, and the black, compacted ash, north of the Thing. The land was so black, it shimmered blue. The words were far back in her mind, a calming list, but she forgot their meanings. "Basalt, rhyolite, andesite." What was the other one?

No grass, no flowers grew here. The moss and lichens were sparse, and the dark, rocky expanse was broken up only by steam coming from far-off vents in the ground.

The magma coursing through this land would have glowed orange and red, rising like the heat from Brosa. The shifting and opening of the earth, spewing fire, would seem like a god's wrath.

Brosa stopped the horse abruptly.

"Get off," he said, loud over the rush of wind.

Eðna sat up straight. "What?"

"Get off the horse, Woman." His fury was still hot. "Now."

She sat stunned, and then slowly drew her sore fingers out from his belt. She shook as she slid off Gull, her legs almost folding beneath her. Was Brosa going to leave her here?

He slid down off the horse and turned on her, and he was huge, violent. "Gods, Eðna."

He ran his hand through his hair. His fingers stuck halfway through, and he held his head as if he tried to contain wild thoughts. He growled. "Don't you see what you've done?"

Brosa never talked this way. Not to his uncle, not to Ginn. Not even to his horse. Never to Eðna. He was going to leave her here.

"Nei." Her voice could not hold. It wobbled. "Nei, I don't see."

With the hair pulled back off his face, she received the full force of Brosa's eyes and thick white scars.

"Any shred of honor I had left was at the end of that line of men." He stopped, regrouped, and his slow, considered words were even worse than his snarls. "You didn't let me get there."

Eðna's chest hollowed and the wind scraped her lungs.

Back at the assembly, she'd seen rocks and blood and Brosa, so scared, so betrayed, and she'd jumped in without thought or reason. She hadn't considered what it might cost him to be saved by her. She shielded him from rocks, but she'd taken his chance to be brave. Stolen his chance to show grace and strength in the face of a gauntlet. Fortitude in the face of being cast out. To prove his belief in the rightness of the law of his land. Courage. Honesty. All those things.

She was left now with his back to look at. Amber wool, across his shoulders, spanned the sky.

"Go," he said, suddenly soft and quiet.

He really did mean to leave her here.

She brushed her fingers over her purse at her waist, with her medication and firestriker inside. She forced deep breaths, forced herself to steadily open the pack that hung from Gull's saddle. She would need food, a knife. Too bad she was all out of whisky.

Brosa kept his eyes on the horizon, his arms crossed tight.

She took a blanket off the horse's back and threw it around her shoulders. If he wanted to leave her, fine, it wouldn't kill her. Nei. She'd trained for exactly this kind of survival.

She blinked to find her position, find a map, but her contacts had been useless for days. Things looked the same in every direction. Even the sky had turned opaque, without a single feature for guidance. She drew up her skirts in one hand and struck out, but not the way they had been heading. Nei, she turned to what she believed to be west. Straight to the ocean.

She walked alone and wordless, away from Brosa, and he didn't stop her.

The ground went by in a miserable blur. Eðna stepped in bunches of moss campion and gold-dust lichens, spread across volcanic dirt that was dark as grackles' wings. Her dress slipped out of her fist, and her skirts dragged and picked up dust.

She only wanted to help him get home safe, get settled, before she went on her own to the sea. But if Brosa didn't need her help, her comfort, he could live without it.

She turned her head briefly and caught a glimpse of him. He walked, leading Gull, far behind, but coming along in the same direction.

Eðna quickly looked away, bent her head to the singed earth. The hem of her underdress, where it kicked out from under her skirt, was so dusty, it looked like it had been burned to ash.

The most recent eruption in this region—north of Thingvellir—was estimated around 200 or 300 CE? She shook her head, tried to dislodge any information she could access, but nothing came. She couldn't remember exact years. The third century, maybe. Yes.

She should have gone there instead, to the third century, and watched the billowing blackness of this volcano eat the sky—a vision of Ragnarok that would be less painful than the force she felt in her chest right now. This force that pushed at her back, like a wave coming off Brosa. It choked her throat and hurt her eyes. She saw the scene again, the rocks flying at his head, that slimy man accusing him, accusing Brosa.

Eðna stumbled. Her ankle turned with a sharp stab, and she hit the ground palms first. A million tiny stones cut into her skin. She choked back a howl of frustration and just sat in a heap, emotion seeping out and spreading like her ashen skirts. Her palms and wrists were pocked with a galaxy of little stone-marks and smeared with blood. She dropped her forehead into her hands, and red light pulsed when she pressed against her closed lids.

Brosa was at her side, kneeling next to her. "Are you alright?"

She looked up into concerned, ocean eyes.

"They were hurting you," she said.

Brosa touched her fingertips, gently opening her hands to see her wounds. "They?"

"Those men." Her palms stung, and she sucked in a breath.

A silent moment passed, and Eðna's heart raced, loud and fast, full of fighting. Her palms glittered with pain.

"Oh, Eðna. You are brave and full of rage." He got down off his knee to sit beside her in the dust. She breathed in his familiar smokiness, his rosemary and soap, and he smiled his darling half-smile. "This is good, já."

She laughed, just a little.

Brosa picked up her firestriker from the ground, and he turned the steel over in his hand for a long, quiet moment. "Do you know what it means, that I am outlawed?"

It wasn't something Eðna had deemed essential knowledge for her mission, and now it was too late to look it up. No one had ever been outlawed in her tiny childhood home. An indistinct memory came, just an image, of a bent man on a hill. "Not really."

"Já, then, you need to know."

Brosa turned to the wind, which picked up now and whipped his hair. He turned his eyes to the somber landscape, and the distant line dividing it from the milky sky. A long time passed, as he turned the firestriker over again, and the gravity of what he might say grew unbearable.

"After this period of four days' travel, any man may kill me on sight and pay no price."

What? Kill Brosa?

"Nei." It had to be wrong. This was a practical land, obsessed with justice, and Eðna shook her head. "Nei."

"Já, it is the truth." Brosa kept on. "Not just if I'm lurking in their woods. There are those who will purposefully look for me."

"Nei." She shook her head over and over.

"Eðna, listen, there is more."

"Stop!" She covered her mouth, as if she could keep any more words from entering the world. The wind filled her head, and she gripped Brosa's arm.

"—Listen!" He pulled away from her touch, his voice dark. "It's important you understand. It is a killing offense to give me aid. No one is to give me food, shelter. Not even my brother can ever do so." He lifted Eðna's hand off his arm and placed it into her own lap. "And neither can you."

She closed her empty hand into a fist. Impossible. She would always help him, always.

"How can you…?" She breathed. "Where can you go?"

Brosa let the firestriker hang from his fingers. "I'll go into the wilderness. Say goodbye to my home, gather my things and go hide."

This was wrong. Everything wrong.

"That's not a good plan."

Brosa smiled, his broad smile that could break open a vault of clouds. He opened his arms wide, to invite her to look at the pitted, rock-strewn land all around. "Have you told the gods your plans?"

Just like her father, laying on humor and charm to hide the truth. She closed her eyes against the vision of Brosa and Jon juxtaposed, so much the same.

Something hard sat in her throat, and her words came out crumpled. "You said you didn't know me."

"Oh, Elskan." Brosa dropped the firestriker and took her hands, closing his fingers around her wrists. She shivered with the brush of his cold silver bracelets and sting of gravel on her palms. "You were with me in the highlands that night. At the trial, you were a breath away from being condemned together with me."

"You were protecting me?" But she was just trying to protect *him* from the men with rocks and hatred, and in the process they both got thrown to the wind, across this stark land.

"Why did you not tell me you saw those dead men?"

Eðna looked down at their hands, holding tight to one another. "I thought you would send me home before I got a chance to speak."

Brosa let go of her hands. "Ja, you're right. I would have." He exhaled, ran a hand through his hair again. "The gods know, I never planned for such a life. Maybe I'll find a cave near the sea, after I get you to the water."

He wanted to deliver her to the coast. The place where she'd come through to the 10th century, where she'd first seen the corpses and felt the seductive pull of Brosa's boat, even before she'd seen his face. His gorgeous ship, with its curves that shone honey-gold in the sun, so much like the colors of Brosa himself.

"Your ship!" Eðna's eyes opened wide. "You can leave on your ship."

"Slow down, Woman. I have no idea how. With which men. Or when." He brushed his hands on his wool, and dirt crumbled to the ground. "I need to see my home, get my belongings, and take you to the sea, so you can go to your own place. We have these four days before it begins."

Eðna echoed him. "Four days."

"Though there are some men who might like to get an early start on me. That's why we're traveling over this black ground. It's bleak, já. But a faster way to Hvítmork." He stood and reached for her hand. "Can you walk?"

She tried her ankle, gradually putting all her weight on it. "Já, I'm fine—"

"—You're fine," he said, at the same exact time, and smiled.

Brosa picked up the rest of Eðna's things—the knife and cloak and scraps of dried fish she'd flung everywhere. He left the berries, tiny and dry in this massive land.

"There are woods up ahead," he said.

Eðna lifted her eyes, but no forest filled the horizon. A few wizened birches stood alone against the moonscape. "Those are woods?"

"Já, well, this is not the greenest part of the land. But the ground may be warm there, with unseen water."

"They look like my woods from when I was little." She turned in a circle. "The whole place was a lot like this."

Brosa turned to take in the surroundings. "This is what it was like, where you lived as a child?"

"We had a bit more grass. Just enough to keep the animals alive."

He shook his head. "Any sane woman would leave it."

She smiled to herself and followed his strides up the hill.

None of the gnarled birches were any taller than Brosa. Flat rocks the size of coffee tables had been thrown by explosive force and honed by wind. Brosa dumped the pack beside one of them, with the food and drink and blankets he'd thrown onto Gull before leaving the assembly.

Eðna peeked inside the clump of trees. Twisted limbs hid an understory of thickly tangled juniper, dead and brown bushes mingling with the living. Gull began to nose through them, chewing on small bits of grass that poked through the evergreen skeletons. Brosa was already knee deep, stooping to collect sticks and twigs.

"We can sleep here," Brosa said. "I'll make a fire for you, to warm you in the night."

"I'll be fine," she said. She would be tucked in against him.

"I know," he said. But he didn't mention holding her. He hadn't drawn her into his big arms even once.

He stood and wiped his hands on his thighs, and a memory struck Eðna, so quick and vivid, she put a hand out to catch herself. A memory of Brosa the first day they met, limping toward her in the highlands, wiping his hands on his thighs to get dust off. So much dirt and dust on his shirt and in his bound-up beard. He said he was digging. In the highlands.

She'd pushed it away, all this time. She'd ignored what she herself had observed. And then stones were raining on him and nothing else mattered. She and Brosa were fleeing, and fighting each other. But now that they rested... She shook her head, but she couldn't force the images away. The dust on his back that day, as she rode with him on Gull. Eðna had lain her own cheek against Esa's bones.

Brosa hadn't held Eðna since they left the assembly. Nei. But he had once held a dead woman.

Brosa sat on a rock and sighted down the length of his knife to check its sting. Just beyond the point of the blade, he could see Eðna settling herself. She laid a cloak down on a flat rock and smoothed it with her palms. She knelt and tucked her skirts around her knees. Smoothed the cloth again.

The woman was a storm, clouds always mixing. Enraged one minute, crying the next, from banshee to maid. Determined, moving toward her dreams like an arrow. But she would stop for him, give him a shy smile that she showed no one else. He could watch her weave braids all day and night, her hands moving on the leather in beautiful rhythms and patterns.

What did she see when she looked at him?

He dropped the blade to his lap. He didn't want to contemplate that just now.

The knife needed honing, and he took out his stone.

At times, Eðna saw everything about him, so that he felt she knew his very bones. And then she failed to see what she'd done to his last shred of honor. His elskan, his good, sweet woman, stood up for him, full of rage. It cost him his honor and pride. And yet, it was a glorious thing she did, placing herself between him and danger.

Now she unwrapped dry fish and cheese and placed it on her rock.

He hid a smile. This was Eðna. She would set up their meal here in this bedraggled wood, as if they ate in a grand chieftain's hall. Outlawed on a bleak plain, they would eat dried berries from a table covered with a wool cloak, smoothed flat as fine linen.

He scraped stone against blade.

She hadn't spoken a word since they stopped here, but thank the gods she agreed she would leave him when they got to the sea. In truth, maybe they should go there now, but Hvítmork made sense first. He would need food, drink, clothing.

Gods, at least she didn't talk of going with him to the woods. He would not keep her any longer. Not with any of a dozen men eager to kill him, or worse.

The song of the stone moving across his knife seemed to lift and join the wind, and an unease grew in his gut. She hadn't spoken a word for an hour or more. His Eðna, always talking of plans. The woman was far too quiet. He gave up sharpening, and silence spread like wool, until he heard nothing but the trickling, meager stream and rippling of the blanket's edge in the breeze.

Her words were soft and small when she finally spoke, almost out of earshot. "You really did it. What they said you did."

Já, then, the silence might have been better.

Eðna pressed the cloak even tighter against the rock. It was flat as his honed blade already.

"You did that to your…" She let the cloak go and dropped her head into her hands. "To Esa's grave?"

He would have to answer Eðna sooner or later, but the single word he needed felt like a stone. "Já." To his own ears, he sounded pathetic. "She and Arulf were all I had that was mine."

Eðna wrapped herself in her own arms. She sat just outside his reach, and yet it felt as though she turned away on a distant ship, and he stood stranded on the shore.

"You remember my brother and his wife in the new hall." He saw Heirik and Ginn there, back on that simple day, when he was so ignorant. He thought he might seduce Eðna into staying with him for all his life. "I said I had no place there anymore."

The more he spoke, the farther Eðna seemed to sail. He moved toward her. Crouched beside her rock.

"The night you came, I had gone to the hills to…trade. My brother and Ginn have not had a child. I thought…I could..." Could what? He'd meant to trade his own family to the gods, so they would give a family to Heirik instead. But just now, crouching in this pathetic stand of trees, he knew that was not his true reason.

He took up a stone, weighed it in his hands.

"I was tired." He blew out breath and words. "I had nei more will. To laugh and slap men's backs. To smile at women and drink the ale. I dug into their grave, já. I didn't mean to ever return."

Brosa ducked to look at Eðna, to get her to lift her chin, but she would not. A cold moment passed, and she finally brought her eyes up to meet his. He saw understanding come, as if she drew aside the veil of words she wore. Slow knowledge of just how close Brosa had come to bringing on his own death that night. The night before they met.

Gods, he had to lighten this day. He winked and smiled, the way that men and women all liked. "When you called out in the hills, I thought you were Hel come to reap my soul."

She laughed—a sound more beautiful than wind-sigh in the trees—and she eased her grip on herself. "You did not, really."

"I truly did." He pitched the stone as far as he could. "I thought you would take me to the next life."

Eðna looked at her scraped palm. "I was nothing so powerful."

"Já," he said. "You were."

It took all his will not to lift her chin and kiss her.

Nei. He could not keep her any longer.

She turned and hurried to dig in the pack for food. With the sounds of wooden cups and knives rattling, he almost missed her quiet question.

"Your baby was in there, too?"

The stab was quick. "Of course he was. With his mother, as he should be."

"Please, I didn't mean you…" Eðna dropped the pack and came to him on her knees, placed her hand on his thigh, churning up a wave of shame and lust, even as they spoke of the dead. "I just don't know how it's done."

She hadn't meant to question his honor. She knew his heart and spirit were good, but she didn't know the logic of burying a child. She wasn't of this world.

"He was so small." Brosa dipped his fingers into the sluggish stream. "I buried him with his mother, so he would not be alone in the everlife."

After all, Arulf was his mother's, já? The babe had been with Esa for many months, but with Brosa for only a moment. The babe had hardly been his child. A bitter thought.

He let drops of water fall from his fingers.

Eðna got up and straightened herself as best she could, and Brosa looked up to her beautiful eyes.

Nei. He would not sit here before such a woman and lie to himself. He was a better man than that.

The moment he and the boy had spent together was long enough for them to become father and son. He named Arulf after his own father, showered his small head with the water that made them so, and Arulf would always be his child.

His only one. He would never do such a thing again.

"I'll find wood." He stood, and dust rained down on Eðna's table and cups.

"Já," she said. "Okay." That was all.

Brosa went into the sparse trees, to gather whatever might burn. He kicked at half-dead brush, weighing it in his mind. It was small tinder, but he could light it, perhaps burn a pile long enough to warm some stones to put inside her blankets for the night. Things would be better when he returned to the stone-table and ate with her. She would understand.

Eðna nudged one of the stones in the small fire-ring that Brosa was constructing. As he collected rocks and placed them, she neatened them, fixed them so they aligned with the others until the circle was complete.

Brosa came to crouch beside the fire ring. He shaped a bundle of twigs into a ball small enough to fit in his cupped hands.

He had good reason to stay on the other side of the ring of stones. Eðna's questions, and his raw answers, hung like the lowering clouds. She'd asked about his… Esa.

Eðna shifted one of the stones with her toe and almost laughed. During this bleak and ragged day, alone with Brosa on the wild edge of existence, she still choked on the word wife, even in her silent thoughts. As if it mattered that he'd once loved someone they said was so beautiful and breezy and light.

Brosa rolled his sleeves up to work. His silver bracelets shone bright on his dusty wrists, and Eðna's heart broke again. She imagined him dressing that morning—just yesterday?—in the family's booth at the assembly, putting on his best clothes for the trial, silent and alone. He'd known, hadn't he? That something this bad could happen. He'd smiled and acted nonchalant for Eðna's sake.

Now, he took bits of touchwood from his pack. The dried fungus crumbled in his fingers, black and flammable, and he struck metal to light it. He shaped the tangle of twigs in his two palms and lifted the bundle to his mouth, to blow easily and feed air to the tiny spark. So gentle, the way he held the beginnings of fire in his hands.

His shirt was cut like her Da's, down to his knees, and with a high neckline and linen ties that kept it closed under his chin. Even when those ties were undone, exposing the simple Thor's hammer and another mysterious leather cord at his throat, it was just a small taste of his skin.

She'd seen him push his sleeves up to work many times, to dig the fire pit for the seer's feast, to set to eating and drinking with his uncle, to lift a small boy and toss him, catch him. But most often his wrists were covered with the bracers she'd braided. His tunic was even longer than his shirt, and wrapped with a thick leather belt. His pants were tucked into leg bindings that twined around his calves, from knee down to ankle.

Gods, he was so hidden. She hadn't noticed it before.

Brosa looked at her over the glowing handful of tinder, and his hesitant smile sent swift currents of blood through Eðna's body. What would the rest of him look like, without all that linen and wool and leather tied up under his chin and wrapped around his legs? Without his thick belt hung with blades and tools?

"—Stop!" She said it out loud. Gods, this was not the time. It would never be the time.

"Gods take it!" Brosa growled, and stamped on the small flame. He stomped and stifled the fire he'd so carefully coaxed to life.

"Eiðr could find us even without the flames, nei doubt. But sending smoke into the sky just begs him to come."

Eðna looked far up to Brosa's face, but the sun obscured his expression. He stood so tall above her, his hand halfway through his hair again, stuck in the tangles.

"Why did you start the fire, then?"

"I wanted you to be warm." He dropped his hands, exasperated. "I thought I could, but…the risk is too great."

Brosa unbuckled his cloak. He shrugged to let it fall from his shoulders, and then he lifted it to the wind. It got caught in the air currents and waved and snapped above Eðna's head, a brown, woolen sail against a looming, lavender and steel sky. The cloak was unbelievably large. Brosa secured it across two big rocks, forming a fort.

"Try it," he said. "The warmth from the ground will be trapped inside."

Brosa stood with his arms crossed, waiting for her to crawl into the makeshift fort. Her skirts got caught in themselves and she struggled on her knees to get all the way in and turn to Brosa. "Come." She reached for him.

He handed her a thin roll of furs. "You can sleep on these. I'll keep watch."

She peeked out from under the cloak, and one corner of the fort sagged over her head. He stood with his boots planted wide on the rocks, his beautiful lips pressed together.

He wasn't going to lie next to her. Not at all tonight.

He was angry, já, of course. Svana and Eiðr had destroyed Brosa's life. If he didn't feel a churning sickness and rage in his gut right now, he would not be normal. He'd truly be a monster if he felt no guilt and hopelessness. And yet, he wouldn't take Eðna's comfort, her protection, even though he desperately needed it.

Gods, he must have felt this way about her all through these weeks together. She'd refused his help and comfort so many times, her chin held high. Adamant, pretension.

She ducked back into the fort and unrolled the furs.

He was right, the ground was warm from subterranean water, but it was hard and uneven. She lay there, a rock digging into her hip, and she reviewed all the times she'd pushed Brosa away, every one of those moments making this absence so much worse.

She closed her eyes and listed the lost chances. The day they met, he would have held her up when she was afraid. At the river's edge, the day he fed her with his hands, he would have kissed her. He'd been so close, she felt his beard against her chin. He would have given her his own mint and rosemary taste, instead of placing cheese in her mouth. So many moments in the woods, when he rested casually with his back against a tree, he would have dropped the wood he was carving and come to her in a heartbeat. In the dark hall, he would have held her close, pressed his body to hers. Gods, the thought made her turn in her furs, restless, mind churning.

Eðna looked out beyond the wool roof, and the gray sky rolled out, endless. She searched the distance, the indifferent black land and far-off steam.

How did she get here, to this place where she cared so much?

She closed her eyes and listed clean things. Sheets, blankets, linen tunics, pillows, a mattress, not too soft but much softer than this. A view of glistening glass and bustling work. She would soon be safe in her impeccable home, where no rocks dug into her back and no one pursued her with an ax. She would have a table to eat at, not a boulder.

Gull's soft snorts and Brosa's pacing, mixed with the sounds of the land, were so steady and familiar now, they dissolved into silence. So quiet, Eðna felt Earth shift in its slow process of grinding and settling. Moving on a time scale that made her own 1000-year dive seem insignificant, like a tossed pebble. Ginn believed that Saga sent them both here. But it seemed vain to Eðna, that a goddess would care. Two women out of time were of no consequence. Would Saga even notice her here? If Saga were real.

Eðna experimented with the logic. If there were truly a goddess, which there was not, but if there were, had Saga purposefully carried Eðna to the time she wanted to reach? The time she was fated to go? Or had she flicked Eðna with one supernatural finger, sending her spinning and flailing? A hummingbird thrown by a tornado, accidentally landing on its one desired bleeding-heart bush in an endless forest of thorns?

Soon she would go home and not give a damn. Her mission—*revised* mission—remained the same as before the trial. Get Brosa settled, then get out of this savage, backward place.

Until then, the furs and fort enclosed her in Brosa's scent. He had wrapped his warmest possessions all around her like a bower, and she curled up inside, wanting him.

Brosa drew the land's warmth up through his boots. He could not stay still. He scuffed big circles in the dirt, looking out in every direction. Flipped his knife, again and again, though his uncle was not here to compete and boast about his grace. He shook his boots and scraped them against rocks, quiet so as not to wake Eðna, until not a grain more of dust or stone could be shaken from them.

It would be the darkest part of night soon, and he searched in the dimming light, alert for anyone who might come and attack before the proper time. All he saw was the endless land, as dark as the sand at the fishing camp. He stooped and gathered some of the coarse dirt. It was made of fine black bits, like the coast, but dry. He rubbed his fingers together, and the grains fell, soft and fine as a woman's hair.

He lifted his eyes.

It surprised him, as it sometimes did—how graceful the world was in its curves and hollows. The expanse around him filled his heart. He led Eðna on this barren route so he could keep watch in every direction, and still, without grass or bloom, the land stopped his breath.

He sat on a big rock to watch the light shift over the ground. He could just see the far-off geysirs hiss and snort, like the great beast that he imagined the island to be. The sweep of the land let his thoughts flow, and his body eased and slowed with the island's breath.

Overhead, clouds formed and broke. Thoughts in Ymir's skull. The giant was in a pensive mood, and they moved slowly.

Brosa leaned his elbows on his knees, and let his knife hang from its strap.

Ginn told stories about the sky and world. She said it was like a child's wooden ball that turned in unseen hands, and the turning made night and day. Strange. But weighing the idea now, it was no stranger than the waking and dreaming of a giant. In truth, the clouds looked more like tufts of steam than thoughts, and they did move in time with the wind.

He let his breath go from deep in his throat, and in the cool of near-dark, the smallest cloud rose from his own mouth and drifted, until the air and the night took it. He breathed. The steam moved. In the empty space where his breath had been, something wavered on the blade's edge of making sense, something about clouds and their ways.

Eðna turned in her sleep, inside the poor shelter he'd made for her. He should have taken her to the sea long ago. She would be home in her ice hall by now. But he ached to have her sit in his home with him, the place where he grew up, just one more time.

He was still at last, and his mind drifted as slow as Ymir's, until his thoughts were nothing but colors and the sense of Eðna turning in her sleep, of all things turning. The sky darkened until it met the silver-black land and melted into it, like metal at the forge.

ᛊ

Svana pushed on through the empty land, racing her horse faster and farther than it should go. It was a pale ghost of the horse she would have ridden in better days. When she was lovely and walked at a slow and dignified pace. Now Eiðr rode hard in the lead, and all the while he seemed to search the land under their feet, as if wights might reach up and snag his legs and trip him.

If only they would. He would fall off his rearing horse and bash his head on a rock.

Svana had been so close, on the cliff. She could have watched Eiðr drop into that endless expanse, a screaming speck. She wished for his arms thrown out, shock in his eyes as he fell and fell. But he had refused to come up to the cliff's edge. "I have no time for looking now, Woman. We need to beat Ulfsson to Hvítmork."

Svana knew, Brosa would be at his house. He was honorable and led by his heart, not his mind. He would worry about Eðna, já, but he would want to take her to his boyhood home. It was too bad. If he truly were at the sea's edge, Svana could watch Eðna drown at Saga's bidding, and then Svana could jump onto Brosa's ship and they would sail on to their rightful life.

Svana tried once or twice with small suggestions to steer Eiðr away from the house and toward the sea, toward Brosa's ship. Seaward, to justice. He did not listen.

Svana's poor horse heaved, suffering with such running, stumbling on stones, and Eiðr still pushed them on. He spoke again of the house at Hvítmork, of how he would tie up Brosa's cousins who stayed behind to guard and keep the hearth. "We'll surprise the stupid goats, tie them fast, so they will not aid Ulfsson when he comes."

"But, Brosa will not—"

"—Enough!" Eiðr drew his horse up, and it reared and complained. Svana's weak horse skidded to a halt too. "I have heard you speak of Brosa too many times." Her beloved's name was filthy and wrong in Eiðr's mouth, and he spat it like foul skyr.

"Husband, I want you to find him—"

"I said enough." Eiðr spoke gently now, an eerie green light in his eyes. "Give the animal a rest, Svana. We've arrived."

Svana looked in every direction. A black-dirt world of nothing lay everywhere, and at their feet a steaming pool no bigger than a dye cauldron. Too small and too hot for the horses to drink. Nei matter, at least her sagging animal would get a moment of rest. She slid down off the horse.

Eiðr pushed her to her knees.

"What are you?—"

"You have talked of the sea enough times, Woman. You are somehow aiding Ulfsson."

Svana struggled to stand, but he held her down, his hand rough and tight on the back of her neck. She twisted in his grip, so she could look up into his sneering face. The wind moved his greasy hair, and his eyes showed no pity. What did he mean to do to her?

He let go of Svana so he could dig in his pack. "I will know for certain." He dropped a small iron ring into the water. It sank to the rocky bottom, dull and black as the stones. Eiðr pressed down on Svana's head, so that her nose was just above the surface. "Get it, Wife."

The pool bubbled like cooking water, and the steam turned to sweat on her cheeks and eyelids. She could not see the ring, only the shifting, hot mist and her husband's dusty boots.

"Eiðr, please. You're angry at Ulfsson. Let me soothe you—"

"—Still your mouth! If you are innocent of aiding that fool, you'll find the ring. If your hand comes out empty…" Eiðr stopped, his voice choked with emotion.

What? What would Eiðr do, if she couldn't stand the water and she pulled her arm out?

He let go of Svana's head. "Find it."

The steam moved in a rising wind, and the ring slipped in and out of view. Svana's hair blew into her mouth, and she swallowed, throat dry, sick with dread. She looked for anyone who might stand for her, but Eiðr's two men, the only witnesses, were smiling with dumb delight. An ordal, here in the wilderness, in front of no court but these idiots.

She had to do it. If she refused, she might never leave this dark land—or maybe she would leave, without an arm, or worse.

Her hands shook, and it took two tries to get her sleeve rolled up.

The gods had been playing with her like a cat with a bug, but surely they were on her side. They would not let her fail. She called to them, swiftly, silently. To Freya for justice. To Skadi for the touch of cold snow, and for speed. She murmured to any guardian spirit that was hers, had always been hers, but had not revealed itself to her yet. "Please come."

A soft bless came on the wind—not words, but the faintest sound of women chanting, the way they had in Ginn's grand hall. Svana caught one last glimpse of the ring and plunged her arm in.

The water felt warm, and it seemed the ordal would be easy. But suddenly it was hot, so hot. It stung as if she cut herself with her kitchen knife everywhere at once, sliced and stabbed her skin, bathed open wounds with lye soap. She yearned to pull her arm free. Fought against the fierce desire.

Why was she doing this?

The ring. Get the ring.

It slipped out of her fingers, and she stirred the water, stirring and scalding, forcing her hand down when every part of her screamed to yank it out. Forcing sounds down in her throat so Eiðr would not mock her. Nei. She would not give him her cries. She stirred the water, searching, searching, and humming with the chanting of the seer's women inside the wind. She burned and burned.

"Svana Sting-Eyes."

She snapped her head up and growled. Who taunted her now?

And all around her was calm.

The air was still. The men were gone, as if taken by the chanting wind. All that remained was a fox pup—whole and gray, no longer bloody and blind on her nithing stick. Its small dusty body matched the dark ash-land, so that she could have missed it, except for its brilliant blue gaze.

It sniffed at the steaming water, and its ears pointed forward, curious.

"Stinging eyes," the fox said. The old teasing.

Svana snapped, "It means clear-seeing, too."

"Clear as that pool?" The fox pointed its nose toward the water where it steamed and curled around her arm, and Svana laughed like a harpy.

And then she saw things in the mist. Brosa strong and fierce, fighting ten men with just a shield and a blade. She saw him on his ship, brave gaze turned to a far horizon. She saw Eðna curled up cold and dead in a pile of ash, like a bird in a singed nest.

Svana did not see Eiðr. His death was of no consequence. Nei, only Eðna's. The woman, with her frozen blue lips, was the way to justice.

The fox spoke calmly. "I forgive you for my neck. You needed my voice. Now you need my snout."

With its nose, the fox nudged her arm.

Svana's finger caught the ring.

She tore her arm free of the water with a shout and held the ring to the sky. The clouds were as black as the iron, and wind and cold rain seared her skin. Thunder broke in the land beneath her knees.

Eiðr stood dumb, his arm with no hand hanging at his side. He was a small and grimy man. If her husband wanted to go to Hvítmork then so be it. Brosa would snap him like a stick.

"Whatever it is you think I am doing, you can see I'm innocent."

"For now," Eiðr said.

What did he mean by that?

"You found the ring, but your arm is burned. If you were free of any fault, you would be unharmed."

Would the gods play with her forever? She let her stinging arm hang at her side. She carefully did not touch it, did not cry.

"Give me the ring, Woman. Let's go."

One day she would be free of Eiðr. Today, her life was her husband's to rule, and he was more cruel with each day that passed. But he could not see that she had the fox. The fox was her own.

Eðna traced letters in the dust with a stick. She sat beside the measly stream, barely a trickle under the enormous gray sky. Tiny, but it bubbled with delicious heat from an underground spring, and she warmed her toes and breathed in the woolly-smelling steam.

Brosa snored. He laid curled up beside a massive rock, where he'd slid down into sleep. He'd finally agreed to let Eðna take watch for a while, with a solemn agreement that she would wake him in a couple of hours.

As if she would wake him.

Hair spilled over half his face, his tension gone. So exhausted, he hardly moved, but his chest rose with steady breaths, sure and alive. His body was finally easy and free in the absence of worry. There would need to be another volcanic eruption, magma racing their way, sending red rivers out to drown him, before Eðna would shake him out of this peace.

With her stick, Eðna drew an egret's long, strong legs wading at the edge of the streamlet. Graceful, snow white birds, associated with water, though they did not swim. A few simple drops of rain landed on her drawing and on her hands, and she looked to the sky.

Brosa said that tonight, the second night of their flight, would be their last before reaching Hvítmork. Another day after that and they would be at the ocean. Just two more nights to hold each other—a final bit of comfort before they parted ways forever. She wouldn't go and curl up against him right now. She'd vowed to keep watch. She wouldn't think about the bigger reason to leave him alone, to not go fit herself into the circle of his arms. He didn't want her to.

She sketched a wing. Maybe she was wrong—again—about what things meant between a man and a woman. Brosa called her Fine One, and he touched her face as if she were made of precious glass, delicate and fleeting as steam. Had she been a distraction? A last comfort on the way to his trial?

Well, he got a surprise, já? She stuck with him longer than he expected.

She flipped her stick the way that Brosa did his knife, and caught it over and over. By the time he woke, she would be good at this. Then she could try a blade. A handful of rain drops came again, and the steel clouds pressed down, unsure if they should pour. The few drops that came down joined the steamy stream.

She should have avoided him right from the start. From the first moment he called to her in the highlands, or even sooner, when some impossible seductive force drew her to his ship.

That first night, riding on that stolen horse to Hvítmork, for a brief moment she'd imagined that she went to some far planet or gray moon. But really, she'd gone farther than that. She'd traveled not only to the past, but into memory. She'd dropped into a 10th century longhouse, já, and into her fears, as though they were physically real, a dark room, surrounded by mud-and-grass walls. She'd flailed and spiraled through time, and landed in a mire of feud, and of betrayal as big and awful as her Da's. She searched for the words, for this bundle of emotion she felt toward Brosa, toward her father.

Nothing.

Brosa turned toward her, as he often did in his sleep. Hopefully, he basked in dreams of sunny fields or expanses of calm ocean, friendly waves bumping the hull the way Gull nosed his ear.

Eðna rose quietly and took the shawl from her shoulders, folded it and with the greatest care slid it under Brosa's head.

At last, full morning came, and at least one thing was as Eðna expected. Brosa was angry that she hadn't woken him. When she said good morning, he grumbled. He knelt by the stream and turned away from her to splash water on his face and rake his fingers through his hair.

He tied his bracers tight using just one hand. The leather turned and locked into place with an ingenious twist, the way his brother did it. He pulled his hair back tight and tied it in a knot. "We have to go."

It was the last thing he said for a long while. They took turns riding Gull, and after some time, tense and silent, they came to grass. The plants were sparse at first, but Brosa and Eðna and Gull left the volcanic land, the tufts became closer together, taller, greener.

Eðna dismounted to give the horse a break. Brosa trudged ahead, and pale wisps fell out of the knot in his hair and curled in the misty air like snowbit tendrils. Eðna yearned to neaten him, and she waded through the grass, thinking of order, and then of nothing but untying that knot and combing her fingers through his waves, darkening to gold now in the soft drizzle. Braiding the sides of his hair for him, the way he often did himself, pulling his hair up off his face, but letting the rest fall over his shoulders.

The rain began to truly fall. She turned up her sore palms and caught it. Her revised mission remained, so why was she like this?

Eðna looked to the heights, as if the hills might answer, and at the top of a far rise, dark figures stood against the steel clouds. She tensed, but they were not men. Two sheep, one with a single horn that curled up from his shaggy head, the other horn missing. Behind the sheep, the sky roiled.

A memory tugged at her. She'd seen something like this before. On her way to the city with Brenna, so long ago. Little Eðna stumbled along behind Brenna and her boyfriend Gren, dragging her blanket as she made it up a big rise in the land. At the top, there was...not sheep. No. It was Brenna.

Brenna stood in silhouette, turned toward Gren, and she leaned into him with every bit of herself. Every thread of Brenna's being was bundled up in her man. Even her dress moved in a breeze and caught itself up in his legs.

Infatuation.

Yes! Finally, that was the word for this. This sudden, intense longing that had blinded her to everything but Brosa.

He was kind, já. A gentle flirt and a strong defender. Undeniably gorgeous. Lonely in a way that Eðna understood deep in her body, where something she had not formerly defined as loneliness crouched inside her, too.

People called it a crush. Yes. She did feel crumpled, smashed flat as the grass. But now that she knew its name, she could escape its effects. Her loyalty lay far beyond Brosa, her contribution to something so much bigger than herself, so much bigger than him holding her, his mouth, the way he kissed her so soft and then changing, deepening, more.

—Stop! Again and again, she had to stop following these paths. They all started with the lab and ended with desire.

Soft rain gathered on her eyelashes and her nose.

"Don't worry," she told Gull. "I'm leaving. As soon as I can."

The number of trees increased, and they left the dark plain and climbed into verdant fields. The birches' white bark was chipped and underlaid with rain-deepened colors, darkest brown and copper. She counted 347 trees before softening her focus to see them as one. A giant living creature, shifting in slumber and ruffling its feathers.

She would describe the forest to Vera that way, like a great bird preening, and all the smaller beasts were part of it. The grass, in places, was as high as Brosa's waist, and it swayed with the chaotic gusts of wind and rain. The land here, this world, was more messy and gigantic than anyone could have comprehended.

"Eðna, come back from the trees." Brosa's voice was rough from disuse, softened by rain. Irritated. "We need to move faster."

Another long incline of mossy, rocky hills loomed above them, with enormous green humps that could break a leg. Brosa was at her side, finally, for the first time in hours, rearranging the packs on the horse. "Get up on Gull."

He stood so close now, so good, his warmth and presence and skin. *Infatuation.* She named the condition, willed it to pass.

Gods, she was weak, naive. Brosa had ignored her, stalked off ahead, hadn't spoken to her all day, and still she swooned over him. Now he was giving her orders.

She growled. "No way." She lifted her head and pushed on into the rain. "I can walk."

"Come, Woman. The hills are turning to mud." Water coursed down his face into his beard. "Get up and ride."

Eðna looked again up the long hill. The grass bowed under heavy gusts. The moss would be slimy, the way hard. The idea of riding Gull was tempting.

But when did Brosa decide he was in charge of her?

"Nei," she said, pressing on. "I could run across this island in my slippers and shift."

In a second, Brosa's hands were around her waist, lifting her onto Gull.

Eðna kicked. "Get off me!"

Gull stomped and shifted, and Eðna cursed and closed her eyes against Brosa's stupid insistence. He would not tell her what to do. She jammed her knee into Brosa's gut, and he huffed and growled back at her, and a wind came and howled around them so that she had to shout. "I can walk in mud!"

"I want you on the horse, Woman!"

He got Eðna up onto Gull, halfway, sideways, and she struggled, and then stopped—

—Brosa was so alive. Shouting at her in this downpour, trying to set her on the horse, his eyes were bright and vivid, finally. At last, Brosa was angry. Luminous, like the first time she saw him.

Eðna dug her fingers into his hair and pulled him to her. She pressed her mouth to his, and he murmured *good* against her lips, sweet pressure, a thirsty kiss. Rain beat against the back of her head, but Eðna tasted summer. Rosemary and angelica on Brosa's tongue. Water coursed down onto their faces and into their mouths, and they were somewhere else, a golden field, a hearth. She saw home fires and all the stars of her childhood. Brosa pressed his forehead to hers, and they breathed together, in this different place.

"Elskan." He ran his thumb along her wet jaw. "I promised some things I should not have." He burrowed in close under her hair. A place for a man's secrets. "Before I knew the outcome of my trial."

"What are you saying?"

He said more words, but thunder broke and swallowed them. The ground was coming apart, and Eðna dropped into it, her mind, her heart, sinking. Rain ran in miserable dribbles underneath her dress.

She'd stayed with Brosa through everything, laid in his arms, given him her mouth to kiss, her hands to hold. Now, he set her on the horse like putting away a stack of blankets on a shelf.

"My dreams were simple," he said. "But they're gone to the crows now. I have nothing to offer you." He gestured around himself, as though his meager belongings were laid out in the mud. "Not even a blanket or a piece of fish. Tomorrow, I'll leave you at the sea."

The sea. Right. She was going there, as planned. As if none of these things with Brosa had happened. As if she could just kneel in the sea-foam, look up into Brosa's eyes and plunge her hands into the water, with the press of his lips still fresh on hers.

Not a chance.

Oh gods, what had she done? Like Ginn said, she'd gotten tangled up with him. And now she saw it. She could not leave him. Not to an unknown fate. The lab was a foreign country, so far from this windswept, thunderous field. Her landing at the sea's edge was so long ago. The fishing hut, the dead men, Brosa's ship limned with golden light.

His ship.

He could leave Iceland.

"Your ship! I can help you get away on your boat."

When they left the assembly, Brosa said he didn't know which men would go with him on the ship. She could do it, yes, she could help him get to Norway. "I can be your crew."

"Gods, nei!" His voice matched the storm. "You are not going anywhere with me. You're going home."

Eðna swayed in the wind, through another growl of thunder. "I'm strong," she said. "We'll make it to Norway—"

"—Hold, Woman." Brosa silenced her. "You are going home. You don't belong here."

Eðna's throat closed. She sat completely still and hollow, and rain poured down her face and into her mouth. She was at the trial again, Brosa turning away. *I don't know this woman.*

She didn't belong here.

A stream of information in her eyes, any content at all, would scrape her mind clean, scour her soul, but there was nothing. Just her raw self, hot with shame that she had not understood what Brosa felt, what he meant when he said that he'd give her his worth, his life. She'd thought once again that she could help him, that she did belong with him more than she had belonged anywhere in a long, long time.

"Fine." She choked. "Just get away from me."

"Já," Brosa said. "I will, right after you agree to ride this horse."

Eðna saw Ginn on the vids, back in the lab, talking about the chief. How he sent her away, sent her back to the 22nd, because he feared for her safety. Pushing her away again and again out of terror that he might lose her.

"You're afraid." Eðna said it to the rain, so Brosa might not hear, but maybe he would. "Just like your brother."

Brosa turned on her, his eyes wild. “This is not my brother’s kind of fear.” He spit water with every word. “It’s nei fear of unformed things that could happen because of his mark. This is real danger, Eðna. Men with weapons. A bare land, not even a fire for warmth.”

“Okay then, I will ride Gull.” She sat up tall, tugged the laces tight on her bodice, and then turned the horse toward the sea—the way she thought the sea must be. What did it matter anyway, if she just left now?

She and Gull started walking, but she halted the horse.

She pressed her eyes shut with two fists. What a mess. And Brosa thought he could fix it by getting rid of her. Her Da was always like this, saying he wanted the best for her, never letting her choose. Always trying to get her to do things—ride her horse, drink her milk, learn to shoot.

She felt her father’s arms around her so viscerally, as if he were actually here. *Good job, Eðna.* His hand over her hand. *Now point the bow upward just a little.*

A hard, familiar rush of guilt came. She left her father alone, without a shred of loyalty. And it did matter. Regardless of what Brosa wanted, it mattered to Eðna, and she would be loyal this time. She would complete her job, to see Brosa to safety, and only then would she go.

She turned Gull toward Hvítmork once more and walked on ahead. Brosa stayed behind for a while, then walked after her, wordless.

Eðna settled into the saddle, and let the horse take her, and Gull walked on a steady, sure line, as if he could feel the pull of his own warm stable, so near now, over just another rise and then another. The wind settled, and the rain slowed until it became a drizzle again. The drizzle turned to mist and then dissipated. Black clouds shifted and broke, and the sky open into a dull gray-green.

She let Brosa pass, to lead the way, but they didn’t speak. Now, he walked ahead with his drenched head bowed under the enormous sky. The land had been crushed under the storm and reshaped, and an endless expanse of lush, dense grass spread away in all directions, all blown flat by the wind. Every blade laid down, and Brosa moved among them, dragging his fingers along. He lifted the stalks, and the leather ties on his bracers mingled with the green. The grass waved as he went by, and laid back down with a damp sigh.

Soon they would get to Hvítmork. Over one of these hills, the land would drop away and down to Ginn's farm. The great hall would rise, ominous and hulking. The place where Brosa and Eðna had once hidden behind the high seat, where Brosa pressed his forehead to the runes carved into his brother's chair. The hall where Eðna saw Ginn's hand slip underneath the hem of Heirik's shirt and heard the chief's ragged breath against his wife's throat. When Ginn kissed Heirik, his black hair enclosed them, so that even in Eðna's memory they turned away, and she could not know the secret of how it worked. How souls and skin fit together.

Brosa walked among the knee-high rocks. He slid his palms over their rough, familiar curves, and damp moss came away.

He drew memories up, as if the rocks themselves had saved his old thoughts and gave them back to him now. So many hiding and hunting games, crouching right here with his small bow and blank arrows, waiting for Heirik, so he could shoot him. He'd written paths and maps with his fingers in this sand. Sat here with Svana, out of view of the world, edging toward her, curious.

He lifted his hand from the rock, as if he could stop the flow of memories of that woman. He felt in his ribs and his hands, that she was to blame. She had more to do with him being outlawed than he yet knew.

Nei matter now. He threw off thoughts of her and stooped to pick up the smaller rocks that lay scattered at his feet. So many times he'd used these stones to build halls for the elves, the sun on the back of his neck sending sweat down under his shirt as he worked. So many halls and hearths built and joyfully torn down to start again. He felt, as a child, that the elves might not be real. That these halls he built were for play. But there are things a man can't be sure of.

Gull snorted from far behind, and Brosa closed his eyes.

Back there was Eðna. And he'd hurt her, again.

He'd hidden the truth from her, drew her into his arms when he had no right, turned his back on her at the trial, turned her away again now. Failed her so many times, he'd rather not count.

That she wanted him, after all he had done, all that had passed, he could not fathom. Stubborn Eðna, tense as a mast-line. Brave to pull him in and press her mouth to his like that. Gods, the thought threw sparks across his skin. He closed his fist on moss. Nei matter his mind's vow to send her home. His body had made no such promise.

She walked now, with her head down, letting Gull find his way beside her. She had her dress tied up in its big knot, and her hair spilled everywhere, dark and made for hiding, whispering underneath. He'd lightened them both with his tale of mistaking her for a spirit the day they met, but in truth, she was that powerful. She'd risen from his land, ink-haired and fine, and she'd breathed new life into his chest.

It would be good if he could show her what he saw, show her his thoughts and memories. If he had a way to give her his stories through the veil in her eyes, she could see her own courage and strength. She could see what he was like in better days, too. Strong and gloriously handsome at fifteen, já? So the maids said. He would like to show Eðna that man—the boy he'd been.

It ripped him apart to say she didn't belong here, when every part of him knew she did. That she belonged right here, tucked under his chin with his beard messing up her hair.

He shook himself.

It couldn't be. He'd had to say the words. Had to hurt her enough to make her leave.

He pulled himself up over the last big rock and there, below him, was home.

The rain and wind had left the house as shaggy as his uncle's hair. Shovels and scythe handles leaned against the strong, solid walls, waiting to be repaired. Shining fish dangled from crossed poles, waiting for tomorrow's sun to come dry them until they were crisp. The house dog lifted his ears and head, and stood to stretch, and goats wandered between the house and the homefield, where the grass already grew thick and tall. It would soon grow to his shoulders, then be shorn and dried to keep the animals alive in winter.

He'd witnessed the turn of grass to sheep twenty-one times now, though he could not remember the first few times, when he spent his days curled against his mother's breast, too small to know the names of seasons. Of evernight and harvest.

The sense of a sun-warmed shirt came over Brosa, or a night-blanket tucked tight. This was his place. When he was a boy, this land had simply been the world, its boundaries set by his grandfather's torch and kept true by his brother's walls. And beyond, naturally, the byways to the assembly and coast, the tents at the fishing camp and the edge of the sea. He'd felt his father's boat rock underneath him, matching the motion of his own drifting thoughts and dreams. But that was for play. He had not truly understood going somewhere.

When he went to trade—was it three summers ago?—it was the first time he'd thought of Hvítmork as a place. A bowl in the land, with his house at the center. A thing that could be held up and examined the way a sharp-eyed trader might look at a silver cup.

Many times when he was away, he'd thought of this farm with longing, taking comfort from knowing this house stood strong. Freezing nights at sea with his men, when they knew that not all would wake in the morning, he huddled on the deck and dreamed of this place with its well-oiled doors at both ends, and neat mudrooms where he stamped his boots and rested his scythe. He'd imagined meals and ale, and long slow winter nights of games and women's braids. The stable just there, not far from the back door, and golden Fjoðr coming to him. The forge on the hillside above, and the bath where he'd spent so many hours concerned with how he looked and smelled.

He laughed. Small concerns, seen now from his new situation.

The dog had come up to greet him, and it fit its head under Brosa's hand. The animal urged him along. Brosa turned to Eðna, and his voice was hoarse. "Come."

He sounded like his brother, and so he started again. "Eðna, will you come with me?" And he knew at once, as if the words woke the knowledge in him, that he needed her to come. He couldn't face this without her.

She came to stand beside him, with her smell of leaves and travel-dust. The braver of the two of them, já. She stepped past him, silently, and the dog went with her down the hill. This is how it would become now. Women, men, even the animals, all moving beyond him.

Brosa stamped his feet in the mudroom, though his boots were full of water. He filled his lungs with the smell of iron tools and fresh dirt, home once more. He threw open the door to the inner hall.

Arn and his cousins sat by the heartstone, cups in their hands and voices slurred and happy. The fire had gone to embers, but their faces shone with too much ale, and one raised a mug in welcome and laughed. "The golden boy, come home so soon."

Brosa snapped. "To the stables. All of you!"

They saw something in him, and they tripped over themselves and fumbled to get out the back door.

Brosa bent over the hearth and moved a log aside, and when he stirred the ash, flames grew. With a stick, he took a bit of flame from the hearth, and he lit the lamps that hung from the wall posts. The cups were so small, in his hands they looked like curled, dead leaves, every one of them nearly out of oil. They flared to life, and then settled, in turn.

He smiled for Eðna and spread his arms to encompass the house and all that was in it. "Come, Woman. Sit by my fire."

Her skin was like sweet milk, soft from the rain and glowing in the firelight. She had a small smile on her lips, the way a woman smiled for her husband, and in a breath, the past weeks rushed away as if it were the first day he knew her. As if she'd come fresh from the spirit world and into his house.

A life formed in his mind in an instant, of years together with Eðna, here where his parents made their home, and Magnus and Amma before them. He would carry her over the threshold so she would not trip, and they would sit by this fire and share drink and games, and he would honor her with his work in the day, and his body at night. For a beat of his heart, Eðna was fresh as cream, and he had never hurt her.

As fast as it came, the vision was lost like a cloud of breath in the night. He saw the truth, that she shivered in a thin dress and soaked leather that must weigh as much as a sheep. The dew-soft skin around her lips was more blue than cream, and she held a shawl tight around her like a shield.

"Come to the fire, get warm." He reached for a blanket from the bench to wrap her in.

At his feet, furs were tossed on the floor, and blankets mashed into the dust—the men had not cleaned all week. Ale was spilled on a cloak that lay over one of the hearthstones—blankets and cloaks that were woven by the women of this house, with the work of their hands, and with wool from the sheep he and his brother and uncle raised and sheared.

He kicked aside a heap of fabric and growled, "A man should not be so careless, when he has such a home." He took a lamp from the wall, spilling oil, and went to the pantry.

He yanked the door handle, and it held tight, as he knew it would. He smacked the door with his palm, then pressed his head against the wood and closed his eyes. A man did not plunder his family's own pantry. It was a lesson for little boys, and he knew it well. The women were the keepers of the keys. His Ma, then Hildur, now Ginn.

"I am sorry, sister," he murmured. Against everything that was right and good, he broke the lock.

Inside, he pressed the lamp handle into the sod wall, and the light reared like a horse. He shook out a blanket from the shelf and laid it on the bed. He piled supplies on top of it with no thought or sense.

He should plan for food and supplies to get settled in the woods. A hatchet and arrows to hunt, furs for his bed, honey in case of wounds, but he could not imagine those things. Could not even see what he heaped onto the pile, only memories of this bed, where he'd slept as a young married man, with his new wife. Five summers ago? More? The room held Esa's simple smile, her scent of milk and sea-dew And Eðna's richer scent of woods.

Stubborn Eðna. She would not leave.

She stood at the door now, her hands pressed against the frame as if to hold it open. She looked at him with pity, and it built up his rage.

"Leave me be, Woman."

He pulled boxes out from far back on the shelves. Long candles, wrapped in cloth and stored for winter. Dried lavender from the south, that women used in soap. A box full of clean rags, made from shirts and sails that had worn thin. Balls of poorly spun thread. A key to nothing. Farther back, a small wooden chest, just the size of his two hands. It held things of his father's—all the tools to keep himself clean and well. A silver spool for tooth-thread, a comb for his beard. A clean man respects the gods, his woman, and himself.

Brosa shook his head. Would he ever need any of this? If he lived and grew old in the woods?

Nei matter. It all went into the heap on the bed.

"—Brosa."

He packed two handfuls of dried cod in a clean piece of linen. Grabbed butter rounds that were wrapped in birch leaves.

"Brosa." Eðna's bony hand gripped his wrist. "Stop, please."

He pulled out of her grasp. "Let me be—"

"—Don't," she said. "You don't need to take everything."

But there was one thing he did need. He pushed aside a small stack of blankets and got his hand around the long piece of wood that he'd hidden back there. He drew it out into the light.

"My steerboard handle."

Longer and wider than his arm, it was made of wood from Norway and carved by his father. Brosa had added his own name, when he learned to write it. He ran his thumb over the jagged-edged letters that he'd made so long ago.

The steerboard of a ship was taller than two full grown men, and it stayed in the ship, but every man had his own handle. Out of all the parts of a boat, it was the most alive. This was the piece that responded to a man's touch and will. Its tapered end fit in his palm. "It breathes direction into the sails."

"It's lovely," Eðna said, and she took it from him, gently as if it were a newborn babe. She held a hand out to him and drew him away from the pantry. "Come out now. You have enough." She spoke as if he'd lost his wits, and maybe he had, já?

A dumb beast, holding a careless bundle of goods stolen from his own house. The pantry door hung open and bits of food and sewing needles lay scattered. A spool of thread lay at his feet.

"I am so tired, Eðna. Gods help me."

Eðna lifted the heavy bundle from Brosa's arms and placed it on the floor.

"Sit with me." She led him to a wide bench by the fire, with lavishly deep and warm furs. He laid down along the bench and rested his head in her lap.

She sat completely still, as if this intimacy might disappear if she breathed. Her fingers hovered for a moment, then she brushed his hair back from his face where it had all fallen from its knot. He'd lost the neat point of his beard, and streaks of dirt marked his forehead. A twig or two was buried in his hair, from sleeping propped up against boulders or lying down in the brush. She combed his hair with her fingers, rested her thumb on his temple. His pulse was steady and strong underneath. She sat with him in silence.

Two stories of beds stretched down the whole length of the grand room, and dozens of pale curtains were drawn. The firelight brought out hints of sunset orange and pink in the fabric, each one hiding a private sleeping nest, protecting against the dark nights, the press of people, the glare of day. The posts that held up the ceiling were fragrant, woodsy, so tall and strong. The house was a palace compared to what she had as a child. It stretched so long, the light dissipated and melted into shadow, until it seemed there were no walls at all, and this place was the whole world.

She imagined little Brosa looking up at his big father and uncle, sharpening blades he would one day learn to use, and at tall women with swishing skirts and aprons. Up at the wooden beams above, forming their neat and strong triangles, as mysterious and far as constellations.

He said that grief crouched in every shadowed corner, but there must also be memories of joy and life here. His cousins grew up here with him, and his uncle told stories around this fire. His Ma held him close and rocked him here. It was a place of loyalty, where people stayed. They lived and breathed and fell in love. Heirik and Ginn. Hár and Betta. The bitterness Brosa felt right now was justified, but it was not him. This warmth, this hearth, right here, was his true heart.

"Fjoðr was my horse," he said. "He was gold, like me. A grand animal, fast and loyal. I wish you could have known him."

Eðna wiped tears from her face with the back of her hand. She ached to rest her cheek against his, to wrap her arms around him and give him her strength.

The little girl she'd been, a thousand years from now, had looked into the hearth this way, searching for shapes she didn't remember now. Horses? Or goddesses swooping across the sky? Now, she saw what Brosa must see. His golden Fjoðr rearing up, running to meet him, tossing a mane of flame. Ships blown across a fiery sea, chased by clouds of spirit-smoke. Elegant hulls forming, blazing briefly and turning into nothing.

Eðna brushed Brosa's skin, combed his hair with her fingers, and she watched boats form and dash against imaginary shores. Her heart stirred, quick and dangerous, but she was not anxious. It wasn't fear. It was desire. Not the familiar wish to triumph and achieve and prove herself. Not desire for this man either—not for his hair in her hands, her finger tracing the tender place where his beard met his cheek. Not for his mournful eyes and rough hands, nei. But desire for a life. One of her own choosing, not because anybody tricked her or instructed her, pleaded with her, asked her to stay or tried to send her away.

Brosa could have a life of his own too. It didn't seem that way right now, but he could. He could travel, find a place, have a home. The pain was too sharp to think of him with a wife, a family, but Eðna could see him alone on the shore of a gentle bay, arms crossed, watching the sun rise in peace.

"Já, then." He shook her off, gently, and he stood and took a deep breath. "Time to go."

He tightened the ties on the giant bundle, drew his hair back from his face and knotted it. He walked calmly toward the door, looking forward, not at the benches or beds or fire. Those were behind him now. He stepped out into the wind and fresh gusts of rain, and beyond him Eðna saw there was a storm simmering. She tugged her leather ties tight and prepared herself for the downpour that was about to come.

Brosa turned back to face her, where she stood in the doorway, and he smiled. He looked stupidly happy. "With your hand on the doorframe, it could be our house." he said. "Welcome me home from a hot day of haying, wife." He laughed off the gravity of it. "Give me some ale and food."

His sweetness stirred up fierce tenderness in Eðna, and an indignant wish for something fair. His dreams were not grand. They were so simple. He needed something so small it would disappear down here in this century. Just a life.

"Back in the hills, you said I should forget you ever came into my life," he said. "You must know Eðna, I will never forget you. I'll remember you here on the threshold."

She would remember this moment, too, Brosa giving her that half smile and a wink, like the whole world was their secret. For the space of a breath, she imagined a life. Stepping from this threshold and into his world. She reached for him. "I don't want—"

Brosa cried out and grasped his arm. At his feet lay a big rock, thrown from the darkness.

He swore and shouted, "Back in the house, Eðna!"

ᛋ

Svana peeked out from around the corner of the house and wiped rain from her eyes. She was finally alone—Eiðr and his men had gone around the other side—and it was quiet. Gods, they had talked for hours about how they would threaten and taunt Brosa when they found him here. How they would ignite his terror then leave him to run away and hide and suffer.

If he was here.

At least they did not plan to kill him outright.

Svana's sore hand, wrapped in rags, throbbed with pain that only fed her hatred for her husband. She would have to play this game. Be the obedient and yet fierce wife, help corner Ulfsson.

She gripped an ax that had been carelessly left leaning against the wall. This family thought they were invincible, their house above fear, so that they could leave weapons in the yard. Now, the hapless men who stayed behind to guard the house were tied in strong ropes and with cloth in their mouths, out in the stables.

The blade hung heavy beside her leg.

How much longer?

She rested her cheek against the house, and raindrops and sodden grass cooled her face. In memory, the sun touched her eyelids and the backs of her hands. Not far away stood the stable wall where she'd sat and spun wool so many days. Spinning, spinning, spinning, gazing over the yard that sloped down to the river. The hill where, as a little girl, she'd rolled and rolled, her arms tucked against her sides, until her skirts were a bundle and her head spun.

She'd laid in the grass and idly picked flowers here, making crowns and talking and stirring the soap. She'd walked right here with Brosa when they were young. Up the hill stood the forge, where she'd often watched Brosa and Hauk work as they got older. She dreamed of kissing Brosa while he was still hot from honing his ax. One day. Já, he would come home from working the walls and look to her for his dinner, and for warmth in his bed. She would turn the keys to the pantry one day—the keys that belonged to her mother, and would someday be hers, when she and Brosa married.

Right here, she had kissed him once. They were just trying it, to find out what a kiss felt like. Svana pressed her toe into the dirt and remembered. The game had taken wings and flown in her heart, so that now the thought glowed and warmed her and she was sure, after all these years, that it hadn't been a game at all.

"I'll remember you here."

She heard his beloved voice.

Her eyes flew open.

It was real. Brosa was here. As if he had been drawn up by her dreaming, he stood in the rain just paces away.

His hair was tangled, his face dark with dirt, and his wrists were ringed with grimy silver bands. His finest clothes were rumpled and stained, yet he was brighter than midsummer sun. Right here, just steps away from her, with those broad shoulders that curved in when he bent to work carving, and those arms, so strong that he worked the fields and forge with ease.

Brosa's smile seized her heart. His love for his home, for this place where he and she had once known each other. Svana could drop this ax and go to him right now—

—Eðna stepped out over the threshold.

Svana's stomach soured. Brosa looked at the woman, wistful and stupid, like he'd had too much ale. Eðna pulled her shawl tight, shy.

The loved each other—it was plain.

Svana bit into the grassy wall to keep from growling. Brosa and this woman loved each other, and here Svana stood, a husk. Left behind again. Stuck behind the house where Eiðr told her to stay. Staying and staying, always staying and watching Brosa leave time after time.

She saw Brosa on the sand two summers ago, the night of the whale, his glorious hair blowing in the salt spray. Golden head bent before his brother, kneeling over his ax. Svana felt light then, rising up inside, thinking Brosa would ask for her as wife. But he asked for Ginn. His hands, strong and thick with rings, closed around Ginn's waist, and envy closed its fist around Svana's heart.

If she had the power of Hel, Svana would breathe flames on this house and consume it with everything Ginn loved—and with Eðna—inside. She would burn down the new hall too, and watch Ginn's tears run like blood over her rich blue dress and pale hands. She would rip Eðna's teeth out and scrape her skin away with her own fingernails, until the woman was only bones.

Svana spit grass, and she closed her fingers on the ax handle.

Ready.

A rock hit Brosa in the arm, and he dropped the bundle he carried. His smile was lost in confusion. Then he understood. "Back inside, Eðna!"

From the other side of the house, Eiðr's voice poured like bad milk. "I owed you a rock to the head, Ulfsson. But your woman took it for you." Eiðr and his men laughed. "I'll give you an ax to the skull instead." And then they were on Brosa, grabbing him and dragging him away. Brosa fought against their grip, and he bellowed rage. Stupid Eðna turned in every direction, looking for help she would not find.

Svana stepped out from behind the house. "Eðna Sjódottir." Daughter of the ocean. Another woman like Ginn, with no father, no mother, come from the sea.

Eðna's eyes and mouth narrowed. Her hand went to the hilt of her cooking knife—a poor weapon. "You are Svana," she said.

Svana had never been this close to Eðna, never smelled her scent of dirt and fine herbs, or seen her hair falling free of its braids. Even with her face pinched in anger, she was strong and lovely. Her beauty only stoked Svana's flames.

"Já, you have me." She walked slowly toward Eðna, forcing the woman back into the house, through the mudroom, then into the great room. Svana's hair stuck to her face and in her eyes. Nei matter, she knew every bench and table corner, every bump in this floor.

Svana let the ax swing by her side just like the chief always did, as if she held such a heavy weapon all the time. As if it would be nothing unusual to cleave Eðna's flesh to the bone, to leave her blind and groping for her own eyes.

"Please," Eðna said, her tiny knife ridiculous in the firelight. She glanced between Svana and the door, backing away. The woman's hands shook. "Whatever you want, I'll give you. Let me go to Brosa. He has nothing to defend himself."

It was cowardly, to use Brosa as a way out. As if Svana would simply give up at the thought of his name.

Svana laughed. "You are almost too stupid to kill."

Screams and battle cries came from outside. The voices of men and horses. Vile, ugly sounds. Nei matter. What were Eiðr and his men against such a golden force of a man, kissed by the gods. Svana held her ground. "Brosa is strong and able."

"He's alone! Please. Give me the ax and I'll go to—"

"—Still your mouth!" Svana had once planted the fox's head on a pole and called destruction down on this house. Now, she was here to deal it with her own hands. She had Eðna right here, now, and nothing would steer her from her path. She raised the ax up over one shoulder, and the fox's voice came up through her throat. "You have nothing but grief coming to you!"

She swung the ax, and Eðna screamed and backed away, backed up into the hearth stones. Flames licked her hems, and she whimpered like a child. Threw her hands up to shield her face. Her kitchen knife swung wildly on its wrist-strap.

Svana was not supposed to kill tonight, only goad and taunt. But she was so close. She could just finish the woman.

—From outside, a savage yell rose above the others. Svana knew with a spear to her gut. It was Brosa.

Eðna went to her knees and she appealed once more, crying in the dirt. "Svana, please." The woman spread her hands in defeat, but her words were strong and certain. "He will die."

In a rush, Svana knew it for the first time. Brosa could die.

He would be gone forever—never to laugh again, to work the forge, to sail, never to give Svana that smile that made her skin shine. She would never have the promise or even the dream of his touch.

Svana had imagined Brosa hearty and strong, killing Eiðr and his goat-brained cousins with his bare hands. Now in her mind she saw him as he must really be, at the stable wall, his back against the grass, slipping in the mud. He would be cornered now, with nowhere to go. Brosa would fight hard, but with no strong weapon in his hands.

They were here to taunt, já. A dead man was nei good plaything. But what if Eiðr was overcome with rage and did not hold back?

A sudden gust blew smoke up from the heartstone and into Svana's eyes. They stung, after all, with ash and tears. Her arms shook with the weight of the ax. She couldn't hold it up much longer.

"Let a foul shirt soak," the fox in Svana whispered. "The stain will one day come free."

Gods take it all!

Svana let the ax down slowly. The animal was right. She could kill Eðna another day, and it would be even more satisfying. Right now, she needed her.

She turned the ax handle toward Eðna. "Go." Her voice was rough and thick. "Save him."

Eðna sat still in the dirt for a moment and blinked like an idiot calf.

"Skyndi, kona!" Svana shouted, on the edge of sobbing. "Hurry!"

Eðna nodded. She took the ax, and fast as a swift bird, the woman flew. As if she could go, like Ginn said, by the sky.

Eðna raced outside and turned in a wild circle, blind with rain. Her hair whipped up and away, as if the gusts might rip it from her skull. Horses cried and men shouted, and Eðna stumbled toward the fight, the heavy ax dragging her down. The wind howled a savage sound, like the sound of the tank flinging her through the dark of time. Brosa cried out, and Eðna shouted for him. "I'm coming!" But where?

She slipped and went down on her knees in thick mud.

She crawled, her hands and clothes soaked and smeared, pushed herself up out of the muck and stood. And she saw him.

Brosa was backed up against the grass wall at the stables. Two men faced him, shaggy and dirty and angry. One held a hatchet, the other a knife in his hand. His only hand. Eiðr.

He raised his arm, as if he would make a fist if he could. "...For what you did to my sister."

"I nei harmed your sister." Brosa held his seax ready to fight, but he held his other hand up as if to reason. "You know I loved her."

Eðna dragged the heavy ax and stumbled, slipping, almost there—

—Her head was yanked back. Someone had her by the hair. She struggled to get free, but every twist sent pain shooting through her scalp. The man held her tight, so close she smelled his wet wool and sweat and felt the shape of his ax against her thigh.

"Eiðr!" He shouted. "Look here!"

Eiðr turned, and at the same moment Brosa turned too. When he saw Eðna struggling, he exploded, and with a growl he lunged at Eiðr. The two fought, and as Eðna twisted and tried to wrench her hair free she saw with awful clarity as the second man raised his hatchet. It glinted as it came down on Brosa's leg, and he cried out and fell to the ground.

"Nei!" Eðna screamed and yanked against her captor. The man with the hatchet kicked Brosa in the ribs, hard, and Brosa covered his face to protect himself.

"Morg, enough," Eiðr said, but Morg did not stop. He kicked Brosa again. "Arka!" He called Brosa *sensitive*, and he spit on him.

"Enough!" Eiðr put an arm out to pull Morg back. And to the man who held Eðna he called, "Let her go."

He released her hair, and Eðna raced to Brosa and sank to her knees by his side.

He laid still, eyes closed, and rain misted his face and trickled into his beard. He didn't move.

"Wake up!" She shook him. "Please."

Eiðr came on his horse. It stamped its shaggy feet right beside Eðna and she flinched and cowered underneath the powerful animal. "That's right, shield yourself Woman. Go and hide." Just as Morg had, Eiðr spit on the ground at Brosa's side. "See you again, Blond-Beard." And they were gone.

Eðna rested her palm on Brosa's cold cheek and murmured, "Nei, nei." She stretched herself out and laid beside Brosa in the mud, face to face. His eyelashes were dark gold and heavy with water. She brushed his cheek and left trails of mud. "Please, be here."

The gray rain and mud, and the wait—the looking, watching for him to move, to breathe—stretched into years, and she saw Brosa as Baldr, pushed away in his magnificent boat. The blazing ship moved off slowly into the night-dark ocean, a creature limping away from the land, carrying Brosa's beautiful soul.

He opened his eyes. "Elskan." His voice ground like stones. "Are you alright?"

He was alive.

Eðna breathed, deep gulping breaths. Yes! He was alive. "Yes." She nodded, and joy and fear raced together in her chest, and her fingers left grass stains on his face. "They're gone."

"You're sure you're not hurt?" He ran his fingers across her face, too, just as she did his.

"I'm fine," she said. "Fine."

He smiled and closed his eyes. Another long moment, so long that Eðna thought he might be slipping away again, and she whispered his name.

He heaved a deep breath. "I need to sit."

He pushed himself up and cried out and grabbed his shin. When he took his hands away, they were slick with blood. A gash went right through his leg bindings. The blood ran through his fingers, and he looked at it in wonder, as if he'd never seen such a thing.

"Keep your hand tight on the wound," Eðna ordered. She felt for her kitchen knife, and it was not at her belt, but Brosa's blade lay in the mud beside him. She used it to rip the fabric of her underskirt.

"Night is short," he said. "It's best if we go soon."

She pulled hard and a long shred came off. Eðna spit out bits of grass as she worked. She tied the bandage above the wound, tight around his thigh, with all her strength, and then she tightened it again. She tied a knot, and then another.

"Good enough, Eðna." Brosa pushed her hands away. "You'll make my leg go dead."

She shook with adrenalin, and she breathed deep and nodded. The fight was over. They were gone. She stood and smoothed her dress, and she laughed. Ridiculous. Covered in filth and blood, standing in the yard trying to neaten her skirt.

"A little help," Brosa said. He reached for her hand and pushed off the ground. He cried out in quick, savage pain, and fell back.

"My bones," he said, and he ground his teeth. He leaned heavily on the wall.

He needed medical care, in a hospital. A bed at least, even a blanket, anything. His skin was bluish white. He stared at something far and unknown, and a chill raced up Eðna's back. He looked like he was dying.

Gull came and woke Brosa by snuffling his ear, and Brosa laughed. He nuzzled Gull in return and spoke softly. "I can't walk, Boy."

He looked at the horse appraisingly, and then to Eðna. "You'll have to help me onto his back." With grim resolve, Brosa pushed off from the wall and stood. "We have to leave."

Eðna rested her head against Brosa's back, and Gull carried them down the long slope to the woods. Blood seeped from Brosa's leg bindings, turning them black, and it rubbed off on the horse, so that Gull's golden legs were rusty brown.

When Eðna put her arms around Brosa or held onto his belt, he sucked in his breath in pain, and so she pressed her palms to her own thighs and sat quietly, hot with shame. She was such a coward. Brave Eðna, right. When the time came, again, she cried and covered her face.

Along with the shame, fear and hope stirred and settled, like ashes flying up and then falling, again and again.

She twisted to look behind, but no one was there. Svana, Eiðr, everyone had vanished. The house receded from sight, and then all was hills and grass and lichens forever and ever, and not one man or horse followed at their backs. She and Brosa would make it to the woods. What they would do then was unformed. No plan.

Brosa made some small joke she didn't understand—laughed at himself—but Eðna worried right through it, not eased at all.

She closed her eyes and dropped into a list of their assets.

Brosa had one small blade and his seax, a skin of water, a tankard. The massive bundle of blankets was secured on Gull's back, right behind Eðna. And she had tools and supplies. Not much. Her little knife, her sewing kit, her medicine.

Her Medicine! She could give Brosa something to ease his pain. They could stop for just a minute. Her hand went to her pack. She could—

It wasn't there.

Fear spiked, and she cast around frantically for her pack.

"Woman, be still," Brosa growled.

She was hurting him. But there was nothing at her belt and she could not be still. Every optimistic thought drained away, and she was emptied.

"Nei." She sobbed against Brosa's back. "Nei."

"Shhhh, Elskan." Brosa reached a hand back to brush her leg. "We'll be alright." Even through unthinkable pain, Brosa tried to console her. He called her his elskan, his sweetheart. He had no idea what she'd lost. Her medicine. Their security against anguish and death, her tether to the advances of the future, the one condition she'd demanded of Jeff, to bring antibiotics and painkiller to the past. She imagined the vials lying in the mud by the stables, smashed and broken.

"Breathe," she instructed herself, the way Vera always did whenever Eðna had a nightmare. Brosa believed they would be alright. He was well enough to make jokes, to soothe her, to call her elskan, his sweet girl.

She rested on him and breathed and pretended for a minute that she could really be his love. That it was so simple. She would stay here forever, without the constant pressure of fear, without the anguish of looking forward to the day she would have to leave him. It was all caught up with her burning desire to return to the future, to report her knowledge to the world.

Here, Brosa would be the only person she could tell about everything she learned—her thoughts and observations, her data, her questions. Brosa would listen to her, always, but was he enough? The notion of the glistening lab grasped at her heart, mixed with the ease and pleasure of a fantasy life with this man, and her deep disgust at the ax wounds that seeped blood on the horse.

Blood was everywhere, on her dress, the horse. The day she arrived, and now, blood mixed with a smudgy sunrise the color of wounds. So much blood. She needed her pack. She had to go back and find it.

"Still, Eðna." Brosa touched her leg again, and she rested her hands where they clutched his belt, and tried not to move.

Finally, they reached the forest's edge. The first tendrils of juniper were at their feet, and a few slender, twisting birches stood before them. Angelica grew with abandon, as high as Eðna's chest. A profusion of big, electric green spheres, umbels as big as her head, ready to burst into millions of white flowers, lacy and wild and lovely.

They left Gull there. Brosa removed the bundle from the animal's back.

"He's not truly mine." Brosa ran his hand over Gull's silky mane, and he murmured in the horse's twitching ear. "Fara aftur, gott drengur." *Return, good boy. Leave us.*

Brosa hoisted the pack to his shoulder and shut his eyes against the pain. Ridiculous bravado.

"You've lost your wits if you think I'll let you carry that."

She expected his sweet laugh, or at least a protest, but his eyes, always sparkling like sun on water, had gone flat and dead. His shining force of life had dissipated. She'd seen this same lack of will before, in her mother's eyes, and now Gida's face seemed to hover, for a second, over Brosa's, as on a screen. Through Gida's twisting pain and sadness, her mother had come to this same gruesome peace, a stillness that was not a serene letting go.

"Don't give up." Eðna would not cry now. "Just give me the pack."

"Nei, I won't."

"Give it, beast!"

At last, he smiled. "You can have the pack, Woman. I was saying nei, I won't give up."

Brosa tossed a last longing glance at the horse. Gull was already cantering away, testing the idea of running. Had the animal actually understood him? Brosa—the man she knew, not the one who simply made everyone happy—was so serious and strong. He could talk to horses, and they would actually listen and obey. He would know what to do now.

He put his arm around Eðna for balance. He was soaked in mud and sweat, and his weight, along with the pack, was almost unbearable. With the first step, he ground his teeth together and growled, and it sounded like anger as well as pain.

Good. If he had the sense and energy to be angry, he was still here, alive, with Eðna. He was alive, and he would know where to go, what to do next.

They entered the woods. He dragged his leg with every step. Something must be broken, a bone cracked by the force of the ax. His breath came hard, with deep grinding noises in his throat.

Beside him, Eðna was useless and silent. The roll of blankets, filled with who knew what assortment of food and tools, dug into her lower back. Her whole body yearned to fly back to the house and find her purse.

She needed to talk about making a plan, about what they had in their packs, what they'd left behind, where they were going, but every time she started, she forced herself to be quiet. Brosa concentrated on pushing himself onward, and all these items seemed best unvoiced. She concentrated on the ground.

It felt like hours had passed, but early, thin light was just reaching through the twisty branches. The night touched down for about two or three hours in May. It hadn't really been that long since the fight. At their pace—slowing to a crawl when the brush was thick—they could not have gone far.

Brosa stopped and leaned on one of the small trees. "Good," was all he said.

Good? Right. If this counted for good, they were truly in trouble.

"I need to rest. We can wait here."

Eðna went down on one knee to check Brosa's calf-bindings. They were stiff with dried blood, but they held. He no longer bled freely.

He touched her cheek, drew her to look up at him, and smiled that charming, dangerous smile. He winked, and a hot blush crossed Eðna's chest. He was flirting? Now?

Fine. Anything was better than the ghostly loss in his eyes that looked so much like Gida's.

She brushed his bindings with just her fingertips. "It looks good," she lied.

"You'll be glad to know I have a plan."

"Are you going to tell me?"

"Já, well, it's not grand, but—"

A sharp crack came from farther into the woods, and another. Footsteps? They held completely still for a breath or two, then Brosa broke the silence.

"We need to move on." He drew himself up, and, as he often did, deflected. "We're lucky, já?"

Eðna laughed. "Já, I'm feeling really lucky today."

Brosa grinned, and a little of his light came back. He pointed to the ground. "Foxes were here," he said. "They made a trail for us." Stalks and branches were snapped and chaotic.

"Will this hide our footsteps?"

Brosa laughed. "Not truly, with the way I'm dragging this leg. But Eiðr has gone now, to let his anger simmer. To test me with time."

"What will he do?"

"Taunt me. Make me lose my wits with the waiting," he said. "See how long I can last alone."

Eðna tied her skirts again and tightened her laces. "Well, you won't be alone."

They waded farther into the woods.

Trees twisted in every direction, like crooked bones with swollen joints, reaching up out of the juniper and wildflowers. Trunks branched again and again until they filled in over Eðna's and Brosa's heads. Sun filtered down onto his big shoulders, and cast lace on his back. Strands of mud-covered gold hair stuck to the back of his neck. Eðna was lulled by the uneven movement of his shoulder blades as he limped, and the patterns of breathing and light.

"—Ah, here!" He stopped. "Here is one of my marks." He pointed to a V of branches, high in the trees. Three stones were set into the crook of the tree.

"You placed those stones?"

"None of the boys could see them. Not even my brother." His pride was so sweet. "The largest one will always lead you to the next."

"You know this place."

He raised an eyebrow, not even bothering to answer, and drew out his knife. Of course he knew this place, if he'd placed these stones. Inside this maze of white bark and lush, green chaos, with its whiffs of dirt and mold and scattered light, Brosa knew specifically where they now stood, as if he had a map in his eyes. But it was in his memory, and in his body, in the way he looked to the sky through the leaves. These were his woods, and his love and experience and knowledge were better than any satellites to guide him.

"Look well, Eðna." He cut away a handful of leaves and repositioned a stone. "Learn how it works. You'll follow them back."

Follow them back. Of course. Yes, she would follow the stones back, once Brosa was settled wherever they were going. Once she'd taken care of his wounds, she could leave. She would head out of the woods and to the coast.

"This is part of your not-grand plan?"

"Já," he took another step and winced with pain. "When I am hidden and settled, maybe with some water and food, then you go. Return to the house."

"Return to the house." She nodded, frustration building, a familiar anger at being told what to do. "Return to the house. Like the horse did."

"Eðna." Brosa sounded exasperated too. "My four days' grace are ending. You won't find trouble for aiding me up to today. From here on, that changes."

The woods were a wicked tangle in every direction. Without her contacts, she had no map out of this morass of birches. No traceable recording. Leaves and limbs arched overhead, braiding and crossing in so many directions. She could wander for days and never get out.

"There will be some stones missing," he said. "I haven't been here since…a long time." He touched her cheek. "Your fire-eyes will find the way."

Eðna turned away, escaping his touch and his false lightness.

"Look," he said, pointing his knife at the odd cairn up in the tree. "Tell me if you see."

If her contacts had been functioning, they would scan for patterns. Match the three-rock formation with any similar shapes. The three stones that formed an arrow, with the largest as the leading point. Yes, she saw it.

"There." She raised her chin toward the next cairn.

Brosa was right. She could do it. She could follow these markers out of the woods until she came to the valley, then skip over Ginn and the chief and their house altogether and head straight for home. Right.

She hadn't thought of the future as her home for…how long? A day now? More?

"I can see it," she said, but Brosa didn't answer. He leaned against a tree, his forehead pressed to the bark. His face had lost all color again and he looked blank, exhausted. Brosa had shown Eðna her way out, given her directions, and now he'd lost his strength to go any farther. She could see his will slipping from him like a blanket off his shoulders.

"You think I'll leave you now." She slid her hand into his. "You are a stupid beast."

Without lifting his head, he smiled, just a little. A playful smile, with just the corner of his mouth, so light and easy, but his hand crushed hers.

They moved slowly, sleepily now, and Brosa staggered every so often. They had to get somewhere, soon—some place where he could rest.

"Where are we going?"

He didn't answer.

"I can't help," she said. "If you won't tell me the rest of your plan."

"Ah, já," he searched the woods ahead. "We're almost at its end."

A small rise was ahead, thick with angelica. Normally, climbing it would be nothing. Eðna could sprint it in 20 seconds, but for Brosa, now, it was punishing. His plan needed to wrap up very soon. He was going to die of exhaustion and blood loss. They needed to make camp, get themselves warm and hidden, and she needed to look at his leg. But she just walked beside him, and he concentrated, step after step, until finally they reached the top.

And she stood in wonder.

They looked down into a ravine, in the heart of the woods, dark and cool and filled with mist, with a rushing stream like Ranka's silver thread. Water gathered in a pool that was deep blue in the center, edged with brilliant yellow-green algae. The pool, and stream, were fed by a tiny waterfall, just big enough to crash and froth. The tallest trees Eðna had ever seen, the ones reached by sunlight here, twined their giant trunks and reached, meeting and intertwining over the water. A natural bower. Roots and branches, gnarled black and silver, dipped their fingertips into the sparkling miniature river.

Brosa's breath came heavy beside her. "We'll stop there. On the other side."

Small caves were cut into the rock face on the opposite side of the ravine. They would cross the stream, and then go where? A cave? Was that his plan?

"I'm failing, Eðna." Brosa's voice was thick and rough. "We need to go now."

"Yes, yes right now."

They crossed the water. It filled her boots, and it was warm and even more miserable than the cold shock she'd expected. The stream was maybe a meter across, not more than two, but stronger than it looked. The current sucked at her ankles, her wool bloomers and remnants of skirt hems. The water swirled up over her little boots, and poured down in. With one hand she lifted her soggy skirts, and with the other she grasped Brosa's belt for balance. They slogged up on to the bank.

Eðna finally let go of Brosa's belt, and her fingers were bent and stiff from holding on so tight. Water streamed from their calves, and their boots made sucking sounds. They limped over to a big boulder at edge of the pool, and she pried open her claws and rested.

"We are here," he said.

This was where the cairns led. To a fairytale ravine in the woods, where they rested, wet and streaming, on a rocky shore. All around were flat stones, fuzzy with moss and sprigged with white and purple saxifrage. Crystal light fell on the pool, the rocks, her hands. Eðna was swept up in birdsong all around.

Brosa smiled. "Welcome to my hall."

Eðna brushed her fingers across Brosa's cheeks, wiping away mud from his eyes and leaving smears.

His hall?

He was delirious, shivering and slick with sweat. And he was smiling, his mouth quirked halfway in amusement. Had he lost his mind from blood loss after all?

"Look deep, Eðna."

The face of the ravine was dotted with little caves, crusted with electric gold and glowing pale lichens. A few larger cave openings were draped with moss. Like with the cairns, she searched for patterns, or their absence. A break in the rhythm of branches and moss and stone. And then she saw it, so near that she drew up short. Right in front of them. "A door."

A wooden door was tucked up under the rocky overhang, inside the curve of a little cave. Just about her height, the door was set into a frame built of gnarled birch trunks. Crude iron hinges were just visible under a thick layer of emerald and yellow mosses, silver and rust lichens. The door matched the rocks and woods all around, and unless Brosa had told her, she wouldn't have seen it.

With a twist of fingers and wrist, Brosa opened the door, and Eðna stepped into a dream—a boy's secret fort, a tiny chieftain's home. A few meters deep and just as wide, the hut was framed by the cave itself, but Brosa had added wooden ribs like the rafters of a real hall. A column of dust swirled in the light from a small roof vent. A bed took up half the place. Its posts were carved of silvery driftwood, with wolf-head finials that watched over the room. A straw mattress was topped with dusty sheepskins. Beside it, a huge driftwood stump served as a table.

And there was a chair. A breathtaking, gorgeous wooden chair shaped like a chalice—a precious cup for a Viking princess to sit in and rule over the house. Its strange shape was formed of the same silver, ocean-tossed wood as the bed. Brosa must have collected dozens of pieces of driftwood over time and fit them together so the natural curves of the wood formed the seat. A rug lay at the chair's feet, sloppily woven of thick wool, inexpertly spun. At the heart of the room, there lay a hearth like a bowl set into the ground, ringed by smooth, rounded stones. Each stone would fit in Brosa's two cupped hands.

A house as charming and sweet as its builder, but it had a musty smell, the scent of a forgotten place, of empty months, seasons passing. A pang of loss hit her. Had he built this place for Esa?—

"A little help, Eðna."

Yes, Brosa needed her help. She shook off thoughts of wives and death, and stepped inside.

Brosa ducked his head to enter the hut, and the low doorway cracked his brow. He laughed at himself. He'd never learned, even as his big body grew and this house stayed the same.

He fell onto the bed, and a cloud of dust and bits of old wool made him wheeze. His leg felt like it was licked by flame, his bones snapped, skin torn. He tipped his head back, and the world swung and pitched under and around him. Even his head hurt now, from knocking into the doorframe.

When he was a small boy here, this ceiling was his sky. Now, spinning with pain, he saw ravens and flickers wheel and fly in the rafters. They went up in swirls of hundreds of birds, and then whisked away with the wind, until another flock grew from nothing and began to circle.

"—Brosa."

Someone was calling.

Had Heirik found his hut? Nei, this was his own place! He would not come out.

"Brosa, can you see me?"

It was not his brother. There was someone else here. "Eðna." She shouldn't be here either. She should have gone home.

"Brosa, I need you to change your shirt."

The thought alone, of raising his arms and peeling away his wet linen, made his mind swim. He closed his eyes again. "Sleep."

"I know." She was soft, like puffs of combed fleece. "I know. But I need to look at your wounds and get you dry."

She pulled at his calf bindings, unwinding the long strips, and the pain in his leg screamed. He pushed at her hands. "Too tired, Woman."

She worked a new shirt over his head, and from inside its soft, dry depths, he mumbled, "This is my place. No one comes here."

"I'm here now," she whispered, and the shirt fell over his skin like a cloud come down from the sky to surround and warm him.

"Shhh." Eðna leaned in and smoothed the wet hair off his face. Her rounded lips came together, so hungry to kiss. If he could only move. Já, she should not be here, with her scent of grass and blood and the mix of dirt and salt-sea essence that was her dual spirit.

A dark memory came. The heavy smell of ocean, and a woman, but not Eðna. It was Ginn in his mind. His brother's woman, a silver-haired spirit in the blue of midnight, ankle deep in the sea. Ginn had disappeared before his eyes that night, though he'd thought it was a trick of his sight. She disappeared for a beat of his heart, and then came to be solid again. Ginn's eyes were sick with fear that night, and she held onto him as though he was a bit of land in a vast ocean. He held her tight against his chest so that she would not leave.

The water would take Eðna that same way, but this time he would let her go. She had to go. "I have to get you to the water."

Eðna pressed her hand to his chest, and he took it, held it hard. It fit completely inside his, and a powerful sense of life grew, despite the hopelessness of his situation. "It's nei too late now." A ragged cough caught him.

"Please," she said. "Lay back."

He looked to the smoky ceiling. The draft pulled slow, and a thread of smoke went out the vent, where it would join with the mist from the water. Eðna had made a fire. She held a needle in the jaws of her shears, and she roasted it over the flames. Did she plan to burn and stitch his wound at once?

"Is it that bad, Woman?" His voice was like rough stone, too loud.

"Nei, you are hardly cut."

She was a poor liar. And soon she would dig that hot needle into his skin, and while he'd been through worse, he did not look forward to it.

"My bindings kept the blade from cutting my leg clean off." He tried to sit up. "But a bone is broken."

"Já, I agree," she said, and she pushed him back down into the furs. "Maybe not broken, but…" She looked up, like she sometimes did, trying to find words or knowledge in the air above her head. "Wrenched. Like a wet shirt. Can you straighten it?"

Eðna tried to set his leg right, and he shouted and grabbed handfuls of fur. His head wheeled like the phantom birds, light as air, stomach sick. The room got darker, and his thoughts disappeared into the smoke. He had to say things now. "I won't keep you here."

Eðna pressed her lips together and threaded her needle. "Lay back now," she said. "Don't worry. I know how to sew."

She stuck him with her needle, and he gripped the furs. "I won't keep you." He was slipping away again. He had so much to say. "Not like your father."

Eðna froze, and for a second, the barest filament of spun wool connected her and Brosa. She'd thought many times that he and Jon were alike, but to hear him say it…Not like your father.

She blinked tears away and bent to focus on her work. She had to sew Brosa's wound before the sun waned again and the roof vent went dark.

"Vera, help me," she whispered.

Vera had always handled the costume fittings. Eðna didn't touch people. She steeled herself to handle Brosa as she would a pack or a belt that needed mending.

It was not the same. Not at all.

She'd never sewn up a human, with blood pulsing just under his skin. Never touched a man she cared about, who hissed with pain and whose leg twitched with the instinct to pull away when she passed her needle through his skin. Skin like silk, moving in confusing ways that leather would never move.

She steadied her hands, swallowed hard and made another stitch.

Brosa didn't realize what he'd said. He was drunk with pain. He didn't mean to peel back a dozen years, baring her father's smile, so expansive and bright, while all the while he hid the world from Eðna. Jon's arms outstretched, encompassing his pitiful land, gathering together his thousand lies and offering them, like they were the greatest gift.

Brosa no longer struggled now. He was blessedly, mercifully asleep. After the harrowing walk here, and her amateur medical attention, he finally rested, in a slumber so sudden and deep that he didn't even flinch when she put pressure on his leg and wrapped it tight. He snored.

She snugged the last strip of linen, tied a final knot and rested her palm against the neatly wound bandage. Adrenalin slowly dissipated, and finally she let herself tremble, now that the worst was over. She let herself rest, and let the horror in, the exhaustion.

There had to be a water skin somewhere here. Brosa's bundle had burst open and spilled a random assortment of food and tools and clothing. In the dwindling light, she found water and drank it in sloppy gulps.

What he brought was a shocking mess of randomly chosen things. She knelt in the middle of it all and took stock. Two pairs of finely woven wool pants and giant shirts, iron shears in two sizes and a sharp blade for carving wood or shaving a man's beard. Those would be useful. And food. Handfuls of dried fish and berries, and rounds of something wrapped in leaves, maybe cheese.

But beside those things lay a silver scoop for cleaning wax out of ears, a metal toothpick and bone comb. Lovely glasses with deep blue rims, far finer than anything they needed to get by in the forest. And tiny leather packets full of herbs. Absurd. So stupid, that she would have mint and lavender and a gods-damned ear scoop, but no medicine to ease him. She shook her head at the plank of wood he'd brought along. His steerboard handle. It was carved with runes that spelled Brosa.

Stupid, sweet man. It would be a mercy if he dreamed right now, maybe of building a boat. Of the scent of sawdust in the sun. It would be a powerful, ancient smell, like the walls and posts of Ginn's hall. Maybe Brosa dreamed of brushing tiny splinters from his hands, as he worked on an upturned hull.

In sleep, the pain left his features, and he looked so young, so hale. Hair stuck to his forehead, dark with sweat, and his beard had bits of bark tangled in it. A bruise swelled next to his eye. She followed his gold eyebrow with her fingertips, so much like the first bird's feather she ever touched. Unbelievable. A wing, a man, under her fingers.

His rich-man's leather leg bindings were a bloody pile now. He was right, they had saved his leg and probably his life. Eðna had exchanged them for rags and dumped the bindings on the floor. His wet shirt laid beside them, a muddy lump.

Gods, she had taken off his shirt. She'd undressed him.

Dizzy from blood loss, he had tried to help, and somehow she got it over his head. His chest was bare, except for his Thor's hammer and the other leather cord she had just glimpsed from time to time. It was a firestriker he kept around his neck, laying against his heart. Eðna surged with shock and desire, and she forced herself to set those feelings aside, like they were no more than supplies.

She'd cut away his bindings and pant legs, then. The blood was thick and sticky. It was an emergency, and at the time, there was no room for squeamishness or fear. Or, truthfully, shyness, which was ridiculous. She flushed now, finally free to think about her first real look at his skin, her first hint at what it would feel like to slide her hands over his chest, follow the curves of his waist and hear him respond to her with sucked-in breath and murmured, private words of pleasure instead of pain.

Nei matter, as Brosa would say. It was done, and now he slept.

Eðna pulled her wet boots off and dumped them by the fire. She untied the strands at her sides, to take off her top—the one beloved piece of clothing she'd made for herself, not for any client. Her herklædi, Brosa's Uncle Hár called it. Her armor. An apt word. She held it up to assess, and the worn leather looked like velvet in the firelight.

She peeled her dress from her arms and pulled it over her head. Briefly stuck inside, she struggled to breathe. The ties on her woolen bloomers were soaked, the knots fused, and she had to use the tip of her knife to untie them. Gods, had she been completely dry even once since she came to this time?

She slipped on one of Brosa's extra shirts, and it fell long past her knees. His soft wool pants, the ones he wore under his clothes, were a dozen sizes too big, and she knotted them in handfuls. The cloth was woven so fine, frothy as one of Jeff's expertly steamed lattes. She sank into the dry, soft pleasure of clean clothes and dreamed of a hot drink, a smooth mug in her hands instead of a clammy water skin.

A swift vision came, of Brosa's rugged world, stark black and vivid green, dotted with espresso stands the way Ginn feared. Eðna saw kiosks in the mossy highlands, where sheep roamed and birds swooped and preened. Ginn's fear echoed briefly in Eðna's own chest and throat, and she swallowed all those thoughts with a swig of warm water that tasted like wet wool.

She didn't belong. Brosa had said so.

The future waited beyond the sea.

She looked up as if the lab were visible in this smoky little room. She was so close to getting away. She could have her heart's desire. Unprecedented achievement. The rush of showing the company she'd done it, showing Jeff the images she'd gathered and notes she'd recorded. Right now, while Brosa slept deep in a sea of endorphins, she could walk away and he would not hold her back.

She picked up a wooden box that fit into her two hands. Inside there were wooden tiles on a dowel, so that pictures flipped by. Someone had lovingly burned outlines into the wood. A horse, a sheep, a shield, an ax.

She was no good at being loyal anyway. She might as well leave.

In the morning. She would go tomorrow. Right now, she had to guard Brosa. He was vulnerable, there were men searching for him, and she would take care of him. She would protect him, já.

Her eyes closed. She saw her Ma wrapped inside her father's embrace. In the fields where the sparse grass grew, Jon took Gida in his big arms and she bent her head to accept his kiss, her eyes closed in bliss.

Eðna's eyes jerked open.

She was slumped on the floor with the water skin in her lap. So weary. Too tired to even sit up. She could crawl in beside Brosa, just for warmth. She could protect him better that way, with her own body, even while she slept.

His ribs were hard and his heart so alive, so steady. She curled up beside him and traced his lower lip with one fingertip, barely touching. He had the sweetest curve along the edge of his beard, where it met his cheek.

"Damn it," she whispered. "I don't want to leave you."

She drew the cloaks and furs up around her and Brosa, and she closed her fist around the handle of her little knife. Dry and secure, at last. It would take a while for the heat from their bodies to mingle and gather within the heavy blankets. It only made sense to sleep together. Yes.

ᛋ

Brosa woke to pain. It surged in his leg, and in his skull, like a relentless tide. The frame of his small bed bit into his back, and something heavy rested on his arm. He opened his eyes just some and found it was Eðna there. She'd crawled into the furs beside him. He smiled. Small Eðna, her head was like a rock. Her hand rested on his chest, and all was still.

Night had come, and he could just see her face. She was so close, her breath brushed his skin. The water sang loud below the cave, and underneath the rushing, the forest made its sounds, as always. Twigs snapped at the passage of birds and foxes. No voices of men or dogs, no snorts of horses. He and Eðna were safe for now.

He drank her in like sweet ale. Her brows were relaxed, not drawn together, and her lashes moved like a cat's whiskers when it dreamed. Her rounded lips, so good to bite, were open in slumber, free of all her troubled words and plans. Her hand rested on his chest, light as a flicker. A small knife rested there under her palm, where she had loosened her clutch as she fell into sleep. Brave woman, ready to stand and fight with her kitchen knife.

He traced the bones of her hand. Had he ever seen her fingers so still? Not braiding leather, or Ranka's hair or Gull's mane as she rode? Not clutching or knotting her skirts or smoothing cloaks or furs.

Brosa shifted, and tight bindings pressed his calf. She'd sewn him up like she'd been a healer all her life. And with those same small fingers, she brushed his hair from his eyes and told him he was a good man.

Slowly, with the lightest touch, he placed his hand on top of hers, so that knife and woman and he were one, and he felt the deepest Eðna, the one beneath her waking shield.

When she first came to his world, she was not ready to fight. She thought she was ready. She yearned to be brave and strong. But she needed him. When no one else did, Eðna needed him. Now she grew stronger, more at ease in the land, and he had less and less to give. Would she need him anymore?

In truth, she didn't. They both knew she could leave this hut and make her way to the sea.

Wild desperation raced in his chest, and he pushed away the thought of her leaving. He would think, for now while she slept, about how this felt instead. He pressed a kiss to the top of her head, and her hair smelled of leaves and his own sea-dew that Eðna and Ginn called rosemary.

His breath made her hair move. His own air, and its unseen waves, lifted a few strands. Here inside the hut, her hair was almost black as the evernight woods. She wore leaves and twigs among her forest of messy strands and bits of loose braids. Nei doubt, she would pick the leaves off one by one as soon as she rose from sleep tomorrow and readied and smoothed herself for the day.

Tomorrow. He breathed deep, and the fire pulsed bright in his leg. There was plenty to worry about, and argue about, when the sun rose.

For now, he let her sleep, unbound and free. Like a woman of the forest, with pieces of the woods adorning her like a crown. For tonight, they could live here in the trees. They could lie together, and his pain would pass. He drifted and soon joined her in dreams.

Eðna turned in half-sleep and buried her face in clean linen. Her breath came slow and deep, here beside Brosa, and resonated with his.

Memories of yesterday rolled over her, one by one. Svana's ax, Brosa lying in the mud, his pale skin, devastation, image upon image, but something was missing. Since she arrived in the past, every memory had been accompanied by quick, heart-pounding fear. Now, no fear came. Only a hush, an ease. Contentment.

She'd been brave. She helped save them both, and Brosa had taken her here to his most cherished and secret place. She'd stitched his leg, her hands and needle slick with blood. Those things were finished, and she and Brosa were strong. She was warm, tucked here under his arm.

So warm.

She brushed a few strands of hair from her eyes and it stuck to her cheek and face, moist with sweat. She'd built such a tiny fire. It must be reduced to embers by now. Why was she so hot? Brosa was hot too. She slipped her fingers inside his sleeve, pressed her cool hand against his wrist, and his skin burned.

Eðna's eyes flew open.

"Brosa?" She bolted up out of the blankets. "Wake up."

His eyelashes moved, but his eyes stayed closed.

She pressed her hand to his forehead the way her Ma did in the world before thermometers. He was on fire. Inside his shirt, his throat seared her fingers. His hair was stuck to his forehead with sweat, but he shivered, and soft, sick sounds came from deep in his chest, up through his dry throat.

"Wake up!"

Eðna turned in a tight circle, looking for anything that could help. Their supplies sat in the giant heap they'd been in last night. Primitive and useless. Shears, cups, a bowl of dried fish. A worthless comb, good for nothing.

Her Da had combed her mother's sweat-soaked hair, her head in his lap, her body racked with fever from the "elf shot" that killed her. Gida had whimpered, half asleep, while Da murmured lullabies. Eyelids jumping, thin and weak, just like Brosa's were now.

Fever, infection. Sepsis.

Eðna wiped her cheeks. No. Not Brosa too. He would not die this way.

Brosa clutched at his own shirt with a fist that wouldn't open, and a fierce and simple devotion rose in her chest. She stroked his knuckles, and she made promises. Calm, reassuring, as if he could hear.

"I'll make you well." She pried his fingers open. She swallowed a wave of tears. "It's curable." Yes. If she had her medicine. She had to leave right now, to get her lost pack.

"I'm coming back." Brosa would not answer, but she told him anyway. "Just wait. Please. Just…" She couldn't say it. Just don't die.

She pulled her boots on fast and skidded on the rocks and waded across the stream. Brosa was right. She would follow his cairns back to the house.

Eðna stumbled, crushing plants and sticks. Her cheeks stung from branches that whipped her face. Her ankles turned, slipped, throbbed. Words came far back in her mind—surreptitious, stealth—vague notions, thoughts alighting and flying away. She should be quiet. She should hide. But she was driven by one need, to save him.

She'd confessed, as Brosa slept, that she felt a tender thing. Not that she had to stay with him to help him get well. Nei, some exhausted, uncontrolled words fell from her mouth. She didn't want to leave him. She wanted to be by his side.

All this time, she'd grown comfortable with Brosa, until she actually felt safe inside the circle of his arms. The man who was so alive, sickness and death could never touch him. The universe had taught her an immediate lesson, já? This time and place were not safe. Bodies were not sturdy, not even Brosa's. Bodies failed. And here in the past, there was nothing you could do about it. Ginn was insane, thinking this time, this life, was better.

A thousand sticks cracked under her feet. Brosa's wool pants, so huge on her, snagged in branches, and she stopped to shove her pant legs deeper into her boots. What was the spiritual nonsense Brosa had told her? Become another sound. In the woods, blend with the animals. Slip through the trees gracefully, leaving them undisturbed.

"Please." She whispered under her breath to Brosa's gods and spirits. The inhabitants and guardians here in the forest, the tricksters who were amused by human lives, who maybe were laughing at her right now, entertained by her desperate run.

Maybe his gods would let him live long enough for her to make it back. Maybe Hel would leave him alone, not come to claim and devour him yet. Eðna appealed to any and all of them. "If you are real, please." She scanned the ground in every direction for some small animal whose neck she could wring, to offer up in exchange for his safety.

How long had they walked yesterday? She had to be almost there.

The edge of the woods came suddenly.

Just beyond tall drifts of angelica, the hill rose to the house, and at the top stood a woman—just a silhouette from this far across the grass expanse that Eðna and Brosa had crossed yesterday on Gull's back. The woman twirled, and her skirt whirled around her ankles. She walked with a strange, bouncing gait, pacing back and forth. A baby wailed—a reed of a voice from far away. It was Betta soothing her baby.

Betta. So, the family had returned from the assembly. They knew by now that there had been a fight, that she and Brosa were gone.

After rushing so hard to get here, Eðna stood, hesitant, shoulder-deep in snowblooms. She had no plan. Hadn't thought about a scenario in which everyone was home, and Ginn and Betta might capture and question her. She'd only imagined the stable yard, the mud, searching for the vials of medicine and finding them there.

How should she do this? Her spirit yearned to race toward the house, but—

"Jade cloth, silver moon…" Betta's voice was close. She'd come down to the woods, bouncing the baby on her shoulder, drifting slowly, whispering a lullaby. "Lichens of copper and green…" So close now that Eðna could hear the words she murmured to her child, future words, obviously taught by Ginn, but with Betta's Old Norse lilt. She named the colors of wool, the features of the night.

Eðna couldn't trust her. This woman, who whispered with love of evening lavender and amber cloth. Her claws had once wrapped around Eðna's arm and dragged her into the night.

Eðna crouched in the snowblooms, and the sour smell of whey seemed to emanate from the brush all around her. The loam smelled like pantry walls. Nei. Eðna couldn't afford to spend another night in the pantry. Every minute she waited was a hundred fevered years for Brosa.

Yet. Betta was right here. Betta loved Brosa, everyone did. Maybe she would help. Eðna shuffled through possible scenarios, and in every one, she needed assistance. She couldn't hide in the wildflowers forever.

"Hallo?" Betta's voice was a sharp knife in the dark, and Eðna tensed. "Come out, Woman."

Well, then. Eðna tugged on her laces and stepped out of the blooms.

Betta looked her up and down, not quite concealing shock at Eðna's appearance. "You can talk to me," she said. "The men who attacked you are gone. All is well."

Eðna laughed, an angry bark. "I wouldn't be anywhere near this house if all was well."

Betta shifted the baby to her other shoulder, and she must have seen something in Eðna's posture, or her eyes. Betta looked behind and around Eðna, and a note of worry crept in. "Where is Brosa?"

"Brosa is sick." Eðna swallowed the trembling in her voice. "I need the medicine, the little containers from my pack. The things I dropped, maybe near the stable?"

"How is he sick? My father—"

"—An ax wound." Eðna didn't have time for this. Didn't have time to explain sepsis. "He has a deadly fever."

Betta gave a quick and solemn nod. "Shield yourself in the trees," she said, with a flick of her sharp chin. "I'll bring your things."

She turned and strode up the hill on heron legs.

Eðna rested her back against a tree and slid to the ground, relieved, terrified, yearning to get home to the hut in the woods. She drew her knees up and held herself, and minutes went by.

She ripped up long snowbloom stalks and plaited them. They bent at ugly angles. Not a proper braid. She wrecked her work and started again. Her Ma's voice steadied her, and Gida's rhyme about the sheepdog softly drifted in her mind, guiding Eðna's fingers through the steps of making her very first braid.

Over the fence,
Catch the sheep,
Back we come,
Two to keep.

Eðna melted into her mother's arms, and Gida reached around Eðna to guide her hands through the motions. And yet, Eðna was here alone in the 10th century, crouched in bracken, a broken little braid in her tight hands. She strained at the smallest sounds. How long could it take for Betta to get her things? How long had it been?

Finally, she heard the breath of moving grass and soft footfalls.

"Eðna, come out." It wasn't Betta. Ginn's voice was deep. "You are safe here."

This was it. Eðna came forward, head high, and met Ginn's gaze.

The woman's tattoos were stark in the daytime. The whale's form traveling down one side of her face was vivid and blue. She carried a bedroll made of sheepskins and a blanket, tied tight with leather straps.

"Where's my medicine?"

"Inside these blankets." Ginn shrugged off the pack. "And some soap and bandages, some food."

Eðna grabbed the bundle. She yearned to open it and touch the vials to be sure, but she held tight to the sheepskins and did not look.

"Put this on first." Ginn lifted a small bow and bundle of arrows and held the strap, like coaxing an animal. "Please. Let me give this to you."

The ink on Ginn's face and arm marked her as dangerous, a passionate Viking chieftess, tough and a little insane, but now her silver eyes were soft and fearful. Holding out the bow, her hands seemed small and not so powerful. Eðna must look the same.

She ducked her head and let Ginn slip the small quiver onto her shoulders.

Ginn spoke low and secretive. "Where is he?" She helped Eðna heave the bedroll onto her back. "Is he warm enough?"

The simple question broke Eðna's heart.

"He's wracked with fever. I have to go now, to save him."

"Where—?"

"—Nei matter. It's a killing offense to even talk to me." Eðna tugged on the straps, and the bow and quiver and bedroll rode up on her back. "You and the chief are at risk. Don't ask me."

"Okay, já. For now. Just…save him."

Ginn helped Eðna adjust the pack one last time, and they stood for a breath, silently regarding each other.

"This was your chance to leave," Ginn said, "but you came here."

"Pretend I never did."

Ginn took Eðna's hands in a quick, fierce grasp. "Please, when you go home, think of Brosa if not me. He loves this land. Don't lead others here."

Eðna's urgency rose, and she withdrew her hands. "I have to go now."

She waded into the brush.

Eðna yearned to run as fast as Brosa's dear Fjoðr, but she couldn't get lost now. Time was too short, and she was exhausted. It would be too easy to make mistakes. She went steadily, cairn after cairn.

The sun grew warmer on the nape of her neck, and the arrow fletches itched—little arrows, like the kit she had as a girl. The bedroll felt like the one she'd taken with her, so long ago, fleeing from a different farmhouse, another family. When she'd looked back, her childhood house was just a brownish-green hump receding in the dawn. Brenna pulled little Eðna by the hand and said about Jon, *Forget your Da. Let him go.*

Let him go, yes. She'd left her Da behind without a word, and then her real life had begun. The first time she saw the city, it gleamed and reached with glass fingers, drawing her in.

Like Ginn said, this was Eðna's opportunity to go there now, her best chance yet. She knew the way to the coast by herself from here, even without maps. She had supplies on her back, in case it took a few days to the sea. And then, finally home, to her fantastic glacier-lab. As if she wore contacts, her mind overlaid the door to her clean, snow-white apartment over the simple wooden door of Brosa's hut. The fort where he now slept, pale and fevered.

What made her whisper those words last night? That she didn't want to leave him?

Brosa was a good man, and she would help him heal. When he was well enough to take care of himself, to reach his boat and escape this land, then she would go. She would leave him, and her real life would resume.

He could have a good life of his own. He'd sit by an open fire one day, unafraid, somewhere where he could be free. He'd grow to be an old man, plaiting his white hair into a long braid every day, telling stories to his grandkids. Yes. He would have a family. He'd look up over the rim of his cup and wink at his wife, whoever she was, and slide his boot toward her to touch her with his toes.

It was a punch to the gut, and Eðna staggered.

Where was she?

She stopped and turned in every direction, but there were no more cairns.

She wiped sweat and tears from her eyes. Anyone with a bit of sense and experience in the woods would be there by now. They would know the map of this place, the patterns in these leaves. She imagined the woods as if from above, a winding morass. She saw herself lost forever inside, turning, turning, and Brosa slowly passing into the everlife, alone.

How would she ever find him? How would she live without him? Her breath came too fast, ramping up toward hyperventilation.

She pressed her hands to her thighs and breathed slowly. Calm.

All was quiet.

Not a single songbird breathed. None of the passerines that lived here—the redpoll, the goldcrest, the starling with its deep violet head like a night sky sparkling with lights in their orderly patterns. She searched the branches for any bird stirring, puffing its wings. No one was there.

And then she heard a single call, sweet and clear as stream-water. A tiny bird hopped on a branch. *Flickers*, Brosa called them, like tiny explosions of light in the hearth. So light, so tiny, small enough that she could hold one in her palm. It pecked at a rock that sat high up in the branches. A rock, in a tree. Yes! Three rocks were placed in the tree. She pictured the three stones as an arrow, and she plunged into the brush again.

"Thank you, *flicker*."

Eðna limped the last few steps to the stream, ragged and exhausted. The hut stood among the rocks and tiny caves, camouflaged by leaves and moss and water. Brosa was in there. Dead or alive. Her heart picked up, as though hurrying now might make all the difference. She crashed into the dark hut and found Brosa, just as she had left him. Near death, but not gone yet. She burst out crying and laid her head on his burning chest. He was alive.

Brosa pushed Eðna's hands away. "Leave me be."

She was at his bedside, fussing over his leg. "I need to see." She picked at the stubborn knots with her kitchen knife. "To check."

"—Get off me, Woman." He threw her hands off, and his voice thundered in his little house, enough to bring the beams down.

Eðna backed away. She knelt there on the dusty floor, eyes wide. Gods, he was a dumb beast. He'd failed to think of an ambush? Now he'd raged at Eðna, his woman, the only one by his side.

"Fine!" She stood, and a heap of rags fell to the floor. She threw future words at him. Curses, nei doubt. But nei matter what they meant. She should have gone home. She should not have come back here.

Eðna sat down at the threshold, looking out to the woods. She held herself close, her knees folded up inside her arms.

All around her, light streamed into the hut, and it shone on the things they'd brought. Weapons and tools were stored in orderly rows against the wall. Food in the small baskets he'd made as a boy, one full of dried berries and butter cakes wrapped in leaves, another bristling with stiff dry cod. Two blankets were folded and stacked on the chair, clean clothes piled on top. A little lamp burned at his bedside. He stretched his leg straight, and pain flared where she had sewn his wound with a row of stitches so even and fine.

Swift, brave Eðna. While he slept like a useless cat, she had found her way through the woods, faced Ginn, cured Brosa's fever with her medicine, cleaned their clothes and made a home here.

He let out a deep breath and heaved himself off the bed. He ground his teeth against the pain, but it did not burn the way he expected. It was dull from the wound's bane she gave him. She called it pain-killer. He limped to the door and settled himself down beside her, her small shoulder against his arm.

"You should have gone home."

Eðna turned on him, eyes bright with anger. "And you should have died. But I healed you."

"Oh, Eðna." He brushed her cheek with his fingers, and she jerked away.

Her voice broke with anger. "Do you think that of me? That I would go home and leave you here to die alone? The animals could bury you with a few berries and your ear scoop, to send you to the next life?"

"Shhh." He took her chin, turned her toward him.

She pushed at his hands. "I'll look at you when I want to."

His Eðna, unlike any maid he'd ever met. He pressed his face to her hair and whispered into her dark tangles. "I should have thanked you for my life."

She nodded, her breath catching in her throat.

"In truth, I am ashamed. I was too full of thoughts of things that can't be. Laying in the mud, a weakling."

"—Stop." Eðna spoke to the woods. She did not truly speak to Brosa.

"Look at me." He smiled. "If you want to."

Eðna shook her head nei. But she leaned into him, and Brosa's body welcomed her as though she were part of him. He put his arm around her, and she rested her head against him.

A handful of the small flickers came, as always, eyes shifting, wings opening, heads ducking underneath. They moved lightly across the stones just beyond Eðna's feet, so close that one of them tapped its beak against her boot. Eðna breathed slower, quieter. Spoke soft and low. "I wanted to hold it—the little one that Ginn killed."

Brosa said nothing, just sat with her and watched the little birds hop and peck.

Strange, to have her here at his secret hut, and yet good. Eðna tucked herself in beside him, and they watched the birds fluff their wings and turn their heads. The powerful sound of water rushed behind their small voices. Eðna's strong will eased the ache in his leg, though she said it was her pain's-bane. It was her. She drew the burning from him, like she herself was a healing rune carved in bone and set against his side.

So many times, he had sat in this same place as a boy, and then later as a man. His body grew large and sturdy, almost too big for this house. He had come here in joy, to dream about racing his new horse Fjoðr, and later to think about the news that he himself would become a father. His mind could expand to hold so much joy in this place. He could spin dreams that reached all the way to the sea. Later still, so many days he sat here inside these walls in grief—or worse, feeling no grief. Empty as a bowl.

He came to welcome the loneliness. His chest could contract with the ache of loss, without anyone seeing him grieve. Only these flickers, settling their wings.

Well, not these very birds, já? They did not live as long as a man. Maybe their ammas and granddas, strutting across these stones as Brosa listened to the slow movement of the woods. Eðna yawned, and he smiled and settled his chin on her head. To share his secret place now was strange, but right and true. To have these moments with Eðna, before he healed and she went home.

He would grieve when Eðna left. It made a stone form under his ribs, but he had to face it. "You can't stay here."

Eðna didn't move. Did not look up to him, just stared into the woods and said, "I know."

The rock in his chest was heavy and hard. She was only agreeing with him, já? Agreeing with what he'd told her many times over the past days. She was stouthearted and would do what must be done. But to hear her say it, hear her give in to the truth and speak it out loud…Eiðr may as well have run him through with a spear.

Eðna's voice was muffled against his side, where she burrowed into his shirt. "Hold me until then?"

Since the day they met, he had yearned for her to say such a thing. But she came to him too late, with just a day or two to live as a man of worth. She still wanted him now, and gods, he wanted her with the great passion. Like his uncle said, it threw him like a horse, again and again until he was sore and broken.

It would only make things harder when Eðna had to leave, if he told her now the things he'd said just weeks ago about the life they could have. Not now that everything had changed.

How could he breathe her scent of leaves and woods, kiss her face, her brows, taste her mouth? Whisper the secret words a man speaks only to his wife—about a family, tall grass, a house by the sea. How could he do these things that he and Eðna both wanted, knowing she would go so soon?

Yet, how could he not? His thoughts circled like hawks.

Eðna sighed and settled against him. And just as he did as a boy, then as a man, he watched the shapes of light come and go.

ᛊ

Svana flicked her wrists and sent a big fleece flying high over her head. She asked for a bless, not for good crops and healthy cows, but for Brosa. "Freya please, let him be alive."

Her Ma always did it this way, after a sheep was sheared. Hildur held each fleece to the sky, and spirits filled it with their breath. They would skim the raw wool with their loving, unseen fingers, and the fleece would float gently to the ground. Little Svana would lay underneath and look up through the thin places, where the shearing had gone wrong, and sun came through and spread over her face. She rolled away just in time before the fleece landed.

This time, twigs and grass fell in her mouth. She spit and struggled, so unlike her Ma. The fleece did not fill with spirit breath. It fell on her head, a smothering heap, smelling of dust and dung.

Was this a sign? Did it mean Brosa was dead?

She pushed stray hair from her eyes. She was beginning to see Brosa's death in every missed stitch and every drop of spilled broth. She saw him lying in the cold mud as she and Eiðr rode away from the fight. Every waking minute, with every breath, she yearned to know. Had he escaped? Worse, had he come so close to death that a door opened to the everlife, where Hel would receive him with her cold arms?

Svana rocked herself at night and thought the words over and over so Eiðr would not hear. "Let him live. Let him be well."

Across the bright valley this morning, she begged the fox to tell her. She summoned a memory of a herding call her Ma knew from the old country and she sang for the fox to come. She shouted, too, in case the song was wrong. "Come out!"

She watched and waited, the fleece lying at her feet, her skirt whipping her ankles in the breeze. The white woods shone like fish. Inside, the forest was dark. If the fox was there, he was silent.

There was silence from Hvítmork too. The chief and Ginn turned inward, closing the doors of their great hall, locking in their pain. It would burst out one day and flow into the land, and something would finally take place to end the endless—this simmering feud.

Until then, work went on. Despite all the blood and death, there was food to make, boots to clean, wool to spin and weave. Svana swept and cooked just enough to get by. She worked her loom with slow hands, always listening for words dropped like crumbs, about Brosa's fate.

The fleece at her feet was heavy and full of dust. It had been rolled in a sack for too long. On her hands and knees, she spread it out in the grass. She drew the corners out, where the legs had been, and the form of a sheep, flattened in a kind of death, appeared in the grass. It was almost as long as Svana herself, and almost twice as wide. She set to picking out the small sticks and bits of chaff, dead grass where the animal had nuzzled its food.

She separated the wool. Bits that were matted, threads that clung to one another, went into a pile for working into the insides of shoes and winter capes. The glistening wool, with the longest threads, would be spun for cloth.

Spinning wool, simmering feud.

The tail end still had stray bits of old mud, dry as rocks. Svana drew her shears and cut away the ruined parts. If Brosa was dead, it was her fault more than anyone's. Svana herself had thrown him to wolves. Uncle Hár told stories of such creatures. Dogs bigger than men. One wolf would span the door of a grand house. Beasts with teeth like rows of sharpened arrowheads. Snapping, salivating.

—Stop. She should not work too fast, not clean too well. It would raise suspicion. She made a lazy wife for Eiðr. With his hand missing, and his family disgraced in the eyes of the chief, Eiðr was pleased he had a wife. A woman in his house, in his bed. A girl who had been lovely for a while. And him, with a beard as full of filth as this fleece! Everyone knew Eiðr was ugly but smart.

Svana cradled her sore hand. She had passed his test with the ring, but he still suspected her of something, though he had no real crime he could name. She had to take care. She hated him, and as her hatred grew, so did his cruelty.

She sat up from cleaning the fleece and looked to the far line where grass met woods. Inside the snarl of trees, next to a stream and foss, sat Brosa's fort. If he was alive, he would be there now. Eiðr had no knowledge of the place, but Svana knew it well. She had followed Brosa many times.

It was on the way there one day that she first wanted him. The day she became a woman in her thoughts and desires. She was twelve, and she followed him like a little lamb. She'd slipped through the trees after him, as she'd done before. Brosa stopped often to stand on a root and reach up to adjust the rocks he kept in the branches. And when he reached, his shirt climbed up and his back looked strong, his waist suddenly leaner than last time she'd looked. His calves were filling out his bindings, and when he went onto his toes to reach up into the trees, he looked almost like his uncle Hár.

Something opened like a snowbloom inside her that day, back when Brosa was still possible for her. When it seemed like the most natural thing would be for Svana to step up by his side, strew flowers as he carried her over the threshold and gave her the keys to their house.

She brushed the woolly curls of the fleece with her fingertips.

Did Brosa miss her now? Alone in his fort, did he think of her? After everything, after all she had done and all he had suffered, still he might think of her sometimes. Or was he not alone? Was the woman Eðna still with him? Just like Ginn, the woman had cost Svana her rightful life, stole her rightful husband, her joy.

Anger was sharp in Svana's heart, and yet her thoughts spun sure, and a thin thread began to take shape in her mind. Eðna…just like Ginn… Já, Eðna *was* like Ginn, a thief and a beiskaldi. But also like Ginn, Eðna knew how to leave this land and go farther than any normal woman could ever go.

Could she take Svana with her? To her cloud-home?

"—Wife!"

She whipped her head up. Eiðr came on horseback. A feeling came up in Svana's throat that stung so hard she could not speak. She held her burned wrist, tucked it into her lap.

Eiðr brought the horse so close, Svana felt he might stomp on her, and he looked far down at the top of her head. "I go to hunt today," he said. Another job that Rakknasson gave Eiðr to taunt him. Eiðr could not draw a bow.

Carefully, so carefully, Svana asked. "You are going to the woods?"

"Já, Woman. Hunting is done in the woods." He sneered at her stupidity, but then he smiled. "In truth, Morg and I are going to worry Ulfsson. I have news that he limped away from our attack. He lives in the trees now. We'll find him, circle him and make him squirm like a fish."

Svana almost shouted with joy. Brosa was alive!

She caught herself in time and kept silent, but happiness bright and fast as a river rushed through her body. She ducked her head, so Eiðr would not see her smile. He would surely hear her relief if she spoke, and so she shut her mouth tight against the tide of joy.

Eiðr spat out, "Have a meal ready at dusk."

She nodded, and she found her voice. "I hope you find him." It was the truth. The only true thing she'd said to her husband in a very long time. Perhaps Eiðr would find Brosa, and Brosa would kill her stupid husband himself. There was nei worry that if it came to a fight Eiðr would prevail. Even if he had two hands, he could never beat Brosa. He could not harm him nei matter how he tried. Brosa was strong as a mountain, golden and hale as harvest grass.

He was alive.

She bent her head to cleaning, and Eiðr did not see her happiness. He took off on his skinny horse, and Svana was left to shine bright as a lamp.

She would go to Brosa. She knew how to follow his cairns, knew the way to his fort, and she would bring him food and soothe his wounds, sing to him, protect him. She would make right all the damage she had done, and he would be well.

She snipped and snipped at the wool, skirting the fleece, sorting the pieces. The door to the everlife would remain solid and closed, and Brosa would rise from his injuries. Eðna would take to the sea, to journey back to her place alone. Svana would not need the woman's help after all. Nei.

The fleece was becoming clean under her hands. This wool would one day become a shirt. Or nei, it would become a sail to catch the wind. Her own thread could carry Brosa away from this island, with Svana standing at his side, brave face to the sea, with nothing but the ship's wolf between her and another life.

Eðna struggled with the little bow. For the seventh time today, she untangled it from a gnarled branch.

What was she doing? Eðna Jonsdottir, hunting for animals.

She blew stray hairs out of her face. It was not like she expected. Like everything.

She'd trained to hunt in case it was necessary. Worlds away, that training seemed like a naive dream, too embarrassing to recall. No one in the 22nd century could have guessed what it would feel like to hunt in real wilderness, in the dim of night, with the threat of stark hunger and the knowledge that it would get worse if she didn't catch anything soon. She'd never practiced moving through dense forest in a man's long wool pants secured awkwardly around her waist and tucked tight into delicate ankle boots that were made for a princess, not a hunter.

Disjointed memories and images from the arcs came to her, as if her mind were a screen—bowhunters talking about stance and grip, images of animals' dead eyes, of blood in the brush and leaves. Here, now, the trees around Eðna became antlers thrusting up from the earth, attached to something unfathomably big underneath. And she was small, rushing around on top of it, disturbing everything.

She wouldn't catch an animal this way. And she wanted to, so much it hurt.

It had been over a week, definitely. Time had become imprecise, and the light hours and dim times blurred, as indistinguishable as separate beads of water in the falls. Days were long and vivid, nights short and used for gathering.

During the light hours, while Brosa slept, Eðna sat in the chair, stiff with worry. He'd explained what Svana's taunt meant. *Let a foul shirt soak.* The Viking practice of letting a man twist and wait like a wet shirt was incredibly effective. Eðna fell asleep sitting up every day, with a knife in her hand, wondering when, when.

Brosa spent his time healing, hurting, hiding his pain, as Eðna rationed the painkiller. Sometimes he exploded with frustration and rage and bellowed things like goat's balls and spat out "Hrodi!"—which meant something like *fuck* and also *snot.* He snapped orders. "Get me a good stick, Woman!" She found him a walking stick, and he heaved himself out of bed and practiced moving around, searching for berries and tinder, "like a child of three years."

Eðna spent her time helping him to stand, to lie down. She cleaned his forehead with linen dipped in stream water. Soothing touches, consoling words that he batted away like insects. Finally, she left him to his anger and took the bow and arrows.

She might as well try. Even with Ginn's bits of food, and the things they had grabbed in the pantry, they would soon run out. It would be an even greater risk for Eðna to go all the way back to Hvítmork to get help from Ginn.

Nei matter, as Brosa would say. This yearning to catch something came from somewhere deeper than Eðna's hungry stomach. She would succeed, surprise Brosa, please him and please herself. She ached to bring something back to the hut and beam and say "Look, I did it."

Her shirt snagged on a branch again. She dropped her bow to pick carefully at the fabric. It took hours to alter Brosa's pants and her dress so they were useful. The last thing she wanted was to sew again, head bent in the dark hut, working tiny stitches with an iron needle.

She got herself free and raised her bow again.

"Every creature makes a home," Brosa had once told her, back when he taught her to walk quietly in the woods, so long ago it felt like a year. "Keep your eyes open for nests, burrows."

He showed her how to practice her aim, not with dirt mounds like she did as a girl, but the way his own Da showed him. Ulf had told the children to choose a tree and then turn on it, surprise it, shoot it. When Brosa told Eðna this, his darling smile grew with the tenderness of his memories. So unlike hers.

She sighed and lowered her bow. This was a childish game, mortifying even here alone. She sighted another birch, missed it and tried again, arrow after arrow. After missing six times, she waded around in the brush to find them all. This part—the collecting of failures like a bouquet of star-blooms—wasn't difficult. The arrows never went far. Every time she raised her arms and pulled back the string, deep truths and promises made her muscles fail.

Never shoot a tree. They were precious.

Her father's voice was always so golden, like liquid light. Brosa sounded so much like Jon, but he said entirely opposite things.

She chose another birch, shot and lost an arrow right at her feet—a shot like a six-year-old would make. A fine start, Eðna. Her Da was always positive, always loving. Always lying—

A screech snapped Eðna awake, and she yelped.

It came from the ground. At her feet, in a nest of twigs and fluff, sat a bird, staring up at her. She'd almost tripped over it. The nest was a swirl of sticks that formed a perfectly-fitted bowl. The bird's plumes were rusty brown and gray, with white speckles that made it disappear into the birch bark all around, so that all that stood out were its bright eyes. Eðna stared back, drawn into the living, pulsing yellow gaze.

She should kill it. She could bring it home to Brosa and pluck off those gorgeous, fascinating feathers. Throw away that beak—a waxy shell—and she and Brosa would eat.

Her hand closed on her knife. She would not even need an arrow. She stood right above it, and the bird looked up as if willingly, peacefully offering its throat for her to slake her yearning to feed and impress Brosa. To heal him.

The bird let out a warble, so sudden and insane that Eðna jumped and crashed into the tree behind her. No wonder she hadn't caught anything. So stealthy, já? Yelping and jumping and losing her arrows, wading through crackling sticks and detritus to find them.

The bird settled in its nest and cooed, sweetly now, as if singing her a song. So not afraid of Eðna. Gods, she was such a bad hunter, the bird was consoling her.

Back when she trained, she knew she might have to kill a bird, if she was in trouble and needed food. Birds were an abundant source of protein here, and there were few nutritious plants and just one land mammal. But here she was, her forehead pressed to a tree cushioned with moss, sick and hesitant while a bird sat right at her feet. A beloved, breathing individual. A mythical creature she had longed to see, to touch, all these years. And another truth came—even stronger than her promise to not shoot trees.

She could not kill a bird. She could not eat one. She would starve first.

She laughed like a madwoman, and the bird ruffled, then settled. Já, she might actually, really starve, if Svana and Eiðr didn't come soon and resolve this feud, this fight, one way or another. The waiting was insufferable.

Here in the woods, the birches were patient. So serene, so still they were covered with mats and clumps of electric green moss.

The moss did not worry. Its miniscule stems reached for sun. They shimmered with her breath and tickled her nose, tickled her mind, and a stored fact came. Starving Icelanders made moss into stew.

Eðna lifted her head. Real, lush moss was everywhere.

Was this the edible species, the right kind? She accessed information in her eyes. No response. Right. She wouldn't be able to accurately, positively identify it.

She smoothed the tree-moss before her. Velvety moist, fresh food. She scraped some into her pack, and then more, until finally she scraped like she was a wild thing until her pack was overflowing.

Gods, she longed for such strange things now. To walk in silence. To eat moss.

To confirm the movement of breath in one man's chest as he slept. To place her lips to that warm spot behind Brosa's ear, under his hair, just one more time—the place where a woman's secrets were meant to go. She told him about her desire. How it hurt when she sometimes climbed, exhausted from worry, into bed beside him. His body reacted to hers, rising with desire too, before he turned away to sleep.

The bird ruffled and settled again, and Eðna wiped stray hair out of her eyes.

"Takk," she said. "Thanks, bird." She set to walking quietly back to the fort.

Brosa cinched his pack, and he leaned into his walking stick to stand. His leg was on fire from bending to search for small fungus at the bases of trees and in between blades of grass. Each tiny cap was small as a finger—not much food, even if he found a hundred—but he could cook them with butter and fish.

He heaved himself up a short rise to the hut. The snowblooms here were darkening with the season, turning deeper green until soon they would burst open with white flowers. He had gone many times with his ma to pick these plants. Now was the time to harvest the whole plant, just above the dirt, for cooking. The stems could be stirred into soup.

Brosa laughed. Eiðr might come any time and cleave his skull. On his death day, they would sing of him in battle with the mushrooms and stalks.

The gods knew, he could get himself and Eðna killed by stumbling around with his lame leg, cracking every stick and bending every limb in the forest. Some fear of death was smart, já. But after days and days of this, he was losing his wits, nei mind his dignity. That was all but gone.

An Icelander, grandson of Magnus, among the first in this land. The child of strong women, his grandma Amma and his mother, the sharp and graceful Melrakki. He winced just thinking of her wicked raised brow. His ma would be crossing her arms right now and glaring at him, while he picked flowers and sat like a fool on his bed, an indoor man, a coward. Squandering all the strengths that she had made sure he possessed.

He crushed a handful of snowbloom buds in his fingers and white petals spilled out.

What could he do? He couldn't make a run for the sea now, with his leg broken. He could not go to Eiðr to end this madness. That would shame his brother and himself in the everlife, to do such a thing. And what about Eðna? What could he do with her? She would not go away, and it broke his heart and yet made him the luckiest of men, even as he crouched here in the woods.

Hundreds upon hundreds of petals fell from each crushed bud.

His mother had given him a strong will, to breathe deep and join in song. A strong body to fight and roam and love women. She'd given him the knowledge of how to mend as well as cleave. Given him the strength to write, to wield runes.

Eðna had been impressed that he could write. His hull drawings made her eyes widen with respect. Why had he waited so long to show her? The lost days seemed like years thrown to the crows, when he could have shown her his worth and strength of mind so much sooner. The brittle bits of paper now lay rolled in his hut beside the steerboard handle where he had carved his name.

Brosa closed his fist, and the petals stopped falling.

The steerboard, já. What he needed was some direction.

A guiding rune would show him what to do about Eðna.

He yanked a handful more of the snowblooms and took them to the hut.

Brosa brushed the sheepskins and made a flat space on the bed. He would not carve the sign in wood or stone. It should not linger. The shape would invoke guidance, so it would work in this time and nei longer. He used the snowbloom petals to draw. He let the tiny bits fall gently from his hand.

His uncle told stories of Odin's advice. "When the sun sets, honor the day." Praise a weapon once it is tried. Ice, once it is crossed. Ale, after it is drunk. A lamp, once it is burned. These things happened, and were honored once they passed.

He nudged the flowers into shape, forming the rune, and petals stuck to his skin. Those things were honored once they had passed, já, but there were always more blades and cups of ale. Day after day, axes were tried, drink was praised, lamps burned low. None of it truly ended.

He placed the blooms and remembered his Uncle's voice, gruff and soothing, giving him Odin's words. "In the wind, chop wood. In a breeze, row to your ship." And with a lifted, bushy brow, "In the dark, talk with a maid."

Eðna.

Even Odin's advice brought Brosa around to her. His rune took shape, and it guided his thoughts back to his woman time and again. She would tell him with her eyes, when he saw her. And he would act then—get on his feet and take her to the sea, or get on his back and beg her to come to bed with him.

He looked to the rune. In truth, his heart was not in the sea journey. His death day, and Eðna's, were fixed. He should not fear all that might come between now and then.

Eðna walked in the wild, placing each foot lightly before pressing her weight into it. Her movements, her whole self, felt more fluid now that she'd talked with that bird. Brosa would not mind that she came home without an animal. He understood Eðna. He believed in her absolutely, with the kind of faith he had in goddesses and spirits.

But goddesses and spirits were not lovers. Nei, he held Eðna at the same distance, too.

Even as she brushed his hair back from his forehead, when his pain haunted him, he closed his eyes and said, *When will you go?* and her chest went heavy and dull. Did he really want her to leave? Or was he begging her to stay? He'd said he was not like her father. He wouldn't push her, one way or another. He'd give her the truth about life, and he would let her decide.

"—Hold."

Eðna froze. It was a man's voice up ahead.

Hrodi!—fuck-and-snot—she had to hide.

In every direction, the trees were gaunt, their trunks thin as bones. Not a single rock or large stump stood nearby. She found a downed tree to get behind. She squatted among the convoluted limbs and wished for invisibility. Her heart and breath were flying like horses, her mouth suddenly full of sand.

The voice came again. "Do you hear?"

Senses strained, she searched for odors of leaf mold and mens' sweat, listened for brush crunching. Where were they? How far away?

"Stow your ax." Another voice, quiet, grave.

"We've waited long enough"

"I want him to suffer, Cowfoot!" The man was exasperated. "Goad Ulfsson, bring him out. Kill him in open air, not end him like an animal limping in the woods."

The man speaking was Eiðr. He would not kill Brosa today. Good. But he would do something to make Brosa suffer, to taunt and enrage him. Eðna looked to her shaking hands, and remembered a story Ginn told, about how the angry man Ageirr had taken her hostage.

—Oh, gods. If Eiðr found her, they would taunt Brosa by using Eðna. They would hold onto her as a hostage, hurt her probably. Use her to draw Brosa out, to provoke him until he raged and struck at them. She could almost feel the man's breath on the back of her neck, the night of the ambush. Would they bind her arms, beat her, maim her the way Heirik maimed Eiðr?

In the most likely future, Eiðr's cousin, startled, would simply shoot Eðna on sight. She would watch her own blood seep from an arrow in her chest, and murmur a plea to any of Brosa's gods, that he would get better without her. That he'd remember her.

She checked her bracers, and they were tight. She unsheathed her knife and slipped her wrist through the strap. Her thighs ached, crouched and ready to spring. The woods had suspended itself as the men passed, with their voices and crunches underfoot. The birds and small animals hid their faces and quieted their voices, but Eðna could not quiet her breath and her small sounds of fear.

Before she sensed him, the man's hands were around her wrist. She gasped and pulled against him, but he was so strong.

It was the dumb one, not Eiðr. The one called Morg. He yanked her to her feet and crushed her back against a tree. She brought the knife up, but the man caught her, and he held both her hands in one of his own. The blade dangled, useless, and her sleeve flapped free. He'd snapped the thread and torn the cloth.

"We knew we would find you." He pressed himself against her, his knee between her legs. Metal beads in his filthy beard rattled in her face. "Wolves will always scent the cowards."

Eðna struggled against his grip. She would be brave, honor Brosa. Not show fear. "What do you know of wolves?"

Swift and sudden, he yanked on her knife and the cord broke. She cried out. And the man pressed her own blade against her thigh.

"Enough, Morg." It was Eiðr. "Hold your blade."

Morg removed the knife from her thigh and slipped it into his own belt. Still, he held Eðna tight.

Eiðr leaned casually against a tree, his arms folded. He eyed Eðna like she was a specimen of some kind, learning her, memorizing her features. It was a violation worse than Morg's foul breath and grimy hands.

"She'll carry my message."

Eiðr came closer now, and with his one hand he ran a finger down Eðna's cheek, pressing hard, smearing a trail that stank of sweat and sickness.

"Hold her braid," he said to Morg. The man pulled on Eðna's hair hard, wrenching her head back, and with her own knife, Eiðr cut her hair. He sawed at her braid, and she wept and shook. He held up a big piece of her hair and admired it in the sunlight. He brushed her cheek with the ends of her shorn braid.

"Go to Ulfsson, wherever he is. Go and tell him that we are close. That we can touch you."

Eiðr nodded to Morg, and the man let her go. They turned their backs and left her alone.

Eðna slid to the ground and held herself tight, choking on tears. She watched them go.

It would be so easy to sit under this tree forever. So easy to just rest, to let her tears run out and dry on her skin. But Brosa would come looking, and he would give himself away.

She pushed herself to her feet.

Eðna ran.

She slammed into trees, her loose sleeve ripping on branches. Underfoot, brittle plants and sticks cracked like bones of small animals. Would Eiðr and Morg turn and follow her?

After a long time, she came to a massive rock and she ducked behind it. With her arms around her knees, she hid. She gagged and took huge, gulping breaths, but had to be quiet, so quiet. Eðna waited, every sense on alert, not sure if Eiðr and Morg were after her.

She didn't hear them.

She calmed her breath. She counted and breathed quieter and quieter, until her own respiration faded into the forest and she heard nothing. Not a rustle. Not even a bug.

And then…birdsong. The animals abruptly came back to life with a flourish of noise. The forest was all clear.

She took a long route, slogging through brush in four different directions before going back to the hut. By the time she heard the waterfall and saw the vapor rising from the roof, she was sleep-walking, covered in mud, her face soaked. Was she crying? She didn't care anymore. She only wanted Brosa. She yearned for him to come rushing and encircle her with his arms. She skidded down the hill to their door and stumbled over the threshold.

Brosa stood at once and pulled her into his arms, and she cried into his shirt.

"What's wrong, Elskan?" He spoke against her forehead, kissing her over and over. "What happened?"

"They caught me."

"What do you mean?"

"Eiðr and that pig, they caught me."

He held her away, and she saw him search her face, her clothes, her hair. He saw her braid. Brosa growled and looked around wildly. He punched the wall, and then he actually roared. Huge, angry, filling up the room. Eðna backed into the wall, her hands up to hold him off. She trembled, and she felt Morg's hands all over.

"It's me, Elskan." Brosa took her hand, and she felt Morg's fingers close on her wrist. She pulled away.

Gentler still, he said "Please. I didn't mean to rage at you." And then his voice broke. He took what was left of her braid in his hand. "Did Eiðr…Did he…?" Brosa could not even form the words to ask what Eiðr had done.

"He touched my face, my hair."

Brosa ran his thumb along Eðna's cheekbone, spreading her tears. He brushed her forehead with his fingertips, and then her eyelids, her cheeks, her jaw, rougher now, as though he could clean Eiðr from her skin. Brosa took her face in both his hands, and he kissed her. A kiss like thunder and the waterfall outside, with the force of all the rivers rushing to the sea, and Eðna opened her mouth, her thirst so deep.

He drew away so he could look at her. "Forgive me." And Eðna wasn't sure if he was sorry about Eiðr, about his violent reaction, about his kiss, still burning on her lips. He sat on the bed, and he held her by the hips, pulled her close so that she stood touching, her legs against his legs. "Forgive me," he said, and he pulled gently on one of the laces at her side. The tie fell open. Brosa let the cord fall from his fingers, slowly, savoring the undoing. Eðna's breath caught, her body so bright, so ready for him, so fast.

She touched his cheekbone, his jaw, the way he had done hers, and felt the shape of his words, forgive me. The shreds of her sleeve brushed against his beard. An image of Ginn and Heirik flashed and was gone. This was not the same, not at all. Her and Brosa. For each other alone.

He untied her other lace, just as slowly, and then drew her into his lap.

"Your leg," she murmured against his skin. "Does this hurt?"

He growled like a forest animal. "Nei matter."

His hand covered the back of her head, his mouth, so easy, met hers with a kiss like wings settling on her lips. His taste of rosemary and stolen honey. He wound a few strands of her hair in his fingers and gently pulled her in. He spoke against her mouth, "Come, Woman."

And she knew now, all the things she'd wondered. How his skin felt underneath his shirt, how their bodies fit against one another, safe and tight, his body so ready for her, too. This kissing and yearning and love all together. Ten thousand things to know. She smiled into their kiss, thinking of him saying there was so much to learn here.

His hands were on her back in her hair, his mouth on her throat. "Astvjeka." He said she kindled his fire. She had not really known—all this time since Brosa was cast out—had not known what she was asking for. He laid her back in the furs, and she began to learn.

Eðna woke to birdsong and steel. To fox and bear fur slipping over her naked skin, and the subtle warmth, on her nose and forehead, of sun through the open door.

Brosa sat in the chair—his big body just barely fit—and sharpened his knife. With his hair a mess and his shirt open, gods he looked good. She could still taste his kiss.

He smiled, teasing, easy. "Good morning, syfjaður barn." He called her sleepy little one. A sacred moment after what they had done last night, and at the same time playful. Her own smile felt sloppy, intense. She sat up, holding furs to her breasts, ridiculously modest and shy. But sure of herself, too. A strong sense of her abilities pulsed with her heartbeat. Brosa's eyes reflected what she felt. He was stronger now, too.

She looked down at her hands, her chest, and a constellation of little white blossoms stuck to her skin.

"There are flowers in the bed."

"A bless," he said. His voice, his closeness, made her skin sparkle.

He ran his fingers through her hair, and he leaned in to kiss her. He tasted of the angelica he used to clean his teeth, and she smiled, remembering he was called vain for his cleanliness. He was truly beautiful and he tasted good and oh gods, this was right, so right.

"I am the happiest man today, Eðna." He brushed her hair with his fingers, and the ends tickled her shoulder.

The ends. Her hair. It came back in a rush, how Eiðr had sawed her braid off.

"I'm happy," Brosa said, "and yet I would kill Eiðr on sight. And by the gods, I admit I'm scared."

"I am the happiest woman, and I don't want to think about Eiðr." She tugged on her shoulder-length hair, short on just one side, and she searched the table for the iron shears. "Please fix it."

Brosa drew back to consider her hair. "Well, it is a mess, and this side is…gone." She saw him struggle to make light.

"Do what you have to do. I won't live with it this way," she said. Not half, not different on each side. Not the way Eiðr had made it. "I want it to be cut by you, not him."

"Já, then." Brosa was sweet and gentle. "Turn around and I'll make it right."

He sawed at her hair with his knife, and she gasped and grabbed the furs. She was back in the woods with Eiðr, with Morg's beads rattling in her face and Eiðr sawing, sawing.

"It scares you," Brosa said. "We can leave it, Love."

"Nei." She swallowed and held her head high. "I'm fine."

Brosa smiled, and he cut her hair. He cut it until it just brushed her shoulders on both sides. The air was cool on her back, and her head felt light and strange.

He looked at her, and he smiled. "You are beautiful, Fine One."

He laid down his knife and took her hand. And they sat, unhurried, silent. She felt a massive turning coming to pass. She had turned toward Brosa, his land, his place, and now his body, as though she had turned to finally, truly look into his eyes.

"I'll go hunt," she said, but she made no move to get up. "I'll bring home food."

"Nei, you won't." Brosa looked at her pack on the floor, overflowing with dirty moss, and he laughed. "We're going fishing."

Brosa tied his pant legs up with string. He left his boots behind and went out onto the rocks in bare feet.

He rested a hand on the door frame, and he looked to the trees in every direction. They'd waited until dim night to leave the hut. They wouldn't go out in the day any longer, not after what happened to Eðna.

In truth, he did not know what he'd do if he saw Eiðr lurking there. His heart raced with yearning to cleave the bastard's skull, but his body was weak. He could not fight now, even if he had to.

The woods were empty, on the edge of night.

He walked down to the water, leaning on his stick. Eðna walked by his side, trying to help. He didn't have the heart to tell her to leave him be. He could walk to the stream, but her hands, her strength, her sweetness felt good, and halfway to the water he stopped to kiss her berry lips. He buried his hand in her hair, and she tilted her head back to rest against his palm. She smiled against his lips. Her laughter caught him in the heart, and he forgot every thought in his head.

He held her away so he could just look. Her dark brows and mess of hair—shorter now than any woman's hair he had ever seen—were so different than the blond women of his family. A good woman, fine and beautiful and gods, she was here, she was his.

Where was he going?

Ah, já, fishing.

"Good, then." He shook himself free of his staring. "Some fish!"

He handed Eðna the net and showed her how to drive sticks into the bank at the narrowest part of the stream. He looped the net loosely so it would not tangle. When he stood, he kissed Eðna again.

"Is this how you fish?" She teased him.

"Alright Woman, you wait here. I will tell you when to pull the net."

He walked away from Eðna, upstream. The water washed his feet in warmth. The current was fast this time of year, but the stream was shallow and he could hold his ground. At about the length of four men, he turned to face her.

"As I am," he looked down at his leg, "I'm suited to his kind of fishing." He steadied himself on the rocks. "I'll stand still for a while, then fumble and stomp to flush the fish. When I say so, you close the net."

She nodded—Serious Eðna, ready to close her net—and Brosa waited until the water returned to its natural course and the tiny fish nibbled at his ankles. Then, he let loose an outburst worthy of ten drunken men. He smacked the water with his stick and drove everything toward Eðna. He swept his walking stick under the plants that hung on the banks. Small fish darted and flailed, and he kept smacking the stream, driving them into Eðna's trap.

"Now," he shouted, splashing toward her. "Close it."

Eðna staggered and fell to her knees in the bright water. She came up with the net in her hands, full of struggling fish, and she held it to the dim sky.

Brosa squinted to get a good look. They were small, but he was proud nei matter. The fish were theirs. Something he was able to give Eðna—this knowledge, and a bit of food.

She was soaked. Truly, she looked like a madwoman, standing in the middle of the stream with her skirt tied up and water running down her arms and legs. She held the squirming net out from her body, as if it smelled foul, and he burst out laughing.

"Shut your mouth," she said, but she smiled, and she came toward him. She stepped lightly in the shallow water, and it formed circles and currents around her ankles, wetting the hems of her underdress. It would be good to lift those skirts, feel her legs underneath. The thought breathed an ember to life inside him. A part of his spirit that had dwindled and faded was growing again.

She came to him, kissed him, and then she ducked her head to tuck herself against his chest. He pressed a kiss to her head and they stood in the water, his stick at his side, and her net of fish. He looked overhead at the branches. The trees joined arms across the water, hanging heavy with dark leaves. The sky through the leaves was clear and dark, the air quick and warm.

He looked to their hut. It was truly well hidden, and he could just make out the door. Inside, it held all the things that they owned, the bedside table with its feathers and cups, the baskets full of sharpening stones, their blankets and furs. They had those things, and they had this piece of forest they could see beyond their door. Stream and pool and dirt and sky. This peace was theirs. The silence of the woods that was not quiet at all.

When they first met, Eðna had said he was so alive. She didn't know then, how he had waited for death that day. Now, outlawed and broken, his life had just begun.

Eðna climbed the ridge that curled up and around and became the roof of the hut.

As the days and nights passed, her forays had turned from hunting animals to seeking fuel, and every night she had to hunt farther and longer to find dry wood.

Each night, she came up here first, to look at the forest. There was a tree whose multiple trunks bent and touched the ground. She liked to climb it when the sun was getting dim, before she headed out to search the woods under cover of the quick summer evening.

The peeling bark was slick with steam, and Eðna hung on while her boots slipped, finding another foothold, and another, until she was more than two meters up. From here, she could look down over their world.

The stream raced with the speed and volume of midsummer. Water gathered in the little pool, and beside it sat the giant stone that Brosa called the setberg—a stone shaped like a high seat a chieftain would use. They sat there sometimes, in the evenings.

Birds went swiftly from tree to tree, and her heart flew with them. She saw the last faint twitches in the brush before nightfall, the fluffing of feathers and scattered little explosions in the treetops. From up here, the setberg looked small, and she watched the sun move across it and the wildflowers around it bend in the breezes. The forest around the ravine was thick, and in the evening it woke with the movements of foxes beginning to hunt.

When she was little, she'd dreamed of looking down from such a high place. She yearned to see and understand the patterns of life, the orderly plaits of sheeps' pathways crossing and coming together. From up here on the ridge, the foxes' tracks were just gentle impressions. She hadn't expected wild animals would make such orderly trails through the woods, but the foxes hunted toward North with the magnetic forces of the pole.

If she could just show this to Jon. She would breathlessly tell him what she knew now. *Look Da, this is how foxes really go.*

There were no patterns of men or of women. Every evening, the woods were undisturbed by Eiðr, Morg, Svana. The forest felt safe and right and good.

Tonight, Brosa was well enough to walk up the ridge with her. He stood now at the foot of the tree and looked up to her.

"When I was a little girl," she said, "I dreamed of riding a high-shot arrow and looking down on the paths of animals."

"This tree is good for such a thing." He patted the trunk, as if to test its sturdiness. "I climbed it many times as a boy. I felt I could see as far as Heimdall could, far over the sea. My uncle told us Heimdall needed less sleep than a bird and he could see all the way across the whale road and over every land."

Eðna's feet dangled, and she breathed deep looking over it all. Brosa leaned against the tree, and they both watched the ravine change into night, until she couldn't stop herself from speaking.

"You don't think I know what I'm doing."

Brosa smiled up at her. "Walk with me a little," he said. "Let me show you the wood."

Eðna slid down off the tree branch and walked with him. They made their way slowly, carefully, Brosa sometimes stopping to lean and rest.

Eðna brushed hair from her forehead and blew strands out of her mouth. "I know how to find sticks."

"Já, then?" Brosa leaned on a tree to rest and gestured with his chin. "Look up, Woman. See those fallen limbs?"

Eðna looked up, and she stopped and turned in a dizzying circle. Stars glowed and sparkled. From down here, they looked like glints of light caught in a net of tree-branches.

All this time Eðna had looked down. She'd observed patterns below her perch in the tree, while overhead a chaos of dead boughs and sticks interlaced their fingers with the trunks of live trees. Bark peeled in sheets that were dried by the sun, big enough to pry free and burn. Perfect wood lay snagged in the crooks of other trees. Disordered patterns crisscrossed, so different from the orderly paths of foxes down below.

"They're dead and broken," Brosa said. "But off the ground. They'll burn well."

Brosa reached as many dry limbs as they could carry. Closer to the ground, he showed Eðna how to find kindling that would snap and how to examine the ends of larger limbs to look for cracks.

"For dry fluff you have to dig, like a winter sheep."

She laughed. He had a way of seeing things that was completely unlike hers, and with each thing he showed her, she saw it too. So, she became a winter sheep, digging and searching the forest floor for dry bits of bark and feathers.

Back at the hut, Eðna let go of the corners of her skirt and tinder tumbled out onto the floor. A woodland assortment of juniper needles, dried moss and lichens, little scrolls and chips of birch bark and the tiniest wisps of down from an abandoned nest all landed on the floor beside the fire pit.

She sorted it into piles of tinder and kindling and fuel.

Brosa came in—he'd washed his hair and face in the stream. He wore clean pants, and his hair glistened, the streaks of white blond glowing in the moonlight coming through the door. He was a wonder of a life force, filling up the room with his grin and his smell of rosemary and soap.

"Good then—a fire." He lowered himself carefully to the bed and stretched his leg. "Since you live here now, you need to know how to strike one up faster."

"I've lit a thousand fires."

He laid sticks parallel to one another in the stone basin in the floor. "You told me yourself. In your city fires start themselves."

"I know how—"

"—I know" He cut in. "You are fine. But there are things to learn still." He gave her a broad smile and began stacking sticks across the top of the others. "You never collected all ten thousands of birds, já?"

Eðna blushed. Why had she ever told him that number?

"I will show you how to strike up a fast fire and hide the smoke."

She thought of the roof and the hot water that ran so close. "But the steam already hides it."

"Já, but this way of making a fire kills the smoke, so there is not so much to hide."

Eðna raised an eyebrow. "You can make a fire without smoke."

"My Da taught me." He arranged bits of bark and fluff in his palms and rolled it all into a small ball. He transferred the little nest to Eðna's palms, and then he added a bit of touchwood. He struck his firestriker, and a spark flew into the touchwood and started to glow.

Eðna held the warm mess of moss and bark and downy feathers in her cupped palms, and Brosa leaned close, almost touching foreheads, to blow on it, so carefully she barely felt a whisper of his breath. So savage, so gentle.

In her previous life, she'd hated the whole necessity of bodies, but sitting across from Brosa like this, leaning into his warmth, he was so familiar and good. She wanted him to lean into her like this forever, wanted his scent of herbs and clean shirt. Of woolly water. Her blood rose just thinking of his hips and hers together. Right now her body and his, together, protected the little spark in her palms.

"Give it your breath."

She exhaled, sending the tiniest puff of air into the handful of tinder. The orange speck grew and then subsided with her breath, and the birch bark curled and ignited. She bent to slide it in under the structure he'd made.

"Place it well," he said. She laid it in the bottom of the depression, inside the structure of sticks. "The shape of this hearth makes the fire grow without stoking."

Suddenly, everything lit. The flames grew fast and hot. Something about the structure and air-flow in this rock depression made the flame leap and become turbulent.

Brosa placed the pot on the fire. "Another thing you don't know is that a woman must keep a firestriker on a cord around her neck," he said.

"Oh, já? A woman must?"

"I saw, after the assembly, you had a poor striker in your pack. I've been meaning to give you this one." Brosa drew the long leather cord from out of his shirt, the one that held the small striker. The little curved piece of iron—curled back on each end—had pressed against Eðna's chest many times when they laid together. It was made for a much smaller hand than his, but she had not asked why.

She ducked her head, and he slipped the cord over. His breath touched her cheek and moved small bits of hair around her forehead. The small weight of the firestriker fell against her chest. She took it in her fist and leaned in again to press her forehead against his.

"So you are always warm," he said, "even when I can't be with you."

Quiet fell. Why would he say such a thing? She would not think of it—of a time when Brosa could not be with her.

"So!" Brosa broke the solemn moment. He rubbed his hands together. "Now for some tea."

He crumbled angelica seeds and bits of pilfered lavender into wooden cups, and the fragrance filled the hut. Eðna took off her leather top, curled up in the chair and tucked the furs in all around her. She breathed the scents of herbs and sheepskins and sank into warmth. She fit in the cup of the chair so perfectly. Like the little firestriker, it was made for someone small.

And it came to her, the answer she'd wondered about, to the question she'd never asked. It was a woman's firestriker. A woman's chair.

Eðna shifted, not as comfortable now. Was this Esa's seat? Was she sitting in a dead woman's chair? A woman Brosa had lovingly built this for. Eðna ran her hand along the carved arm.

"I made so many trips to the sand to find that wood," Brosa said. "A piece or two at a time."

The small lines around his eyes were different when he smiled now, without as much flesh around them, since they'd run low on food. His cheekbones were strong, almost stark. He poked the fire with a stick, and his eyes sparkled with reflected flames and driftwood thoughts.

She opened her mouth to ask, but he spoke. "My family was never here." Like a quick knife, he went straight to Eðna's worries.

"You never brought your… Esa?"

"When I wed, I hardly knew Esa. This was not for her to see."

"Oh." Eðna's skin flushed, awkward as a stork. "But you made this chair for her, didn't you?"

Brosa laughed. "I have been making that chair for more than ten years. I hid the wood, so my brother would not find out about this place. When I started, it seemed so big. Now, I can't sit in it."

Eðna knew that Brosa adored her. The way he touched her in the furs, held her face in his two hands, the way he spoke to her, so low and soft in her ear, she knew his heart. And yet, she burned to be sure. "You had no choice but to bring me here, I know. You wouldn't have shown me this place otherwise." She couldn't help but poke at it like ashes with a stick. "If you didn't even know Esa well enough…"

"—I know you." Brosa lifted his cup to his lips, and he said to her over the rim. "You don't like talk of Esa."

Eðna stopped with her own cup to her lips, and lied into her tea. "That's not true."

"Já, well." Brosa half-smiled that maddening, secretive smile. "We can talk of other things."

Pressure gathered in Eðna's chest. Was this jealousy? Could she really be jealous of a woman who was gone?

She coughed, regrouped, and something Vera once said came to her, came out of her mouth without thought. "I've heard that making something is a form of hope."

Vera told her that crafting something—a dress, a shawl, a knife—was an optimistic act. It implied a future, where the item would get used by someone, hopefully used well. She traced the carvings on the chair with her fingertips. What was Brosa imagining when he collected these pieces of driftwood and carried them all the way here, so far from the sea?

Eðna had never understood the notion, but now, feeling the embrace of this lovingly-made chair, she knew Vera was right. When Brosa lashed the first pieces together, he imagined it would hold a body.

"This." Brosa spread his arms to encompass all the things in the hut. The flame threw changing light on what they had—the items he took from Ginn's pantry, their few clothes, the small things he'd carved over the past weeks. "My hope was this."

He truly read her mind sometimes.

"All the hours I built that chair, tore it down, made it again. One day, I would bring my true elskan here and just sit, with her in that chair. Watch the steam rise from her cup and bless her lovely face."

Eðna shook her head. "You are not real. Men don't say those things."

But in a small place behind her heart, she knew they did. She remembered her Da whispering to her mother about the color of the sunset reflected in her eyes. And Gida ducking her head and smiling. Humming later as she worked.

"Ah, but I am real." Brosa winked. "You know I'm flesh and blood."

And as if she still had her contacts, Jon was superimposed over Brosa, another big flirt, raising his arms wide to prove to little Eðna. *I am here. I exist.*

Maybe this was what Brosa called the everlife, because Eðna must have died and dreamed this world. How else could she be here in this impossible situation? Maybe she'd sucked up sea water and drowned at the threshold to the past, and in those last moments, instead of seeing her life flash before her eyes, she'd made up this—this fairytale fort and impossible man.

Dark gold hair fell across his brow and brushed his shoulders, and a single damp curl tangled in the Thor's hammer at his throat. Oh gods, he was right, she had so much to learn here. The spark that caused him to be so outrageously alive was big and unknown, and she could take a lifetime to study it. It was bigger than waves, greater than 10,081 birds.

She settled into her chair and closed her eyes. As if her soul truly left her body, she soared above and saw the heat signature of this hut, its slim trail of smoke joining and twining with the water vapor. The woods all around cradled their little house. And she saw inside. The sheepskin-covered bed and tiny bowl of a hearth. Saw herself curled up in a gnarled driftwood chair, feet drawn up, wearing a man's big woolen pants, a wooden cup of tea warming her hands. She saw Brosa, sitting by the fire ring, wounded but healing, smiling for her, deep in the woods in the nest he'd built of sticks and moss and lichens. She widened her view and saw the bird she'd met when she was hunting, the one that had sung to her and offered its throat. It slept now, its head tucked under brush-colored feathers—able to fly, choosing the ground.

ᛒ

Brosa held Eðna, and it became day again, always. Every time they woke, they went to the threshold of their small house, and he stood with his arm around her strong shoulders. They drank their wildwood tea and watched the steam climb up out of the water outside their door. The water-wraiths would mix with the smoke from Brosa's hidden fire. Eðna's short hair brushed against his arm, and he was whole.

Every day, the light stayed longer. So, the days still rose toward midsummer. That was all he knew about their passing.

Eðna gathered wood or food most nights, though she often came back with little. She was skilled now at walking with the sounds and paths of the animals, and he relied on the signal they agreed on—a bird call—to know when she approached. But nei matter her stealth, there wasn't much to catch. She would not kill one of her blessed birds, and though it was dangerous not to eat them, perhaps mortally stupid, he would not say so.

He worried about Eðna. Any man would. It was nei fantasy of danger. She had been caught by Eiðr before.

But she needed to go search for wood and berries and foxes, likely so that she could roam the woods and get out of this hut. He would do the same if he could. As it was, he could not do much more than collect berries and tinder, fish in the stream, feel the leaves and sun on his face. He lived mostly as a winter man, making and fixing things like he would in the evernight, when snow kept them housebound and tied to his uncle's stories.

Now, he held a length of tree trunk over his knee, two els long and as big around as his arm. It was an older tree that had fallen but was still green—a good find. "Takk" he said, like a fool talking to a tree, and then began to scrape the bark with the edge of his knife. The soft insides would become cord, and then a net that would feed them.

Bits of bark fell everywhere as Brosa peeled it. He would need to sweep the hut floor later, but he'd made a fine broom just yesterday, so it would be quick. He worked best this way, out of sight, less vigilant. On his bed, where he could stretch his leg.

Eðna told him she walked the woods in widening circles, watching the edges of their territory. He smiled. She must look like a sheep dog, sniffing at the edges of their place, but he wouldn't make the comparison unless he wanted her to turn her back on him, maybe smack him.

He straightened his leg, and his bones creaked like an old door. He winced at a sharp stab of pain, but it was a quick spark, nothing more. He was healing well.

Eðna had saved his life more than once. It was plain as that. Perhaps his leg would never be straight and true like the other. And under his dusty wool and bindings, there was a new scar to add to the rest that he had gathered since he was a boy. Nei matter. Eðna had healed Brosa's skin with her stitches, saved him from fever, and she would not care if he had another scar or limped all his life until his hair was white.

She burned with love for him, just as he did. He shook his head at such a rare gift—one he thought he would never receive. He had cared for Esa, but he knew now that the love-rage was not something that could grow between a man and a woman.

Had fate's winds blown him another way, he would be married to Esa still, and he would love Eðna as his woman of the heart. Já, that would not sit so well with her. He laughed. It was lucky he'd become an outlaw. He did not need to marry for alliance or trade. He was free to love Eðna with his whole self.

The birch bark revealed a pale, slender body underneath—the naked, tender heart of the tree. It was a color found nowhere else, somewhere between ocean and cloud, light, and yet not pale as death. It shone with life. Using the tip of his blade, he cut a line from top to bottom and began to peel the underlayer of skin.

It glowed green in the flickering light. Oil smoldered in a leaf-shaped lamp, casting light on the tree's inner skin, and on the things they had gathered, the home they were making. Lamplight on leather—his belt tossed on the chair. His seax in its sheath of rare hide he had burned with his mother's needle, with lines like winding rivers and streams. Beside it, the bracers that

Eðna so finely braided, like a woman's thick, brown hair. The old mass of driftwood for a table. He had dragged it here as a boy, his legs aching, breathing like a horse, regretting the idea with every heave. It was set now with two cups he'd traded for in Norway, made entirely of frost. Eðna called it glass. With rims dyed deep blue, so that a man put his lips to the winter sky. A rich man's cups. Even more powerful here in this small place.

His childhood mug sat on the bedside table too, made of wood, with no handle. It was worn with use, where his small hands had held it every day, and then his larger hands as he became a man and drank massive swigs of ale, each swallow as big as this entire mug, and he and his uncle laughed at how small he once was. Most often, he used a horn instead. Yet, he would not give up his simple cup.

Now, it held a handful of feathers instead of ale. Splayed like a quiver full of fletches, but these feathers Eðna collected for her interest, for beauty. Feathers from the wings of common birds.

The longest were the color of dry mud, some with pale tips as fine as needles. These she thought might be redwings, and she laughed and said Brosa was like the male who made nests in caves. Or he was perhaps a bowerbird, who collected shining things like rings and bright berries, to lure a wife. Among the real feathers stood one made of wood—the one he had carved and worked until it was as finely grooved and slender as the others.

Over the past weeks, he'd truly carved many things. His knife handle had become sleek in his hand, the way it did in the dark months, when he did nei more than work on handles and blades.

He had made other gifts for Eðna, too. Baskets against one wall, for tools and dried fish. He weaved them tight with young twigs that could be shaped and twisted. They looked a great deal like nests. He was not sure Eðna would like the resemblance, or the clumsy work as compared to the fine things she could braid and weave herself. When he gave the baskets to her, she turned one over in her bone-thin hands and smiled. While he slept that day, she filled it with sharpening stones, in order, coarse next to coarse, fine with fine, neat and tidy.

In the dark corner were his most valued possessions—his containers made of clay, each the width of just two of his fingers, filled with the black liquid called ink. The pots were stoppered tight with thick rounds of hide. The ink made all his plans possible. A surge of fear ran through him every time he opened a flask, that he might fumble with his large hands and drop it.

The hands of a frost giant!

Like an arrow shot in his mind, he heard Svana.

Gods that was long ago, when he was first growing, his body expanding, so that everyone worried he might grow taller than the house. Svana placed her tiny hand against his to measure the span. She must have must been no more than twelve.

Eðna's hands were just as small, even as a grown woman. Her fingers were fast as eels and strong as tight-plied rope. She was good at all things that needed such hands. Working leather, untying stubborn knots, striking up a fast fire—she had gotten to doing it faster than any man or woman, save himself. Brosa made touchwood for her, dried as best he could without the use of the container his uncle had built. Eðna kept her striker around her neck, close to her body. She would always be warm.

It was what he could do, while he healed. Make things for her, make a home here. Keep her warm, with this roof and these walls and hidden fire, with the work of his hands, with his body surrounding hers, joining with hers in the night. Gods, he had nei reason to think right now about her touch, while he worked and she roamed. Her soft hesitance, the brush of her hands on every part of his body.

He growled and shifted his leg. He needed a net, and so he bent again to coaxing strings from the wood.

His steerboard handle, with his letter carved into it, leaned against the back wall with his inks. It crouched in shadows, much like he did himself, wondering if it might someday turn a ship. Might work itself into the waves, draw against the power of the sea and make a road, a way forward, out of nothing.

A familiar struggle rose in his chest—the yearning to escape the limits of this place, to go forth into his land and to see far distances. And yet, reveling in this life with Eðna. This time together that he never thought they would have.

The birds that made her eyes most bright were some she had never seen—the herons and egrets. She talked of them in a kind of trance, the way anyone might speak of the gods, of their power and willfulness.

Herons visited in cold weather, near the sea's edge, and one day they might go there, ja. For now, they would stay here, content together. Their stomachs were empty, but his hands were full of her body. His mind and heart were full of her, too.

A delicate net took shape in his hands.

Here, now, was good.

Eðna wrung her dress in the stream, and it disturbed the moon's reflection. Water dribbled back into the dark water and sped away into the night-forest.

The wildflowers grew so tall, and the birch leaves so green and thick, an emerald and turmeric sea in the daytime. But the stream's edge was still not completely hidden, not completely safe during the day, and so she washed in the dim of midnight.

Brosa was off gathering tinder and fuel. He walked well now, but he was slow, and the pain came back if he tramped in the brush too long. He spent many of his waking hours making things, repairing nets, adding images of birds to the engravings on her chair. He'd carved two spoons out of soaked birch, one for each of them, fashioning stems like whale's tails and scooping out their soft insides. He sanded and smoothed the intricately embossed comb she used before bed, when she took her short braids down and climbed into the blankets beside Brosa. She turned to him, and they gave themselves to each other, lost themselves.

Midsummer had past, certainly, and there was a bit of true, dark night now. At this hour, she would not be seen, but what would she look like if she were? If someone from the future zoomed in on a satellite image, what would they see?

A wild creature. A woman of the tenth century, outlawed and hungry, crouched by the water in her dark leather armor, with ragged, shorn hair, and mud spread on her throat and cheeks to blend into the stones and trees. A woman who washed in the night and searched for food, for fish in the farther reaches of the current, berries and even foxes in the brush. Though she still hadn't caught a fox, she moved with real stealth now, her arrows sharp and ready.

She smiled. Her Da would call her a maiden of the forest, and he would boast of her skill now.

She looked to the dark sky, and a swift sting of tears came in the back of her nose. Jon and Gida would love all of this. This cool density of real woods, their hut wrought of fragrant wood, furniture carved with the heads of sacred animals, even this wet dress she'd just washed in such clear, warm, abundant water and the worn, wool pants she wore to hunt.

These pants had been ten sizes too big on her the day she first wore them. Now, they were more like twenty. She tugged on the rough linen cord at her waist, and a cramp seized her stomach. Eðna bent to vomit, but not much came.

It was like this every time, and it had happened three times now, this sudden strike of pain and nausea and, with it, terror. It was so much like the beginning of Gida's appendicitis. And three times was a pattern. Something was wrong.

She cupped her hand and brought stream water to her lips. She rinsed twice, three times, until her mouth was clean. If only she hadn't feared sickness so much, hadn't willfully pushed out all knowledge of bodies, learning only basic first aid for this mission—

"—Elskan." Brosa surprised her, and her hand went to her heart.

He stood over her, and she saw him for a second as a creature just like her. His cheekbones were sharp, his face hollow, but his hair was lush, and limned with silver moonlight. "Leave that," he said. "Come sit with me."

He still had a habit, picked up from his brother maybe, of giving commands. Gently, but they were not questions. She smiled. They would have to keep working on that.

Eðna settled beside him on the setberg and rested her head against the cool, curved stone. Brosa laid his head in her lap, and they looked at the dense world of stars that seemed to shimmer and shift. For now, she would forget about sickness and just look.

"Now, tell me again," Brosa said. "The parts of a boat."

"Nei." She twined her fingers in his night-silver hair. "You'll just tease me again."

"I am not teasing." He definitely was. She could feel his amusement. "I want to know how many you've learned so far, of the ten thousand things I promised to teach you."

"Beast."

"Já, I am." Brosa turned in her lap to face her. "Start at the bottom of the boat." He trailed his fingers along her leather top, and she arched so slightly into his touch. "Kjolr," he said.

"Fine." She pushed his hand away. "Kjolr." And in her future language, "keel."

"The bites."

"Beams." She listed several more parts in a rush. "Ribs, klinks, thwarts, knees, oarlocks."

"Easy, Woman." He smiled. "You cannot rush a boat."

"Sails." She kept on. "Steerboard."

Brosa's hand stilled, no longer flirting, and Eðna was sorry she'd added that last item to the list. They didn't talk about the steerboard much. The handle—the piece of it that leaned against the wall of their hut—was a reminder of a young man's dreams of the sea, of Brosa steering his own way. Things that seemed impossible now.

But he'd brought it here to the woods. He'd carried those dreams with him along with all the things he grabbed, the combs and string and games. He took such a random assortment, but the steerboard handle was on purpose.

He never said so, but a small piece of him could still fathom a future in which he would need it. Could imagine a road out of here, across the sea. They didn't talk about any of it, and so they didn't break the spell of these days and nights together or snap the remaining thread of hope.

"Nei matter." Brosa kissed her palm, and his beard tickled the inside of her wrist. "You are right. You know the parts."

"I know."

She felt his mouth curl into a smile, where he rested against her. They would speak of it one day, but not tonight. The stars were thick, only a breath of space between the clusters. The long, lavender smudge of the Milky Way angled up and across their view.

"I saw this kind of sky when I was little," she said. "But not for years after that. Not in the city."

He lifted his head to look at her with his brows drawn down. "You never saw the sky?"

"Only pieces, slivers between buildings. And no stars."

"The stars are gone in your time?"

"Well, nei." Eðna rested her own hand over Brosa's and curled her fingers around his. "The stars are still there, but there's so much light from all the things that people have built. The city shines brighter than the stars, and so you can't see them."

Can the stars see us?

She had asked her mother, back when she lived far out past civilization, in the heart of the island.

Later, she looked, breathless and wondering, at satellite images. Looking down from space, the ring of Iceland was a glowing band, a circle, and at its center, the uninhabitable place. And yet her family lived there. The contradiction at the heart of her land, her father. Maybe her.

The cities themselves looked like constellations. Lights covered the earth in various densities, with brilliant clusters where throngs of people lived, and smaller clusters, farther apart, where humankind had extended its cities and homes into the water. The lights grew smaller and farther apart until, far out in the ocean, you could see individual sea-steads.

Brosa tugged gently on her laces again, always loosening her armor. Her body softened everywhere, readying for him, but her mind was caught on the man-made stars and the patterns of civilization seen from space. Zooming in, you could see single boats, and small fleets tied together into villages, with massive sails and tendrils of green growing over their edges.

"Sea-steads!"

She struggled to sit up, but Brosa was heavy, and he pressed a palm to her chest.

"Calm, Woman. What are you about?"

"Sea-steads." The word was almost a perfect Viking kenning, with the juxtaposition of ocean and homestead. "Homesteads—whole farms—on the ocean, floating far out on the waves, with everything you need to live."

"Everything?" He laughed. "In your time, they raise cattle on the sea?"

Eðna smiled and pressed her palm to his cheek, his beard. Sweet Brosa, picturing cows at sea. "Well, nei. We don't really have cattle. And I don't think cows or sheep would live well on the sea."

"Ah then, you don't know about Amma, my grandmother," he said. "And my Grandda Magnus. They came to this island with sheep and horses on the deck of the boat you saw at the fishing camp."

"Your ship." His grandparents had made a hopeful journey, on the decks of the very boat she had been drawn to when she first washed up in this time. "Your same ship."

"Well, every board has been changed by now. Every nail shaped new on the forge. But já, in spirit. The wolf is the same."

"See? It's the same. Your ship is a floating home at heart. It's meant to carry a family, a farm."

"I suppose so."

"We would have to leave our things here, but we could have new chairs, shaped like this setberg but made of driftwood, with soft pillows of linen and our fur blankets around our shoulders. We could sit on the deck and watch the sky change."

Brosa settled deeper into her and joined her dreaming. "The whole deck could be soft with rugs and sheepskins, for pushing you down and rolling on top of you."

She pushed at his hands, but he slipped his fingers up under the crossed laces and, one by one, pulled them free.

"You can carve beautiful benches." Her breath was erratic now, his fingers against her ribs, through her thin shirt. "There can be chests with iron hasps. When we travel fast to new places, we can secure our things in them, our drinking horns and carved feathers." Eðna was nearly breathless. Too many words tumbled out. "We'll stow away our bowls full of berries and things we traded for. Take them out again when we find a calm place to stay."

"Well, my deck would fit a proper home," he said. "Bigger than a boy's fort."

"I could make some new kinds of knots and stitches, figure out a way to open the roof, so we could lay down in our giant bed and see even more stars than we see from here."

Brosa brought her laces to his lips, and she shivered as though he kissed her bare skin, lying on the deck of their ocean home, surrounded by all the colors of the sea. They would lay in their blankets, with the edges of their salt-seasoned canvas roof rolled up for stargazing. Tent walls of creamy fabric surrounded them, and blankets and pillows all the colors of Betta's dyed fabric, her birds-egg silver, mustard green and deep magenta. All given by Betta and Ginn as a farewell bless.

They would take an abundance of butter and creamy goat's cheese, and the ocean would give them so much to eat, they would be round and full. Eðna would have a clean white dress that billowed, and she would lean over the shieldwale and trail her fingers in a green and darkening sea, outside the grasp of Svana and Eiðr.

"The wolf will watch when we sleep," she said. "And no one will find us." She sat up. "We have to go soon."

Brosa disentangled his fingers. "You are serious, Woman?"

"Já, see? It's a way we can live outside the reach of everyone."

Brosa sat up, too, and covered her cheek with his palm. "I thought we were telling stories, like my uncle."

"You could make your changes to the hull," she said. "Like in your drawings. Make it even swifter, so it cut the waves like an eel, and then it could change and unfold and become still when we wanted."

Brosa would stand at the helm, arms crossed, content in his floating home, doing nothing but watching the sky move. He liked to do that.

Here on the setberg, he kissed the soft inside of her wrist, her arm. "I didn't know you meant it in truth."

"It would work," she said. "It would be—" And she lost her breath as he kissed her throat, her jaw. Eðna closed her eyes and opened up to Brosa, and as he kissed her, she sank into her vision. Her arms around him on the deck of their homestead, his braid coming apart in her fingers and in the salt-wind. An orange sun dropping behind their silver sail. And below them, all the creatures of the sea arranged in their orderly strata—schools of tiny fish flashing in unison, eels slicing past, deep whales, and deeper still, a kraken.

No need to hide. They would live in the open, in peace.

Brosa picked up his knife. He knelt by the hearth, and he examined the blade in the flickering candlelight. It was sharp as the finest sword and glinted well. He roasted the knife in the flame the way Eðna had done with her needle when she sewed his leg. A protection, against what he did not know, but he did it—for her—all the same.

He looked to the door to be sure she was away.

There was no animal to sacrifice, small or large, and he would nei kill a bird, not in a hundred hundreds of years. Brosa took a deep breath and held it.

He drew the blade across his own palm. He would trade his own blood for Eðna's life.

She was sick. She hid it from him, já, but he'd seen her clutch herself, wild-eyed and afraid. She was thin now, though her will was strong and fierce. When she spoke of her mother's elf-shot, Eðna's memories and her pain went deep. Yesterday, he woke to find her sitting up in bed, shivering as if she roamed the frozen lands in her shift. Her fear came like a tide and she could not sleep.

Terror flooded Brosa's gut too, until he could not stand his own sloshing thoughts. He could not watch Eðna die. And yet, he could not stand letting her go back to her city.

She thought about going back, he could see. Her fear drew her heart and mind far from here, back toward her shining tall buildings of frost, where there were healers who could save her. She talked of her sea-home, but he could see her going away in her thoughts. Not on his ship, but on the metal boat that brought her here, as it turned to ply the water of time.

He pressed his wound and winced.

He swore he would not be the man that Jon was. He would never make Eðna go or make her stay. But he grieved nei matter which way his mind twisted. He called now on Eir for healing and compassion. He asked her to take his offering, small as it might be. To take his blood, take his sleep instead of Eðna's, and let her heal.

"Make her well," he said, and he let his blood drip onto the candle. He asked Eir for Eðna's sake, but he could not help but add a plea for himself. "I will build her a tent on the ocean, on my honor. Just let her stay."

Eðna threaded her fingers through Brosa's hair and let the golden waves separate and fall. Sun slanted in from the door at an extreme angle, lighting the strands. He slept, his head close to her thigh, and she simply watched. She divided a few strands and braided, idly.

A peaceful moment, as evening came to blanket them in their little home.

Eðna had always been a listener, an observer. Back when she was connected through her eyes and screens, she'd absorbed a million images, and a million minor thoughts and feelings of people she did not even know. Now, it was only her own mind inside.

All the things she didn't miss passed through her head, and then away, out of range of caring. Small things, like the slippery feel of a plastic hairbrush, the smooth surface of a modern cup, the constant hiss of ceiling and hallway vents. Dumps of information from people she didn't know, about their groups and jokes and hurts, all drifted away, and now there were the scents of the woods, of woolly steam, and crushed green everything, underlaid with the decay of dead brush and the tang of dirt. No one else's needs or desires or words or approval. Only the voices and languages of so many birds, and the movements of foxes that lay just at the edge of hearing. The rise and fall of Brosa's steady breath.

Around the room their things encircled them—little cairns of the blackest stones, the steerboard handle, with a little bowl of wilting snowbit petals on the floor beside it. On the table, her bouquet of birds' feathers in a cup. Most of the feathers were real, but one was carved from a slim piece of wood. Brosa had made it for her, back before she even paid him attention.

She drew a feather from the cup and worked it into the braid she was making. He would wake up with it in his hair and laugh.

Sweet Brosa, so humbled here. In all the endless hours he spent in this hut, or within a few meters of it, he'd collected and made so many things. He'd made this home for Eðna, full of petals and feathers and little carved wonders. A nest full of things that would make her comfortable, make her happy, and in the light that was just now turning from honey to plum, they did.

Her stomach seized with a cramp, and nausea came and tossed her insides. Eðna stood, a hand to her belly for calm, for protection. Brosa stayed lost in his dreams.

She could not sleep. She wrapped a dark shawl around her shift, and stepped into the purple of night. The water trickled and misted here around the hut, and all around, every white wildflower petal glowed as if she had infrared vision. Long ago, her contacts would have put a Latin name beside them, *Saxifraga rivularis.* A name that had nothing to do with how such tiny petals looked electric white in the falling night, like a million lanterns that belong to the land wights she craved to see when she was little.

Eðna stepped around them, her bare feet gripping the rocks. The stream's rushing became louder, and the splashing of the miniature foss.

When she and Brosa cast off to the sea, the water would sound different. Waves would slosh against the hull and shieldwale, gentle, not rushing and riffling like this tiny river. Here, they could stand in water up to their ankles. Out on the sea, fathomless darkness would carry them. And there would be so much life. Fish just below, swimming like mercury. Implacable birds rising and falling. Wings and waves. Words came—dereliction, duty, betrayal. They were present and then gone. The future language became a point on the horizon of thought, slipping, slipped, beyond. Eðna stood in the glorious night and shivered—

—Something was off, something near.

Eðna froze and listened, and she felt movement in the trees, heard soft sounds, almost lost in the rushing of the stream. Sticks crunched, and out from the woods stepped a fox.

Eðna let her breath go. The fox was round and inquisitive like a pup, and its dusty gray fur looked velvet-soft. Its eyes flashed piercing blue, almost as though they were lit from inside. The fox tilted its head to examine Eðna, and the white insides of its ears flared with light, too.

"Hallo, fox."

It tilted its head even farther, an almost impossibly curious angle. It lifted its snout, and as if it heard a call from off in the woods, it turned and left.

Eðna would laugh if she weren't still tense, her throat dry with fear. She was scared, she and Brosa both, so much of the time. They pushed it back behind their hearts, and yet here she stood. Her knife gleamed in the moonlight, and she gripped it tight, hands shaking, heart slamming.

The woods were her home, but they were dangerous too, so dangerous that she and Brosa slept every night with weapons at hand. And as much as she felt her bare feet connect her to this land, and as brightly as her body shone with the touch and love of a good man, it was not safe. They couldn't go on like this forever.

ᛊ

Svana worked her cooking knife back and forth, gnawing a small bough of living wood. She knelt on the forest floor next to a pile of sticks and cords. Her eyes darted between the work in her hands and the entrance to the small hut across the ravine. It looked empty, but nei doubt, this was where he would be.

All those weeks ago, when Svana skewered the fox's head on a nithing pole, a stray wind had turned it against Brosa. How could she have known Brosa was in the highlands? How could she control the wind?

Now, she would make it right. If it was not too late.

"A bless," she whispered. She wrenched her knife, and the green twig splayed open, tough, fighting its doom. She formed branches into a ring and set to adding crossed lines the way she'd seen Betta's Da do it when someone was sick. A mending shape. She looped two sticks together and wound a bit of cord to make the first crossing.

She struggled with her desire to come here, these many days and nights since she learned that Brosa lived. Eiðr was wary of her, and he might follow. She would give away this hiding place. But she yearned to get a glimpse of Brosa, so she could know he was well.

The woman might have gone to the sea, but he was here. He had to be here.

She set the half-wreath in her lap. Which would be best? If he was alone, all for Svana? Or if Eðna was still here, with her dark key to another world? A heavy, powerful key.

Svana looked up from her work and narrowed her gaze. After so many years of following him here, she knew how to separate his fire's smoke from the steam that climbed from the rocks across the water, as easily as she separated strands of her own hair to make a braid. His smoke was darker than the steam, smudged with the spirit of ash. It could be seen if you knew where to search for Brosa. If you really knew him.

Just as she thought this, the smallest puff rose from the hidden roof. Svana's heart stormed like hoofbeats, and she gripped the mending wreath so hard it bit her fingers.

She breathed quiet words. "You are here."

She watched his smoke rise as if she were in a seer's trance. He was in there. He was near. And then Brosa ducked his head and came outside.

Svana surged up on her knees. The desire to go to him was strong as a gale, throwing her forward. She got to her feet, the wreath hanging from her fingers, and the wind pulled her toward Brosa.

There was motion in trees, near his hut, and then out of the woods came another person. Eðna. She was so small, she stood only to his shoulder, and she was thin as a straw. All bones and eyebrows. And her hair! It was gone up to her chin, like a thrall.

Eðna looked up to Brosa, and he bent his head to kiss her.

He kissed like a hungry god.

Jealousy flared bright in Svana's chest. When Eiðr took her mouth, it was foul—a kiss to get past. She'd never been kissed the way Brosa kissed Eðna now with his whole body. He took the woman's hair in his fist, and Eðna kissed him in return, running her hands all over his hips and back. And here Svana stood in the trees like an outlaw herself, pushed out again. Backs turned on her. Svana Sting-Eyes.

As if Brosa could hear her envy, he snapped his head up and looked her way, and Svana was struck by an unseen hand across her face. The wreath dropped at her feet, and she stood stunned.

Brosa was a dead man.

His cheekbones were sharp as flint, his face so hollow that he looked like the chief. His beard was twisted tight in a ripped bit of cloth, and his glorious waves of hair were now stiff and matted. Brosa's shirt hung loose on his shoulders, his body no longer rounded with health. Through the dirt on his face, his white scar shone bright as snow and vile as his brother's bloody stain. His eyes stood out black as death and yet alive with an eerie passion, seeking, glowing like coals.

Her jealousy died in her throat.

"Nei." Svana trembled and backed away, shaking her head. "Nei." She could not stop speaking the word. "Nei, nei."

Brosa was nei hungry god, and nei dead man, but he was not alive either. Far, far worse, he was a draugr, returned from the grave—Esa's grave—to torment and eat the living.

Svana had heard of such spirits only in Hár's stories. The revenants, who took the air straight from the mouths of the living. Dragging their mountain-heavy bodies through the land, they drove animals and men howling mad into death. As a child, she'd held tight to her Ma's promise that she would never see one. But here Brosa stood without flesh. He had laid down with bones, and now his own stark bones standing out from his body were the price.

Svana wrapped her arms around herself, bewildered deep in the woods she thought she knew. Birds sang all around, and Brosa-the-draugr was right there across the water. Eðna was a thrall to him, shorn and willing, and Brosa had already started to take her air. Soon, Eðna would be struck with illness and suffer until she died and vanished with him, riding mad into the everlife.

Another wave of fear washed over Svana.

Eðna.

Eðna was her enemy, já. Svana wanted to rip the woman's skin from her skeleton, but Eðna was the only person besides Ginn who knew how to truly leave this land—pass through the door to another world. Eðna held the iron key that could close that door. If the draugr consumed Eðna, Svana's last hope would die.

As if her fear shot across the ravine, the woman Eðna fell to her knees. She wrapped her arms tight around her stomach and retched and spit up bile on the stones.

Svana's mouth fell open.

Her fear had hit Eðna like an arrow to the gut! Brosa knelt beside the woman now, drawing her hair back off her face. So gentle for such a dark creature.

Svana trembled with the power moving through her—the life of the warped, ruined mending shape that lay at her feet. She opened her hands, and her palms were slick with berry juice that looked like blood. She snatched up the wreath and threw it as far as she could, to send the blessing toward Eðna. It dropped to the forest floor, and Svana stared at it for a long moment, then ran.

Brosa smoothed the form of a tiny hull under his knife. His thoughts tossed and changed direction like the wind that might rock and throw such a boat if it were full size.

A day and a night had passed, and Eðna was sick again. Again, she sat up worried when she should be sleeping.

He left his work with nets and fletches to lie, and he worked on this child's toy. When it was shaped and rubbed with sand, he would wrap cloth around it and give it to Eðna, and he would tell her. He would give her the truth that he'd been keeping in his mind these past two days.

He was sure now.

He had called on the gods and given his blood so that Eðna would not die. He hung his head and laughed. The gods had answered him, já? With a trick. A cruel one, a twist poetic enough for the best skald.

This was not the sickness that claimed her Ma. Nei. Brosa had seen this before, and he knew well what it meant—the hunger, the aches, the stomach griping. Eðna did not seem to know or remember these signs. Maybe her fear overwhelmed her sense. Or maybe this kind of sickness did not exist in the future? In a far world without trees and stars, it could be they had done away with women's pains.

The little ship hung from his fingers, listing on its tiny sea.

"What do I do?" He asked the ceiling, as if the goddess Eir were there herself, laughing at him. Every part of him—his mind, his hands, the very spark that drove his heart and would last into the everlife—all of him yearned to tell Eðna what he suspected. That she was not dying, that she carried their child.

Eðna would want to go live on the boat, or sail to the old country. And just those few days ago, when he made his sacrifice, he had yearned for the same things she did—to stay together in peace and pass all of time beside one another.

Now he was caught like a fish in one of his own nets, circling, never finding a way out. How could he let Eðna suffer as Esa had? He could not hold another son on his knees and name him with his first and last breaths. Worse, Brosa's throat closed at the thought of a daughter, with wisps of dark brown hair stuck to her perfect forehead, fire eyes holding his for just one moment, her whole hand the size of his thumb.

He'd heard the stories of his own Da, and what he did when Heirik was born. When he saw the blood would not wash off of his son, Ulf drew his blade and ordered every man and woman to leave. He bolted the doors—the only time Hvítmork has ever been barred and locked.

Nei doubt everyone thought Ulf would kill the child, but instead he named him. Heirik, after his own grandda. The men of his family were named in turn: Heirik, Magnus, Ulf, then Heirik again. His own son Arulf. One day, perhaps Heirik would have the chance to name a son. Father after father, every one of them doing what they believed was best.

If Eðna thought she was stricken with what passed for elf-shot in her world, could he just let her be? Could he lie to Eðna, agree she was deathly sick, so that her fear drove her to her city? Their child would be safe there.

Brosa bent his head to carve, but his knife wavered, his hands too big and clumsy.

Birdsong came, loud and close, and he looked up to find a flicker that had wandered into the hut. It perched on the bedpost, standing on the head of a wolf, and it set its black eyes on Brosa. Oh, Eðna would love to see this—a bird come all the way into the house.

If she went to her city, with its houses piled one on top of another until they reached unfathomable heights, she would never see such a thing. Nei small birds would come when she had glass windows that did not open, in a world where all birds were dead.

Angry, brave Eðna. She must have been a fierce little girl, her head bent to sewing, her mind full of plans. She set a new course the day she left Jon. If she had not run from him, she would never know the city, never know her second mother, Vera. She would never know Brosa at all. Never know birds.

Stupid beast. What was he thinking? It was the worst betrayal of Eðna, not to tell her everything he knew.

It was not her mother's death that truly grieved and frightened her. Nei. It was her father's lie. A lie so big, it spanned the world. Jon hid the beauty of the city from his own little daughter.

It was the worst lie. Until this lie, now, if Brosa kept his knowledge secret. If he tricked her into going to the city then he would be no better than Jon.

He closed his eyes and let his head fall back, hard against the wall. "Frigg!" It hurt more than he expected, and he rubbed the back of his head.

He would tell her when she came home. He would not wait. He would not fail.

He set to finishing the boat.

Brosa heard the brush moving and Eðna's bird call. She was home from scavenging, and he welcomed her with his own call in return.

She set down a full skin of water, and she untied her skirt and let handfuls of berries fall into a bowl. Not enough food to make a new life. She needed milk and butter to feed the child.

She looked to the little boat. "What are you making?"

He said the words, before he could retreat. "You are not sick."

Eðna stood still as a rock, her skirt in her fists. She spoke in a small voice. "You've seen it, too." She dropped to her knees before him, let her head fall into his lap. "It's sharp pain like my ma had. I'm weak and—"

"—Shhh, Fine One." Brosa brushed his thumb over her anxious brow. "You are not sick."

"Já." She sniffed like a pup. "I am."

"Nei," he brushed her hair off her forehead. "I know what ails you."

Eðna sat up on her knees and wiped her nose. "What do you mean?"

Brosa pushed wet strands of hair behind her ear. "You are going to have our child."

Eðna's dark brows drew down tight. She was quiet as the frozen lands, and her gaze turned inward so that Brosa could do nei but wait.

Once before, he'd made plans for a family.

How many summers ago, five now? Back then, he'd held images in his mind, the way a seer must see, a vision of himself holding a boy of two or three years. Brosa stood in the tall, green field's-mane and showed the boy the farm. The child had pale hair like Esa, and a sturdy body like Brosa himself. Now, his thoughts turned to a brown-haired child. To love and pain beyond reckoning.

So slowly, Eðna's hand went to her belly, and Brosa saw her test the idea of a child. Would she rage at him now?

A slow smile came to her lovely, fierce mouth, and he saw Eðna find what she herself knew to be true in her bones. The frost in her eyes melted, and she looked at him with such trust, tears drying on her face, a dark blush across her chest.

He had done the right thing. Eðna was his woman, and he had honored her with the truth.

He offered her the wooden boat.

She held it in two hands, up to the light. "Take us somewhere," she said. "We need to go now on your ship, make our sea-home—"

"—Nei," He took the boat from her and set it beside him. "I won't put you on a ship now, flying wherever the wind may blow."

"We'll go to Norway. We'll trade."

"I am not a trader, Eðna. And a ship is nei place to have a child." He took her hands. "I'm a builder."

And he knew the truth then, as it fell from his tongue. With those few words, he spoke his own nature for the first time. "I need to make things—more than feathers and toys."

"I know." Eðna tightened her hands around his. "Let's go now, somewhere where you can build. You can make your boats and make a house for us, for our…family."

A sudden breeze came to play in the strands of her hair, tossing the shadows and light on her berry lips. The gods truly toyed with him. Eðna looked to him for plans and hope, yet here they sat in the fort he'd made as a boy, on a bed with wolves and ravens he'd carved so long ago. The chair—it was decorated with wings now, added for Eðna. This whole hut carved through. They'd been here weeks, months. What more could he cut?

Eðna let go of his hands and pressed her palms to her body. She was too light, too thin to carry a child.

All these circling, tossing thoughts came to rest. There was one possible course of action.

He could not take her anywhere but the water's edge, where she could go to the future, where it was safe to have their child—a babe that had his mother's dark brows and eyes, and Brosa's big chest and strong arms. His brown-haired child that he would never see.

They would go somewhere, but not where Eðna hoped.

He would not say so yet. He nodded, and he drew old knowledge up from his past, like water from deep under the ground, about how to act to make people happy. How to smile in just that way that put a woman at ease. He put that smile on his face and reached for the berries. "Well, then," he said. "What did you find to feed the child?"

For now, Eðna would not see his worry, and his stupid, sad joy.

ᛊ

Svana closed her fist around the handle of her little hatchet. The room was dim, with a thread of moonlight through the vent, and she trembled in her bed, ready to kill, while Eiðr the stupid beast snored beside her.

Since the day she saw Brosa as the draugr, she had not slept. The way his coal-eyes sought in the trees, he must have seen her. Uncle Hár said that the walking dead were hungry for food and for life, and they roamed the land seeking both. They could only be stopped by chopping their heads clean off. So Svana waited every night with this blade by her side.

Waiting, waiting, to feel his heavy body dragging in the land.

Finally, he arrived.

A single heavy knock came at the door, and the hinges strained and creaked. Svana waited, taut as a rope. The door swung open just a hand's-breadth, splashing moonlight onto her big loom and letting in the dim mists of almost-day. The strands of the loom came alive with a fearsome blue light and showed her Brosa.

He was in the form of a golden cat. He jumped up on the table, knocked over the pitcher of cream and licked it with his cat tongue. When he raised his cat head, the loom-light flashed in his black eyes.

Brosa-the-cat dropped from the table with a thud that moved the earth, and he went to the loom, and he walked in and out of the strings. He rubbed his head on the frame and turned around and around, in and out and in and out.

Svana tightened her grip. She should do it now. Spring up from her bed and hack at his neck while he was wound up in the loom, but she could not move. She watched, dumb as her husband, and held her breath.

So many times she had watched her Ma weave. Svana and the other girls would play with the stone weights, while the women sorted and tied and wove their strings and stories. One time, Brosa came and slipped a loom weight onto her finger as a ring, pretending to be a fine trader, but she knew it was not pretend. It was a gift of devotion.

The cat pointed its ears and rubbed against the loom, and she knew. Draugr or nei, she could not hack his head off. He was her beloved, her sweet Brosa, and this was not his fault. His wound had brought him too close to the threshold of death, and Hel had gotten her boot in the door and stolen Brosa's soul.

Svana lay silent and stiff in bed, and watched as the loom strands twined in and out, weights clacking like dried fish on a line.

In the morning, she crouched beside the loom, hatchet close at hand, and stared at the tangled mass of threads and weights. The valley was dark green now—from here inside the door, she could see it roll away and to the woods.

Brosa had finally come, já, but still here she was, alive and breathing, and still he roamed, hungry, in the land.

She held her breath, touched a fingertip to one of the weights and drew it back fast. She was not singed, not turned to ash or frozen and cracked like a winter stream. The weight just swung a bit and then settled. She lifted another string and a dozen more came with it.

"Frigg." She went to her knees. This would take hours of coaxing to fix.

Where was the fox last night, when she hesitated? When she let her heart keep her from carrying out her plans. Her courage wavered, and now Brosa was nei doubt back to his hut, slowly taking the life from Eðna—the keeper of the key Svana needed.

She wiggled her fingernail inside one of a thousand tiny knots and started to pry.

Gods, she had taken action many times, never sitting like a coward in the bath, a lazy man at his hearth. Time and again her actions turned back on her. She had set a nithing post, sent men to kill her own husband, passed Eiðr's test in the scalding water, held Eðna under her ax then let the woman go. Yet last night, she failed, thwarted by a single memory of pretending these weights were rings.

She saw him again, young Brosa, behind the house. He slid the loom weight onto her finger. She walked around showing the family, and Hár smiled and kissed her hand. Told her she would one day marry a trader and have dozens of such rings.

Now in the light, she saw the truth. They were just rocks with holes in them.

"Fox!" She yelled out the door and into the land, so loud her throat was raw. "Where were you?!"

A great stamping of hooves came, and Svana's heart clenched in her chest. Was it the pounding of the draugr's unearthly weight? Was he coming again? She snatched up her hatchet, but before she could even get to her feet, Eiðr came over the rise.

Just her husband.

Nei reason to get up, then.

She slid the hatchet under her skirts so he would not ask.

Eiðr let his horse go and came to knock dirt from his boots. He stepped in Svana's light. His shadow lay heavy on her and the loom.

"Strange news," he said.

Svana did not get up to serve Eiðr water or help him get food. She was sick to death of his news. All of Eiðr's news these days—all his talk—was about Brosa. How he would goad him, when he would kill him, how weak and soft Ulfsson was, how Ulfsson must be missing his torcs and wine. He had no idea that Brosa was already gone beyond death, beyond any injury Eiðr could deal him.

Svana picked at another knot. "What strange news?"

Eiðr wrenched a piece of bread from a flat old loaf on the table, and he sat and spoke through chewing. "Morg was at the fishing camp. A silver bird came to the sea's edge. With long legs and a sharp beak that opened to the sky."

A bird.

Svana struggled not to scream at the cowfoot. "Hundreds upon hundreds of birds come to the water's edge every day."

"Já, wife. I am not stupid." He chewed. "This bird came from nothing. It did not fly or land, it was just…there. Morg and Magnus waded out to it, deep as their bindings, and it did not move. It let them touch it all over, and it was solid and cold as knives. Made all of silver."

Svana crossed her arms against a sudden chill, as if her own fingers moved over the sea-sprayed metal. "A bird made of silver?"

"Hard and bright." Eiðr drank straight from the pitcher. "Like Ulfsson's fine bracelets." Disgust was plain in his words.

Eiðr was near as bad as Svana, with his obsession. Every morning, every day, he talked of Brosa's wealth, his looks, his horse. Even this unnatural bird, so far from the forest, reminded him of Ulfsson.

Svana swore she would not speak, had sworn it a hundred times over. She pushed and pushed her anger down, but now the words burst out. "You can't see a valley without Brosa lurking in it."

Eiðr laughed, a single savage laugh. "And you, Woman. You would see him in the bottom of a bowl of cheese."

Svana closed her mouth tight. Eiðr had never spoken so plainly about her feelings. His wife longed for another man, and so he hid his jealousy out of pride. Now, her yearning for Brosa was laid out flat and raw as a gutted fish.

And he was wary of Svana, nei matter that she had passed his test. Nothing she could do would be enough. Her burned wrist was all the proof either needed, to call Svana untrustworthy. She wouldn't say anything more. Nei. She must not.

And yet. "You are feeble with it," she said.

She sat up on her knees and met Eiðr's green eyes, and the words kept coming out, just like the day she set the fox's head toward Hvítmork. "Your obsession with Brosa is far stronger than my own. All day, you seethe with the desire to hurt him. At night, you toss in your sleep and send sparks out of that arm, melting our candles and turning our stews. Last night—"

"—Silence, Woman!"

"—What does a strange bird have to do with him? He is not even near the camp. He's in the woods, half a day away—"

Svana stopped.

Gods, what had she said?

Eiðr stood, and his voice was softer than she'd ever heard it. "How do you know that?" His dusty boots shushed against the floor. He came to her, slowly, shush by shush, step by step. "Have you seen him?"

"Nei." She could only whisper. "I know only what I hear you say."

Eiðr came close and stood beside Svana, his dirty boot digging into her knee. Rough and sudden, he buried his fingers in her hair, ripping her braids apart. Pain flared, and she swallowed a cry.

He pressed down on her, down through her crown of torn braids, down through her bones and into the ground. He leaned his body into her, and her cheek was crushed against his coarse pants. With his empty wrist, his stump, he brushed the strands of the loom, right in front of her eyes, as if they were strands of hair he gently brushed off a woman's face.

"Take care, Wife. Your loom is tangled."

Eiðr let go.

Svana watched him go to the woods, to his stupid schemes.

Trembling, she looked again to the loom weights and saw the tangled truth. Eiðr was getting worse. Soon he would hurt her. She would live in dishonor, with a man who laid his hands on her in violence. Forever spinning. Spinning and weaving.

Nei. She could not sit any longer and wait for that fate, a fair wife, cooking enough, cowering at night.

Svana set her eyes on the forest's edge. She felt the fox there, point-eared and silent. The fox who had given her his voice, his snout, his power. She saw now, clear as the wind, he had not forsaken her. He'd given her the tool she needed—a silver bird. The bird would mean something to Eðna—Svana felt it in her spine, and she sat up straight with the knowledge.

Love kept her from killing Brosa last night, but she had to put steel into her heart. She would go to the hut once more and she would save Eðna. She'd tell her of the strange bird and they would escape the draugr, and everything and everyone else in this land. The fox's silence told her, she had the strength to do what must be done.

Eðna counted six small arrows, laid out at her knees. She knelt in the woods, readying her tools to search for food. She had her few supplies—the wrist bracer she'd cut and made narrow as her wrist got skinnier, her small bow, her knife hanging by its strap.

She cleared a space in the brush to get at the dirt. Her nails were short now and tinged with earth. She spit into her palm and mixed a paste to spread on her cheeks. More than ever, Brosa insisted she hide as best she could as she moved through the trees.

The breeze dried the cold mud, and her stomach lurched.

She smiled this time. She was going to have a child.

She needed to catch a fox today. She needed to devour something, any kind of food, even a handful of leaves. Brosa said fox meat tasted sour and swore it was stringy, but Eðna would eat great bowls of it right now. With her pinkie, she dabbed dirt on her lips, and it tasted good. She took another taste. Yes. She could eat just a little.

What was she doing? Kneeling in the woods eating dirt.

She let the crumbs fall from her fingers. She would only vomit it up and give it back to the earth.

She pushed hair off her face, and wisps stuck to the drying mud. She tied her hair with a leather cord and set off to hunt.

Berries were everywhere now, but they were sour and she couldn't keep them down. Same with the little bits of fish and butter they had hoarded. She was sicker by the day and wasting food.

So much like her Ma, right before the *appendicitis*, the *peritonitis* and *sepsis*. The way the aching hunger and nausea and abdominal swelling built up fast, and one day Gida struggled to eat and breathe. Eðna had been struck with fear, thinking she would curl up and struggle like that, while Brosa would try to ease her with his lists like lullabies, and comb her sweat-soaked hair.

How could she have been so wrong? So insensitive to her own body?

Simple. She'd ignored her body out of fear after Gida died.

When Vera took her in, she was so patient with Eðna, so encouraging, but Eðna could never measure a man for a tunic, never touch the nape of a woman's bare neck as she pinned hand-woven trim. Vera did those things, and Eðna braided leather and put away everything that had to do with skin and blood and life.

She, Eðna, who never even wanted to have a body of her own. Could she really carry a child?

She pushed lush leaves out of her way, so much fuller and greener now, and she saw Betta's little one in her mind, squirming happily on a blanket in the grass. Such a tiny animal, a delicate and horrifying thing, so pink and alive. He could be hurt so easily. Could get sick. Gods, she went from fearing her own death to worrying about this yet-to-be-born child.

Nei, she would not. She pressed her palm to her chest. Closed her eyes and cleared her mind. Soon, she heard the thousand small movements everywhere, the breath of air through leaves, scuttling of a world of insects, calls and croaks of birds far overhead, and closer too, in the trees. The heartbeat of the child underneath her own pulse.

She heard her mother's voice, the way she greeted her every morning. *Hallo, Eðna. My sweet girl.*

"I'm here, Ma." She told the trees, and the leaves shivered as if to answer. The wildflowers brushing Eðna's knees shushed with every step.

Eðna had collected flowers and meadowgrass on the day Gida died. So naive, thinking a circlet of petals and grass could make everything better. She snuck up to the house to surprise her mother, and was almost to the door when she heard her parents talking. Her mother's voice sounded pale and strained. Gida begged, *Jack, please.*

It was the first time Eðna heard that name. *Jack.*

Here in the woods, grown-up Eðna silently nocked an arrow and drew her bow, and her parents' conversation came to her again, clear as if her mother and father stood beside her, whispering in her ear.

Nei, Elskan, her father pleaded. *Let me.* His voice was strangled with pain. *They have medicine*, her Da said. *Surgery. They can treat you.*

Eðna stood still as a stone. Her parents had said things that made no sense. Words little Eðna had never heard before. Words that grown-up Eðna had forgotten.

I want to die here, Jack, where the spirits can find me. Where the sky is full of gods. Her mother was steady and sure. *Don't make me go.*

Back on that day, little Eðna had crouched low to hold herself in a ball, rocking back and forth. She had the sense of something big and misunderstood, lurking underneath and all around. She didn't know what it was. Now she knew—it was the truth about the city, about their lives. And Gida's faith. Eðna hadn't remembered that part—how Gida believed that their lives out on the farm were worth dying for.

Her muscles burned with the weight of the bowstring.

Gods, what her mind had hidden from her all these years! The rest of that conversation, the part that mattered. Her father hadn't let her Ma die. He'd pleaded for her life.

Eðna had put the memory far back in her mind, along with everything physical, any intuition about her own body, any sensual joy in touching another. She'd buried everything her mother really said that day. Gida wanted to live out her last moments in a place where her beliefs mattered, where her gods would gather her. It was not Jon's decision. It was Gida's own wish.

Eðna lowered her bow and looked at her own hands. They were fine-boned but strong, a gift from Gida. Her feet stood lightly, balanced, settled on the forest floor with ease, like a graceful bird. An elegant, powerful egret.

Leaves rustled. Barely a swish of breeze in the trees, a soft touch of movement out of the corner of her eye. She turned with fluidity and ease and shot a fox.

The animal spasmed, leapt once in the air, then fell still. Eðna waded through the juniper to reach it.

It was skinny and wild and dusty ash-white, fur the color of driftwood on the sand. The fox's eyes were open, and Eðna closed them. She ran her hand along the animal's side and felt its bones so close to the surface, the deep and sudden lack of movement and soul. Eðna turned her own gaze to the sky, unafraid now of the swooping powers that might be there. They were Gida's gods, and she could not fear them, or disparage them, ever again.

With the back of a hand, she wiped away mud and tears, and each gleaming leaf in the forest came into focus. The trunks all around her were peeling white and glowing inside with copper and bronze and the pink of raw meat. The taste and texture of clay was on her lips.

The fox had lived and died unremarked, not part of written history. So had Gida, and Gida was happy with that. She'd lived a good life, and it was enough.

Eðna had come here seeking knowledge, and she found it. Yes. She wanted her dream with a desperate clenching in her chest, wanted to arrive back in the lab and show that she'd done this, she'd been here and discovered and learned.

But she also found freedom, tranquility, courage. Time had opened up for her, making space for her to sit and watch the light change, to travel the volcanic lands with an outlaw. Space to braid Ranka's hair and find compassion for her own ten-year-old self. That morning, on the way to the assembly, she'd woken for the first time with the impression of Brosa's kiss on her lips. When he flirted with her in the morning, it sent a thrill through her veins. Washing his hands, hungry, smug. It was just right.

Yes, time had made space for her to find contentment, down here in this well of woods and years that could bury her forever. Would bury her one day, and she would turn to dust, and that was right.

She brushed the fox's fur.

A life unobserved could be beautiful, and she would not give hers up. Not even for this instantly beloved, impossible child that lived in her. Or maybe especially for the child.

Brosa didn't say so, but Eðna could guess—he wanted her to go to the future, to the city. He must know, there was no way she'd leave him, no way on earth she would go to the future, only to live to be an old woman, white with regret. She would not take all the gorgeous, boring, miraculous days away from Brosa and herself and their little one, even if those days turned out to be few in number.

Her Ma always said Eðna was stubborn. Já, so she was. She would stubbornly fight to stay here, nei matter what her man thought she should do. If that made her like Gida, then yes, she was her mother's daughter. And if being fiercely happy and at home in this rough land made her like her father, then she was Jon's daughter too.

She bent to the animal at her knees. "Þakka þér," she murmured. Thank you. For what the fox had lost. What was now hers.

Brosa pulled the net from the water, and three tiny fish flashed and struggled inside. Three fish, each one smaller than his hand. He threw the net on the stream bank and sat beside it.

This had to end. He and Eðna were slowly starving and being driven mad by the waiting, always ready like a nocked arrow.

They were content here too, já. They had become one here and made a warm home, but they could not go on this way, cowering in their den as the days became shorter. Last midsummer, he and his uncle were riding out to the walls, building them up where they'd crumbled and washed away. He'd sheared a sheep or two, proving his worth to the women. Last harvest, he worked ten fields. This year would find him in the woods, waiting for the snow to fall on Eðna, waiting for winter to lock them inside a hut not much bigger than the pantry that she feared.

Nei, he would not wait for that.

He drew his walking stick to him, and he heard Eðna coming through the woods. Had she finally caught a fox? Ugly tasting meat, but it would feed her and the babe. He pushed himself halfway to his feet, to greet her, but his heart stopped in his chest and his backside hit the ground.

It was not Eðna.

Svana's eyes struck him first. Those sky blue eyes that always sparkled with pretty joy or lazy contempt, were now fierce and afraid. Her hair—always so neat in its tight braids and whorls, soft as new butter—now stuck out in broken pieces. Her small mouth was the same as always, pink and shaped to kiss, but no smile curled her lips. She stood in the water, shaking as if it were a winter's night, and she held a kindling hatchet pointed at him. It swayed with her anger.

"I will not let you steal Eðna's breath." She waded toward Brosa, against the current, hatchet pointed. The hems of her sky colored dress, torn and gray, trailed in the water.

Brosa looked past her, to the woods. "Have you brought Eiðr? To end me."

"Nei!" Her eyes went wide. "Nei, I don't need that cowfoot's help. I've come to..." She swallowed. "Finish you myself."

He had nei patience for whatever madness this was. "As you see"—he spread his arms wide—"I have no weapon and I need a stick to walk. You had much to do with this, I know it, Woman. You took anything that might have made me worthy of a family, all that made me Ulf's son, my own horse, for the gods' sake, everything is gone. I have nei but three small fish to eat—"

"— I'm here to send you." Svana stood her ground. "On your journey to Hel."

Brosa's brows drew down. "You make a man into an outlaw, then visit him in the forest to feed him to the ravens."

"Not a man," she said, now just a horse's length away from Brosa, ax pointed. "I see you are a draugr."

Brosa bit down hard, but could nei help it. He burst out laughing. "Well, you stripped everything from me, maid, but I'm still a man."

"You are the hungry dead."

"Já, well, I am hungry, but I'm nei dead."

Svana stood in the stream and looked at him, and in that moment he saw her understand. Tears came up like a boiling pot, and she lowered the ax and rushed the last few steps to kneel in the water at his knees. "Brosa, Love, all my plans turned back on me. Turned on you. I thought your brother would be blamed for the deaths on the sand. I wanted Ginn to suffer the way I suffer."

She touched her forehead to Brosa's hands, and a rush of home came over him like a great wave. She smelled of soap and lavender, a plant as rare as ink and glass beads. Gods, she must have hoarded the tiny, dry buds for two years. She'd gotten dressed in her finest to come here and kill him.

She looked up and Brosa met her red-rimmed eyes. "Forgive me," she said.

He saw Svana was sorry for action she'd taken, já, but what he saw more clearly was the unforgiveable result. Svana had stirred a boiling pot and brought misery down on his family, and he was not the only one cast out. Eðna was outlawed, too.

"You sent me, us, here to die."

"Nei," she said, tears flowing. "Nei, I never meant for you to be accused of murder."

"Nei matter what you meant," he growled. Svana had sent them here to cower and to die.

In truth, Brosa had committed the worse of the two crimes he was outlawed for. He had disturbed Esa's and Arulf's bones. And if not for Svana, he would have taken that secret with him to Hel one day, and he would have missed this life, nei matter how short, with Eðna.

All these past weeks, Eðna had grown thin, but she was fierce and capable. Settled, no longer scared. They spent their days sitting close, watching the sun off the falls and talking about the world outside the woods. It was Svana who held his hands now, but in his mind he felt Eðna's bone-strong fingers clutching his, her hands braiding his hair. When she lifted his hair off the back of his neck, she always kissed him there. He saw all the carvings he made for her, the comfort they gave one another, the way she fed his lust, if not his stomach.

"I do forgive you, Svana," he said, and he brushed one of the hundred tears from her face. She never could hide her crying.

Svana pulled a small bundle from her pack. "I brought these things for Eðna, in case you had taken her life force. Some cheese and butter."

He laughed and opened the bundle. "You would take my head and give Eðna the cheese?"

"You were a draugr," she said. "Cheese would not feed you."

"Já, well, it will now." He took a small bite of a round of butter, saving most for Eðna, and he spoke with his mouth full. "Now, you have to go. It's dangerous to come see me."

"Já." She smiled. "Not as dangerous as I feared."

A heartbeat passed, and then they both laughed.

"I am relieved you won't need to remove my head."

"Nei matter. I couldn't. I care for you too much." She ducked her head, trying to shield her heart, but he knew her. "I always have."

He would break her heart again, but truth was best. "You are my sweet sister. We grew up together. But we were not given to each other. And we didn't feel the love rage that grabs the heart and every thought."

Her eyes were wet and blue as a winter bath. "I did." She pressed her hands to her ribs. "It's so heavy."

"I know," he said. "I know your meaning."

In truth, she was beloved as a sister, and on his honor, he protected his kin. But what could he do for her when he had no power, nothing to give or bargain for her release from Eiðr?

As if she heard his thoughts, she answered, "Take me with you—with both of you—away from this land." She raised her palm to stop him from speaking. "You need to leave. Eiðr is through simmering, and he is ready to act, to kill you and Eðna both. He's more cruel with each day. He may send me to the crows soon, too."

She stood and picked up her hatchet. It hung by her side and water streamed from the blade and her dress. Brosa saw her change—or perhaps his thoughts about her changed—from a cherished girl to a woman resolved. "I am glad I don't need to kill you, but I must leave with you. I won't stay here another day. I can get a crew. Only two men, but with me and Eðna—"

"—Shhh, Woman." He stood and wrapped his arms around her tiny bones. "Shhh."

Svana spoke the truth. He and Eðna must leave soon and go somewhere safe for the child to be born—a real house, where women could be with her. Maybe the small village where he'd first landed years ago, the very first place he had seen beyond this island. Wooden planks reached out into the water, so that his ship came right to the welcoming land without wading. Warm fires sparked there in strong houses, with light streaming into windows built into the walls. The women wore good wool dresses, and they smiled over their fat, sweet babes.

He could build Eðna a decent home like that, with good people all around.

His heart broke.

Just for the moment, he'd let himself dream again. He could not allow himself to think about days to come. It would hurt all the more when things did not turn out that way.

He looked over Svana's head to the small piece of forest where he and Eðna lived. Even if Eðna and the child returned to her city, Brosa still had to go away. Eðna would want him to determine the course of the rest of his life. The steerboard rested at the back of the hut. It took a crew of twenty men or more, but Svana's offer might be a start.

Svana relaxed in his arms, nei longer shaking. He breathed in the scents of the longhouse again. Of women and their lavender—his mother, Esa, Ginn—of men and their soap. Hundreds of baths with his uncle. He closed his eyes and thought of casting out into the waves to leave it all behind.

It was an unformed future, but it was something he could do. For Eðna—to honor her courage—he could live to remember her. For Svana, with her broken braids and filthy dress, he could do this. After living in this hut, happy as a house dog, but with nothing he could give or do for anyone, now maybe he could help.

"Já, Sister," he said. "We will. Eðna and I will take you with us and go."

He did not mention that if Eðna saw sense, she would be on a different journey.

Svana let out her breath. She stepped back, letting go of his embrace. "For your help," she said, "I will fix this." She laughed and tugged on his twisted, bound beard. "Your woman doesn't keep you very well."

"—Brosa?"

He was startled by Eðna's voice. He hadn't heard her signal.

A long moment passed, long enough for him to see his situation. Standing in the stream with another woman's fingers twined in his beard. A long enough moment for him to see Eðna, so proud. Her small frame stood as tall as the sky, a shieldmaiden of the forest, with blood on her hands. Her dark hair was like a bird's wild nest, full of leaves and twigs. A dead fox hung at her belt, its life dripping down her skirts.

He had time to see all that, and to watch Eðna's face fall, watch her fold up in pain at the sight of him and Svana. And then her pain turned. Eðna growled from deep in her chest. In one motion, she dropped her bow and lunged for Svana.

Svana slipped her fingers out of his beard and ran. She crashed through the brush, and Eðna ran after her, both of them gone into the trees. Brosa lurched after them, stumbling in the water. His leg failed and he fell to his knees and roared. Eðna's savage, wordless yells came to him, from farther and farther away. She was gone, and he could not follow.

ᛊ

Svana raced through the woods, and branches slashed her cheeks and neck. They left trails of pin-prick pain, and tears stung the hundred open wounds. Eðna was closing in on Svana. The woman she had come to save now chased her.

But Brosa was alive! He was nei draugr!

Svana had touched him and knew it to be true now, not by spying or hearsay. His solid hands, his thin but living body, had been right there in front of her. He'd bent his head to comfort her, wrapped her in his arms, and now she was certain he lived, and certain he would never take her as his own. She was a sister to him.

She smiled, even as she fled. When she and her mother came to Hvítmork, they had no one. She heard the whispered words. Bare is the back of a girl with no brother. Now, she had one—the strongest of brothers, a god among men. She thought she would grieve for all her days if he took Eðna as his woman, but now she knew better. Brosa called her sweet sister, and her chest was warm with it.

Still she ran.

The branches scraped her skin, and her ankles burned from twisting. Svana stumbled on a root and fell to her knees, and Eðna's fingers closed like talons around her shoulder. The slick chill of a knife pressed against Svana's breast, where her dress met bare skin. She waited for the cut, for her blood to run into this wood-brush and away.

Eðna held her knife steady, and she pressed herself against Svana's back. Svana's skin tingled with the touch of her breath. "We're happy here," she said. "What do you want with us?"

Eðna's heart was a second horse, thundering against Svana's back. Their hooves flew together now, in time with one another. Eðna's knife pressed tighter, and Svana's fear spiked.

"I came to save you." Svana laughed. "To warn you."

"You're here to betray him."

"If you mean my lousy husband Eiðr, then you are right. I'm here to betray him."

Svana looked to the sky and waited for Eðna to decide. Would she listen to Svana? Or slit her throat like an offered sheep?

This bit of sky might be the last thing Svana saw in life, but at least she knew the truth. She would not be Brosa's woman, but she was his kin. And she knew now, what she wanted was not him, it was a different life. These two years she had swallowed so many wishes and dreams. Spent endless mornings mending, making soap, cleaning Eiðr's foul clothes, spent so many nights in his bed, his never-hand spreading evil over her skin. What she wanted, more than air itself, was to leave.

Would Eðna's knife be the way?

The fox had pushed Svana, as if with a butt of its cold snout, to come here alone. To do what she had to get done, using her own strength. And she had found some peace, já. Were she and the fox done now? Would he let Eðna's knife set her free?

The release from this life did not come.

Eðna let her go.

Svana whirled to face her and backed away, her hand going to her own small knife at her belt.

Her breath halted at the sight.

Eðna had changed, even more than Brosa. She was half forest spirit, half Hel herself. Her bones stuck out from under her eyes and across her cheeks, where dirt was smeared in trails. A hungry and shadowed face with a mass of hair like tangled sea plants. Her sleeves and dress were smeared with blood, her skirt tied in a filthy knot, and a fox lay lifeless and stiff from her belt, swaying among her skirts. The woman's knife was clutched in one bony hand. Her eyes glowed like embers, like the fire inside Hel's head, a creature from Hár's night stories.

Nei. Svana calmed her breath. She would not make the same mistake. Eðna was hungry and fearsome, but she was human.

"I have stirred up anguish." Svana held her palms out with no weapon. "But I've come with news—something to tell you—and to ask for your help."

Eðna laughed. "What help can we possibly give to you? Thanks to you, we have nothing."

Svana looked to her hands where she had so recently held a hatchet. "I just want to leave here," she said. "All I have wanted these two years is to go away."

Eðna shook her head and laughed, a disgusted and angry sound. "All that you have done, the lives you've wrecked, Brosa near death. A good man's life broken, all so you can leave Iceland?" Eðna's hand closed on her knife again, and tears formed at the corners of her eyes. "Why him?"

"It was not meant for him. At the start, it was for my mother." Svana was surprised by her own words. So many weeks ago this had begun in Hildur's name. The first time she called on the fox. "It was only my Ma and me. I had no father. At the assembly when I was just a girl, Hildur got the gift of running the house at Hvítmork. She wanted me to take the keys from her when I was old enough—it was her driving wish that I marry Brosa Ulfsson." Svana shook her head. "She wanted it for so long, I thought I wanted it too."

Eðna's fierceness flickered, like the flare of a lamp running out of oil. Talking about Hildur, it did something, it softened Eðna, and so Svana went on. "There are lands all around this island, people who would give me a chance. I could make a life."

She raised her eyes once more. Tree fingers entwined above her, and the sky beyond was blue and bright and fair. For the hundredth time, she wished to be up there with the clouds.

A breath passed, and then another, and finally Eðna let her knife drop and hang from its strap.

In that moment, Svana looked at Eðna and she saw herself—a girl, not Hel after all, nei even a fierce forest maiden. Eðna was a mess, with broken braids and red hands, but she stood tall, her knife hanging, palms open, peaceful as a pool. "My mother was Gida," she said. "She wanted a certain life for me, too."

Svana nodded, and Eðna did as well. Eðna spoke. "You said you have news."

"Já," Svana said. "It's about a strange bird."

Eðna's brows drew together. "A bird." She sounded just the way Svana had, when she first heard Eiðr say it.

"Nei a sky bird or a water bird. It was unnatural. It came and went at the edge of the sea." Svana met Eðna's eyes. "The way you did."

Cold climbed the back of Eðna's neck, as though frost crystallized there.

The way you did.

"A world full of birds come and go," she said. "Why should one strike fear?"

"It had no feathers," Svana said. "Only bones and beak. It stood in the foam on long, thin legs that shone like a sharp blade, and it did not move."

"A bird without wings? That shines like a knife." It was superstitious nonsense. A million brilliant and varied birds visited the island in this century, coming to the coast to feed, to lay eggs and hatch their chicks. "The men had too much ale."

And yet, the words echoed. *The way you did.*

Svana was grave, and Eðna could see her conviction. This bird was more than a drunk husband's figment. "It opened its mouth wide, straight up to the sky. The bird had three legs, and it stood for a long time. It let the men touch it. Then it was gone. It did not fly, just was not there."

It sounded like an egret, wading on its elegant legs, and yet grotesque. A three-legged bird made of blades. She tried to imagine a lovely heron but made of silver, with three legs, its head tipping back to open toward the stars. Something about it reminded her of Jeff. His excitement over something he'd devised.

Oh gods, it was made of metal. It was steel. It wasn't a bird.

It was a camera.

Svana spoke with quiet certainty. "You know this bird."

Eðna did. She herself had come the same way, with a mission no different than this terrible egret's. To look into the sky and see if it could be done—if it was possible to go to the past and return. Yes. The bird had to be a camera. That's why it stood so long, waiting for near-dark, enough to see stars. Pictures of the sky were all Jeff needed to map, trace, date. He had sent the camera—on spindly, shining bird legs—to try to pinpoint where Eðna may have gone.

The camera had done a better job than Eðna did. It had returned home with its information.

Eðna looked to her knife, brick-dark with dried blood. Her hands were filthy and strong. She murmured Ginn's words. "A horde will follow."

When Jeff saw the night sky as it appeared from Iceland, circa 922, it would begin. Equipment would come next. Parts for things, pieces to make 22nd century shelters that would unfold, ugly and wrong on the black sand. Technology, gleaming like no honed ax-edge or man's big ring. Stuff would continue to vomit out from the sea. Food, furniture, chairs tossed into the brush, legs sticking up like dead, apocalyptic bugs. Jeff's old-fashioned computers, new and deadlier than any knife or spear. The espresso stands Ginn foretold. Yes. They would appear one by one, starting right there at the fishing camp—its simple tent and hearth replaced by a glass kiosk, with welcome screens flickering.

"Everything is unraveled," Svana said. "My plans. They came apart like a weak hem."

Unraveled yes, everything. Jeff himself would come, in his ripped jeans and t-shirts, with his disarming, uneven smiles. And others, not so sweet. Men and women in costumes would gawk at Brosa's resplendent boat. They would climb over its curved sides that he'd sanded and repaired with his two hands, together with his father, and wreck the smooth places that his thumbs had traced. Food wrappers and scuff marks would litter his burnished decks. Heedless people would run their hands and fingers over the sacred wolf's head of his family.

Everything Brosa believed in and yearned for in his entire life would be like thirty seconds of nothing under their boots.

"Nei," she murmured. Emotion crowded Eðna's heart, came up in her throat. "Nei, I won't let it happen."

"Eiðr is coming for you soon." Svana spoke quickly now. "I can help you get a small crew, poor men who wish to leave as much…"

Svana talked more, but Eðna had turned inside herself, her heart dropping deeper and deeper. An hour ago, she was content. She would have a child, a home, a sea-stead. Live out her life with Brosa. She would give him this fox, and tell him she would stay forever. She looked to her belt now, and the stiff animal looked scrawny and cold.

She'd heard so much about Svana in Ginn's vids, and in whispers around Hvítmork. Svana, whose skin was once like cream, with hair the color of sweet butter, the girl who now kept a lowly home for a dishonored man. Didn't Eðna know the same rage and helplessness?

As if called by Eðna's thoughts, Svana stood up taller. All of the girl's anger, her dishonor, her loss all fell away, and she rose from the brush as if rising from the sea—a warped mirror to Eðna herself. Her own fear, and yet need, to get away from her farm. The loneliness, so hard it made her cry, soundless, in bed at night.

Possible futures were laid out like "take" and "leave" piles on the pantry bed back at Hvítmork. A child, a sea-stead, a bright clean lab. A thousand filthy fingertips running across the bow of Brosa's boat. Images tossed together like a sloshing sea of moments, so that Eðna was ten again. She remembered Brenna's stick, swirling in the dirt. All around the island, there are people who could have saved your Ma. Svana's words, so much the same. There were lands all around this island, people who would give Svana a chance at a life.

The way Vera had given Eðna a chance. Yes. First there was Gida, but Eðna had a second mother. She whispered her name. "Vera."

Eðna answered Brosa's birdcall from far off in the woods. He must have chased after her and Svana, but lost them on the way. She followed his song until she spotted him, limping through the brush without his walking stick.

Her love. She saw him, and the wonder of the woods washed over her. The density of the green, chaotic world, and of her place in it, and his. The thrill of living birds flying in Gida's gods-filled sky. One of them called overhead, a longing sound. She saw her man in the land, coming toward her, and she knew that she had to do it. The terrible thing that she planned.

Part of her wanted to dash into his arms—the other part wishing she could hide forever. Everything she had to say, everything she now had to do, was going to break his heart.

He looked pathetically sorry. "Elskan, please, I—"

"—Nei matter," she said. "I'm not angry about Svana."

Brosa stopped, confused, and Eðna watched his eyes as he slowly realized there was something else, something different.

Did he see her mother's peace in her body, her eyes? See her ease, now that she no longer struggled against the world? Or maybe he saw her fear of the camera, and her resolve. The heart-wrenching thing she would have to do now.

"What is it then, Eðna?"

How could she even start?

"Sit with me," she said. They found a downed tree where they could sit together. Not their beloved setberg, but big enough. Eðna drew the leather cord with her firestriker from under her dress and held it tight. She drew on Brosa's belief in her, his warmth and safety.

"I told you about my farm, but I haven't told you the rest."

Brosa tucked a piece of her hair behind her ear, rested his thumb on her cheek. "What is the rest?"

He had no idea how soon it would begin, how bad it would get.

"So many changes will come to this land." She ducked away from his touch. "After too many fires and too many halls and houses and ships, the forest can't recover. A few hundred years from now, our woods right here will be gone." She couldn't stop. "When I was born, the land was almost stripped bare, and the naked land itself was covered with buildings, all around the edges of the island. You can't see a far horizon in any direction."

"Shhh." Brosa took her hands, and she let the firestriker hang. "Já, then, we will never go there to your time. We'll go to the south, in my ship, and the gods will give us a strong wind and a place for all three of us."

"That's not enough." Eðna struggled, and she stopped to gather herself. How could she say it? "Svana told me, Eiðr saw something at the fishing camp. Something that came from my time. It means that men and women will follow. They'll destroy everything here."

What could she do? Options divided, becoming a fork, and then six strands, twelve, twenty-four, a hundred. A whirled, sticky nest of possibilities. Numerous, but not limitless. No matter how she turned it over and over, one thing had to be done.

"I have to travel back where I came from." She called on her mother's bravery and resolve. "Without you."

Brosa's arms closed so hard around her, she felt her bones might break. "Nei, nei. I…" He faltered.

"—I can come back."

It was a promise she could not really make, but she blurted it out. She had to, had to protect their hearts somehow. "Ginn said she returned in the very moment she left. I'll go to the lab, stop Saga's river—block the way behind me—so no one can ever come again. I'll be back in a heartbeat."

"Love," he said, and his voice cracked. "Can we not just go make the sea-home you dream of?"

"But there is all this that will be lost. These lichens and mosses, our hut, my birds." She pushed a bit of Brosa's tangled hair behind his ear, just as he had done for her. Gida's faith welled up in her heart, and Jon's expansive love. "I have to do this for the sea and the land in your eyes, the light in your hair."

"Could we not live side by side with these men and women?"

"They're not generous and kind like you." She shook her head. "People in the future. Their eyes are covered with linen full of words, the way I was when I first came here. The trees will never be their bones. The streams will not be their blood. Your ship will become a..." How could she describe a museum? "A skeleton, never to sail again, only for dead men to climb all over and touch." Rich people with their costumes and twitching eyes. His proud wolf, shamed and rendered powerless.

"Those men and women are not your fault, Eðna. They are not your people."

"Nei matter," she said. "What kind of life would it be for us? To live with ourselves, when I could at least try?"

"A fine life." He kissed her forehead, desperately trying one way after another to get her to stay. "A simple, good life with each other."

"Nei. It will never be good." Even for her and Brosa, if they ran away to Norway or much, much farther, and let the future people overrun Ginn's land. "How could we hold our daughter's hand and tell her about how the woods once were? About what her father and mother once were, before we gave up and let the people come—"

"—Silence, Woman."

His words hit her like a hurled stone, but she pressed on. "It is like you men say. Only a coward waits like a sheep in its pen."

Brosa dropped his head into his hands, and he looked like a great and brilliant beast going down to its knees. They sat in the silence of the woods, with its bird calls and shushing leaves, and Eðna said nothing more, just waited. When Brosa looked up, tears cleared trails in the dust on his cheeks. He held her gaze for a long moment, and then he nodded, slow but steady.

"Fierce Eðna, you are right. And I have been the sheep for too long." He smiled, a sad and loving smile. "Nei more."

"Good." Eðna raised her chin. She would not cry.

They sat in the heart of the woods on a mossy rock and she laid it out to him, her idea, and all the wild hope it was built on. They talked about possibilities, faced heartbreaking risks. But the plan was really no plan at all, because when it came down to it, every outcome depended on something they did not, could not, understand.

They simply didn't know how any of it worked.

"I have been thinking these past days." Brosa took out his small knife, and began to draw a line in the soft bark of the tree they sat on. "About the unseen ocean, the one you must travel."

Eðna tensed. "Why have you been thinking about it?"

He carved a wave form. "In the cold of night, our breath makes steam that floats away, já? Smoke from the fire gets pulled to the vent. We don't see the air," he said, grinning, his despair turned briefly to excitement. "We see the steam move and the smoke move, and so we know the air's ways. So, I've been thinking."

He traced the wave again, and added another, waiting for Eðna to see and understand.

She only stared at the crude drawing.

"We see you move, Eðna."

"I move," she said, under her breath. She moved close beside Brosa, so she could see the waves the way he saw them. She traced their rough peaks and troughs with her fingertip and let his logic unfold. "It's like the air that carries the smoke. The ocean carries the boat."

"Já!" He smacked the stone with his palm. "You see."

Brosa knew about waves. He had deconstructed and rebuilt his own ship, had dreamed of and sketched hulls that would make boats move efficiently across the water as it sloshed and changed shape. He'd ridden the whale road and studied its choppy motion, and he'd seen it as a system. He saw beyond it, too, to the idea that even unseen air formed waves, and that time formed waves, too. Eðna was the boat, the evidence of its violent currents. Her being here was the proof of patterns and forces they believed in, but could not see.

"My uncle says Saga sits on the banks of the river of time, but he's wrong. You and Ginn, you come and go at once, in the span of a breath." He pointed to the waves, to their crests. "Time is nei river where you pass by and are gone."

Eðna finished for him. "It's an ocean."

Brosa was so alive with the work of a problem to solve. So strong and gorgeous he sparkled. Eyes wet with ocean colors, sleeves loose around his wrists, golden braid drawn over his shoulder, with bits of hair stuck in his open shirt. A body like a cathedral made of trees, so elegant and grave and full of faith.

"Do me one thing," he said. "Stay there long enough to have the child."

Eðna froze.

Yes, it was what she suspected. He wanted her to stay there, in the future. He didn't want her to come home.

"Nei, never." There was no way she would do that.

He held her tight, and he spoke into her hair. "When you said you had to leave, my heart begged you to say. But my mind…You must know, staying there is what's best."

"I will not stay there."

"Out on the sea, waves move in circles," he said. "They come around. You said yourself, you return as though no time has passed—"

This was why he'd been thinking about how time worked, how Eðna traveled. He wanted to send her back. Her and the baby. Despite arguing for a way to live in harmony with the people from the future, despite listening to all she told him about how awful it was, he actually wanted to send her there.

She cut him off before he could speak another word. "—I'll become a bug under their gaze. Twisting in the dirt. Our child will be looked at the same. If I stay there even a moment too long, you will never see us again."

Nei matter the shapes and patterns of waves. If she didn't follow her plan, destruction would come here. The future men and women would break Brosa's heart, and he would fall fighting them. Brosa would never get to Norway, and he would die at a stranger's hands, at Eiðr's hands, or at winter's hands.

If the one impossibly crazy scenario, the one that shone brightest in her mind, could work, then everyone and everything here would be safe. Their home—hers, Brosa's, Ginn's—would be hidden from the 22nd century's greedy eyes, and Eðna and Brosa could live out their days together.

Eðna wouldn't think of that—not yet. She could not think about Brosa smiling that broad smile, looking at her across a proper, indoor hearth, winking at her and making her blood run hot. Or imagine him holding and sheltering a baby, so incredibly small, curled against his chest. Scenarios too delicate to bear. Wishes like a skin of ice. She blinked them away.

"This is my one chance," Eðna said. "But I have to come right back, in the very same moment that I go."

"Já, then." He held her hands tight. "I believe you." He rested his forehead against hers. "But Elskan, if you block the whale road behind you, how do you know you'll return here, to the right time? With no spar to sight the sky. No steerboard."

She had no idea.

She would have to be like Gida, courageous and full of faith, and like Vera, optimistic and full of hope. She would have to admit that this terrible scheme depended on things she could not sort or order or understand. She smiled for Brosa, kissed him where his braid lay, against his throat, where secrets were meant to go. She whispered against his skin. "I just will."

Eðna stepped into a maze of cloth. A frame full of fabric hung in the sun outside Ginn's great hall. It was the perfect place to hide—dozens of dyed lengths of fabric, each taller than Eðna. She could stay here for a while until she figured out how to get Ginn's attention.

Or more likely, Betta's. If Ginn's grand house was the epic gods-carved building that rose beyond this bower, then this, here inside the fabric, was Betta's own hall where she alone had the keys.

Eðna was not afraid this time, not like she was the last time she snuck back here to get the antibiotics that could save Brosa. This time she was here to talk, to make a plan, a deal.

The delicate handspun wool was worked so finely, the fabric was almost sheer. Late sunlight slanted through, washing Eðna in color—her hands speckled with gold, amber, and the palest green. A few of the lengths were dyed a deep, heartbreaking apricot-pink that looked like a sunset she'd seen with Brosa, when they once walked together freely in open fields. She'd seen Brosa's face glow with this color, and they had both looked to the far horizon.

They hadn't seen such a thing in so long. Eðna pressed her cheek to one of the curtains, but it slipped away.

"You're as strange as Ginn." Betta's voice came through the cloth forest, and Eðna opened her eyes and laughed.

"Maybe after all this time in the woods, já."

"When you came," Betta said, and her breath made the cloth shiver. "Your eyes jumped like a bird's."

Eðna laughed again. Brosa once told her she blinked like a hen. She was just accessing information, something from another life.

"Well, I thought I was glorious." Right. And completely lost and uptight and alone.

Betta held little Haldi on her shoulder. He was so much bigger than last time Eðna had seen him, his chubby legs now squirming, yearning to crawl. Had she been in the woods that long? Would her contacts even work? Would Ginn's?

"What has changed?" Betta's eyes and bones were sharp.

"Changed?"

"You must have a reason, to put us in danger."

"I know," Eðna said. "My presence here is dangerous. But I'm actually here to protect you. Protect Ginn. And I need her help."

Betta shouted beyond the cloth. "Ranka!"

The girl peeked in—she'd been lurking and listening—and her eyes widened at the sight of Eðna. Betta sent her to get Ginn.

Eðna sat with her legs crossed and waited. In this moment, the world's fate hung like this cloth, fluttering, uncertain. She picked up a piece that had fallen to the ground, a pale cast-off, and folded it in two, then four. What on earth could she and Betta talk about while they waited, if not life and death?

"You make this color, green," she said, running a finger along the grain. "Ginn taught you other names for it. I heard you, last time I came here. You were singing a lullaby of colors."

"She taught me sage," Betta said. Her voice was full of love for Ginn, her eyes full of devotion and protectiveness. "And pea." The word was tart on Betta's tongue.

"Pea." Eðna said. "So small and round. More yellow than the green in this cloth." Months ago she would have looked up the pea's Latin name, the plant's growth habit and habitat. Now, she just smoothed this bit of cloth in her hands and wondered at the color.

"You were a hen. But now you look like a mother fox, fierce and thin."

Eðna looked up from the cloth. So much for talking about small things while they waited. "As you say, weeks in the woods have toughened me."

"Nei, that's not so. The weeks have softened you." Betta shifted her baby to her other shoulder. "A mother fox is courageous, not fearless."

Maybe Betta was right. Eðna hoped so. She was going to need all the courage and softness in the world.

Baby Haldi mewed, and Betta kissed his head and shifted her weight from foot to foot. "Many times, I thought I couldn't have this." She meant her child. "I had to fight for my life, for my heart. You will fight for your child, too."

"How did you know?" Eðna was so still, the words so delicate. "About our baby."

Her body looked the same. Flat and gaunt from eating berries and moss and stringy meat. But it held a life. A girl with arched eyebrows and a pointy chin. Or a boy who would look like Brosa, shining and handsome and funny, with a grin as wide as the sky. All of Eðna's terror, despair, anxiousness, all melted into a vision of a little Brosa. His sun-kissed curls melted away the cold in her bones. Hazy warmth made her smile, private, only for her child.

"I know what I can see," Betta said.

Eðna lifted her head, the intimate moment gone.

"What else can you see?" How gorgeously warm and instantly protective Eðna felt when she thought about her family? How desperate she was to balance everything, to find a way, to fulfill her promise, her dream, and yet everyone else's needs too?

"Brosa will make a strong father."

Eðna sought out the girl's hawk eyes. Could she actually see things turning out well? See Brosa with a child at his side? See the outcome of Eðna's wild plan.

Nei. No one could do that. Nei matter Betta's perceptiveness, she could not guess what Eðna was plotting, and certainly not the result.

"It's true, he'll be a good Da." A gauzy curtain stirred, and Ginn stepped out from behind it. "If Betta says so, then it will come to be."

Ginn dropped lightly to the ground and sat on her knees across from Eðna, her keys and beads jangling. She folded her ring-thick fingers in her lap. "I stood outside for a moment and listened. Your voices were rising like light from inside the wool."

Betta glanced at Ginn. "I have to go clean Haldi." She lifted her child and slipped away.

Eðna looked off through the cloth. "Do you really think she knows the future? Any better than you or I do?"

"Well, a nearer future than the 22nd century," Ginn said, and she picked grass blades. "But já, she sees something that other people don't."

Eðna went back to her folding. "She could see that I'm going to have a baby."

Ginn stopped picking grass and sat still. "I know. I wish you everything good." The fabric whispered in a light breeze, and she turned her face toward it, as if she could see through the cloth to the open doors of her grand hall. "In the new house, I will have a child."

And then Eðna remembered something Brosa said—that the night he laid down in the grave, he was giving up his life so that Ginn and Heirik could have the baby they'd longed for these past two years. What might Ginn have suffered, lost?

"It will come to be, Litla." Eðna murmured the words she'd heard Heirik say, from the day she overheard him in the hall.

Ginn went still. "Where did you hear that?"

A blush crept across Eðna's chest. "I'm sorry, I… It was so long ago. One day in the new hall, the day before the seer came, Brosa and I. We were hiding."

Ginn narrowed her ice-eyes. "It was a private moment."

Eðna ducked her head. "We didn't want to be there. We just panicked and hid, and then it was too late. I'm sorry." She smiled. "But you should have seen Brosa. His eyes were closed so tight. I thought he'd disappear into the ground rather than watch you."

Ginn pulled her arms tight around her knees. "My husband was speaking only to me."

"Já," Eðna said. "I know now, what it is to have a man talk of safety and devotion."

"Don't make me cry," Ginn said, and she wiped her nose.

Eðna wiped her own cheek with the back of her hand. She took a big breath. "Já, so. About safety and love—"

"—You've come about the camera."

"You know about it?"

"My husband and I know everything that happens in this house and on our land. Nothing escapes us."

"That's disturbing."

"It's what we live with." Ginn laughed again, and yet, she was serious. "He's always lived with it. The duty to know everything about his people, his land, his animals, and to act or not. I take some of that burden. But he can't really take mine. He doesn't understand what I fear." Ginn spread her fingers in the grass, as if to sense something moving in the land. "It's coming, isn't it?"

"Has Betta seen the people come from the future?"

"Nei," Ginn said. "She sees me, and she knows something terrible is wrong. She has no reference for what it would be like, no more than Heirik does, to have tourists here." Ginn smoothed her skirt. "They can't imagine what we know. What destruction people would wreak here, for nothing but amusement."

"Unless we do something." Eðna was fierce.

"We will fight." Ginn's conviction was just as fierce. "We'll fight those who come, with everything we have. The gods will be with us."

Was Ginn crazy?

Heirik was infallible, supernatural, and Ginn lived with pure faith in the gods, and a belief in love that was a force of nature. Even so. Even if all the men and women of this land rose up to fight beside them, they were still human. And they would die. They could never fight off the future.

"I'm going back," Eðna said.

Ginn was shocked. "You would do that to Brosa?"

"I would do it *for* him. I'm going to destroy the machine."

Eðna needed Ginn. She needed her help and her strength, and now, in this taut moment, she realized that she needed Ginn to believe in her. She needed Ginn's respect and understanding. "I see how you are with Heirik," she said. "You would do anything for him, já? To save his land and place and time?"

Ginn placed her palms carefully on her thighs and took a breath before answering. "Of course."

"Even leave him."

Ginn gripped her dress in two fists, her face gone pale. Eðna saw herself in that gesture—she had that same feeling when she thought of leaving Brosa. A bottomless feeling, colorless, clutching.

Ginn lifted watery eyes to Eðna. "Já," she said. "I could make it with you to the lab again."

"Nei! Nei." Eðna took Ginn's hand. She'd misunderstood. "Nei, you don't need to go. I just…I need to know you understand—you're the only one who understands what I have to do."

Gods, how powerful Ginn was, kneeling here within the cloth. The first woman to travel through time. Even if Eðna went to the future with all her recorded experiences, sensations, hints at how the contacts and the runes and the machine interacted. If she told the world that time was an ocean. Brought heaps of maps, silver arm bands, glass beads and ax heads—even actual instructions for time travel—still, she would not be the first to have achieved this miracle.

A few months ago, that thought would have made Eðna furious with jealousy, but now she felt free. In fact, she loved Ginn for it. Ginn had paved the way—the whale road of time—for Eðna herself to experience this life.

"But," Ginn asked, "don't we need two of us, to destroy the way here?"

"Já, but it doesn't have to be you and me. I need your contacts." She caught Ginn's eyes. "For Svana."

She told Ginn everything. About how Eiðr and his men would ambush them at the coast, about the scrawny crew Svana could pull together. Eðna and Svana would go to the lab, while Brosa and these men would fight their way to the ship.

Danger and desperation and hope against all reason, all whirled together into one plan. And Ginn vowed that she and the chief would bring all their gods-given power to bear on making it work. Ginn would end her feud with Svana, get a crew of two dozen strong men, and the most powerful would fight. The chief and his men would do anything—would lay down their lives and go to Valhalla—to clear a path for Eðna and Svana. To get them to the ocean's edge. Ginn's eyes were white-hot steel.

Eðna had seen vids of Ginn on the night she convinced Jeff to send her here to the 10th century the second time. Ginn walked with a calm confidence, in the black dress of a Valkyrie, passing through the mist that issued from the hallway vents. Loyal beyond measure, with pure faith in her course. Determined eyes, one of them encircled by her sinister-looking tattoo. A tiny iron cage hung from her wrist, lurching with the motions of the small animal she would sacrifice to come here, to come home.

"I hope I will be as strong as you."

They held each other's hands. Ginn's were lovely and heavy with rings, Eðna's skinny and strong-boned. She and Ginn understood each other. Nothing lay between them now.

Brosa closed the door of the hut behind him. Down at the setberg, Eðna sat inside a thicket of tall snowblooms. Past midsummer now, they waved in the breeze far over her head.

He closed his fist around the gift he'd made and slid it into his pack. There was not much time now. They would leave in the morning, and he had so much to say. He ran his hand through his clean hair one more time, straightened his best shirt, such as it now was, and went to her.

White flowers threw shadows on her shoulders. She was so fine and lovely wearing his old linen shirt, sitting on the berg and using the blooms to make a circlet. She murmured as she worked.

"Are you calling water spirits?"

Eðna looked up and laughed. "Nei, I am not." She turned back to her work. "If I tell you what I'm doing, you'll tease me."

"Nei, then, I will be grave and not smile." Brosa smiled. "I promise."

Eðna laid the flower crown in her lap. "I'm sending a message to my Da."

Brosa sat on the stone beside her. "You can speak a message to him? From here?"

"I don't know. He may never hear or see it, but if these contacts can save anything—if there's a chance—I want him to know about this place, about us." She looked at her hands, played with the flower crown. "I want him to know about me."

She was no longer angry or stubborn about her Da—a man Brosa could nei imagine. He had thought about Jon many times, but he could not fathom the man who made Eðna. "I wish I could know him."

Eðna looked out over the pool, at the falls, and then she sat up straight. "Wait." She brightened. "You could talk to him. Through my eyes."

Brosa raised an eyebrow. "Talk to your Da?"

"I have the contacts in," she said. "Just talk to him as if you're talking to me."

Brosa shook his head like a dumb beast. Still, sometimes he could not fit these things into his mind. All the things Eðna said were possible. They were still strange and unknowable as the plans of gods.

"Please," she said. "I want him to know you."

Gods, Brosa was unworthy of her, that was sure, and in truth, he didn't know if he wanted Jon to see him. He had washed his hair, put on his least tattered shirt, combed his beard, but still he lived as a savage. His face was sharp as his brother's—so hungry that Svana had thought him a draugr. But Eðna looked so pleased. If she wanted him to talk to Jon in the future world behind her eyes, then he would.

"Well, then." He straightened up a bit, ran his hands through his hair.

"Oh, come on," Eðna said. "You're not that good looking."

"Ah já, I am." He winked, and she smacked him and then brushed snowbloom petals from his face.

Brosa settled on the stone, so he could look at her level and sure. He had no thought about what to say.

"Jon." A dumb beginning. He resettled himself and looked into Eðna's eyes. They were more familiar to him than anything, but he made himself believe they were her father's eyes instead. He imagined the man that Eðna told him about—a charmer, a liar, and yet, a man who loved Eðna. A father whose arrows flew straight and whose chest expanded to fill his daughter's sky.

"I wish you could see your daughter," Brosa said. "Instead of my rough beard." He laughed and tugged on it. "She's much better looking. But, here I am."

"You sound just like him." Eðna laughed, a sound as light as leaves in a breeze, and it sent a chill up the back of Brosa's neck. Would Jon truly hear that laugh one day? It was beyond any act of the gods that his uncle ever spoke of. A man so far in the future, hearing these words, hearing the air enter their chests and the sound of her laugh.

"Eðna is a powerful thing," he told Jon. "Brave and beautiful beyond reckoning. Scornful as a sheared lamb, too."

Eðna moved to smack him again, but he took her hand and stilled it. He covered her cheek with his palm, and in the sudden hush, he spoke to both Eðna and Jon at once. "The curve of her jaw and chin fit into my fingers like she was made for me to hold. To honor."

Brosa saw her eyes, já, but beyond them, her father's. "She tells me you may hear my voice one day. I know you can't answer, but maybe that's for the best, já? Everything is up to her, anyway, but I do hope she'll be my wife."

Eðna's eyes widened. He'd surprised her, and she couldn't even speak.

"We don't have much time left," Brosa said. "So I hope she'll give me an answer soon."

"You want to be wed now?" She turned to look around her, always looking for an answer as if it stood beside her. "We live in the woods, and we're going—"

"—Quiet, Woman, I'm talking to your Da now."

Brosa drew the tiny ring from his pack. "I have this I carved for her, of a whale's bone." He had measured her fingers with his own many times. He carved the ring with waves all around, and formed a wing that would lay against her finger, up to her knuckle, a strong ring for Eðna. He had worked two runes into the inside—her letter and his—because she liked that he could write.

"You made this?" She lost her breath, her words.

"I did have days and days alone while you hunted and looked for wood. I had this bit of hvalrib in my pack, I was going to use to make a game piece." He spoke again to Jon. "And that's it. I have nei much else to give her. But she seems to want me anyway."

"Shut up." Eðna sniffled. "The image will be all blurry now." She wiped her eyes.

He covered her hands with his one. "Well, Fine One, do you think Jon would approve of an outcast? What do you think he would say?"

Eðna looked in Brosa's eyes, and he saw that she worried about tomorrow. She wanted a better plan, something he could not give her. But he would give her this anchor, if she would take it. A marriage. His worth. He waited for her, and he willed away every thought of duty and danger and fear, so that he saw only Eðna, felt her hand on his cheek now, too.

Her voice broke on her words. "My da would say yes," she said. "A thousand times."

Brosa could not move, could not speak, stunned by the joy of her.

She wiped her face with the back of her hand. "We can't really get married, though. Don't we need the chief and a sword?"

"I have my knife." He drew his seax from its sheath and laid it against the length of his arm, wrist to elbow. "It's not my grandfather's fine sword, but it will stand for it. We have snowblooms all around. And I walk well enough, I may be able to carry you across our door."

Like a flash of sun on water, he saw it—Eðna in his arms as he stepped carefully through the door of their hut, and he saw Esa before her as they stepped into his brother's house, petals trailing from the bundle in her hands. Hár said that Saga sat with Odin on the banks of the river of time. But he saw now, the truth he had told Eðna, that time was not a river. It was a vast sea that stretched to the horizon before him and behind, without end, its waves circling, churning, carrying and flinging mortal men and women through their lives. A choppy sea, where moments like this could fold together like waves, Eðna and Esa, their weddings, the moments that made their lives.

"Before the gods then, I give you this blade, Eðna." He laid it in her lap. "To hold when I am far from home. To keep safe for our sons and daughters." His voice cracked. Eðna—not he—was the one who would go unfathomably far from home. She would hold the fate of their sons and daughters in her body. What could this knife do?

He pushed away the image of Arulf's small face, and thoughts of the unknown face of his child to come.

"Put on your crown, Woman."

She placed her half-made circlet on her head, and she looked to him, and every glorious and beautiful thing in the world fell behind, all nothing compared to her. Sitting with her legs crossed on the setberg wearing his own big shirt and with petals in her shorn hair. Time was an ocean, já, and this moment was its calm center. Nei matter what came to pass next, he would stand beside Eðna and she beside him, and he would fear everything but back down from nothing.

"It looks funny," she said. "Doesn't it?"

"You are a goddess of the woods." Brosa slid the ring onto her finger.

It stuck. It would not go over her knuckle.

Tears sprang to Eðna's eyes. "My fingers are too thick."

"Nei, nei, Elskan, you don't need tears." Brosa held her hand tight. "I will just work the inside a little more. When you get home." He drew a cord of leather from his pack. "Here." He threaded the ring on it and Eðna ducked her head so he could put it around her neck, next to the firestriker.

He tied strong knots for his wife, so her ring would never fall from her neck, not even when she traveled the violent sea of time. She lifted her head, and he spoke not to her Da but to her alone. "Astkvan." His wife of the heart. He slipped his fingers into her hair and pulled her close. He kissed her, and a snow of flowers fell all around.

Eðna and Brosa stepped out of the forest.

The wide valley opened before them, and Eðna breathed deep, as did Brosa by her side. They saw the far distance for the first time in so long. Clouds flowered overhead, a gentle opening and turning, in an electric sky so blue it burned. The fleecy undersides were lit with gold, and a hundred hills, velvet and green, gently rolled away toward the sea. She reached for his hand, and they started the long walk to the whale road.

They'd left behind many things, after all. Now the hut sat alone, but not entirely empty. A small pile of wood waited by the firepit, and the touchwood that should always be there beside the ring. A stunning bed and chair waited for someone, someday. Another boy of ten years? Eðna smiled thinking maybe Ginn was right, that in her new hall she would make a family. Maybe Ginn's son or daughter would come here one day and sit in Eðna's chair.

Nei matter that they left so much behind. Still, she carried a pack full of the things they would need. The furs and hat and socks she needed to travel in the freezing water, and the bits of food and tools for this two-day walk, and beyond, for the time when Eðna and Brosa could leave this land.

Eðna wore her leather armor over Brosa's old shirt and pants. She had her calves bound like a man, and her bow and arrow slung across her body. He had the steerboard handle strapped to his back and his walking stick in hand.

They kept to the woods' edge and walked all day.

In normal times, they would ride horses for this journey. Brosa told her about the trips he took every year with his family.

"When I was small, my Ma placed me on a sled with my cousins and bundled us all in wool. We were tucked in between casks of ale and grass baskets for collecting eggs." He leaned into his stick and smiled. "I nei had to walk like this." But it was risky enough to walk, let alone take animals with them. Brosa could not handle walking in deep brush, and so they walked on the edge.

For the first while, Brosa beamed with an almost manic cheerfulness, then he settled into determined optimism, pointing out plants and clouds and telling stories of the gods. Of Loki trying to eat faster than fire, and of Skadi's father, whose eyes became stars for her to look at every night. He made Eðna laugh telling her about the time when Thor drank so much, he lowered the level of the sea.

It was like him, to fight through fear with charm and diversion. His mood was a gift for Eðna, an attempt to say goodbye without sorrow, just in case she never came back.

Late on the first day, they came to the rocky landscape that divided Hvítmork from the sea. The family's well-worn byway was visible, but still Eðna and Brosa kept to a different path. They wove in and out of boulders the size of full-grown sheep, and the ground between them was strewn with rocks as big as fists.

Brosa had to slow to handle the terrain. After an hour, maybe two, they came to a thick-stoned climb, and Brosa stumbled. He fell to his knees, with a roar and a curse. "Goats-balls!" He shouted and threw his walking stick across the rocks.

Eðna crouched beside him. "Come, husband." She helped him stand and sit on a boulder and she bent to pick up his stick. "Are you okay?"

He growled. "This is folsku-ferd, Eðna." A fool's expedition. "You are setting off into danger beyond fathom, and I can't even walk. How can I protect you?"

"Protect me?" She sat beside him. She turned the stick in her hands. It was smooth where Brosa had gripped it for so many weeks.

"A proper man would walk ahead," he said. "Look for danger."

"—Stop." Eðna pressed her fingers to his mouth, to shush him. "You truly are a fool if you think I want a man out ahead of me. I'm not a fledgling. I want you beside me, not in front."

Brosa's smile came slowly, reluctantly, and she saw him admit what his heart knew. "Já, you are nei fledgling." He kissed her palm, solemn and sweet. "I'd be the luckiest man to walk beside you. And you are right, a fool not to."

Then his half smile turned into a wicked grin. "In truth, I could even walk behind you, since you are so brave. When we get to the sand where Eiðr lurks, you go first."

She yanked her hand away and smacked him. "Beast."

She handed him his walking stick, and they set off again.

That night they laid sheepskins on the ground to sleep inside the trees, but they could not close their eyes. They sat together, leaning against a strong birch. Men lurked nearby, just outside of their reach, those they knew—Brosa's uncle, his cousins Magnus and Hauk—and those they were not sure of. Nei doubt Eiðr, Morg and Svana were all near, making their own way to the fishing camp, readying for the ambush they had planned for the sea.

They'd reviewed the Viking logic, and now Eðna understood.

Eiðr knew Heirik would be hiding at the coast. He would draw the chief out and goad Heirik into doing something rash. If Heirik struck first, that would give Eiðr all the permission he needed to kill. It would be his turn.

A chill breeze swept the night, and Eðna pressed herself tight to Brosa's body. She realized too late that she would have no more moments alone with her husband. He wrapped his arms around her and whispered soothing words, and finally they fell asleep inside a circle of armed men.

Early on the second day, they made it through the rockiest part of the journey and came to the top of a great valley, blanketed with rich green grass and white, round flower-heads. Down the center the massive byway—a path that was wider than ten grand halls—had been trodden into dust over three generations of treks.

They came to a halt, and Brosa pointed with his stick. "The ocean." It was a thin, dark thread laying across the horizon. A chill breeze came in that instant, as if whipped up and sent by the sea to seek her here. Eðna resisted, but it called her.

"You and I will not die," Brosa said. "But if it so happens, send your last breath out to Freyja and tell her we are coming on the same wave—"

"—Shhh." Eðna kissed him to quiet him, but he spoke softly into the kiss. "We can live in the warmth of her mountain hall. All three of us." A vision of eternity together, sitting around a crackling fire in a cozy supernatural house where their souls would reside—his, hers, the baby's.

It was his plan. He needed one, just as much as Eðna did. And his plan was to appeal to Freyja, ask that they not be separated in the everlife.

"Alright. I will tell her."

Brosa nodded, then leaned into his stick and went ahead, knee deep in grass and wildflowers. He walked away, and her eyes stung with love and dread. It was the last time she'd see him this way, with nothing but her own naked vision, her own devotion. She opened her pack and took out Ginn's contacts.

They lay curled up, small and dry and containing all of Eðna's crazy hope. She gritted her teeth and put them in her eyes, and she blinked against the pain. Nothing happened. No words or numbers scrolled, no warnings or reassurances, but she was as ready as she could be.

They topped the last rise, and the glittering ocean spanned the world ahead of them. It turned Brosa to a silhouette, his body dark against the glint of a million silver ocean tips. Stinging-white light glanced off the water and flared all around. His ship stood, formidable and gleaming, its wolf-head curving high over the water. It's shape was just like the tiny one Brosa had carved.

Eðna shrugged the pack off and threw it to the ground. She suddenly needed that little wooden boat. Brosa gave it to her to take on her journey, but she'd tucked it down in the pack instead. In case she failed, she wanted him to find it one day and remember them together. Now, she fiercely needed to take it with her instead. She pawed down to the bottom of the pack and found it.

The swell of the hull fit into her hand, and she held it up to the sun. She closed one eye, and the illusion was complete. The proud and elegant Viking ship sailed far out on the water, safely grazing the horizon. Their sea-home. Soon.

Eðna tucked the boat into her pack and descended the long, shallow slope to the sea.

It would be soon—the ambush they expected.

She swept her eyes over the curve of tiny caves that enclosed the beach. The black sand stretched away in both directions, diminishing to a fine strand to the South, and to the North a gathering of boulders thick with brown seaweed and moss. Puffins and razorbills were scattered on the cliffs, and some dark and unknown birds peppered the sky, but there was no human motion anywhere.

They were all here, nonetheless. Svana, Eiðr and his cousins ready to attack. Ginn, Heirik, their men, ready to draw attention, draw the fight up the beach. Despite Eðna and Brosa staying close under the shelter of a cliff, many eyes were on them now.

She threw her shoulders into walking. The flowers were up to her thighs, and she pushed through them. When she first arrived here, these very blossoms were closed like fists. Now, a million miniature flowers had burst open in supernovae of tiny petals. Their big stalks bent under her boots, and blossoms stuck to her calf bindings.

She could almost hear the tension, like a high-pitched whine. She and Brosa were already at the fishing camp, now, right beside the tent where she first saw the dead men. The sea was just a few meters away. How would the pieces of the plan interlock and turn so fast? Was it possible?

"Murderer!"

Eðna ducked at the first shout and covered her head. It came from above. And another voice. "Defiler!"

She and Brosa looked up. Eiðr, on his horse, rode high on a cliff overlooking the water. From down here, he seemed as big as the one-handed god Tyr. His animal reared, and he raised his arm to the sky, the absence of a hand more chilling than any war-clenched fist. Another man joined him—Morg. The man who had grabbed Eðna in the woods. He looked a hundred feet down into Brosa's and Eðna's eyes.

It was strangely calming. Finally, the ambush had begun.

Eiðr and Morg surged down the hill fast, their horses churning up dust and flowers. Two more men came out from below where they'd been hiding among the giant rocks. Four men, as expected.

And then, a wordless cry came from across the sand—a war cry that chilled Eðna's bones and moved the ground under her feet. Heirik led a dozen men some on horseback, some running, roaring with rage.

Brosa dropped his walking stick and drew his ax from his belt. "Get in the water, Eðna." Panic clawed at her chest. After all the planning, all the goodbyes, it still felt too fast. She wasn't ready to leave him. He shouted at her. "Now!"

And then he turned away from her and charged to the fight.

Eðna turned in every direction, horror mounting. Men shouted on the slope and horses thundered on the beach. Every force inside her begged to call Brosa back, to make him turn away from the fight, toward safety. He rushed, through pain and fear, into danger. A resolute warrior, going to fight by his brother's side.

It was working. The clash started to the North. They'd bought the women space and time.

Eðna had to go. Now. She would be back in less than a second, charging up the beach to fight at Brosa's side. But she couldn't leave. She had to see him one last time. She turned in the water, no way she could fight the urge, the burning need to know. Did her love live? Was he winning this fight or dying?

She needed to see with her own eyes.

Saga let her.

Time slowed, as if the goddess showed Eðna everything in a slow unfolding, unfurling. Honorable Brosa fought, one hand on his ax and the other holding the steerboard handle as a desperate shield. A dozen men slashed and beat each other all around him, and blood flew in slow, graceful and horrible arcs. Heirik fought on his swift, dark horse—infused with the power of every god in one man. He came to fight at Brosa's side.

Brosa and Heirik were together, still and alone in the midst of a raging battle, washed in a sea of gore. In this molasses moment, Eðna had time to see Brosa's expression. He was not afraid. He didn't beg his brother for help, for protection. He looked to Heirik with simple sadness. So sad, so sorry that they would not be together again. That things had gone this way. In Brosa's eyes, she saw a lifetime of devotion. And in Heirik's eyes, the same.

Heirik nodded, and then he raised his chin in warning. Brosa turned, twisted his body, swung his seax and slashed at Morg. Morg, who had torn Eðna's hair from her scalp, who'd held her braid so that Eiðr could saw it. After everything, still, Brosa was sorry about Morg, too. She could see her husband's pain, even though it was Brosa's knife that slowly, so slowly, slid into Morg's chest.

Brosa watched Morg die. He didn't see Eiðr come from behind. Eiðr hit Brosa in his leg, and Brosa went down on his knee. Eðna lost sight of him among the men on the ground who were crawling, groaning. Brosa her love was down among them. She willed him to get up. "Please, please love."

"—Now, Eðna!"

Ginn's voice tore Eðna away, and she snapped to the present, time whipping by, urgent, quick. So quick. Svana slogged toward Eðna, her skirts dragging in the water, a small hatchet in her hand, deadly determination in her eyes. It was time.

Eðna breathed. She would be back in a blink. Her going and returning should look just like a flicker—one more trick of the optical nerve among the thousands of ocean glints. She would be here again, would find Brosa among those men, save him, fight by his side.

Eðna pulled Svana close, pushed her to her knees, pushed her hands down into the sea. "Be strong," Eðna said. To Svana, to Brosa, to herself.

They tapped out.

ᛋ

Svana woke in a place.

Inside her skull, hot needles stabbed and burned. Furies slashed at her mind, with fingernails like shards of ice. Panicked horses screamed, and she pressed her fists to her head, but could not dull the shrieking. "Svana!" The horses wailed. "Skyndi!" Over and over they wailed, a relentless tide. On her knees, her head in her hands, Svana pleaded with all the gods to make it stop.

"Stop," she murmured, and she rocked herself. "Stop."

Svana knew about this. Eðna told her she would hear alarms, but they would not be the war cries of men. They would be steady, horrible braying. She breathed deep and slow, as they had planned, and she opened her eyes.

This was the place—the great hall that Eðna said they would find. In every direction, there was nothing. No sky. No grass. No wood. No ocean. No rounded shapes of hearth or bench or animal. Nei, not even colors of a fire or midsummer, only the silver of blades.

The air had nei smell of any kind—not smoke or cow or grass—and she put her hand to her chest to be sure it rose and fell. So cold, her skull froze and her breath turned to clouds. She turned on her knees, crawled in a circle at the center of the hall, and the place was the same on every side. Svana sat up on her knees, and her head wheeled like crows. There was no way past this horror, nothing beyond.

She smiled.

She was somewhere else.

Finally, she had come unfathomably far from her miserable life, and she was in a place where Ginn would never, ever go.

She closed her hand on her little hatchet.

Svana looked for the one wall made of frost, like a cup, but thin and clear and tall. If Saga willed it, then Svana would see a man through this wall. She'd see him right through the frost—a man that Eðna told her was taller than the door to Svana's house, with blood-and-blond hair and summer-sky eyes. He would wear fraying shirts with no sleeves or bracers, and his arm bands were inked into his skin like the images on Ginn's face.

If the man was not here, things would be harder. But if he was, Svana knew what to do.

He should be here. The shrieking alarms would bring him. She shaded her eyes—so many things glistened like sudden light off a pool.

There!

There he was.

"Jeff." She said the name that Eðna had taught her. Behind a wall that was not a wall, Jeff stood tall and lean. He turned, and his mouth fell open.

The shrieking stopped, and there was an unearthly hum. Not the rolling murmur of a house full of men and women in sleep, not the hum of a women's spinning-song. Nei, it was not a human or animal sound. It was steady, coming from all directions.

Svana crawled to Jeff, dragging her hatchet, so slow, she felt her bones and dress weighed more than ten horses. She fell onto her elbows, and her face hit the floor, but nei, she would not stop. Svana pushed up onto her hands again, and Jeff came toward her, rushed to her, knelt in front of her. He smelled of unknown flowers, and of something bitter and warm. His hair was not the color of blood, but of honey and berries, and his wide open eyes were exactly like the sky. Gods, Svana had gone up after all, into the clouds.

Eðna shouted, and Svana and Jeff looked up. Eðna threw future words, and Jeff stood to go to her. He spoke back to Eðna, words Svana could not understand, but she could hear his wonder. His questions, Eðna's pleas.

This was the time, while the two of them talked. Svana got to her knees. She had to reach the place where Jeff worked, the thing called the machine.

Behind the frost wall were all the things Eðna told of. Tables she could see through, and chests built not of wood but of silver that shone bright as the richest armbands, with flames flickering inside tiny windows. Powerful runes covered the frost, as if a child had drawn pictures on a frozen river. One of them moved, and Svana shouted and jumped back. The runes were alive inside the glass! She reached for the shapes, and her breath clouded over their moving forms.

"—Jen," Eðna said, and Svana came to attention at Ginn's old name. "Safe." Eðna spoke to Jeff, and her voice was muffled from the wall between them, but Svana heard a few words she knew. Another name, *Vera*, Eðna's second mother. And then she heard her own name, *Svana. Safe*. And one more word she knew. "Please," Eðna said. She spoke unknown words that made Jeff stop and listen. "I did it. You owe me one."

What kind of man was Jeff? Did he weigh lives like nothing but stones? Did he know compassion?

Saga dipped her fingers into the water of time and she slowed the current, and they each stood, still as winter. The machine hummed, and Svana heard within the sound the heartbeats of foxes and men. Of her own fox, who had not followed but had given her the strength to come here. Jeff reached out to Eðna, so slowly, and Eðna stood strong and wild in her forest rags. Time crawled, long enough for enormous flocks of birds to pass, for whales and their calves to cross the ocean.

Jeff nodded. "Já, Eðna," he said. "Okay."

He came to where Svana stood, to the machine. He touched the runes on the ice wall, and they jumped and Svana covered her face with one hand, gripped the small ax in the other.

Could she really cross this man? A man who made runes move under his fingers? He could crush her life in his hands the way Ginn did, but worse, a man this powerful could crush her everlife too. She would writhe in loneliness and agony forever.

Nei. She was strong. Look where she had come!

She gripped her hatchet, and put steel in her thoughts and heart. Eðna risked her life for what was right and good, and for Svana's sweet brother Brosa. Svana could do this much for him, too. She swallowed hard and stood ready. Jeff said words she couldn't understand. He made the runes move.

And Eðna disappeared.

Svana's mouth fell open, but she had no time to watch like a dumb cow. She raised her little ax over her shoulder. Svana looked for her fox, not for help, but to show him her strength. She heard her Ma telling her *good* when she spun her first thread. She saw Brosa sitting among the rocks in the elf hollow, beautiful and strong in his land. Saw herself, rushing, courageous, into the water, ready for a strange new world. She swung hard and buried the blade deep, cleaving the machine like a horrible skull of steel and sparks. She worked the ax free and then slashed again and again. She closed the door behind them and turned the key. She destroyed Jeff's machine.

Eðna opened her eyes to cold, white nothing. Not a sound, not anything she could see.

She expected the blindness, just like last time she came through to the past. Except this was not like last time. This blindness was white and sharp, and it stung like a million needles in her eyes.

She shook her head, and her inner ears exploded with pain. Her hearing returned, with a sudden howling, screeching wind, almost worse than the deafness.

A force pushed her forward on her knees, against her back, over and over. It was waves. She was at the ocean's edge, kneeling in the foam. Freezing water, cutting wind. She struggled with her dumb brain. Yes, this was expected when she traveled in time. Back to Brosa.

Brosa.

The thought of him crashed with the next wave, all of him, Brosa. His ax held high over one shoulder, the steerboard handle held in front of him, a desperate shield. She had to get up and fight at his side, against Eiðr. Now. But she was so numb. So tired.

Eðna pushed herself up out of the sand. Her hands should be wet, but she couldn't feel them at all. And the whiteness seemed to swirl and whirl.

"Shelter first." She remembered learning a long time ago. She needed to get up and away from the water. "Warmth."

She staggered to her feet, wrapped her arms tight around herself, bent her head and trudged forward. There would be a slope up away from the water, and little caves there, if she was in the right place.

The wind screamed like furies and spit ice in her face.

Ice?

Cold and solid white. This was snow!

Eðna lifted her numb hands, and she could see them. She wasn't blind. She was inside a snow storm. Now she could pick out dim sights beyond the swirling snow. The white world moved in slowly turning shapes against a dark sky. She could see.

Her relief evaporated in a second.

This was not the exact moment she had left, underneath the late summer sun, in the midst of raging weapons, shouts and fists. This was winter. This was wrong.

The wind knifed its way in under the fur brim of her hat. "Warmth," she mumbled. Yes. That was critical now.

She trudged on, and finally plowed straight into the wall of little caves. With swollen fingers, she felt for a cave opening, welcoming and familiar. "I'm here." Here, já. Here on a beach with a cave. But was it the right place? And time? "Confirm temporal location."

She blinked, and something hard cracked inside her eyelids. Her contacts were freezing. She pried them out with stiff fingers, and thought she might rip her eyes from her head. She got the contacts free and let them go, taken by the wind.

She looked up to the night, and finally she could see.

It was the contacts blinding her. Now, the black expanse of sand leading to the fishing camp was visible. Three dark humps stood far down the beach, pointier than boulders. They had to be the hut and two tents. Yes! She squinted, but could not make out the ship. No elegant bow rising from the waves. Dread lifted its head. "Saga, please."

But it had been summer. Brosa would be gone by now. It was past the season when it was safe to sail.

She could be decades too late. There might still be a fishing hut here, and yet Brosa might be in Norway, a white old man, or beyond to the south, or to whatever afterlife had come. And yet. "Let him be here."

She no longer felt her feet, but she moved, somehow, toward the blurry shapes of tents that floated in a limitless ocean of wind and snowflakes.

Here, Eðna!

It was her father's voice. Jon's fingers closed tight around her arm. Her Da whipped her up into his arms, and her little skis clattered to the ground. She could almost see her them against the white ground, but the snow ate at her eyes. Jon carried her now, crushed her tight against his chest, and she felt her Da breathing hard, in determined gulps. Was he sobbing? She tucked her head against his shoulder and hid her face in his strength. Her father saved her.

—A fresh wave of snow smacked Eðna in the face, and she came alive and sputtered. Jon was not here. She was not a child, and she would save herself.

She walked, forever.

At last, she blundered into the wall of the fishing hut. Her fingers were all but gone—curled up, senseless, inside her fists. With the backs of her hands she felt along the wall until a door pushed open and she tumbled inside.

The hut was completely dark and still as a grave. No fire crackled in the hearth, no men here, but the little building shielded her from the wind and she was instantly, infinitesimally, warmer. She dug her arms inside her clothes, untying her leather and ripping Brosa's old shirt, pushing it aside to get her icy hands under her armpits. She just needed a fire. She needed to get a fire going, in the dark, with fingers swollen and numb.

She felt Brosa place the necklace over her head. She leaned into her beautiful husband, his big chest and smell of smoke, and he tied strong knots. *A woman must keep a striker at her throat.*

She smiled while she fumbled to get the firestriker out. Next to it, on the cord, hung the bone ring with its sweeping wing. "Takk, Husband."

Eðna knelt by the dim hearth, and she closed her eyes tight, let them get accustomed to the darkness. When she opened them, she could see the sparsely filled room. Just the fire ring and a single bench. A crumbling, tiny pile of touchwood was right where it should be, near the hearth, and she murmured thanks again, this time to the men who kept the hut in proper order.

She fumbled lighting a spark, but her hands were still too numb, and long moments passed, marked only by changes in the pattern of howling outside and the rhythm of her foggy breath.

The touchwood, and then striker, fell gracefully to the floor, slow as lovely snow.

The dead men lay here, so long ago. Now she would join them. She'd die in the same place. Someone would find her here, maybe Ginn and Heirik. Or maybe Brosa had waited for her, had not left the island, and he would find her here, blue, preserved. He would kneel over her body, gather her frigid, stiff limbs and rock her. Rock her, and with her, their baby. Would he lay himself down beside her, like Baldr and his wife side by side in death?

Nei.

When she first met him, he was covered in the dust of Esa's bones. But he had changed since then. All the glorious, sun-kissed, green weeks, months, they had lived in their hut, it had changed them both. Brosa had dreams now. They were simple—to build things, to one day have a family—but he had them. And he wanted those dreams enough to fight.

Oh gods, a family. Their baby. Was it still alive, after being pummeled by time and storm? Eðna had risked everything, for something far greater than their two little lives, but here at death's hearth, she couldn't push the child away anymore. Finally, she would let herself imagine a girl with blond curls and a smile like her Da, running toward Eðna through green grass up to her waist. Eðna would let herself lie down now, just for a minute, and she and her daughter would braid grass and make wildflower crowns.

—Eðna opened her eyes.

Nei. She blinked herself wide awake. She would not give up. Cold was a simple, curable condition. She gripped the firestriker and tried again, and this time a spark came to life in the fluff and fungus. The tiniest, most tenuous spark. She exhaled the most careful wisps of air, almost no breath at all, until it grew into an orange glow. Small, but substantial enough to catch. She added more dust and splinters of wood from around the floor, set the little nest in the firepit and added bits of driftwood from the pile. The hut came to dim life around her.

Eðna laughed like a madwoman. She did it!

She could see now. A stack of cloaks and furs sat n than a meter away. She dragged the lump of blankets up over her wet clothes. With her last bit of will, she pried her boots off and dropped them by the fire. And that was all. Now, finally, she could sleep.

In her dream, she would be a snowy egret, spreading her enormous, pale wings like a fan. She sheltered herself and her baby, and fell asleep under her own wing-blanket. As she slipped away into egret dreams, she smiled. Some spirit would come for her, but not Brosa's Hel. Hel came for the cowardly dead. Eðna was no coward. Finally, she was loyal and free.

Brosa wrapped his laces up his calves with numb hands. His fingers were stiff, and thin as grave bones. Hár always told him he'd grown soft. Nei more. Living alone in a tent set on the wind-tossed deck of his ship had made him lean.

Tonight, the world shrieked like desperate wraiths, and the boat pitched and pulled at its anchor. The tent canvas came undone, and salt-wind whipped in, freezing his face and beard.

He sat on the fur bed he kept ready for Eðna, and he bundled himself in boots and bindings and bracers to go and look for her again. Once in the winterlight, once in the dark. From here where he was anchored—just a few boat-lengths out—he had a view across the coastline, and on most days, he could see where she would emerge from the sea. But not today, with the air solid with snow.

Days like this, he had to go look.

Nei matter, he no longer felt the needle pricks of cold and ice in his beard. He was beyond such things. He didn't feel any pain sharper than a dull ache. Weather and loss had turned him to raven rock.

He tightened his bracers with Heirik's one-handed knots.

He had not seen his brother for weeks now, since the last time he and Ginn skied here with food and ale and more blankets. Ginn had touched Brosa's cheek and called him a sheep.

It was a sweet name, out of affection. But in truth, she was right. He was not hardened like bones, after all. He was toughened like a sheep, alive and stubborn, pawing down through the snow to find what it needed to live. He smiled. A sheep like those that Eðna thought he herded, the first day they met.

Even the notion of a sheep reminded him of his wife. His first glimpse of a far-off, ink-haired spirit, full of wonder at the touch of feathers, and yet brittle as sticks over things she could not control. She must be seething right now, with something she could not control keeping her away.

He had everything waiting for her. All that she said she wanted in her sea-stead was here, most of it delivered by Ginn, who was so grateful for Eðna's and his sacrifice. He ran his hand over the shining wooden lid of a locking chest with iron hasps, packed with clean linens, and lengths of fine cloth that shone like bright water. Fabric spun from the bodies of insects, though he was not sure he believed the traders from the east. Wool rugs, three deep, covered the deck, and he sat on a full bed of the softest furs.

He closed his eyes and waited for the rush of fear to pass through him. The dread that sometimes rose and sloshed like sea water in his gut. He put his mind through the steps of building a boat, laying the keel, fastening the strakes, overlapping their edges like waves coming in to the sand. He wrapped his arms around himself and dreamed of the scents of steamed birch, and the wool packed between the planks. He spoke gently, falling into sleep, about the beams and ribs, the knees and thwarts. The steerboard. He pulled the handle to him sometimes, and woke with it pressed to his chest.

He eyed it now, where it lay beside Eðna's trove of linens, and he laughed. A man who'd been born to hoist horns of ale and sing with men, flirt with women, tell stories by the hearth. Here he sat with nothing but a board to talk to, to hold.

With frozen fingers, he strapped snorskori to the soles of his boots. Made of the teeth of many foxes, they would keep him steady in the snow and ice. He lifted the bedroll onto his back, a familiar weight after so many times searching. The extra blankets would warm Eðna. She would be wet when she got here.

All he had to do was find her, bring her back to this boat and wait until Ginn and Heirik visited once more. They came every few weeks, with food and asking for news. Once Eðna was here, his brother and Ginn would gather the men again, who would be his crew. They would bring enough food for Eðna and the child and himself, to live until it was warm enough to sail. And then he would take his wife away from here forever. Find a village. Have a life.

Eðna would be happy to know he had a plan.

The ceiling of the tent pressed down on his head and humbled him. The wind howled and whipped up loose snow into the forms of wraiths. One of them entered the tent, and he lifted his foot to let it pass him by. It skittered like a live thing across the floor.

Brosa stepped into the demented wind and was snow-blind. Nei matter, he knew every step along his deck by touch. He felt for the shieldwale and went to the rowboat.

"Hrodi." His bracer came loose and fingers of winter reached inside his sleeve. He grumbled like his uncle, most of the time now. With his teeth, he tried to tie the leather, and he bit his wrist and snarled. One day, Eðna would help him with these things. When they were long gone from this gods-forsaken coast.

He did not look forward to his walk up and down the water's edge, feeling his way, the wind tearing at his face and fighting against his heavy pack. He could blunder into the sea and freeze. But for that same reason, he had to go. If Eðna came today, she would wash up in a deadly ocean, with only moments to make it to land. She needed him.

With a thud, the rowboat slid onto sand. The sea sucked it back, but it held, and Brosa stood. Ice like seal-oil greased the rowboat's deck, and even the fox-teeth shoes could not hold. He slid and went down with a shout, and pain shot like an arrow through his leg.

He sat and looked to the sky and snow fell, relentless, in his eyes. He saw his situation. A man alone inside a storm, sitting on his backside, surrounded by the handmaidens of Hel calling him and lashing at him. It felt as though the wind ripped the skin from his face.

There'd never yet been a day this bad. He should go back to the ship. Claw his way up the shieldwale and get to safety. Wait for the storm to settle. He could look again tomorrow.

For four months she had not come. Why would she suddenly come today?

A bird called, fierce and desperate, and Brosa came awake. He shook his arms to stir his blood. If he started thinking Eðna might not come today, then there would be no reason for her to come tomorrow either, or the day after that.

He wiped his face with the back of his bracer and pushed himself to his knees, groaning like an old man. His beard probably did look white. He would look ancient when he found her. Would she think that thirty years had passed?

He smiled into the wind, and his teeth cracked.

Eðna could come any day, já, even this one. He trudged up the coast to meet her.

The white was endless, and inside it, he felt he could struggle for eternity and not find or recognize anything. Not Eðna, not his boat, not even a stone or branch of driftwood. Frost formed in his lungs, and he labored to walk, slower and slower. Soon, a spirit would come pluck him like a seed from out of this world. He could just see it ahead, luring him. A glimmer of light, from out of the snow. He staggered toward it, and it grew into the outline of the fishing hut, aglow in the storm.

Someone was here? They'd made a fire.

A wave of heat rolled over Brosa when he opened the door. Ice-melt ran from his lashes and into his eyes, and he blinked them clear. A small fire crackled, and something lay beside it—the spirit that had come to take him to the everlife. Human in form, she had fallen here, broken. He blinked again and knelt to look.

Frozen, ink-dark hair so cold it cracked in his hands. Lips as blue as a juniper berry. Curled into a ball like a kit in its den. It was her favorite way to sleep. He'd waited so long, his mind stumbled on the truth. It was her. She was here. "Oh, Eðna."

He took her up in his arms, and she lay heavy, stiff, not waking, not moving. Her cheeks were pale as still water, or milk underneath the cream. Her brows did not arch with fire or laughter. Gods, just a while ago he'd sat on the ground in indecision while she froze to death here. He felt her cheek, pushed her hair away and leaned in to feel her breath.

It couldn't be. The gods could only be so cruel to one woman and one man.

"Brosa?" The smallest hint of breath, and her whisper, brushed his skin.

"I'm here." He pressed his cheek to hers. She was alive!

But he could hear the grave in her voice, the beating of ravens' wings in her ragged breaths. Eðna was very cold, disappearing like frost from a glass. He might still be too late.

He threw off the bedroll, and his furs and cloak. He tore at the knots and snapped the leather ties on his bracers to get to his wool tunic.

He made Eðna get her arms up over her head, get out of her armor. He peeled the wet clothes from her body. His tunic was bigger than a dress on her. Like one of the dolls Hár carved for the children, just a slip of pale birch and scraps of cloth.

"Astvjeka min." He held her tight, soothed her with his words. He threaded his fingers into her hair and cradled her head. Bent to kiss her forehead, where she liked to be kissed, and rocked Eðna slowly, as if they floated in their sea-stead home. He looked into the fire sputtering in the small hearth and asked his gods to be kind.

He held her for some time, and the wind outside the hut howled, then slowed and stopped.

And slowly, slowly, Eðna moved her fingers. Her thumb moved across the back of his hand. She stroked his skin and warmed it so that pain shot like needles where she touched. She murmured soft words. "Did I make it?"

"You're here," he said. "At the fishing camp."

He pulled the blanket up higher, to her chin, but she pushed his hands away. She noticed her sleeves—that she was wearing his tunic. "What have you done?"

"Put dry clothes on you." He tucked her blanket tight. "I'm saving you, Woman."

Her brows drew down deep, and she struggled to push the blankets away. "I'm fine."

"Eðna—" he started. He'd never seen anyone less fine. Brosa crushed her close and couldn't speak anymore. His throat was full of joy and relief and still choked with fear like a stone, and he rocked her until he could again say words. "I knew you would come."

He smoothed her hair, and she stopped struggling and rested.

"We did it." She sounded drowsy and ale-heavy. "Svana destroyed it. No one else can come."

Brosa smiled for her. "You will be happy to know, I have a place for us." He brushed her lips, pink now, with his thumb. "And I have a plan."

She laughed, the most glorious sound he'd ever heard. "You have a plan?"

"It's not much of one," he said.

Tell me." She curled up, tucked in against his chest. Gods, she smelled like seawater. Just like the day they met.

"Já, well," he said. "I made the boat for you, the way you wanted." And he told her all the parts of the sea-stead, the bed made of feathers and fur, the locked chests and linens. Wool blankets, shaggy cloaks, carved bone combs and a full cup of wooden feathers, sketches of hulls and wings. And Eðna slept and grew strong.

Brosa rubbed the smooth wood with a cloth he'd dipped in seal oil and the finest sand. This cradle would shine. Eðna said he sanded so much, it would outshine the stars, and that he needed to let it rest. Nei matter. His heart was in the wood, and that was good.

When the babe came, he would sleep nestled between him and Eðna in the night, like children do, but sometimes he would need his own place to lie down. Brosa would surround his child with these strips and curves of wood. The strong bird that Brosa carved at the foot of the bed would slice the waves of the child's dreams. A bed like a boat, to be driven by wind and waves, and by the strong will of any babe that came from Eðna.

Weeks had passed, and they were left to themselves here, anchored just far enough from shore to be free from feud, and yet close enough to receive food and news from Ginn and Heirik.

Here in this tent, they were surrounded by so many things he'd made during their time in the forest hall, things he'd carved and built. He still smiled at the thought of this skiphus. Like his wife and he himself, it was full of what the women called contradiction. A vessel built to go, made into a home to stay.

Stay, já, but only until the thaw. In a few weeks they would push off and seek a new place. Eðna had finally agreed they would live on land, though they did not know where.

His great grandda Magnus, and his Amma, came to this island with sheep and horses on their decks, and that is how Brosa and Eðna would go, with animals and silver and food given by his brother and Ginn. He laughed to himself thinking of Eðna surrounded by sheep in her floating home, and perhaps a goat to chew on her pillows and blankets. He could almost see her scolding the animals, her dark brows pulled down tight.

Uncle Hár had often goaded Brosa, out of love. He said Brosa's dreams were soft, or that he had none. In truth, they were just simple. He wanted the things any man might have if the gods were kind. A sturdy house, strong woman, warm hearth, cloaks for their shoulders and fish for their pots. A good ale after a day of hard work.

Soon. The skies were lightening, and he felt winter loosening its grip on the water, so that it moved freely now, not sluggish and sleepy. Almost ready for him.

Brosa looked to Eðna now, where she stood at the bow. Her back and shoulders were so sturdy, her eyes turned away from the coast where they were moored, yearning seaward. Her hair was longer now, just some, dark and thick below her shoulders.

Nei different than any other day. Yet, he felt he had been slogging toward this moment through a cold and relentless tide. Now, they were both here, and she was his.

He had not doubted she'd return. A courageous woman can outlive a thousand men.

Brosa went to her, stood behind her, and she murmured "Hallo, husband." He lifted that short, heavy hair over her shoulder, so he could get to skin to kiss her, and she sighed and leaned back into his arms.

"Did you see the flashing fish? They're circling."

She was still fascinated with the creatures below. The fish he had seen hundreds of times in his life were new to her. She traced their paths with her gaze, wanted to know their ways. He had learned as a boy how they would move, so he could catch them. He'd learned the movements and swells of the waves, so he could feel them in his body and control them, some, with keel and steerboard and hands.

Eðna would steer with him, when the time came. It was her own dream, after all, as simple as his, to steer her own life. Find her desire and follow it.

They stood together and watched fish come and go.

A great quiet came. He nei longer heard the small slap of water against boat, but this was not the peace and stillness that came with flat water. It was silence, a massive presence. He lifted his eyes, and he stared in dumb wonder. The surface of the water, as far as he could see, was a mass of black wings and eyes that flashed like firestrikers in the night. The birds he called fish-arrows—a staggering number, beyond reckoning—rode the waves. Black necks rose like dragon prows curving up out of the water, hundreds upon hundreds of throats, one upon another.

He spoke softly into Eðna's hair. "Look, wife." She raised her eyes and gasped. She spoke the birds' future name. "Cormorants."

So many, it seemed that Brosa and Eðna could step off the boat and walk across the water on their backs.

Brosa wrapped his arms tight around Eðna and set his chin on her head, where she fit so well. "Your ten thousand birds." They watched them rise and fall, rise and fall, without sound, and they waited for the time when he and Eðna would strike out alongside them, and together steer their small family home.

Eðna woke alone. A rectangle of early sun laid across the blanket, and she stretched her legs so she could just reach the steerboard handle that Brosa had built into the footboard of their bed. She traced their letters with her toes—the Es and the B.

She had a bed.

Luxurious, even after all this time—over a year—and still sometimes when she turned to Brosa in the night, her bones and joints remembered the thin mattress in the fort, or the chill that crept into the tent on the deck of their winter ship. She heard the creaking of the frozen masts and howling wind. Here, this house was always warm, and it had sturdy timbers built of oak. The posts and benches were all lovingly carved with wings and waves.

The leather window shade was rolled up, and the salt smell of the sea came rushing in, along with the scents of the lavender and rosemary she'd hung to dry. Layered over it all was the familiar smell of wood planks steaming in hot water, so they could be bent and formed into the shape of a hull.

On the table, Brosa's plans were laid out, with rocks holding down the corners of the brittle paper. Sea shells were spread out, white as bone, and each one had a dark blue rune painted on it. Small glass vials of ink lay carefully closed and stored in a wooden box. Later, the women would come and practice writing with Eðna, while they talked and drank tea.

She tugged on the laces of her leather top and went to the threshold. Chickens strutted along the planking between her house and the one across the way. Half-woven baskets leaned against a bench, big round bodies with the unwoven spires of reeds sticking out in every direction, reaching for the sky.

To her left, there were no other houses, just the bay. Its small, persistent waves nudged the shore. Tiny fires burned on the wave-tips, reflecting the still-rising sun, and the last wraiths of mist curled up off the water and burned away.

On the sand, a half-built boat lay cradled in wooden supports. Sun warmed the wood, and it glowed like bronze. Most of the planks had been bent and nailed to the hull, and the boat was filled with heavy rocks, positioned so it would dry to shape. It was a long ship for a rich trader, and one of Brosa's own designs. In cross-section, the hull matched the form of a bird, its wings upraised.

Other than the boat and the tent for steaming wood, the beach was empty.

She had some time.

She slipped on her boots, grabbed her small bow and quiver and stepped outside.

The boat-builder's house—their house—was at the very edge of the cluster of dozens of huts and tents that made up their port village. Their yard sloped to the water, just a few strides from their door, and down to the dock, where small boats were tied up. Rising above them, an elegant skute floated, serene and still, waiting for repairs.

Beyond their yard, a small forest began. Eðna tromped through tall grass and wildflowers to get to it, and her boots darkened with dew.

From up here at the edge of the trees, their house looked graceful. Its long slope of thatched roof swooped down like a spread wing, descending to touch the sand.

She hiked her skirt up and tied it in a knot, and she stepped into the woods. Filtered sun made lace out of her plain wool dress and skin. The air was cooler, the light crisp and precious. She trailed her fingers in the leaves and water ran down her wrists.

Her traps were empty today. Nei matter, that was fine. They had plenty to eat, and more than enough furs, an abundance of dry coziness, everything they never had during the first year of their lives together.

Eðna came to her small clearing, where she always stopped and sat very still. She breathed softly. And soon the forest sounds came, the singing and chirping and scuttling. More, different animals lived here, beyond foxes. The hares, alert and powerful, bounded away at the sight of her, but if she was very quiet, they would come to the edges of the clearing and chew at leaves and watch her in her silence.

All those months in the fort with Brosa, and then the weeks they lived on their sea-stead anchored near the land, shivering, at times very afraid, she had learned that it was alright to do nothing. To simply sit.

Eðna closed her eyes and let the sun warm her face. She breathed deep of the wild stillness, absorbed the press of trees around the clearing, and turned her face to the oval of sky. And if she was quiet enough, her former self—the woman of the woods—seemed to come to her. That hungry creature that hunched by the water's edge with mud on her face.

The best parts of that woman stayed in her now. The contentment, the willingness to fight, the newness of love and touch. She felt such compassion for that girl, who let her parents in after so many years. Now, her mother was in her hands, her Da in her heart. Her father would have breathed deeply in this clearing, too. Her Ma would be so proud of what Eðna had done, what she'd been willing to give, for this.

She rested her palm on the fallen oak. The trees were so different here, not the birch and ash of Iceland, but still they called out her memories. Running as a child and counting as she touched every tree, limping to the hut with Brosa when he was wounded, spotting his cairns. The first time Brosa truly touched her, he'd pressed her hand to bark and held her there. She ran her fingertips down the scratchy, bumpy trunk of this big oak that might someday become part of a hull.

"Þakka þér." She whispered thanks.

A flare of warmth hit the back of her neck, as a cloud passed away. She should get back. Day was fully here, and Brosa would want to get his hands on his tools. She had work to do, making knots and lashings for the biggest boat they were repairing, or perhaps working rivets on the forge or leather bracers for the next market.

Brosa was on the beach when she got home, inspecting the unfinished boat with his back to her. The lilt of his voice reached her at the edge of the woods—that way he had of speaking in lists, like a lullaby. Like the waves that would one day carry the vessel whose parts he named.

"The keel," he said. "The planks and klinks and ribs."

Familiar tenderness washed over her, the way she always felt when she saw him this way, with the bay stretched out before him—in the landscape, in his home. His body was strong again, and his hands were smooth from working the wood. His calves held tight in their bindings, the beloved curve of his hip, where just now their child rested. One small, chubby foot kicked him over and over in the small of his back.

Their daughter looked over his shoulder and saw Eðna.

"Hallo, Gretta." Eðna waved her fingers.

Brosa turned, and he smiled, that growing smile that started from the smallest quirk of his lips, like a wink, a secret, changing to a full, beaming sun. A smile he gave to Eðna and no one else. Egretta struggled and reached, her unburdened smile as bright as Brosa's, her golden waves of hair mingling with his. A girl and her Da. Eðna's bowerbird, her egret, their ocean-blue eyes so much the same. Yes.

ᛋ

Svana moved through the passages of the glacier-hall. Her dress swept the floor, fine and blue as a rain-soon sky. Rare beads and bracelets adorned her chest and arms, so she would blend in among the men and women outside.

One more escape.

That was all she needed, and she would be free.

Eðna and Ginn had explained that Svana would be studied and questioned if she did not let Vera hide her. And Vera was kind, já, but she had Svana weave and sew, weave and sew, until Svana wanted to spit and scream, "This is not it!" Not what she risked her life to come for.

She wanted the air of this far, far land on her skin. She wanted to see this glittering building from the outside and throw her head back to wonder at its height. She wanted the world of machines and books and people beyond counting. The world Eðna and Ginn told her about, and all the other places and times that it contained.

After all she'd risked and won, she still could not feel or have these things. Her life depended on a woman who put her to work, and a man, Jeff, who held her fate in his hands. She would not live that way another day.

Eðna and Ginn had told her many useful things, too. How to use screens, how unseen keys and alarms worked, how the lab closed and opened, what Jeff was like, what drew his mind away and made him weak. One night, when he was with a woman, Svana slipped into the lab and switched her new contacts—full of birds and learning exercises—for Eðna's. There would be no more trace of what Eðna discovered.

Just like when Svana traveled here through the sea, she would again wear Eðna's eyes within her own. Perhaps one day she would find the man *Jack* and give him Eðna's messages.

She turned a corner.

—And threw her arms out. The passage stretched out endless before her, a hall like the yawning mouth of a white wolf, full of mist that spewed from vents in the walls. The floor slipped away, like the cliff's edge under her boots, and she was sliding, sinking, into the vast clouds. She felt again the immensity of glaciers and mountains, of ice that looked like fingers seeking in the land, and she was small, too small.

She took a breath.

It was just a long hallway. And in truth, she was small as a speck in this world, but she was not alone.

She touched the sleek, gray fox that laid over her shoulders. Its voice no longer sang or raged through Svana's throat. Its blue eyes no longer pierced the sky or sent destruction across the land—they were closed. He was cleaned and tanned and peaceful in death.

One last time, he gave her something. A memory. It was herself, a little girl swaying at the top of a shaggy grass roof, promising herself she would go far, far away.

On that roof, she'd seen something true, and she felt it again later, when she stood on top of that cliff in the volcanic lands. She felt the safety in vastness. She did not have to be afraid, nei. She could walk through this blinding mist and melt into the great world outside, and no one would ever find her.

She ran a finger down the fox's snout, and she stood tall. He had not given his head, his voice, his very life for nothing.

She walked now with the power of two worlds. She wore the furs and jewelry and delicate boots of a rich and powerful woman. At her waist, hung a set of thick iron keys, forged with black teeth like a monstrous grin. Underneath, she wore the clothes of the future. In her boot, she'd tucked the *cash* that Eðna had left in her room so long ago, paper that people like Jeff still traded. And on the surface of her eyes, she wore the slivers of spar that would let her navigate all the worlds outside and know everything.

Soon, she would be there. She would meet the men who wore uniforms the color of new blood and blue steel, who played at fighting battles that happened long after Svana's own birth. She would meet women dressed as warriors, as leaders who ruled worlds bigger than the sky, or those who wore gossamer white dresses and brilliant ribbons and shawls, who did complex dances and ate *sandwiches.*

She would decide who to talk to, because they looked interesting, not because anyone made her. She would choose who to be, from anywhere and any-when. She would drink bitter drinks topped with steaming cream and eat round fruit that ran sweet as honey down her wrists and chin.

The fox would be with her always, but his work was done.

She came to the main hall, with its doors big enough for a giantess to pass, made all of the finest frost-glass. She did not stop to look out, did not pause here at the threshold. Svana opened the door and stepped outside.

MANY THANKS

To my readers, for your passion about this story and your patience while I wrote it. Thank you for your notes, thoughts, ideas and links to gorgeous images and amazing artifacts.

To my family, Martin and Sebastian Brown, for your ideas and love and time together. Martin, you are the best editor. To my dear friends, Michelle, Claire and Brian Kroll, Kim Topazio, and Corey Blue, for all you do and for believing in me.

To friends who helped me with many aspects of this book, from sharing knowledge about spinning, shearing and bowhunting, to proofreading. Thank you, Konane Mookini, Rachel Lundstrom, Chaitanya Muralidhara, Nancye Bonomo, Yvonne Ellsworth, Sarah Jordan, Sarah Gilbert, Jackie Benjamin, Natalia Uribe Wilson and Chad Honl. And to early readers Tana Lovett, Julie Bracker, Jenn Runion, Heather Monroe Kinne, Stacy Crockett, and Kelly Flowers.

To Brian John Park for the stunning cover, and to Angela Quarles for creating my e-books.

To Shannon Okey, for believing in my first novel and publishing Beautiful Wreck. You helped me start on this path.

To Tom Dority for his work editing the first volume of So Wild A Dream.

To the kind people at Desk & Mug, Groundwork, and Taborspace for all the quiet and coffee.

To a smart, cool person I've never met but whose work has had a great impact on my stories—educator, fight re-enactor and historian William R. Short, author of Icelanders in the Viking Age and the man behind hurstwic.org. I recommend you visit there to look around in wonder.

ABOUT THE AUTHOR

Larissa Brown writes speculative fiction grounded in history, but with a touch of time travel and epic love.

From the open fires at an Oregon Renaissance fair to the ruins of a Viking longhouse in Southern Iceland, Larissa's rese arch has taken her across the world. She's invented Old Norse words, made Viking mouthwash out of angelica root and attempted to learn the ancient needle art of naalbinding.

Her first novel, *Beautiful Wreck*, takes place in a fictional 10th century Iceland – a world of rugged beauty and ax-hewn justice. All About Romance named it one of the best books of 2014. *So Wild A Dream* continues the saga in the same White Wo ods world. Larissa is also the author of the novella Tress, a gothic horror fairytale love story.

Larissa posts photos of her #writingspot on Instagram to share the adventure of writing, and she's the proud owner of the addictive online generator What Does Your Hero Smell Like? (found at herosmellslike.com.) She can often be found writing, or creating designs for hand knitters, at a coffee shop in her hometown of Portland, Oregon.

RECEIVE NEWS

And SEE MORE NOVELS & KNITS

www.LarissaBrown.net
FOLLOW ALONG

Instagram: **@larissabrownauthor**
Ravelry: **LarissaBrown**
Twitter: **@vikinglovestory**

Made in the USA
Coppell, TX
30 November 2022